THE CONSIGNMENT

ALSO BY GRANT SUTHERLAND

DIPLOMATIC IMMUNITY

GRANT SUTHERLAND

THE CONSIGNMENT

BANTAM BOOKS

THE CONSIGNMENT
A Bantam Book / March 2003

Published by
Bantam Dell
A Division of Random House, Inc.
New York, New York

Book design by Lynn Newmark

Library of Congress Cataloging-in-Publication Data
Sutherland, Grant.
The consignment / Grant Sutherland.
p. cm.
ISBN 0-553-80187-2
1. Persian Gulf War, 1991—Veterans—Fiction. 2. Illegal arms transfers—Fiction.
3. Weapons industry—Fiction. 4. Pentagon (Va.)—Fiction. 5. Africa—Fiction.
I. Title.
PR9619.4.s88 C66 2003
813'.54—dc21   2002027939

Manufactured in the United States of America
Published simultaneously in Canada

10 9 8 7 6 5 4 3 2 1
BVG

Wisdom is better than weapons of war:
but one sinner destroyeth much good.

Ecclesiastes 9:18

ONE

PROLOGUE

Christmas that year we went up to the mountains, just Fiona and Brad and me. There were a few inches of snow on the ground when we arrived Christmas Eve, but the sky was clear, so after we'd unloaded the car Fiona and I took a walk together down by the river while Brad chopped some logs for the fire.

We went down the track, stepping over fallen branches, the bare woods were quiet all around us, even the murmur of the river was muffled by the snow. There were deer tracks beside the river, we waited awhile but the only creature we saw was a squirrel; it scurried along the leafless maple branches overhead, showering us with heavy white snowflakes. Fiona bent forward and shook her hair. I wrapped my arms around her waist, pretended to pitch her toward the icy river. She shrieked, then struggled, and we fell back on the soft white blanket. She laughed and scooped snow into my face. As I got to my knees, she shoved me and I went down again, and she ran, laughing, up through the woods.

Fiona laughing. I can still remember that.

Back at the shack, Brad already had the fire going, he was

stretched out on the sofa, his head in a book. Fiona hung up her jacket, telling him he should get out while the weather was good.

Weather's fine right here, Mom, he said.

She rolled her eyes at me, then went to the kitchen to unpack the food and drink. Christmas Eve in the Rourke family. I didn't have the heart to bring it down. Christmas morning, we unwrapped our presents, then Fiona drove down to the store to make a call to her mother in Cleveland while Brad helped me with some minor repairs to the shack. Since starting college, Brad seemed to have spent every vacation on a field trip out of state, it had been a while since we'd shared any real time together. When he was a boy, he'd been proud that his father was a soldier. When he became an adolescent, my profession turned into something of an embarrassment for him. That phase passed too, but nothing since had moved into its place, except, maybe, uncertainty. An unsureness of where to position me in the scale of adult relationships, at what point to fix me between hero and villain, friend and foe. So that Christmas morning the two of us crawled over the porch, hammering down loose nails, making small talk, and circling the possibility of some new connections between us that might replace the ones that, through the passage of time, we'd lost. When Fiona returned from the store, we set down our tools, with the real work not even begun.

Maybe that had something to do with why, after lunch, I found myself setting out alone up the hill behind the shack, and, after twenty minutes, turning up the path toward the mountain pool that was sheltered by a ring of boulders. The pool where my father, one summer, taught me to swim. Now I scrambled around the snow-capped boulders and looked down at the iced surface, surprised at how small it seemed. I picked up a rock and threw it, it bounced on the ice.

My father had once been a soldier. He'd fought in France when he was Brad's age, then returned home and gone to college on the GI Bill, and after that he spent his working life in insurance. When I turned eighteen, and told him and Mom that I was going to enlist, he took me aside and confided to me that it was only meeting Mom that had stopped him from reenlisting after college. The Army, the way he spoke, seemed to be the life he'd missed out on, the one he *thought maybe he should have had. Their support for me never wavered. Through my cadetship at West Point, my first commission in the Rangers, then the Gulf War, and on through my hospitalization after Mogadishu, they stood by me. For Fiona it wasn't so easy.*

When we married, I promised Fiona I would leave the Army sometime around my thirtieth birthday. I told her that by then I would have fulfilled my youthful ambitions, I would have served my country and experienced life as a soldier, yet still be young enough to launch myself into a civilian career. I told her I was not an Army lifer.

I was, it turned out, plain wrong. By the time I went out to serve in the Gulf War, I knew in my heart that I didn't want any kind of civilian career. The life I wanted was the life I already had. But when I returned from the Gulf I found that Fiona had other plans. She wanted to talk about the future. From the wives' circuit, she'd learned that a number of my fellow officers were resigning their commissions. She gave me their names. I attempted to sidestep the issue. She reminded me of the promise I'd made when we first married. I told her that my feelings had changed. We argued, and in the heat of one exchange she revealed that she'd been seeing a shrink ever since my departure for the Gulf. She said she simply couldn't cope with the idea that I might be killed.

The awful truth was apparent to both of us. Over the years of our marriage we'd each made discoveries about ourselves: me, that I was born to be a soldier; Fiona, that she was not born to be a soldier's wife. But when I stayed in the Army, she stuck with me. We still loved one another. If Mogadishu hadn't occurred, we might have been okay.

But in Mogadishu I took a gutshot during a firefight in the back-streets of the city, I was flown home and hospitalized. It was while I was convalescing in the military hospital after surgery that Fiona laid it on the line to me. She wasn't going through that again. Never again was she going to sit glued to CNN, watching Apache helicopters firing missiles, and wondering whether her husband was dead or alive. Never again was she going to be taking handfuls of pills just to get her through the day. Never again was she going to be breaking down in tears during a regular evening session with her shrink. She wasn't mad at me, it was simpler than that. She just couldn't take it anymore. I could either accept the instructorship at West Point she knew I'd been offered, or she wanted a trial separation. If I went on active service again, she would divorce me.

When I came out of the hospital and told her I'd taken the West Point job, she was so happy she cried. I was okay with it too, at first. It was only as the years passed, and the graduation ceremonies started to blur, that it started to eat at me.

It wasn't just that I got jaded. Guys I'd served with in the Rangers had moved on with their careers, some in the Regiment, others to the Pentagon, and a few, even, to Delta Force. They were out in the world doing things I might have done, while I carried on the same old routine, drilling the latest intake of cadets on the West Point range. I got to feeling that I'd repeated my father's mistake, that I'd inadvertently sidelined myself from my own life. Without telling Fiona, I started applying for other postings. But everywhere I applied, I found I was joining the end of a very long line. The military was downsizing, the scramble for permanent positions was on in earnest, making a vacancy for a West Point instructor wasn't high on anyone's list of priorities. I knocked on every door. I proposed myself for any kind of deployment. I was turned down everywhere. I felt beached, stranded midlife and midcareer. On my thirty-ninth birthday, I gave myself another year. One more year, I promised myself, and if the Army couldn't find another place for me, I would see what the civilian world still had to offer.

A month later the World Trade Center came down, the Pentagon was hit, and for me, like for so many others, everything changed.

Looking down at the iced pool Christmas day, three and a half months later, I remembered my father and his lingering regret for the soldier's life he'd almost led. Now he rested alongside my mother in a California graveyard, while his own son's son, Brad, was already a man.

I tossed another rock onto the pool, and the ice cracked, a hazy white web across the water. Then I scrambled back around the boulders and retraced my steps down the hill through the snow.

I took my boots off on the porch, went inside and hung up my jacket. Brad was lying on the sofa, reading. Fiona was in the armchair by the fire, her legs tucked up beneath her, perusing a magazine. I got myself a whiskey, then I came out and stood near the fire and told them what I had to tell them. That I'd resigned my commission. That I'd taken a job in the civilian world, that I was embarking on a new career. They received the news, as I guessed they might, in stunned silence. The fire blazed high. The snow on the roof shifted. I swirled the whiskey in my glass and told them exactly what it was I was going to do. Brad gave it a moment, then he closed his book and got up and left the room. Fiona stared up at me like someone very close to us had died.

CHAPTER 1

You'll recognize Trevanian?"

"I'll know him," I said.

"Tell him who you are, background history."

I looked up from my coffee to Milton Rossiter, the major shareholder and president of Haplon Systems, my employer.

"Who I am?"

"Ex-Army, that bit." He skirted around behind our stand, sucking in his gut, then he came back out with a big cardboard cutout of a rifle and propped it against the table. He clicked his fingers and pointed at me. "Hey, didn't he have somethin' to do with Grenada? Maybe give you two somethin' to talk about."

"I was never in Grenada."

Rossiter frowned and went on adjusting the cardboard cutout; standing back, then stepping in to adjust it some more.

The doors of the airfield hangar had been open half an hour, the buyers were streaming down the aisles, there was a lively buzz of business in the air. It was my second fair at Springfield, and my second year in the employ of Haplon Systems. The basic layout of the fair hadn't changed. The buyers entered through the main doors onto a quarter acre of royal blue carpet, where a collection of young women greeted them, offering glossy brochures. From there the buyers moved down one of six aisles into a gridlike array of stands where suited men like me plied them with information and stats, then ran videos to show the materiel in action.

"Trevanian won't be signing up for anything right now," Rossiter told me. "But I don't want him walking away from here thinking we're not interested in his money."

He held up the PC lead and looked faintly bewildered. I went over and stuck the plug into the adapter, then leaned across and switched on the screen. Rossiter nodded as a Mercator projection of the earth appeared, explosive flashes of light bursting and dying across war zones where Haplon weapons were currently in use. Rossiter touched the PC screen as if he were trying out the latest Nintendo—push here for nuclear Armageddon—while I went back to my coffee.

I'd been marketing manager for Milton Rossiter's company for more than a year by this time, I think I knew him pretty well. Normally he dealt munitions the way a stockbroker deals shares, without a second thought. But that morning at Springfield he seemed anxious. His father had founded Haplon in the aftermath of World War II, buying up surplus rifles from redundant arsenals in Europe, then selling them into the U.S. sports market. After that, Haplon rode a wave of profitability through Korea and Vietnam, expanded into production, and when Milton finally inherited the business he'd already been his father's right-hand man for fifteen years. His aim ever since had been to keep Haplon profitable and growing, ready to be handed over to his children, three unmarried women in their twenties whose only interest in Haplon Systems seemed to be the dividend check they each received quarterly.

With his long background in the business, Milton Rossiter's self-belief was normally total, but in the months leading up to Springfield some of his usual arrogance had deserted him. Partly, I suppose, because the construction of the new Haplon plant out in California was falling behind schedule. Not a disaster on its own, but along with some recent Pentagon cutbacks and the shrinking Haplon order book, the situation was causing heartburn in a few of Rossiter's bankers. They were pressuring him to refill the order book. He was relaying the pressure down the line to us.

He left the PC and came back to me.

"Ned," he said, making a face. He set his hands on the table and leaned toward me. "Ned, you look like shit." He shook his head while I looked down at my shirt and tie. "Not your fucking clothes. You. Jesus Christ," he said quietly, the customers flowing down the aisle behind him. "Place has been opened twenty minutes, you've been sittin' there nursin' coffees, rubbin' your goddamn eyes." He clicked his fingers near my face. "Come on. Wake up."

I raised my eyes slowly.

"Jeez," he said.

I got out from behind the table.

"Christ, it moves. You going all giddy like that? Maybe you want to sit down again." Someone in the crowd of buyers caught Rossiter's eye. Rossiter hailed him over the passing heads, then pistoled his fingers at me before moving off through the suits. "Stay sharp, Ned. You miss Trevanian, I will personally fucking slay you."

Around midmorning I saw Trevanian. He was joking with someone down on the Scitex stand, looking relaxed and tan. Clean-shaven and sandy-haired, not quite six feet, he looked just like the mug shots I'd seen of him, only he wasn't in uniform, he was wearing a blazer and tie. When he left the Scitex stand and came in our direction I signaled for Micky Baker, our junior salesman, to rescue me from a Paraguayan time waster, a colonel wearing full battle dress and shades who was requesting a rerun of our artillery video.

By the time Trevanian arrived at our stand, I was pretending to study one of our brochures. He offered me his hand, we did the introductions, then he beckoned forward a striking black woman in a beige slacksuit. She slipped her Gucci purse beneath her arm. As we shook hands, her collection of chunky gold bracelets clinked.

"Cecille Lagundi," Trevanian said. "My associate."

I smiled. Associate. Colleague. Partner. In the arms business, all flexible terms. Straight to the point, Trevanian said they'd like some information on the P23. I sat them down, then slid two leaflets across the table, launching into my spiel. "The P23's an excellent close-range weapon. Probably Haplon's top line. We've been shipping them twelve months"—I gestured toward the PC, the bursts of light and accompanying sound effects—"they're battle tested—"

Trevanian lifted a finger. "We don't need the pitch," he said mildly. We looked at each other. His eyes were pale green.

"The numbers," I said, reaching over and touching the leaflet beneath his hand, "are on the back."

He flipped over the leaflet and studied the numbers, the P23's vital stats. Dimensions. Rate of fire. Range. Everything you could know about the weapon short of using it. While he was doing that my eyes cheated across to Cecille Lagundi. She was looking at the numbers on her leaflet too, but casually. How did I figure her? A female friend picked up by Trevanian on an African tour of duty? One of his U.S. employees?

Jack Trevanian was ex–British army, a free agent who ran his own private military company. This is one aspect of the peace dividend the average citizen never hears about, the swelling band of Jack Trevanians running private companies of mercenaries around the globe. Freebooters who wade into trouble spots where Western governments no longer care to venture. Rebels and insurgents repressed, all checks to Switzerland. When not buying weapons for their own companies, guys like Trevanian spend their time advising tin-pot regimes on how best to equip their ragtag armies. I figured Trevanian's connection with Cecille Lagundi was probably professional, but there were other possibilities. Her security badge said DEFENSE CONSULTANT, but she didn't look like any other defense consultant roaming the fair. She couldn't have been more than thirty-five. Her skin was a perfect, unlined ebony.

She raised her eyes and caught me studying her. She kept her eyes on mine as she slid the leaflet back across the table.

"So tell me why I shouldn't buy it," said Trevanian.

The gun's weaknesses, he meant. I told him that we'd engineered them all away on the draftboard.

"You believe that?"

"No weapon's perfect."

He raised a brow. "You going to tell me what's wrong with the gun or shall I just move on and see Fettners."

Fettner & Sons were our main competitor. We both dealt in the same sort of equipment, a niche too low-tech for the likes of Hughes or McDonnell Douglas and too high-tech to be undercut by the cheap foreign manufacturers. If Trevanian had gone down to the Fettners stand and placed an order, Rossiter would have skinned me alive.

"It's not great over distance," I admitted. Gesturing behind me, I offered to take them behind the screen and show them the weapon. "If you want, we can take it out to the firing range, you can let off a few rounds."

Trevanian remarked dryly that the Springfield firing range—a temporary structure bulldozed out of the earth beyond the hangar—was only fifty yards long. Not exactly a rigorous test for a weapon whose weakness, as I'd just told him, was over distance. I shrugged, conceding the point.

Trevanian seemed to relax some then. He tossed his head toward the screen. "What else you got back there?"

Opening a hand, I invited them into the Aladdin's cave behind me. We went through the door in the rear screen, up a ramp into a cargo container that had been fitted out especially for fairs like Springfield. Milton Rossiter had even employed an interior designer to ensure we got the appropriately masculine, high-tech effect. The walls were black beneath a polished aluminum ceiling; spotlights mounted on two chrome tracks ran the length of the container. Haplon product was racked on chrome tubing along the side walls. The heavier equipment—the antitank gear, launchers, mortars—was lined up on the steel-plated floor.

Cecille Lagundi seemed slightly lost; she folded her arms and looked around.

I unracked the P23. Trevanian asked if we could strip it, so we moved to the rear of the container, where I got down on my knees and dismantled the gun, talking Trevanian through each stage, answering his questions. When I was done pulling it apart and then reassembling it, I handed the gun to Trevanian. He weighed it in his hands, raised it to his shoulder, and sighted along the barrel to the rear wall.

"Good feel," he said, passing the gun back to me.

We talked some more about the gun. He had that clipped Brit way of speaking, direct, and he asked all the right questions. He probably thought we were getting along fine. After a while he tilted his head.

"You ex-Services?" he asked me.

"Army."

"Poor bastard," he said, and smiled. Then he touched Cecille Lagundi's arm. Give us two minutes, he told me, and the pair of them walked down to the front of the container, talking quietly, while I reracked the gun. I'd been in the business long enough by that time to know when I'd made a sale, and I knew right then they were hooked. They came back to me after a minute's whispered conference.

"We're interested in the gun."

I nodded. Good decision. Wise choice.

"Also these," he said, and she handed him a list and he gave it to me.

Glancing down the list, I felt my heart flutter like a startled bird in my chest. Gatling miniguns, mortars, rockets and rocket launchers, night-sights—and beside each item was a number designating quantities required. A major shipment. I looked up.

"How soon would you need delivery?"

He gestured vaguely, brushing my question aside. Then looking around the container, he asked me to show them what we had on site.

I went and told my sales team that the container was off-limits for the next hour, then returned inside and worked my way through Trevanian's list, talking him and Cecille Lagundi through each item. Trevanian asked the questions, but he always deferred, in the end, to Lagundi, making sure she was satisfied before moving on to the next weapon. I still couldn't pin her down. Her accent sounded improbably Irish, a soft burr. My best guess by this time was that she was some kind of representative for whoever was financing Trevanian's spree, there was just too much firepower on his wish list for it to be going to any private military company. He must have been buying on someone's behalf. Cecille Lagundi must have been making sure Trevanian's client wasn't getting screwed. That's how I figured it.

When we were through, we reemerged from the container to the front of the Haplon stand, and I gave Trevanian my own sales file, the one with the prices and volume discounts clearly marked. He seemed to appreciate the gesture. He put my file beneath his arm, gave me his card, and took mine. He shook my hand, then she shook my hand.

"We'll be in touch," he told me, and that was it, the pair of them walked away. They passed the Fettners stand without pausing.

Milton Rossiter immediately appeared at my side. When I explained what had happened, his smile nearly split his face. He clapped me on the back and told me I was a goddamn star. My palms were sweating. My heart thumped hard. While Rossiter went over to the rest of the sales team to blow the trumpet, inspire them to sell more guns, I opened a drawer and searched for a new sales file.

"Hey."

When I looked up, Dimitri was looming over me, his hands braced on the table. I hadn't seen Dimitri face-to-face for at least six months, a brief encounter at an arms fair out in Kuwait. Back then I'd been surprised by how he'd suddenly let himself go. Now as I looked him over, I wasn't so much surprised as alarmed. His face was puffy. His stomach pressed over the belt of his pants. The rigors of army life, it was pretty clear, were fast becoming a distant memory to his body. In Kuwait, I'd wondered if he wasn't turning himself into one of those salesmen who do most of their business in bars, lots of backslapping and hearty laughter, then a trawl through the raunchier nightspots after midnight. But I couldn't really believe it. That wasn't the Dimitri I knew.

"Dimitri," I said flatly.

"Have they placed an order with you?" His tone was surprisingly belligerent.

I lifted a brow. Order?

He stabbed a finger on the tabletop. "Trevanian and Lagundi were back in your candy shop a full hour. Don't jerk me around, Ned. Did they give you the order or not?"

"As I recall, you still work for Fettners."

He thumbed his chest. "That's my order. My order."

I'd heard some talk that he'd started leaning on the bottle, but I hadn't taken it too seriously. Now I wasn't so sure.

"I haven't taken the order," I said quietly. "But you're asking for my professional opinion, I'm going to. Now get lost."

His eyes filmed over. "You haven't taken it." I jerked my head sharply in the direction of the Fettners stand. Dimitri finally seemed to get a grip on himself. "Right," he said, nodding as he backed away. "Okay." Then he turned and hurried back toward the Fettners stand.

I watched him go.

"Fettners, yeah?" Rossiter, my boss. He'd left the others and now he was standing at my shoulder watching Dimitri thread his way through the suits.

I nodded.

"He see Trevanian over here? Worried he's lost a customer?"

I nodded again as Dimitri disappeared.

"Guy's a loser, right?" Rossiter put a hand on my shoulder and squeezed. "You fucked him," he said cheerfully.

The rest of the morning I spent catching up with old customers, fielding inquiries, and reining in the misplaced enthusiasm of young Micky Baker, our newly minted marketing grad. Around 1:00 P.M., people started thinking about taking lunch in the giant pavilion outside, and there was a general drift away from the hangar. Rossiter came across to the stand and ran a sharp eye over the morning's paperwork: provisional orders, genuine inquiries, and a dozen leads that would probably come to nothing.

"Trevanian's joinin' us for lunch," Rossiter told me, closing the file.

I rose and buttoned my jacket. "The woman?" When his eyes shot up, I lifted my hands. Casual inquiry, I said.

He laughed. "Keep your pecker in your pants. She's gone back into town. Shopping her way down Fifth Avenue, something like that." He remarked that we seemed to be getting low on brochures. I took the hint and volunteered to fetch a fresh box from my car before joining him in the pavilion.

The parking lot was surrounded by a high chain-link fence with barbed wire slung in three looping strands across the top. I went to my car, grabbed the box off the backseat, then I hitched the box under my arm and wove my way back through the rows of parked vehicles toward the gate. Halfway across I caught sight of Dimitri's car, an unmistakable four-wheel-drive Mercedes with a black top and a Yankees sticker plastered midway down the rear window. My view was obscured, but someone—Dimitri?—appeared to be crouching by the driver's door, doing what, exactly, I couldn't quite figure. It seemed as good a time as any to confront him, so I moved toward his Mercedes, telling myself to stay cool, to let him have his say. Just possibly he might have a reason for his earlier display. Failing that, maybe an apology.

Two cars back from Dimitri's I finally got a clear sight of him and I stopped like I'd hit a stone wall. His ass was propped on the footboard, both his legs were buckled up beneath him, and his right hand was up at the door handle. That's the only thing that was holding him up, his right hand, it was jammed somehow, caught in the handle, his torso leaned away from the car, his head lay on his left shoulder, he looked like a puppet with all its strings cut or a man too drunk to stand up. But he wasn't drunk. One eye was glazed, but the other one wasn't even an eye anymore, it was just a bloody mess where a bullet had torn through to his brain. God knows what the back of his head looked like. The blood was pooled under him like an oil slick, there was a spray of pink lumps on a neighboring car.

I stood there with the goddamn box under my arm. I stood there some moments taking it in, absorbing the searing shock. It was Dimitri. That twisted body suspended there was my one-time West Point roommate, Dimitri Spandos. I felt myself going under, swayed, then managed to will myself back. Back to the world around me. To the parking lot. The arms fair. I went into automatic.

My hand, heavy as a lump of iron, rose. I touched my clammy fingertips to my forehead like I'd forgotten something. Then I turned and walked straight back to my car. There I put the box on the hood, unlocked the passenger door, and reached in to search the glove compartment. If anyone had been watching, if there was a security cam, then maybe—God help me—maybe my pause and retreat from near Dimitri's car might be interpreted as the action of some dozy, forgetful sap who'd passed near the scene but noticed nothing. Palming the perspiration off my face, I grabbed an old garage bill from the compartment, then I stood up and made a show of folding the bill into my breast pocket. After relocking my car I set off with the brochure box across the parking lot again, keeping several rows clear, this time, of Dimitri's silver Mercedes. When I went through the gate the security guy didn't even look up from his comic.

The hangar had almost emptied, most stands were deserted now that lunch had started out in the pavilion. I dumped the box at the Haplon stand, then retreated to the johns, where I pulled a thick wedge of paper towels from the dispenser before locking myself inside one of the cubicles. I took off my jacket and shirt and hung them on the back of the door. Then I braced my arms against the wall, hung my head, and breathed deep—long and steady, in and out—and tried to quiet my wildly clamoring heart.

Jesus, I thought. Oh Christ.

The main door to the johns opened.

"Ned? Are you coming out the tent for eats?"

Micky Baker, he must have seen me come in. I raised my head.

"Yeah. But don't wait. I'll be along."

I heard him wash his hands. He tried to strike up a conversation, but when I ignored him he got the message and left me alone. The door closed behind him. I finally pushed off the wall and took the paper towels one at a time and wiped them across my chest, under my arms, and everywhere else the perspiration was coursing off me. After a minute it seemed to be easing, so I balled the last few towels in my fist and swiped them over my neck and face, then I put on my shirt and jacket again. I collected up all the soaked paper and dumped it in the trash can on my way out.

I had to go through the motions, I knew that. I had to put in an appearance.

But on my way over to the pavilion I lingered a moment at the edge of the grass behind the hangar. Off to my right was the parking lot. Straight in front of me, fifty yards away, the grand pavilion. To my left, the temporary firing range, the red earth banked up like a levee, the last shots blasting off and echoing off the hangar wall. I looked from the range to the parking lot and saw Dimitri's Mercedes two rows back from the chain-link fence. There was a direct line of sight from the firing range to Dimitri's car, all a shooter would have had to do was turn around and fire. But that was a maneuver, of course, that would have been seen and prevented by the rangemaster and any number of other people standing near. A couple of yards farther on, the line of sight was blocked by several armored personnel carriers that had been parked between the hangar and the pavilion throughout the morning. While I watched now, the drivers began moving the vehicles out to the runway, preparing for a later demonstration.

Micky Baker called my name from over by the pavilion. I took one last look at the firing range, then went to join the Haplon team for lunch.

They found Dimitri sometime between dessert and coffee. A security guard hurried over to the Fettners table, then seconds later the toastmaster rose to make an announcement: Anyone and everyone who had fired weapons that morning was requested to report at once to the firing range.

"Oh, for chrissake," said Rossiter, a chocolate mint halfway to his mouth. "For what?" He turned to me, his brow puckered.

Gillian Streiss, my deputy marketing manager, departed our table along with half a dozen others, there was a general air of annoyance that some unexplained screwup had spoiled lunch. A minute later there was another announcement, more a demand this time: It was imperative everyone who had used the firing range should report, the rangemaster had a list of names, it was necessary he speak to each one of those people immediately. Around the pavilion another twenty or more people got reluctantly to their feet. Rossiter tossed his napkin on the table.

"Look after Jack," he told me in a peeved tone, then he excused himself to Jack Trevanian and went out to report to the rangemaster.

A small crowd was gathering at the Fettners table, Micky Baker went over to see what he could find out. I was left facing Trevanian over an untouched bowl of peaches. He raised a brow in question. I turned my head in dumb reply.

Micky came scurrying back a moment later. "Some accident on the firing range," he reported. "One of the Fettners guys—" but that was as far as he got because then the sirens started. We got up and went outside to see.

Two squad cars and an ambulance were making their way through the parking lot. Word was already spreading out from the Fettners guys, Dimitri's name was suddenly in the air. People were saying he was shot, badly wounded.

After a minute I left Trevanian with Micky Baker and went back into the hangar and sat down at the Haplon stand. There was nothing I could do then but wait. And so I waited. The next quarter hour, people wandered in and out of the hangar, the day unexpectedly cut loose from its moorings, suddenly drifting. The police gathered the Fettners team together and interviewed them all. The likes of Micky Baker started spreading the word that maybe Dimitri was more than just badly wounded. Around two P.M., there was an announcement over the loudspeakers: The fair was closing early, anyone who wanted to could leave just so long as they checked their security tags at the main gate. Then four names were read out, none I recognized, three men and one woman who'd neglected to report to the rangemaster.

I delegated Gillian Streiss to pack up our stand, then I gathered my papers together and told Rossiter I was leaving.

At the main gate I checked my security tag, the guard consulted his clipboard and waved me on through. I drove out to the turnpike, put ten miles behind me, then turned off at a giant Wal-Mart sign and made my way over some speed bumps into the parking lot of a mall. I parked and reached into the glove compartment and took out my "scramble-and-squirt" device, a box of electronics the size of a book of matches. Then I reached farther back and took out a rubber cup and fixed it to the device. I put the whole thing in my jacket pocket and got out and crossed to a pay phone, where I picked up the receiver and fixed the rubber cup to the mouthpiece. Then I inserted two quarters and dialed. After two rings a machine at the far end came on and I got three long beeps, the signal that the machine was ready to receive.

I hung my head. I gathered myself, then spoke. "Blue Hawk is dead." I repeated it once, then I dropped my finger onto the phone bar, breaking the line.

CHAPTER 2

Colonel Alex Channon sat silently through my recital of the sequence of events out at Springfield. His elbows rested on his desk, from time to time he raised a hand and tapped his knuckles against his mouth. When I was done his gaze slid on by me, and for several moments he contemplated the bare wall. Then he reached over and switched off the digital recorder. He looked like I guess I must have looked when I lost four men from my unit in the Gulf War. Diminished. At least partially broken.

"You called from outside the fair?"

A pay phone, I told him. Ten miles from Springfield.

He didn't acknowledge my reply, just sat awhile staring at the recorder beneath his hand. In the twenty-something years since he'd walked to the rostrum in the West Point lecture theater and delivered the first lesson in Intelligence to me, Dimitri, and our fellow cadets, Alex Channon had climbed steadily into the upper branches of the Pentagon tree. He'd once been a military adviser to the National Security Council, one of the uniforms you sometimes glimpse ducking out of picture as the Secretary of Defense announces some policy shift to the media, and now he was the Pentagon's place man in the Defense Intelligence Agency, the DIA. But the years of his ascent had worn him. He remained lean, but his hair had thinned and grayed, and the lines of his face had deepened. He had large responsibilities and he carried them gravely. He was the kind of guy most people would be relieved to know still had influence down in Washington, but at fifty-four years of age he hadn't made General, and his time was probably running out. Though he gave a few guest lectures at West Point each year, the small office there where we always met was really just his reward for climbing so far up the slippery slope at the Pentagon. Retaining close links with guys like Colonel Alex Channon gave the academy a certain clout around budget time.

After he turned my story over, Alex's shoulders sagged. His crisp uniform shirt crumpled. "Holy hell," he said softly.

"I'm not so sure the shot came from the firing range." I mentioned the armored personnel carriers, and the fact that they'd been open for general inspection all morning. I told him about the way the gunshots from the firing range echoed off the hangar. "One or two stray shots, maybe a silencer. No one would have noticed."

He looked up at me as if it was an effort just to concentrate on what I was telling him. Until that day, I would have said that Alex's decision to send me and Dimitri undercover in the arms trade had worked out better than any of us had any right to hope, that the two years of Hawkeye had put some real numbers on the board. Hawkeye. Dimitri's suggestion, as I recall. A big fan of *M*A*S*H*, he'd made the suggestion as a joke, but it stuck to the operation and became the official code name. After I resigned my commission, and Dimitri left Delta Force, we served some time training with a bunch of Defense Intelligence operatives, preparing for Hawkeye as if we were about to be dropped behind enemy lines. The operation was meant to be over in six months, but each quarter Channon had had the time extended. Now, between us, Dimitri and I had assembled a virtual encyclopedia on the ruses used by the arms trade to skirt the decrees of U.S. and international law. The Customs Service had found our background work invaluable. The Pentagon had been reassured that two of its own guys were on the case. Until that day, I really believed that our work was A1 quality, that we were doing just fine.

"Did Dimitri ever offer you money?" Alex asked me suddenly, leaning his forearms on the desk.

I squinted. "When?"

"Anytime."

"No."

"Have you ever been solicited to bribe a client?"

"Alex—"

He put up a hand. "Ever?" he said. His gaze was direct.

No, I told him. Never. "And if I had, you know I would have reported it to you."

The way he looked at me, Alex Channon didn't seem so sure. His focus narrowed. "Have you ever accepted a bribe, Ned?"

"No."

For a few beats, his eyes stayed on mine. Then he muttered, "Best news for weeks," and he slid the recorder into a drawer.

I cocked my head. I asked him, naturally, what the hell he meant by that.

"That guy you reported tailing you last month," he said, ignoring my question. "Have you seen him again?"

"I said it was just a feeling."

"First feeling like that you've had in two years."

Once a month Alex flew up from Washington and received a face-to-face report from me. Between times, on a weekly basis, I used the tiny scramble-and-squirt recorder he'd given me to deliver my reports over the phone. It was a recent weekly report he was referring to. My first few months undercover I'd reported several tails, but as my undercover life merged with my real life, my sightings of these shadows dwindled, then disappeared. It was an unexpected and alarming moment, the month before Springfield, when I found myself leaving the local 7-Eleven and craning over my shoulder to catch a glimpse of someone I felt watching me. There was nobody there, but I reported the incident to Channon anyway. It was only later that it occurred to me the spectral figure was probably the projection of some more acutely personal anxieties.

"What would you say," Channon asked me now, "if I told you Dimitri reported some guy tailing him too?"

"Are you telling me?"

He dipped his head and waited for that one to sink in. Dimitri had a tail and I had a tail. And now Dimitri was dead.

Channon rose and came around his desk and dropped into a chair. He grimaced and opened his hands. "Okay, here's the story. A couple of months ago I got a call from Dimitri. Urgent. Priority one, he says, get my ass out to L.A. to see him. Which I do, of course. And I walk into the appointed hotel room at the appointed hour and Dimitri's up on the bed eating pretzels, watching TV. Only he's not alone in the room. There's two guys in dark suits standing across at the window. I couldn't believe it. Two guys I've never seen before. This is meant to be a safe meeting, just me and Dimitri. Then Dimitri introduces them. A pair of agents from the goddamned IRS."

I squinted. Internal Revenue?

"Christ," Channon went on. "Dimitri didn't even have the guts to tell me himself. They had to do it for him." The IRS, according to Channon, had picked up discrepancies between Dimitri's tax returns and some investment accounts he had. His occupation led them to look a little closer. "They even put a tail on him for a few days. A guy going around after him picking up the paperwork on his transactions—credit cards, checks—they recorded his withdrawals from cash machines, got a fix on the times, and traced his account back through the bank."

"That was his tail, the IRS?" I was thinking about that feeling I had at the 7-Eleven.

Channon nodded. "Makes you weep, doesn't it? And by now they've got him by the shorts, they know something's not right. So when they come knocking on his door they're not just after back taxes, they want to know where this free money he's got's coming from. And the way they're talking, Dimitri figures they've already got a fair idea. And he figures—correctly—that it's not just a fine he's looking at. So now he calls in the cavalry." Channon thumbed his chest and screwed up his face. "The mystery man from Washington he's told them about. Me. The guy he's working for on government business. I was his escape route."

"He didn't need money."

"Every gambler needs money, Ned."

We looked at each other. Dimitri's inability to restrain a corrosive gambling habit was what had led, years earlier, to the collapse of his marriage. I'd never told Channon that. Dimitri had sworn to me that he'd slain the demon, and I'd believed him. But from the picture Channon was sketching—a guy floundering out of his financial depth, grasping for cash—it sounded like Dimitri's habit had risen from the ashes and gotten a disastrous new lease on life. Channon had clearly made some inquiries of his own. I was appalled.

"Why'd he set you up like that?"

"Why didn't he warn me? Because once I was there I was real. I couldn't deny I knew him. He'd whistled, I'd arrived on the next plane. What was I doing, just visiting? Dimitri figured once I was there I'd have no choice, I'd have to lie for him. I'd have to say the money was the government's, anything to get him out of the IRS's clutches." He shook his head. "Hell, he was in dreamland. The IRS had their teeth in him up to the gums, they weren't going to let go. Once I produced my bona fides, they showed me what they had on him, stuff they hadn't shown Dimitri. Jesus, you didn't have to be Columbo. Dimitri was some kind of bagman—at it for at least a year—giving and taking bribes, cutting a piece for his own commission." Channon lifted his eyes and spoke with real bitterness. "So that's the story. Two years too late I find out you've recruited me a goddamn crook."

I flinched. A few weeks after the collapse of the World Trade Center and the strike on the Pentagon, Channon had summoned me down to Washington and made me an offer. It was a strange time. The usual civil restraints on the Pentagon and the federal agencies had been temporarily brushed aside, their leashes were off. The DIA decided to take the opportunity to do something about the increasing amounts of U.S.-manufactured materiel turning up in the wrong hands internationally. Alex, somewhere in the back of his mind, must have made a connection with me.

During the Gulf War, one of the emplacements in our unit took a direct hit from the Iraqis, four grunts were killed but there were no identifiable remains. Our ordnance guys did some forensics on the wreckage. Their conclusion was checked, rechecked, then finally buried in some obscure Pentagon file while the U.S. Army set about the more urgent business of getting a few hundred thousand battle-weary troops back home. But I knew. And my fellow officers, including Dimitri, all knew. The missile that had taken out our men came from one of the biggest and best arms manufacturers in the world. It was top-quality product, made in the U.S.A. It wasn't just Iraq we were fighting out there in the Gulf. The truth is, we were joined in battle against the weapons of every major arms-manufacturing country on earth, including our own. On our return home, Dimitri and I visited the bereaved families of those four men to offer what solace we could. Brave sons, killed in the line of duty. Death instantaneous. No suffering. One mother refused to let us into her house, but mostly there was a stoic acceptance from the families that was humbling, and which I recalled often during the weeks of flag-waving and welcome-home parades that followed. I wrote a letter to Channon, the only senior figure I knew at Intelligence down in the Pentagon at the time, berating the folly of trading our weapons into the hands of our enemies. He was kind enough to phone me. He assured me he sympathized, and that my concerns were widely shared down in Washington, and he told me why nothing could be done. When I cornered him in his West Point office years later, and pleaded with him to open a door for me back into active service, that earlier memory must have been stirred.

He summoned me down to Washington in October, put Hawkeye before me, and told me the operation needed one other operative, a second make-believe arms salesman. The first person who occurred to me was Dimitri. As cadets at the Point we'd been close, then we'd served together in the Rangers. Back then Dimitri had been more than just a supremely good soldier, he'd been a friend. I'd seen him through the collapse of his marriage, watched as the emotional impact of that rupture finally killed his gambling habit, and I'd listened a year later to his self-lacerating admission that he had only himself to blame for the loss of his family. That was when he told me he was trying out for Delta. He'd totally screwed up his personal life, he knew that. From that point on his professional life meant everything to him. He hadn't succeeded as a husband or father, but as a soldier he knew he could be one of the best. When Delta Force took him in, he proved it. He accumulated medals and battle honors from missions all over the world, his reputation in Delta was second to none, even in the ranks of the elite he stood out.

I used to hear about him, though my contact with Dimitri during those Delta years was intermittent. Most Delta operatives tend to stick with their own. But the summer prior to 9/11 he'd called to tell me that his operational career had come to an unexpected end. He'd taken a bullet in the shoulder during some mission down in Colombia, his shattered collarbone had to be pinned. It hadn't healed well enough to go back on active service immediately, and he told me that if it didn't improve fast, Delta was going to offer him a place as an OTC, an Operators Training Course instructor. He said he was going to turn the offer down. He'd thought about approaching the CIA to offer his services, he told me if they didn't want him, he'd try his luck in the real world. The timing seemed fortuitous. I called him in October, he thought about it for a week, then signed up for Hawkeye.

"Ned." Now Channon lifted a finger warily. "Do you promise me you didn't know Dimitri was screwing around like that?"

I gave him my word that I hadn't known. Channon studied me, and finally nodded to himself. I asked if the IRS was tailing me. He conceded that it was possible.

"Not that I've breathed a word about you to them," he said. "But that's just me. Christ knows what Dimitri's been telling them." Channon rose from his chair, agitated by the thought of Dimitri in private session with the IRS. "There's a part two to the story," he said, facing me over his desk. "Dimitri cut a deal with the IRS. They were coming down on him so hard, he knew the only way he might crawl out from under was to offer them something real." What Dimitri had offered them, Channon explained, was a chance to bring the hammer down on the arms companies actually giving and receiving the bribes. "Dimitri got the IRS to cut him some slack till the next fair. He told them that's where he could do the spadework, set some bad guys up for the IRS to knock over later."

"The next fair," I said.

"Right." Channon made a face. "Springfield."

A new light suddenly illuminated Dimitri's death. That morning, and for the previous few weeks, Dimitri hadn't been working solely on Hawkeye.

"He wasn't working for our operation, period," Channon corrected me sternly when I ventured the remark. "Once the IRS showed me what they had on Dimitri, I suspended him. I made it absolutely

West Point uniform, were on their way to the mess. Bright as buttons. Laughing. Still at that stage when the famed Honor Code held them with the unshakable force of born-again revelation. Upright and keen, barely more than boys. Kids for whom war, like so much else of life, was still just a theory. Their faces fresh, engagingly open, and so incredibly, unbelievably, young.

"You're sure you want this," Alex said, finally turning back to me.

As I nodded, there was a knock at the door. Ernie Small, the Point's head of Infantry, looked in. I stayed in my chair. Under Channon's instructions I'd made a habit of dropping in at West Point at various times, touching base with old colleagues and generally showing my face around. Channon's idea was that my presence at any time wouldn't then be a matter for comment. He didn't want our occasional meetings to be clandestine, he wanted them to simply blend with my life. The best cover, he told me, was no cover. Channon knew his business. The tactic had worked. Now Ernie Small simply winked at me, asked jokingly if I was chasing my old job, then reminded Channon that fifty cadets were over in the main lecture hall waiting for his pearls of wisdom. Channon made a face. Ernie smiled and withdrew.

"You pull out now, no one's gonna hold it against you," Channon said when Ernie was gone.

I didn't reply.

He studied me, then rose to his feet. "You phone in each day, every day. You give me a full brief. And next time you hear me tell you you're coming in, that's it." He jabbed his finger onto the desk. "You are coming in. Clear?"

I dipped my head. He let his look linger on me a moment, as if he still wasn't quite sure about something. My response to Dimitri's death? My insistence that I wanted to go on? At last he gave it up and glanced at his watch. He told me the hour he expected my first call.

"What if there's nothing to report?"

He looked up slowly. "Just phone me," he said simply. When he saw that I got it, he nodded. My call would be my report. Confirmation that Ned Rourke—unlike Dimitri Spandos—was still in the game.

CHAPTER 3

Our family home was a brick-and-tile place on Ellis Street in Yonkers, lawns front and back, with tall hedges on both sides to screen us from the Walters and the Bidwells. The street was tree-lined and peaceful, the trash collection Mondays the sole point of drama in the week.

We bought the house back when I was a West Point instructor. I never expected to like it, but my life up till then had been so footloose that the settled calm of Ellis Street, the almost soporific blandness of the neighborhood, grew on me. The passing years did their work and rooted me to the place. The Haplon factory was just over the state line in Connecticut, so we kept the house after I resigned my commission, and I commuted up there daily. I never told my wife or son about the double life I was leading. I knew that any hint that I was back on active service—overt or covert—would probably collapse our marriage and ruin our lives. And Channon's orders had always been to keep the operation strictly to myself. It was safer for everyone that way, he said. For me. For them. And he was right. In spite of everything that has happened since, I still believe he was right, it really was safer. Whether it was better for everyone is another question, one I didn't properly consider until Dimitri's death. And by then, as I discovered, it was already too damn late.

"Maybe It was gambling trouble." My wife Fiona was seated at the breakfast bar eating muesli and reading the latest *Scientific American*. I'd just showered and dressed after my routine morning exercises—sit-ups, skipping rope, then some stretches—and these were Fiona's first words as I walked into the kitchen. "Olympia told me the kind of money he used to lose," she said, looking up from her magazine. "Maybe Dimitri went in over his head."

I remarked that Dimitri had gotten over his problem a long time ago.

She sniffed. "He said."

"Yeah."

"And you really believed him?"

I gave her a dark look, and Fiona dropped her gaze back into the magazine. When I'd gotten home the night before, I'd given her all I really wanted to about Dimitri's death—that it was a tragic accident, a loose shot from the range—and the last thing I needed was to chew over the remainders of his long-failed marriage. I took some ham from the fridge and a carton of eggs. Nodding to her magazine, I asked what was new in the wonderful world of geochemistry.

"Well no one there got shot yesterday," she said.

She turned another page. I got the frying pan out of the drainer.

"He really was the pits," she murmured.

"Can we leave this? He hasn't been dead twenty-four hours. You think he was a slimeball? Fine. I don't want to hear it just now."

I received a less than sympathetic look.

"Right," she said.

I turned and reached up to the plate rack. I asked what she had on at work that day. Fiona relented a little and gave me a quick run-through of her schedule: office in the morning, lunch with some Geometrics clients, then down to the lab for most of the afternoon. Geometrics was the company she worked for, a specialist in testing geological samples. Their office and lab were just two blocks from home, one of the reasons we bought the house in the first place.

My wife's career, let me say right off, was a real lesson in how far sheer guts and determination can get a body in this world. Back in the early years of our marriage, when we moved from base to base around the country with our baby son in tow, Fiona never once complained. But as our boy got older she decided she wanted more from life than the usual round of coffee mornings with the other officers' wives, followed by housework, then half a bottle of gin in the afternoon with Oprah. She started studying again. Some correspondence courses first, then she got herself on some program the U.S. Army had going, and within a couple of years she was launched on a degree course offered in modules by some college out west. Just chemistry at first, but we used to go camping a lot in those days and she got interested in all the different types of terrain we hiked through. After six years' hard grind, she graduated in geochemistry. From there she picked up work wherever I was posted, but it was a frustrating time for her, having to leave her job whenever the Army moved me on. When I took the West Point job after Mogadishu, it wasn't just the guarantee of my personal safety that made her so happy. At last she had stability in her life. Her own home, and her first steady job since our marriage.

She started in the lab at Geometrics and worked her way up. It was a small company back then, developing new techniques to evaluate rock samples for the mining industry. When Geometrics boomed, more promotions followed. After five years Fiona was their head geochemist, managing the main lab and overseeing their international facilities. Quite an achievement for any woman; for one like Fiona, written off by her family when she accidentally became pregnant at seventeen, simply amazing.

Now she made a note in her diary, then came over to the percolator. Dropping some bread in the toaster, I drummed my fingers lightly on the bench. I asked if Brad had been down.

"Haven't seen him," she said, and she gave my drumming fingers a do-you-mind kind of look. I decided I was not prepared, at a quarter of eight in the morning, to face yet another outbreak of low-level hostilities. I beat a retreat down the hall and opened the side door to the garage.

"Brad!" I hollered. Our son Bradley had been holed up in semi-independent quarters above the garage since the age of sixteen. We built the conversion for Fiona's widowed mother, Charlotte, but when

Charlotte made the only spontaneous decision of her life and hitched up with a widower from Denver and married him—all this a month before she was due to move in with us—Brad hauled his desk into the conversion and claimed it as his own. A place to study, he told us. Before long the rest of his junk was making the short migration across the house, concluding some weeks later with the grand finale, the dismantlement and disappearance into the conversion of his bed. Seven years later, a high school diploma and a college degree behind him, he was showing no sign of moving on. Now he was working on his doctorate, an inquiry into the meaning of lumps of Mesolithic rock discovered in a layer of Precambrian. "Brad!" I hollered again, but there was no answer, so I climbed up and rapped on his door. "Eggs and ham. You want some?"

When he called me inside I found him sitting at his desk, freshly showered, wearing nothing but a pair of white briefs. He was tapping away at the keyboard of his PC.

"You want to leave that alone for five minutes, come and have some breakfast?"

"Has Mom left?" he asked without turning.

His mother, I told him, was still down in the kitchen.

I glanced around. He had more books stacked along one wall than I'd read in my entire life, and more again on the shelves. A couple of trophies up there too, from college baseball.

I nodded to the PC. "You don't get enough of that nine to five?"

"Tell Mom to wait, can you?" He scratched the stubble on his jaw, his eyes fixed on the screen. "I'll be down in two secs."

I could have asked him what he had to say to his mother that he couldn't say to me, but what, finally, would be the point? The emotional parameters of our family had been firmly entrenched for years, the special bond that existed between Brad and Fiona was one I'd long ago accepted as exclusive. It was more than just the mother-and-son thing. Physically he resembled me, tall and lean, but Brad and his mother were intellectual kin. It was no surprise to anyone when he decided to major in geology at college, by then he'd been involved in an informal private seminar with his mother on the subject for years. She never forced it on him. It started way back on our family camping trips. He gradually lost interest in fishing with me and took to wandering off fossicking with Fiona, armed with a hammer and a sample bag. If I thought about it at all, I guess I thought that most kids have phases, that in time he'd come back to me, we'd do our things later. Fishing and hunting. Just spending time together like my father had with me. Of course, it never happened. From the age of around ten, rocks, for Brad, were no longer just things you threw at squirrels and skipped over the lake; he could not tell you where a trout might rise or how to stalk a lone deer up a wooded valley, but he could distinguish igneous from metamorphic rock at a glance and give you three good reasons why the lump of stone you held in your hand was neither.

And later, in high school, he spent hours each week down the road with Fiona at the Geometrics laboratory, a kind of unofficial and unpaid assistant. When Fiona set up her study at home in Brad's vacated bedroom, he treated it like his own; using her microscope; walking off with her books and periodicals; borrowing any interesting new rock samples that caught his eye and taking them for an extended inspection out in his own quarters above the garage. It drove her crazy sometimes, but I'm sure Fiona wouldn't have changed those years for anything.

When I returned late from work at Haplon, I'd often find them in her study, drinking coffee and talking, Brad seated with his legs stretched out on the floor in front of him. My appearance in the doorway could generally be relied upon to bring their talks to a premature end. I guess they just didn't have that much to say to a guy who'd been out selling arms all day.

I can't complain. My son grew up and became himself, the man he was going to be, through this deep tie with his mother. But what I wouldn't have given that morning, standing in the room of my twenty-three-year-old son, not to feel that the relationship between us had probably peaked somewhere back in those distant days when I was still a young soldier and he was barely a boy of nine.

"Ham and eggs," he said, nodding to his PC. "Excellent."

When I retreated down the stairs he called after me, reminding me to tell his mother to wait.

Brad arrived In the kitchen five minutes later, his shirttail hanging over his jeans, with a printout in his hand. He placed the printout in front of Fiona, then came over to inspect the ham and eggs sizzling in the pan. He looked over my shoulder. "Got a job," he told me, then he wandered around the breakfast bar and pulled up a stool by his mother.

"This is great," she said after a moment, squeezing his shoulder as she carried on reading the printout. "Who sent this?" She scanned for a name. "Barchevsky?"

Brad picked up a knife and fork, gave a quick drum roll on the breakfast bar. "Da-dah," he said, then dropped the cutlery, laughing, and hugged his mother. "Thanks," he told her. "One I owe you. A big one."

She pinched his cheek, then they bent their heads over the printout, smiling like a pair of kids.

I, meanwhile, was still in my usual place back at the starting post. Brad's Ph.D., as far as I knew, was not due to be finished till the new year.

"What happened to the doctorate?" I asked.

Brad looked at me curiously. "This isn't a for-life kind of job. It's a few months in the field. A couple of mines and some virgin claims, somewhere I can test out a few ideas."

I dished up the ham and eggs. Brad sat down opposite me at the bar, and we ate while Fiona continued perusing the e-mail printout. Eventually I had to ask.

"So who's this Barchevsky?"

Ivan Barchevsky, Brad explained between mouthfuls, was the owner and head geologist of a small mining company. "I just met him the once, but he's a big fan of Mom's. Hey"— he turned to Fiona —"you see they're gonna pay me? I'da known that, I woulda asked for share options. Wayne Mitchell paid off his college loan like that. Summer job out in California, they hit pay dirt, Wayne walks off with fifty thou."

Fiona gave Brad the printout. I asked him where he was going to be working.

"Mbuji-Mayi area," he said.

When I glanced at Fiona she took her coffee cup to the sink. I turned back to Brad.

"That doesn't sound like California."

"Africa." He forked some more ham into his mouth. He turned

the printout for me to see, pointing to a name halfway down the page. "Congo somewhere."

I read it aloud: The Democratic Republic of the Congo. "They're handing out visas?" I said, surprised.

Brad drew my attention to another part of the printout. Apparently his visa had already been arranged and paid for, he simply had to go to the consulate to get his passport stamped. "I'll go in today, they say it might take a few hours." He shrugged. Foreigners.

"Brad, have you read up any background on this place?"

"Sure." He dipped his head, swallowing the last of his breakfast. "There's a whole bunch of kimberlite pipes right on the boundary of the main claim, they're getting magnetic anomalies like you wouldn't believe. Hey, Mom. I mean, just everywhere."

I made a face. "I was thinking more in terms of politics."

"Yeah, well, they had some kinda trouble till late last year, Barchevsky said. But now it's like fine." Brad took his plate to the dishwasher. "You know. Stable."

Stable. A country where the good citizens had spent the previous year slaughtering each other at the rate of several hundred per month.

"Brad—" I said, but he was already talking to his mother. In a few weeks she'd be making her own journey to Africa—Johannesburg, where Geometrics had a lab. It was part of the annual whistle-stop tour she'd instituted three years earlier, calling in at all Geometrics facilities to hear their problems firsthand, making them feel the head office cared, and presenting the annual bonuses. Brad, from what I could make out, was hoping they could meet up in South Africa and go to the Kruger National Park together. I got the impression this wasn't the first time they'd discussed the idea.

"Okay, okay. I'll check my schedule," she finally conceded.

"Great." He came around the bar and grabbed the printout. He addressed his mother as he headed down the hall. "I'll call Joe, tell him I'm not interested in Canada anymore. Catch you later down at the lab." Voice fading into the garage, he told me that breakfast was great.

I pushed my knife and fork together on the plate. Behind me I could hear Fiona going through the routine, wiping down the sink then putting a powder pellet in the dishwasher. At last I turned, one arm resting on the breakfast bar.

"So," I said.

She started talking about dinner; things she had to buy at the store.

"Oh, come on, Fiona, cut it out. Brad's going to the goddamned Congo and this is how I find out?"

"I only just heard myself."

I looked at her.

"What do you want to hear, Ned? That I encouraged him?"

"Did you?"

"He's an adult. He wants to go, he goes."

"And the fact that you teed it up with this Barchevsky guy, that's got nothing to do with it."

"Oh, for Pete's sake." She came and took my plate and shoved it in the dishwasher. She turned the dishwasher on.

I asked about Brad's mention of Canada.

"It was an alternate site," she said. "Some mine up in Ontario."

"Ontario. Well, what's wrong with that? Ontario."

"Weren't you listening?" She gestured in the direction of the garage. "He's got a firm offer for the Congo. He's made up his mind."

"Nothing to do with you."

"Right."

"Where else was on offer?"

Her eyes skated past me so I asked again.

"Nowhere," she said, and walked out of the kitchen and up the stairs to our bedroom. I took a moment with myself, then went on up. She was standing at the dresser, loading her purse.

"Brad tells you he wants a few months in the field," I said, "and with all your contacts, every geologist and mine manager you know, you're saying that's the best you could come up with. Ontario and the Congo?"

"He asked me last month," she muttered into her purse. "It wasn't exactly extended notice."

"I don't buy it."

"What's wrong, Ned?" Her tone was tight now, and mean. She kicked my old sneakers aside as she recrossed to the door. She tilted her head back and looked straight at me. "You're not afraid of what he might see there, are you?"

So now she'd said it. And having said it, she regretted it immediately. She pushed by me and went out to her study.

I'd always tried, for obvious reasons, not to bring any troubles from my work back home. But a spouse can't help learning something of a partner's daily concerns—Lord knows, I'd heard enough of office politics at Geometrics to fill a library—and anyway, I'd have been less than human not to have mentioned the Democratic Republic of the Congo to Fiona sometime. A major African war had been raging there until the previous Christmas, when the exhausted combatants signed a peace treaty. Throughout the conflict, weapons had entered the country through the infinitely permeable walls of international sanctions and UN embargoes. And among those weapons, no doubt, were some supplied by Haplon. Weapons for which all the correct paperwork was in place, but which nevertheless arrived at the worst possible destination. Guns I sold.

Which is what Fiona meant by her remark about me being afraid of what Brad might see. Though there was peace there now, what Brad might see out in the Congo, apart from magnetic anomalies, was the aftermath of a war his father had helped to create. Ravaged towns and ruined lives. Brutalized men. Women permanently scarred by rape. Limbless children.

I stopped out in the hall while Fiona piled papers into her briefcase.

"This is wrong," I told her. "So damn wrong."

She screwed up her face and snapped her briefcase shut.

"Our problems are between us, Fiona. You and me. Not you and me and Brad."

"Just you and me?"

"You and me," I said.

She came into the hall and put her face up close to mine.

"If that was true," she said, "then there wouldn't be a problem now, would there." She dropped her briefcase by my feet and went along to the bathroom, closing the door.

I slumped back against the wall. Six weeks to the day before Dimitri's death, Fiona accused me of having an affair. I denied it, of course. But in the days and weeks that followed, she made my life a living hell of interrogations over supper, silences at breakfast, and casual inquiries loaded with well-disguised traps that any careless answer of mine was liable to trigger. She had sensed that I was lying to her. It wasn't any one thing, more a series of lapses on my part.

Out jogging one evening, for example, I stepped into a phone booth near home to phone Channon. I later learned that Fiona had driven past on her way to the store and seen me: so who was I calling that I couldn't call from home? And twice when I had to meet late with Customs about Hawkeye, I rang Fiona with the lazy excuse that I was working late. Both times Fiona rang back, only to discover from my Haplon colleagues that I wasn't there.

Once suspicion began to roll, it just snowballed. After nearly two years undercover, evasion was second nature to me, but it wasn't too hard for Fiona to catch me in a series of small half-truths, not once she'd put her scientific mind to it. Her suspicions intensified daily. Her field of inquiry widened as she sifted her memory for possible earlier signs of my infidelity. That first time she confronted me with the accusation, I laughed. Six weeks later, I couldn't even raise a smile. Our lives were becoming unlivable.

Now Fiona emerged from the bathroom; she grabbed her brief-case. "And for your information," she said, striding away down the hall, "it was Brad who suggested the Congo. I didn't like the idea. I told him I didn't like it, but now he's got the job and neither one of us can stop him."

"It's a war zone."

"No it's not." She turned and came back. She planted herself in front of me. "And I resent the implication that I'd send Brad there just to get at you. That's not why he's going. He's a geologist. What's he supposed to do, cross out the places on the map that you've been selling God-knows-what to? Most prospective territory left in the world is in those places. What should he do? Put his career on hold just so you don't have to feel guilty?"

"Listen—"

"No." She threw up her hand. "If you've got any more to say, go tell it to your bimbo." She veered into her study to retrieve a forgot-ten file. If I'd told her the truth at that moment, the arguments and recriminations would have ended. But our marriage would have ended too, I never doubted that for one second. So instead of telling her the truth, I remained silent out in the hall. When she came out of her study I put my hand on her arm. She tilted up her chin.

"Going to hit me?"

"There is no bimbo."

She shrugged my hand off.

"There is no woman," I said. "There is no affair."

She peered at me. After a moment her look seemed to soften. She raised a finger.

"Very good," she said. "Very good." She walked along the hall, then turned down the stairs. "In fact, you get any better at it," she called over her shoulder, "you'll be lying like a third-rate goddamn lawyer."

We had been married nearly twenty-four years. When she wanted to push my buttons she knew where they were. By the time I got to the head of the stairs she was down at the front door. I grabbed the landing banister.

"Fiona!"

She opened the door.

"I'm not fucking anyone," I told her.

She regarded me coolly over her shoulder. "You're not fucking me, anyway," she said. "Not anymore." Stepping out, she closed the door gently behind her.

I bounded down the stairs, then caught something from the corner of my eye, and turned. Brad. He'd come down the hall from the garage and was standing by the kitchen, facing me. He must have heard every word. I slowed, then stopped on the bottom stair. We looked at each other awhile without speaking. At last he gestured to the kitchen.

"I brought down a copy of Barchevsky's offer."

"You heard."

He looked away. He said it was none of his business.

"It's a misunderstanding."

He made a face. "I don't need a map, Dad," he said, then he turned his back and loped off toward the garage.

It wasn't hard, at that moment, to see that I'd risked, and possibly already blown, the most important part of my life. And for what exactly? Two years' total immersion in an operation that Dimitri's actions had turned into a tragic farce? I couldn't accept that. There had to be more. I didn't want medals or glory, but when Hawkeye finally folded I had to have more to show for my decision to cloak my life in a lie than a dead ex-friend, a firm handshake from Channon, and a full Army pension.

When Hawkeye began, it was meant to last six months. Six months had become two years, with Channon shifting the touchline quarterly. I'd embarked on the operation knowing that the price was to be a temporary deceit, but that was all. Temporary. With hindsight, of course, I can see that I'd dug myself into a treacherous emotional hole, one so deep it could destroy me. The months I'd spent on Hawkeye. The petty deceptions I'd practiced on my family. They'd become spurs for me to go on with the operation, as if I could somehow regain what I'd lost and be self-justified by some final overarching triumph.

But I glimpsed the truth that morning. Glimpsed it and pushed it aside. Two years of deceit. The sudden fracture in my family. Dimitri's death. I was already in too deep to allow the truth any real life.

Brad disappeared into the garage, I called his name, and the door banged shut behind him. I stared at the wall a moment. Then turning slowly, I hauled myself up the stairs, and got ready for work.

CHAPTER 4

The Haplon offices were housed in a three-story aluminum-clad structure grafted to the front of the Haplon factory. The marketing department occupied most of the top floor, and Milton Rossiter had his office up there too. That gave us good access, but the downside was his access to me.

"Ned!"

My deputy, Gillian Streiss, was going through the leads from Springfield with me when Milton's call came echoing down the hall. Arching her brow, Gillian flipped her notepad closed, then withdrew to her own office while I dragged myself out of my chair.

"Ned!" he shouted again just as I put my head around his door. He beckoned me in, hitting the intercom and bellowing instructions to someone in a far corner of the factory. His jacket hung over the back of his chair. A fax in the corner was churning out paper. "Can you lay your hands on Trevanian's wish list?" he asked me.

I retrieved the list from my office.

"Trevanian'll be here in two minutes," Rossiter said, running a pen down the list, making crosses. "He wants to see the gear in action, whatever we can lay on for him. But definitely this stuff." He handed me the list.

I remarked that it seemed like pretty short notice.

"You wanna tell him it's not convenient or you wanna sell him the damn guns?" Rossiter hit the intercom again. This time he spoke to Darren down on our test-firing range, telling him to expect some customers in ten minutes. "And set up some fresh targets. And while you're at it, how about runnin' a broom over the place before they get there. I was down there this mornin', looks like a fuckin' sty." He flicked off the intercom and faced me. "The Lagundi woman's comin' too."

"Do we have any idea what name's going to be on the End User Certificate? Presuming they place an order."

Rossiter turned aside, tearing off a fax. "Nigeria," he said.

I looked at him. An End User Certificate is attached to all arms transactions, it's meant to guarantee the purchaser's legitimacy and ensure weapons don't end up in the wrong hands. In practice, the guarantee is frequently worthless. There are just too many corrupt public officials in impoverished countries who are willing to trade the appropriate signatures and rubber stamps for a relatively modest fee. And one of those impoverished countries, quite notoriously, is Nigeria.

"So we don't know where they'll go," I said.

"They'll go to Nigeria."

When I snorted, Rossiter lifted his eyes.

"You wanna do this or not? Because if you don't, I can always whistle Gillian in to handle it."

I folded Trevanian's list into my pocket. Rossiter kept his eyes on me steadily as I retreated into the hall.

Trevanian arrived in reception looking like he'd dressed for golf—checked pants and a green V-neck sweater. Lagundi was wearing a white slacksuit and a collection of heavy gold jewelry. She looked like a million dollars. I gave them each a pair of safety glasses, grabbed some for myself, then launched into the standard Haplon tour.

The factory and office block were on a thirty-acre site, the rear five acres of which were a dumping ground for obsolete and terminally broken-down machinery, a legacy from the days of Milton Rossiter's father. The exterior of the main plant didn't promise much either. It was a collection of buildings cobbled together from each decade of the late twentieth century, an architectural eyesore, but the interior really wasn't so bad. The Pentagon can't afford to be seen purchasing from sweatshops, and guys like Rossiter invest plenty to retain their preferred supplier status. The factory floor was always spotless. I led Trevanian and Lagundi around the machine shop, where our engineers were working on prototypes for the next generation of smart mortars. I showed them Big Tom, the automated lathe that had once reconditioned worn barrels from U.S. Army tanks that Rossiter's father later on sold to various regimes in Central America. Trevanian acted interested when I gave him the history, but Lagundi didn't bother.

From there we went out to the assembly lines, stopping behind the guy doing quality control on the night-sights. Trevanian gestured down the line of workers dressed in white overalls, hunched over a long bench, assembling electronic parts. He asked if we were busy. No more than usual, I told him. In fact, it was relatively quiet, we were almost down to a skeleton staff, but there was no sense letting Trevanian know how much we needed his order.

Next I took them out to the munitions line, a separate part of the Haplon plant, set away for reasons of safety. Though we'd never had an accident, there was enough missile propellant and gunpowder stored in our bunker to blow the average-sized neighborhood to hell. It was only a grandfather clause in Connecticut state law that allowed this part of the plant to operate at all, but Rossiter had grown tired of fighting the endless local petitions, and this whole operation was scheduled to move out to the Greenfield site in California before year-end. We watched some specially enhanced mortar shells being assembled on the line for a while, but when Trevanian started casting his eyes toward the giant wall clock, I knew that the recreational part of the tour was over.

Out back behind the plant, the Haplon firing range was about a hundred yards long, grassed banks to either side and a high earth bank behind the targets. Someone was already firing from one of the concrete bays when we entered the gallery. Micky Baker, who'd been standing behind the shooter, came over.

"We're about done." He jerked his head toward the armory. "Darren's gone to get your stuff." Darren, the Haplon rangemaster, the guy Rossiter had bawled out over the intercom. A yard broom, I noticed, was propped by the ammo cases, and the floor was clean.

I nodded to the shooter, asking Micky who the guy was.

"Rangemaster from Springfield," he told me, and when I cocked a brow in surprise, Micky explained, "Cops were giving him the total third degree. Kind of blaming him for how that Fettners guy got killed. He figured he should get his own ballistics done on the pistols from the Springfield range. If the cops ever find the bullet that killed the guy, he figures he'll be able to prove it didn't come from the range." Micky's tone suggested that he thought the exercise was a waste of time.

Tapping my shoulder, Trevanian asked if there was a queue.

"You're done," I told Micky, and he went to tell the shooter.

Darren arrived then, pushing a trolley-load of weapons. While I looked the weapons over with Trevanian, Lagundi pulled up a chair. Micky and the Springfield rangemaster went to retrieve the bullets from the sand traps behind the targets.

"Someone said you knew Spandos," said Trevanian, pulling the magazine off a P23 and inspecting the breech. I looked up. "Outside of business," he added.

"We went through West Point the same time."

"West Point."

"What was he to you?"

"He handled some orders for me awhile back. Wouldn't have picked him for a West Pointer." He was fishing, but when I didn't rise, he snapped the magazine into the gun, then turned to the range. Micky was still up at the targets, sifting the sand traps, so Trevanian replaced the weapon on the trolley.

"We had some Nigerian generals down here last month." I gestured to the weapons. "They didn't ask to see any of this."

"Is that right?" said Trevanian. He couldn't have cared less. Cecille Lagundi, seated behind the first firing bay, gazed up to the targets as if she wasn't listening to our conversation.

Then Micky Baker's voice came over the bunker speakers. *"Ned? You want bodies or circles?"*

I glanced at Trevanian. Half and half, he said. I relayed the instruction over the intercom to Micky, who immediately set to work at the far end of the range. Once the targets were in place, Micky returned with the Springfield rangemaster. When Darren started taking Trevanian through the safety drill, I accompanied Micky and the other guy out of the bunker. I asked the rangemaster how everything finished up with the police.

"Finished?" He ran a hand over his bald head. "Jesus Christ, I wish it was. I tell 'em fifty fucking times the shot couldn'ta come from the range. You think they'll listen?"

I indicated the envelopes he was clutching. "You going to write them?"

He opened an envelope. Inside was one of the bullets he'd retrieved from the sand traps. Then he showed me the number on the envelope: the serial number, he told me, of the gun from which the bullet was fired. "They ever find the bullet killed the guy, I'll have my own ballistics ready."

"I heard they'd given up searching." Rossiter had told me that. I wasn't sure if I believed him.

"Only the cops," the rangemaster replied unhappily. "Those goof-offs dropped it in the too-hard basket. Sittin' on their butts now, doin' paperwork, blamin' me."

"The FBI are out there too," Micky informed me.

"A whole fuckin' team they got out there," the rangemaster cut in. "Guys in suits directin' guys in overalls. They marked out the parkin' lot in square yards, checkin' each square to see if maybe the bullet got buried in the tarmac. Take 'em weeks, the way they're goin'."

"What if they get a match with one of those?" I nodded to his envelopes.

"No fuckin' chance," he said. "No way." He turned and started back to the Haplon offices.

When Micky Baker went to follow, I grabbed his sleeve. When the guy was out of earshot, I asked Micky, "What's he doing using our range?"

"Rossiter's deal. Rossiter called me in, said I should bring this friend of his down here. Let him blast away at whatever he wanted."

"Friend?"

"Well, they seemed pretty friendly." Micky drew away from me apologetically, anxious that the guy left in his charge might be found wandering the Haplon plant alone. I watched him jog off in pursuit of the rangemaster. I turned it over. The FBI's arrival on the scene was no big surprise. Channon would have told the IRS what had happened out at Springfield, and they wouldn't have hesitated to get the feds involved. But the connection between Rossiter and the Springfield rangemaster was unexpected. Unsettled, I returned to the bunker.

Darren gave me some ear protection, then we stood behind Trevanian as he took aim with a P23. When he squeezed the trigger, the gun jumped, and a metronomic thump-thump of semiautomatic fire went pounding into the target. Then he paused and switched to automatic. This time when he fired, the barrel juddered upward, the sound through my ear protectors was like a staccato clatter of drums. An odor of hot metal and burnt gunpowder filled the firing bays. From the corner of my eye I saw Lagundi raise a white handkerchief to her nose and mouth.

When he'd emptied the magazine, Trevanian flicked on the safety and reracked the gun. Pushing back his ear protectors, he went to join Darren, who was peering up the range through tripod-mounted binoculars. Darren stepped aside, and Trevanian bent to inspect the damage. Even with the naked eye you could see the body-target had been raked hip to shoulder.

"Ever have any trouble with the barrels?" Trevanian asked me, still peering through the binoculars.

I told him no, never.

"Fair rate of fire for a thing like that."

"We've never had any trouble," I repeated.

Stepping back, he squinted up the range. Unlike many buyers who came to try out the merchandise, Trevanian knew what he was doing. He wasn't going to be rushed. He went back to the trolley and selected another gun.

He handled the bigger guns well, but his touch seemed to desert him when he moved down the scale. I noticed that he fired just the one magazine from the only pistol on the trolley, and he missed the bull by a mile. Half an hour it went on like that, Trevanian blasting targets, getting a feel for the guns, while Lagundi sat watching, not saying a word. Finally only one target remained, a full-body. When

Trevanian reracked the last gun, Darren invited Lagundi to step up and take a shot. Trevanian declined on her behalf.

"Excuse me?" she said.

He looked over his shoulder. "You don't need to."

"I might want to."

"Well, do you?"

His tone seemed to get to her. She rose, reached into her purse, and produced a Beretta.

Trevanian made a face. "This isn't personal shooting practice. If you want to fire something, at least make it count. Choose a weapon off the trolley."

She crossed to the firing bay. When Darren looked at me, I shrugged. As far as I was concerned she was a customer, she could do what she liked. Darren went and gave her some ear protection, and she clipped back her hair as he gave her the obligatory safety instructions.

"Can she shoot?" I asked, moving to stand beside Trevanian, watching her.

Trevanian bent over the trolley, reexamining the guns he'd been firing. He didn't seem too pleased with her sudden display of independence. When Darren left her alone in the bay, Lagundi raised her pistol arm slowly and took aim like a sports shooter, like she knew which end of the gun meant business. Steadying herself, she sighted, then fired. Her gaze still fixed on the target, she let her arm fall.

"Low," Darren announced, peering through the binoculars. "Six inches."

She lifted her arm, then sighted and fired again.

"Still low," Darren told her, less certainly.

She took aim a third time and fired. She didn't wait for Darren's verdict, she pumped three more bullets into the target, then ejected the empty magazine and returned to her chair. She took off the ear protection and starting rearranging her hair clips. Darren beckoned me across the bay to take a look through the binoculars. There were several white concentric circles on the head of the target, the bull's-eye at the center. The circles were unmarked.

"Below the bull," Darren said. I adjusted my gaze downward and saw it immediately, a grouping as tight and neat as you could hope for. Six bullet holes punched clean through the throat.

"Luck?" I wondered aloud.

"At seventy-five yards?" Darren pursed his lips and turned his head.

I contemplated the target a moment, the hairs prickling on my neck. Then I stood up and glanced over my shoulder. Trevanian was still at the trolley. Over on the chair, Lagundi's pistol lay cooling by her purse. As she finished straightening her hair, her eye caught mine, and she smiled. Then she picked up the Beretta, dropped it into the purse, and told Trevanian it was time they were leaving. He rose, turning slowly from the trolley to face her. If looks could kill, she would have been dead.

CHAPTER 5

Lots of people shoot straight, they're not all murderers," Rita Durranti declared when I finished telling her about Trevanian and Lagundi's visit to Haplon. "I'm more worried they were out at your plant so fast. They're pushing this along like they're in an awful hurry."

Rita was a senior Customs officer, the single point of contact between Hawkeye and the civilian world. She was the person Dimitri and I came to when we needed information or access to the confidential files that Customs kept on suspect arms shipments, and the range of lowlifes, weirdos, and downright dangerous people behind them. In return, and subject to clearance from Channon, we reciprocated with information that the Customs people were in no position to gather. A slightly built woman of Italian descent, Rita lowered her eyes as we walked.

"I can't believe you still want to go on with Hawkeye. Not after Dimitri—" She lifted a hand. Dimitri's duplicity. His death. "I thought you had more brains. Honest to God, I did."

We paused by the inscription stone at Grant's Tomb, then turned to stroll around the paved plaza. It was Rita, with her somewhat strange sense of humor, who first selected the memorial as an appropriate meeting place for any exchange of information connected with Hawkeye. I generally preferred these short, out-of-doors encounters to my occasional preappointed forays into her anonymous office at Customs downtown, but so soon after Dimitri's death, the Tomb cast an undeniable pall.

"You know, the worst part is I never really liked the guy," she said. "It was like dealing with someone who had a piece missing. And I can tell you, he didn't much like working with me, a woman. No offense, but Dimitri was three parts sexist pig."

"There's worse than Dimitri."

"I know. I've dated both of them." She shot me a look. "Maybe the IRS screwed up. If they made too much noise, that could have got him killed."

"Officially, it's an accident."

"Officially, Ned, you're a sales manager."

I let that one pass.

"If you felt threatened, in any kind of danger yourself," she said, "you'd tell me, right?"

I nodded, but her gaze lingered skeptically on my face. I had a lot of time for Rita Durranti. Mid-thirties, and still single, she was tough in that way a woman can sometimes be after growing up with too many brothers. Rita had five: four older, one younger. She only stood about five feet two in her socks, but she was a packet of energy and drive. Her grandfather and father had both worked the Fulton Fish Market, there wasn't much anyone could have told her about the ways of the world that she hadn't learned firsthand by the time she was fifteen. When Channon first introduced us, I admit I had reservations, she seemed too young, too inexperienced for the work. After two years, I'd have been more than a little disappointed if she moved on to the more senior posting in Customs that she richly deserved. If I'd wanted to talk with anyone about how vulnerable Dimitri's death had made me feel, it would have been with Rita. But I didn't. Finally she seemed to get the unspoken message. She sat down on a bench.

"I can't find any mention of Lagundi in our files. I went through everything on Liberia twice. Zip."

"Maybe she's got nothing to do with Liberia."

"You saw Channon's report?" Rita said. I had. Channon's report wasn't actually Channon's, it was the DIA's assessment of where Trevanian might eventually deliver the Haplon materiel. Apart from a crazy predilection for placing numerical probabilities on every half-assed guess they make, the DIA's assessments on these matters is generally superior to the CIA's. And after processing all the information we'd given them—types and quantities of materiel under discussion, and Trevanian's name—they'd concluded that Liberia was the most likely destination. Exactly which rebel faction it was going to, they hadn't quite figured. "How often does he get it wrong?" she said, meaning Channon. "Trevanian's company's active there. That's where there's a war brewing. That's where they need the guns."

I frowned. I told her Liberia was only a maybe. She asked me where I thought Lagundi came from.

"Rossiter says Nigeria."

She nodded. "End User Certificate's Nigerian."

I cocked my head. "I didn't tell you that."

"You didn't have to. I got a copy from Commerce this morning. Just for the night-sights."

"What date was on it?"

She was perplexed. "Haplon filed it, Ned. The date's whatever date you put on it." We looked at each other a moment, then I turned to face the memorial. "You didn't date it?" she said.

"I didn't see it."

She missed a beat. "If there's an End User Certificate, there's an order."

I told her to fax me a copy of the certificate as soon as she got back to her office. My home number, I said. But by this time Rita's trail of thought was catching up with mine.

"Rossiter never told you Trevanian had placed the order?"

"It's his company."

"You're his sales manager. What reason could he have for keeping you in the dark, just sidelining you like that?" When I suggested that there could be a million reasons, she said, "All right. Name one."

I was silent.

"Then let me name one," she said. "Rossiter's found out who

you are." I turned my head in denial. Rita made a face. "Don't do the brave soldier number on me. This is a real problem. If the order turns out to be a breaker, how do we stay on top of it? We can't if you've been sidelined."

"We will."

"How?" When she saw I had no reply, her lips went tight. She pulled a notepad from her briefcase, tore out a page, and gave it to me. "Those are some of the questions I prepared, things I was going to ask you about the Trevanian deal. How many can you answer?"

The questions were extensive. Mostly they concerned preliminary paperwork and correspondence between Haplon and Trevanian that I should have seen. Some pieces I should have written myself. But I hadn't seen any of it. I couldn't answer a single one of the questions. Folding the torn page, I slipped it into my pocket.

"Well?" said Rita.

"I'll find out."

She rolled her eyes.

"I'll get copies of the correspondence," I told her. "Whatever you need. Just leave it with me."

A young couple came by, pushing a baby in a stroller. When they sat down on the next bench, Rita got up and we walked over to the granite mausoleum, then paused by the engraved maps of Grant's campaigns, a temporary exhibition. Maps and campaigns that I'd pored over for interminable hours as a West Point cadet, now long forgotten. Rita studied the maps.

"Did Channon tell you about the two orders Dimitri put through the system for Trevanian?"

I nodded. Channon had told me just that morning when I reported to him on the phone. I told him I was going to see Rita. Channon mentioned the old orders and warned me not to get dragged into any wrangle with Rita about Dimitri's work, he said he was concerned that Customs might make their own decision to shut Hawkeye down.

"And did he tell you I wasn't happy about them?" she said. "Even at the time?"

"He mentioned it."

"Then maybe he also mentioned that Customs came within a whisker of totally withdrawing our support from Hawkeye." My head swiveled, I looked at her. "That's right. And now Trevanian's back on the scene, Dimitri's dead, and you can just imagine what I'm thinking."

"Without your support, there's no operation."

"I know," she said.

My heart fell. "We do still have your support."

She looked at me. She didn't reply.

"Rita?"

"I kept telling Channon that Dimitri wasn't being straight with me."

"You don't know he wasn't being straight."

"Maybe if Channon had paid some attention, Dimitri wouldn't have wound up dead." She turned away from the maps and strolled along by the wall, and I went with her. She clutched her briefcase to her chest. She was clearly troubled, not only by what had already happened, but by what else might occur. She seemed to be puzzling out how she should proceed. At the end of the wall, she stopped and faced me. "Why do you want to go on with this?"

"Because it's not finished."

"That's all?"

"Trevanian's order looks like a breaker. What more do you want?"

"So going on with it, that's your duty."

"If you like."

"Not revenge?"

"On who?"

"That's what I'm wondering."

We looked at each other. Then I said, "If you were going to withdraw your support, you would have done it by now." She shrugged. Probably, she conceded. When I asked her why she hadn't, she shrugged again. I turned it over.

"Trevanian got two dirty orders out under your nose," I said. "That must hurt."

She raised a hand. "You know what? Let's just find ourselves somewhere to sit, you can have a look at the papers you asked for."

We found ourselves an isolated bench. She opened her briefcase and showed me some of the paperwork on those earlier orders from Trevanian, the ones Dimitri had shepherded through Fettners. She also showed me copies of the End User Certificates. Nigerian. The orders weren't half the size of the one he seemed to have placed with Haplon. She lingered with some bitterness over her failed attempts to have Channon lean on Dimitri. After fifteen minutes she came to the end of her story. "Channon said I was imagining things. The arms got loaded on a ship bound for Nigeria, the ship sailed, and that was it."

"They got to Nigeria?"

"According to the paperwork."

"Then they were re-exported?"

She said that my guess was as good as hers. She lifted her hands, who knows? I had a last rummage through the paperwork, then returned it to her briefcase. She clipped the case closed, and we sat silent awhile. Her earlier troubled mood had returned, she was thoughtful as I walked her across to her car. But when we reached the car, she suddenly pivoted.

"Do you know why Dimitri was murdered?"

"No," I said, startled.

"Do you know who killed him?"

"What kind of question is that?"

"That's not any kind of answer."

"Of course I don't know."

She studied me a second. Finally she tugged open the door of her ancient Corvette and tossed in her briefcase. "Back at the office right now, my boss is waiting for me to come and give him the inside story from Haplon. Your story." She climbed in and wound down the window. "I'm going to tell him you've been sidelined at Haplon. And you'd better tell Channon. Neither one of them is going to be impressed."

I tapped my pocket, the torn page from her notepad, all her carefully prepared questions. I told her I'd get the answers for her. Enough to keep her boss happy, I said.

She hit the ignition. "Speaking as a Customs agent, that sounds just great, Ned." She pulled hard left on the wheel, looking out into the traffic and offering me a final thought before she pulled away. "Speaking as me, I'm not so sure it's so great. Dimitri's dead. And if you had any brains, you'd just lie down and quit."

CHAPTER 6

On the managerial and sales side of Haplon, Rossiter employed around forty people, thirty in R&D, and then another hundred or more doing the grunt work on the assembly lines and warehouses out back. From the vantage of my third-floor office overlooking the parking lot I had a good view of all arrivals and departures from the premises, and that evening after my meeting with Rita Durranti I stayed at my desk and watched the parking lot gradually empty.

Working late, for me, was not unusual. Paperwork had a way of building up during daylight hours, when I was often traveling, visiting clients, or arranging the Haplon presence at places like Springfield. At least twice a week I stayed till around ten to clear up the backlog, though in truth it wasn't always necessary. I maintained my nocturnal work pattern in the knowledge that it might one day prove useful should I ever need private, uninterrupted access to anything in the building. On two previous occasions I'd found the cover helpful. This time it was much more than that.

"Home run," said Gillian Streiss, putting her head around my door. "Coming down?"

When I gestured despairingly across my paper-strewn desk, she shot me a sympathetic smile and went on to the elevator.

Rossiter's red Lotus was still parked in the reserved bay by the entrance to the lobby, but I hadn't seen the man himself for over an hour. After shuffling the paperwork around my desk awhile longer, I got up and went out to the hall. It was quiet, but the lights were on down in the big open-plan office where the Haplon sales team was quartered. I strolled along there and looked in. Micky Baker was hunched over his keyboard, his eyes fixed to the screen.

"It's eight-thirty," I said. Startled, his head swung around. "No medals for being last one out. Unless you're e-mailing your mom," I told him, "shut it down." Stopping behind him, I leaned forward to read the screen.

He tapped a pen on his notepad. A list of numbers. "Rossiter wanted an update on these export licenses we've applied for. I've been e-mailing and phoning since four. They just keep jerking me around, passing me up and down the line. Four and a half fucking hours."

The e-mail Micky was composing, in response to being jerked around, was caustic. Not far short of abusive. Reaching over his shoulder, I touched the screen.

"Delete it."

Micky groaned.

"If you send that," I told him, "no one at Commerce is going to get off his butt and reply for a week. Now go home and get some sleep. When you come in tomorrow, rewrite it. And while you're rewriting, keep it in mind that Commerce grants the licenses. No export licenses, no Haplon. No Haplon, no jobs for you and me."

He gestured to the screen. "It took me half an hour."

I looked at him silently. Finally he hung his head and jammed his finger on the DELETE.

"Rossiter's gonna kick my butt," he muttered. I assured him that Rossiter knew Commerce better than to blame a Haplon employee for any delay. Micky plucked his jacket from the chair. "You'll tell him I tried, right? You'll back me up."

I clapped him on the shoulder and guided him into the hall.

When he disappeared toward the elevator, I stepped into my office and crossed to the window. Rossiter's Lotus hadn't moved. After a minute, Micky emerged from the lobby below and crossed the parking lot. After watching him drive away, I returned to his desk in the main office. His notepad lay open by the screen.

There were four reference numbers relating to export licenses we'd applied for, and beside each reference number was the name of the buyer, all national departments of defense. Germany, Australia, Pakistan, and Nigeria. The first three I knew about, but the only whisper of an order we had from Nigeria was the approach from Trevanian. I tore a blank page from the notepad and scribbled down the reference number before folding the slip into my pocket and returning to my office.

Another five minutes and Rossiter's car was one of only six remaining in the parking lot, including my own, and I went down the hall to see what was keeping him. His secretary, Barbara, a notorious martinet, had already left. Rossiter's door was closed. When I knocked there was no answer, so I tried the door and it opened.

I paused, one hand on the door, and looked across Rossiter's office to the filing cabinet. He kept his correspondence and details of orders pending in that cabinet. It was tempting. Tempting but risky. I couldn't afford to have anyone find me in there. While I was thinking it over, there were suddenly voices along the hall behind me. I quickly closed the door, stepped back, and bowed my head over Barbara's desk calendar. Not a moment too soon. Rossiter bore down on me, trailed by Vincent Juniper, Haplon's financial controller. Vincent had aged years in the past three months; dealing with the irate bankers out in California was wearing him down. Rossiter didn't miss a beat.

"Whatever you want, Ned, save it for tomorrow." He nodded Vincent away, then stepped by me into his office. Gathering up his briefcase and coat, he flicked off the lights, then came out, pressing the lock. "Californians. The goddamn happy people. They're gonna give me a coronary."

"Trouble at the new factory?"

"Factory? Great big fuckin' concrete slab, they haven't even finished the roof. Now the electrical contractor's sayin' he wants an extension on his deadline. Just like the builders got. And Christ, those

guys bust their deadline twice. All that new technology they got out there, they can't even get it done halfway right."

We walked down the hall as he continued complaining. Contractors. Bankers. The way Rossiter saw it, the entire world was lining up against him. He jabbed the elevator button, then faced me. "Somethin' you wanted to see me about?"

I mentioned an ongoing problem with the Pakistani order we were working on. I told him it could wait.

When he got into the elevator, I returned to my office and took up a position near the window again. But when Rossiter finally came out of the lobby below, he wasn't alone, he was with Darren, our rangemaster. They crossed the parking lot together. At the Lotus they stopped. They carried on talking a minute, then Rossiter got in his car and drove off. Darren came back to the building.

I dug my key ring out of my jacket. Apart from my own keys, there were three others, copies I'd made when Rossiter had given me his key ring the previous August and sent me to fetch something from his apartment. I'd gotten copies of his apartment key, his office key, and, on a whim, the key to his Lotus. Now I went down the hall to Rossiter's office. When I tested the door, it was locked. Fingering the keys, I found the copy, slid it into the lock, turned, and felt a satisfying clunk. After letting myself in, I closed the door and relocked it. Then I drew the blinds and switched on the desk lamp.

The filing cabinet was a tall aluminum piece by a table behind his desk. I opened the middle drawer. Everything in the cabinet was filed alphabetically, the name of the shipment's final purchaser was generally the main reference in the system. Nigeria. The middle drawer finished at K, so I closed it and tried the next drawer down. The N marker was halfway back. I pulled the divider forward and flicked through the paperwork.

It wasn't the first time, of course, that I'd taken an uninvited excursion through Rossiter's correspondence. Haplon product had turned up in some surprising locations over the years, theaters of war where embargoes were purportedly in place, and the company had been on Defense Intelligence's radar long before I made my entry. Though during my first eight months of employment I hadn't had great access, once Earl Jacobs quit and I took over as head of Haplon sales, the situation improved out of sight. By the time

Trevanian's order came along, I had a real handle on Rossiter's modus operandi, the shortcuts he regularly took through U.S. export regulations and Customs procedures. Most of that knowledge I'd gained through my after-hours dips into his aluminum cabinet. It wasn't so much what he wrote down—he was way too wily to commit himself to paper—it was what he so carefully omitted, or what he told me at our daily meetings that didn't square with what I read later in the documents from his cabinet.

After a minute, I found it. Nigeria. Ministry of Defense. Opening the folder on Rossiter's desk, I quickly flicked through the pages. There were fewer than twenty. I replaced the empty folder in the cabinet, switched off the desk lamp, and took the pages into the hall. After relocking the door, I retreated to my office and turned on the photocopier.

I hadn't copied five pages when Darren suddenly appeared in my doorway.

"Late night?" he said. I looked up and straight back down. I carried on with the photocopying. He leaned against the door frame. "What's with those two down at the range yesterday?" Trevanian and Lagundi, he meant.

"Just customers," I said.

"Some customers. Were those slugs you dug outta the sand trap any good to you?" he asked curiously.

After Trevanian and Lagundi had left the plant, I'd returned to our test-firing range and retrieved the bullets she'd fired. I wasn't aware, at the time, that I'd been noticed. Now I shook my head and stayed silent, but he wouldn't take the hint.

"That woman got the grouping any tighter," he said, "she'da been plugging the same damn hole. Man, I seen Marine instructors can't shoot like that."

I concentrated on the pages feeding through the copier. When I realized that Darren wasn't going to move, I asked him if he'd heard from the Springfield rangemaster.

"Haven't stopped hearing from him. Guy's on a crusade. Seems like the cops are talking about pulling his licenses. He's wild. He won't accept that maybe he screwed up."

"You think he did?"

"Not a question'a what I think. Guy says he's even been questioned by the FBI, they're not too happy someone got his brains blown out at a U.S. arms fair. That shit's meant to happen in other places. You know, Central America. Not here in the land of whipped cream and apple pie."

"Why are they coming down on him?"

"They don't believe in accidents." When I glanced up, he said, "Put it this way. He's got a list'a people who used the range. It doesn't match with what the cops got from their interviews. Some people on his list who shouldn't be on it. Some not on the list who should be. Plus, he can't tell them exactly how many rounds were fired, he's not even definite about weapons used, and calibers. I guess if I were a cop, I'd be thinking same as them. Screwup by the rangemaster."

"You're not a cop."

He laughed. "Right. Which is why I'm actually thinking, Thank fuck it wasn't me running the Springfield range that day." As the last page ran through the copier, someone out in the hall called Darren's name. Registering the voice, I shot a glance behind me down to the parking lot. Rossiter's Lotus was back in its bay. "Wants to show me his new toy," Darren explained with a what-can-you-say? kind of smile. He went out to join Rossiter.

My chest felt hollow. My heart was up near my throat.

Scooping up the papers, originals and copies, I crossed to my desk. I was still shoving loose sheets in the drawer when Rossiter came in with Darren.

"You wanna see something?" Rossiter said, hefting a small leather case onto my blotter. Sliding my drawer closed, I sat up as Rossiter flipped open his case. "Now tell me they ain't special." He gazed down at the pair of eighteenth-century dueling pistols lying on a bed of black velvet. "Perfect working order." He took out a pistol and turned it in his hands, admiring the craftsmanship. Darren joined in, congratulating Rossiter on the latest addition to the Rossiter family collection, while I made a few feeble noises of assent.

What had happened, it transpired, was that Rossiter had bought the pistols at auction, then taken them to be reconditioned by a small-arms specialist a few blocks from the Haplon site. The conversation I'd seen earlier between him and Darren in the parking lot was about the pistols. Rossiter had told Darren to wait, then gone to fetch the damn things.

"You see the sticks?" Rossiter asked, lifting the slender ramrods from the mahogany case.

I saw the sticks. And the pistols. And I saw the ampules of gunpowder that he tenderly plucked from the case, and the heavy lead pellets that he passed me one by one. The stolen paperwork was in the drawer, inches beneath his hand. It was torture. The ritualistic admiration of Rossiter's latest aquisition went on for an age.

"Makes you think, doesn't it?" Rossiter finally replaced the guns in the case. "Have we ever made anything that beautiful? I mean, has anyone the past fifty years?" When Darren suggested the stealth bomber, Rossiter laughed, then he packed the rest of it away and snapped the case shut. He said he was going to leave the pistols in his office safe till he got the cover note from his insurers at home.

When he exited my office, trailed by Darren, I hung my head. He was going to his office. But I'd relocked his door and closed his filing cabinet. I'd followed the correct procedures. Provided Rossiter didn't actually open the cabinet and search through the Nigerian paperwork, there was nothing for me to fear. But for the next few minutes I remained anchored to my desk, a knot tightening deep in my gut. The silence went on a long time. Finally I heard Rossiter and Darren talking. They seemed to be talking quite calmly, and I couldn't sit still any longer. I put my head out and saw them down by the elevator. Rossiter lifted a brow, he looked straight at me. When I smiled he didn't respond, just got on the elevator with Darren. I went back to my desk. After a minute, I crossed to the window, and saw Rossiter and Darren appear in the parking lot below. Rossiter went to his Lotus, Darren to his Ford pickup, and they each drove away.

I breathed in. I breathed out. Then I pulled out the stolen paperwork, split it into two piles, originals and photocopies, and took the originals down the hall to Rossiter's office. I located the key on my key ring, slid it into the lock, and turned. The lock clunked, I leaned against the door. It didn't budge. I pressed my shoulder against it, holding the key tight, but still nothing happened.

I thought, What the hell?

I gave it another try. Same result. Alarmed now, I stepped back and looked at the lock and the door. Then I saw it. Up in the right corner of the door, another keyhole, an old one. It had never been locked any of the other times I'd let myself in for a private look at Rossiter's files. I turned the key in the bottom lock again, and pressed with my shoulder. Nothing moved.

Finally I hauled the secretary's chair over, got up, and peered into the upper lock. I could see right through into Rossiter's dark office. I rested my forehead against the door, closed my eyes, and felt my gut churn. There was no way in. And I still had the stolen paperwork with me on the wrong side of the goddamn door.

The elevator motors suddenly kicked into life. I jumped off the chair, slid it into place beneath the desk, then retreated with the paperwork to my office. I looked down to the parking lot, but there was no sign of Rossiter's Lotus. Then the elevator doors opened, there were voices, and next thing Stan Kolotsky, the super, passed my doorway with a team of cleaners. Seeing me, he backpedaled and looked in.

"Carpet wash. These guys gonna make some noise. The stuff they use, it stinks bad too."

I frowned. Stan shrugged apologetically, then left. A minute later, one of the cleaners fired up a machine. Someone turned on a radio. It sounded like they were settling in for the night.

I rested my forehead on the desk. Rossiter's door, I decided, wasn't going to open until Rossiter reopened it. In the meantime, the stolen paperwork simply couldn't remain in my desk. It couldn't remain in my office. It couldn't, in fact, remain anywhere at the plant, unless I was willing to risk it being found and traced back to me. Finally I lifted my head. Then with more misgivings than I can name, I put the originals and copies into a folder, slipped the folder into my briefcase, turned out the lights, and went home.

CHAPTER 7

My study was a place of refuge throughout Hawkeye, the one private corner to which I could retreat and feel largely unburdened. I had my own phone, fax, and PC in there, but what I mostly did in the room was skip rope and listen to music.

But that night after returning from the Haplon plant, I walked straight by my stereo to my desk and laid out the stolen paperwork and read it. It was a sobering experience. The order from Trevanian's client, as outlined in the correspondence and documentation, had been under consideration by Rossiter for months. And not just consideration, Rossiter had gone ahead and applied for export licenses from Commerce as though the order had already been placed. Some of this, of course, I'd learned from Rita Durranti. What she hadn't told me, almost certainly because she didn't know it herself, was how much earlier, and over what range of materiel, Rossiter had set the paperwork in motion. It wasn't only the night-sights. There were mortars and miniguns. Ammo. Every single item Trevanian and Lagundi had inspected out at Springfield was there in Rossiter's paperwork. And the paperwork predated the Springfield fair by months.

I chewed on my lip. Then I took out the note I'd made from Micky Baker's list, the reference number he'd been chasing at Commerce. I dug around in Rossiter's correspondence and found the matching number. It was the Commerce Department's reference for the Haplon night-sights. But the final two pages were the real kicker, a draft of the headline contract to be signed when Trevanian paid his deposit on the order. I was the Haplon representative who normally signed these things, but here there were two blank spaces for signatures, and beside the spaces two names in bold type. J. Trevanian, on behalf of the Nigerian Ministry of Defense. M. Rossiter, on behalf of Haplon Systems.

"Dinner's in the microwave," said Fiona, making the desultory announcement as she passed in the hall. I heard her enter her own study.

A minute later I'd finished reading, and I gathered together the paperwork, returned it to the folder, then wrapped the folder in a carrier bag. I climbed onto my desk, reached up, and pressed my fingertips against a ceiling tile. I lifted the tile into the roof cavity, inserted the carrier bag through the opening, and pushed it over by the rear wall. Then I eased the displaced ceiling tile back into position.

Climbing down, I wiped my footprints off the desk, took a final glance at the ceiling, then left my study. The moment Fiona heard me approaching along the hall, she closed her study door.

Down in the kitchen I found a frozen casserole in the microwave. On a plate on the bench nearby, a slice of cherry pie. I stood there and considered the dismal scene a moment, then I opened the cutlery drawer. Then I changed my mind and went back upstairs and knocked on her door.

"Your dinner's in the microwave," she said.

I went in. She didn't look up from her reading. When I said her name she still didn't look up, so I asked her, "Are we adults or kids?"

She closed the book, swiveled in her chair, and looked up at me. "Okay," she said.

Okay. It was, as she meant it to be, provoking.

"I'm not lying to you," I told her.

She flicked up her hand, dismissing the whole issue. She seemed too battle-weary to face another argument over my supposed infidelity right then. "Brad's gone out for dinner with Barchevsky," she said.

It took me a moment. "The Congo guy?"

Rising, Fiona switched off her desk lamp. "He wants to run through the itinerary. Give Brad a better idea of what he's expected to do at the mines."

"Brad hasn't even got a visa yet."

"As of lunchtime today he has." She averted her eyes and stepped by me. But if she could read me, I could read her too, and what I read in that moment was concern. Concern and doubt. I followed her into the bedroom.

"You're having second thoughts now? Now, when he's got his visa, when he's all set to go? It's only just occurred to you sending him over there's not such a great idea?"

"Nobody's sending him."

"Have you mentioned this to Brad?"

Kicking off her shoes, Fiona unbuttoned her skirt. "I asked him if he was really sure he wanted to go."

"Oh, you asked him. And I guess he said, 'No, I've just changed my mind.' "

Stepping out of her skirt, she reminded me of my remark about adults and kids. Then she went to her dressing table and slipped off her blouse and started swiping a ball of cotton wool over her face. I sat down on the bed.

After twenty-something years of marriage, I can't claim the romantic fires still burned as brightly between us as they once had. But they hadn't died out either. Sex, until Fiona's suspicions about me reared up so suddenly, had never been a chore. Watching her at the dressing table now, it crossed my mind that if the problem was just Brad, and if this had happened a year earlier, I would have wandered across and rubbed her shoulders. We would have talked, at least halfway sorted something out, before moving on to bed. As it was, we sat in grim silence as she finished wiping off her makeup with harsh, short strokes. Finally she dropped the last used cotton-wool ball in the trash.

"If the mines were in dangerous areas," she said, "Barchevsky wouldn't be employing a geo without any experience like Brad."

"You're rationalizing."

"Oh please. Psychoanalysis?"

"That could be why he's employing Brad. Maybe no one with any experience wants to go."

"There's a peace agreement."

"Made in Africa."

"It's lasted since Christmas."

"Fiona. In the Congo, there is no such thing as peace. Occasionally you get a temporary cessation of hostilities while everyone regroups. But that's it. As soon as one lot gets tired of talking, it's over. Any so-called peace agreement is dead."

She craned around. "You sell arms, for chrissake. You're not a military strategist. You're not even a soldier anymore. Get over it. Stop lecturing me."

"Okay," I said. "The Congo's fine. Safer than Seattle. That what you want to hear?"

She got up and went to our bathroom. When she turned in the doorway, her eyes shone. "Thanks for all your support, Ned."

I spread my hands, helpless. I had nothing left to say.

When I slept, I dreamed about my father and me fishing up at the shack, and in the middle of the dream I woke suddenly and opened my eyes and lay still. Fiona was in the bed beside me, her shoulder rising and falling, cradled in sleep. I listened for a moment, then quietly and slowly rolled onto my back and looked over to the bedroom window. The gauze curtains billowed gently against the pane, pressing against the narrow opening. As I watched, the curtains ballooned, made a whispering noise against the glass, then a cool draft of air brushed my face.

I sat up and swung my feet to the floor. Then I checked my watch on the side table. It was three A.M. When I looked at the curtains again, they were still.

Someone, somewhere in the house, had just opened a window or an external door.

I padded across to the window and parted the curtains. Brad's car was parked in the drive alongside mine, I'd heard him return home around twelve, before I'd fallen asleep. But Brad, I knew, was not in the habit of wandering the house at all hours. Once he put his head on his pillow, he generally slept through until breakfast. A stray cat was passing beneath the street lamp out front, but otherwise Ellis Street was quiet.

Returning to the bed, I pulled on some boxers, then I reached under the bed and got my Beretta. Fiona never stirred. I edged my way out into the hall, flicking the pistol off safety.

It was possible that I'd misread the signs, that I was wrong. Fluke winds do blow. Curtains sometimes move in unexpected ways. But I'd woken so suddenly, so immediately alert, it was a sign I couldn't ignore. It was a lesson that had been pounded into me during special training at Fort Bragg. What your senses tell you in sleep is real. And what my senses told me that night was, wake up and adrenalize.

Padding down the carpeted hall, I checked in the bathroom, the two studies, and in Brad's long-abandoned bedroom. All the windows were closed.

Near the head of the stairs, I stopped and peered over the banisters. Then I reached and hit the light for the downstairs hall. The light blazed on. I blinked, my eyes adjusting fast, and listened and waited for someone down there to make a break for the door. Seconds passed. There was no sound from anywhere. I set myself moving again, going down the stairs, covering the hall.

I repeated the same drill I'd been through upstairs. I checked the windows in the kitchen and the living room. I looked in the dining room too, then I went to the end of the hall and checked in the garage below Brad's room. There was no sign of anything awry. By now I'd started wondering if maybe I wasn't stalking my own shadow, if maybe the previous few days hadn't set my trigger too fine.

I entered the laundry room and reached across the basin and gave the window a cursory pull. It slid smoothly open.

For a moment I stood rigid, the air around me chill. That window was always, but always, kept locked.

Then cutting through the early morning quiet, a car started up, perhaps a block away. The noise started faint and got fainter, quickly fading into silence as I strained to listen and locate it. When it was gone, I waited a few seconds, then I flicked on the light and returned my attention to the window. Some paint on the wood frame was scraped, a blade clearly had been inserted to force the lock. It was neatly done, the work, if I had to guess, of a professional. Unlocking the laundry door, I went outside. The laundry light shone onto the grass, illuminating the footprints in the dew. They looked like stepping stones. One set came from the path behind the garage over to the laundry window. The other set, parallel to the first, went back the other way. The second set, farther out from the wall, were more widely spaced, as if the guy had been running.

I turned south in the direction of the car I'd heard, and listened, but it was long gone.

Returning inside, I relocked the laundry door. The chance of lifting prints from the window, or even of the guy having left any, was somewhere around zero, and I had no intention of calling the police in anyway. So after a moment's fruitless reflection, I simply slid the window shut, relocked it, and went back upstairs.

This time when I entered my study, I switched on the light and made a careful inspection, looking for any sign of disturbance. My chair. The trash can. Desk drawers. Nothing seemed out of place. Finally I put my Beretta on the desk and climbed up and pushed aside the ceiling tile. The carrier bag was still there. I hauled it out and checked inside. Everything was there, untouched. I rebundled it and returned the bag to the hiding place.

Then I got down and dropped into my chair. The adrenaline rush was dying. I was perspiring now, I felt queasily light-headed, a familiar sensation from my Army days. It wasn't pleasant. I closed my eyes and waited for it to pass. Every bit of military training I'd ever had, of course, told me that that was the most dangerous moment, the point at which I was most vulnerable. I should have been thinking, staying alert and energized, but instead I just sat there like your average middle-aged sap, congratulating myself on not having lost the Haplon paperwork.

"What are you doing?" My head swung around. Fiona, eyes heavy with sleep, was studying me from the doorway. She stepped in, cinching the bathrobe cord at her waist. "Why's the light on downstairs?" she said.

"I got some water."

Her eyes went to my desk. She noticed my hand resting by the phone. "It's a bit late to be calling the office."

"I wasn't."

She looked at me. "You don't have to creep around in the middle of the night. Why don't you be a man and just call her?"

"I wasn't calling anyone."

"So what are you doing?"

"I thought I heard something. I came out to take a look."

"Where's your water?"

"I drank it downstairs."

She tilted her head. "You went downstairs, had a glass of water, then came up to your study to do what? Write a memo?"

"This was here." I showed her the Beretta. "I just came in to get it."

She knew I was lying. I sat there, feeling stupid, like the worst kind of heel. It wasn't a big lie, not even very important, but somehow the timing couldn't have been worse. It seemed, at that moment, to stand for all the other lies I'd told her. Lies she knew were lies, and tried to nail, but couldn't.

"Funny," she said. "It was under the bed when I turned in."

"Fiona—"

"Don't even try." There was real scorn in her voice now. "Get some linen from the closet. You can use the spare room." Gesturing phoneward, she made her exit, saying, "You might as well do it now. Go on. Make your goddamn call."

CHAPTER 8

Milton Rossiter took me down to Manhattan in his Lotus. He was going to look at some diamonds.

"All you have to do," he said as we drove, "is sit there."

What he meant was that I should sit beside him in the diamond trader's room and watch for any sign of trouble. If any trouble occurred, my job would be to get Milton out safe and unharmed.

One drawback with being a soldier, or even an ex-soldier, is that people who know your history find it hard to treat you like a regular human being. Attitudes vary from exaggerated respect to downright contempt, but worst are the aging jocks with something to prove. Guys like Fiona's cousin Wayne from Wyoming, who used to spend his days selling agricultural machinery and his evenings working out, getting himself in shape for Thanksgiving, when he would invariably challenge me to an arm wrestle. To keep the peace in the family, I always had to consent. Wayne, grinning, would then attempt to crush every bone in my hand while simultaneously extracting my arm from its socket. Rossiter's take on my history was different, but sometimes equally childish.

He saw my Army background as a selling point for his equipment, he knew my presence at Haplon gave his sales team a measure of credibility with the buyers that no number of marketing graduates or MBAs could duplicate. And Rossiter wasn't averse to spreading word of my supposed military exploits. All lies, of course, he knew zip about the real details of my military career. The Gulf War and Mogadishu were the only operations I'd ever admitted to. Rossiter also enjoyed exploiting my previously unrealized potential as a bodyguard, one that he had on permanent call, and for free. Though he never actually said that to me, it wasn't hard to figure once I found myself being invited along to negotiations with any potentially violent client of Haplon's. On two earlier occasions he'd required my presence at handovers of large sums of cash, transactions that I duly reported to Channon.

I went along with my unofficial role without complaint. Rossiter had the usual blindness of someone who's run his own show for years. He believed he had me under his thumb. One day he was going to be very surprised, but in the meantime my occasional irregular assignment made good copy for my reports to Channon. But dealings in the diamond trade were a new departure for Rossiter.

"I'm guessing this isn't for your wedding anniversary," I said, keeping my eyes on the road ahead. He snorted. "Payment on an order?" I wondered aloud.

"Possible payment."

"Which one?"

"The Nigerians."

I looked at him from the corner of my eye. The Nigerians. Trevanian's order, which, as far as I knew, hadn't yet been confirmed.

"Trevanian faxed me last night," he said. "He wants to firm up the order."

"But he doesn't want to give us money."

"He doesn't have any money. He's got diamonds."

"That's acceptable?"

"It's discussable." Rossiter shifted down a gear, turning south onto the Harlem River Drive. "While I'm pouring money into that fucking pit in California, everything's discussable," he muttered, then he leaned over and switched on the radio to indicate that he wasn't taking any more questions.

West Forty-seventh is at the center of the U.S. diamond trade, a beat that was made familiar to me by Rita Durranti when I first started with Hawkeye. She was collecting evidence against a guy named Jerry Tyrone. He had supply contracts with several African states whose demand for materiel invariably exceeded their capacity to pay in U.S. dollars, a hard-currency gap that the two sides bridged with barter. Gold and diamonds were the only commodities acceptable to Tyrone, and I frequently found myself making the trip down to a Customs safe house near West Forty-seventh to listen and learn at Rita's debriefs of her informers after valuations and sightings of uncut stones that were the coinage of Tyrone's somewhat Byzantine transactions.

But all the time I'd worked for Rossiter, his policy had been to accept only U.S. dollars. His problems at the new factory in California seemed to be making him rash.

As we walked along Forty-seventh, he scanned the shop fronts. I asked him what we were looking for.

"Hersch Building. Nameplate'll say Greenbaum. M. Greenbaum."

"Diamond trader?"

"So he tells me."

We passed quite a few Orthodox Jews—hats, ringlets, and beards—most standing in twos and threes outside the shop fronts, talking. After a few minutes of searching, we located the Hersch Building and went in. When we asked for Greenbaum's office, the porter gave us some tags, then directed us to the cage-elevator. Upstairs, we found the room. I pressed the button.

"Come," said a voice from the speaker over the door.

But when we stepped over the threshold we weren't in an office, we were in a small cubicle of plated steel. A security camera was trained on us from the ceiling. Another speaker was mounted on the wall. I exchanged a glance with Rossiter. Eventually the inner door opened and a small guy with a neatly trimmed beard rose from behind his desk, beckoning us in. Mordecai Greenbaum.

"The others, they haven't arrived. I can wait only fifteen minutes." He checked his watch after shaking Rossiter's hand, then Rossiter introduced me, explaining my position at Haplon. Greenbaum waved that off. Nodding to me, he sat behind his desk and hitched his ankle onto his knee. Then while he made small talk with Rossiter—politics, and the state of the diamond market—I sat in a corner armchair and looked around. The shelves were overloaded with trade magazines, and several oak cabinets were lined up along one wall. There were no pictures, just a whiteboard scrawled with numbers, carats, and prices. The office of someone who wasn't too concerned about his working environment, but neat. Greenbaum was wearing a discreetly expensive suit, the kind you might expect to see on a corporate lawyer or a broker down on Wall Street. A skullcap was pinned to the crown of his head. The way he and Rossiter were talking, they hadn't known each other long.

When the buzzer went off a few minutes later, Greenbaum directed our attention to a monitor off to his right. On the monitor, we watched Trevanian and Lagundi enter the secure cubicle. Greenbaum turned to Rossiter. "That is them?"

Rossiter nodded, and Greenbaum let them in. Trevanian looked hassled, even a little pissed off, but Lagundi seemed like she hadn't a care in the world. She nodded to me and smiled. After Rossiter did the introductions, Greenbaum cleared his desk. He unrolled a square of black velvet the size of a handkerchief and placed it in the center of his blotter. He took an eyeglass from his pocket and rubbed the eyeglass on his shirt, inviting Trevanian to put the stones on the velvet. Trevanian glanced at Lagundi, who turned away from us and retrieved a leather pouch from inside her blouse. She opened the pouch and gently shook the contents onto the black velvet.

Roughs. Uncut, unpolished diamonds. They sat there, a small pile of crystalline pebbles, they weren't anything much to the untrained eye. She pushed them apart with one finger, then lined them up in pairs. Five pairs, ten stones. Greenbaum bent and studied them with his naked eye a moment. Then he looked up at Lagundi, raising a brow. When she nodded, the examination commenced. Greenbaum rolled each stone between thumb and forefinger, peered at it, then replaced it on the velvet. Next he picked the same stone up with a pair of tweezers, put in his eyeglass, and swiveled to face the north window. He held each stone up to the soft morning light and examined it carefully. Nobody spoke. After a few minutes' inspection he dropped each stone onto a set of jewelers' scales on the window ledge, took a reading, and jotted a note in his pad.

After stone number five, Trevanian asked if he could smoke. Greenbaum shrugged, too intent on the grading to care. Another quarter hour went by. Trevanian smoked, Rossiter thumbed through some diamond-trade magazines, and Cecille Lagundi watched Greenbaum like a hawk. It was like a priestly ritual in some private alcove of the temple. The only sound was the occasional mutter from Greenbaum as he jotted his notes. The inspection finally completed, he lined the stones up in pairs again.

"Certificates of Origin?" he mused. Lagundi told him that certificates weren't required. "If you wish to realize full value for the stones, certificates would be helpful," he said. She looked straight at him and said nothing. "You have more?" he asked, passing a hand over the stones.

"You wanted to see a sample," Trevanian cut in. "This is a sample."

"You have more?" Greenbaum repeated, unfazed.

Trevanian gave him a look. Then Lagundi folded the velvet around the stones and took them to the window. To the surprise of everyone there except Trevanian, she took her own eyeglass from her purse. Then she carefully examined each stone, and weighed it on Greenbaum's scales before returning it to her leather pouch. She was checking that Greenbaum hadn't made a switch. When Rossiter realized what she was doing, he said, "Oh, for chrissake." But Greenbaum didn't seem put out. He folded his hands together over his paunch and watched her calmly.

When Lagundi finished, Trevanian stubbed out his cigarette. "Every stone's a D flawless," he told Rossiter. "They've all been pre-graded, every one between five and eight carats. Putting a price on them's not rocket science."

Greenbaum produced a copy of Rapaport Report, the bible of the diamond trade, from his drawer. Trevanian flipped through it, then stopped and ran a finger down one column. "D flawless, five carat stone. Fifteen thousand six hundred dollars per carat," he read aloud.

"List price," Greenbaum interrupted. "Meaningless."

"Call it our opening number," Trevanian told Rossiter. Greenbaum shook his head, frowning. "Opening number," Trevanian repeated. "We'll negotiate the discount from there." Then Trevanian explained how the proposed barter, diamonds for Haplon materiel, should proceed. It was child's play compared with some of Jerry Tyrone's transactions. He wanted to agree with Rossiter on a discount figure for the list price per carat for the roughs. Then Greenbaum, on Rossiter's behalf, would make a selection from the stones that were stored in a Manhattan bank vault. Once Greenbaum's selections added up to twelve million dollars—the price of the Haplon materiel—the trade would be done. "The only number we have to agree on is the discount," Trevanian concluded.

Rossiter asked what would happen if there weren't sufficient stones in their stock to add up to twelve million dollars.

"Our loss," said Trevanian. "Deal goes down the pan, we don't get the weapons."

Everybody in the room knew that was not going to happen, Trevanian hadn't brought the deal so far to just sit back and watch it collapse because of some stupid miscalculation. So now Rossiter had sighted a sample of the diamonds, and he'd listened to Trevanian's proposal. He needed professional advice. He beckoned Greenbaum across to confer. While they did that, Trevanian and Lagundi took the opportunity for a few quiet words together by the window. No one paid any attention to me. The whole situation was making me distinctly uneasy. Did my presence in the room implicate me in any way? Was I inadvertently becoming party to the proposed transaction, and was that what Rossiter intended? To compromise me?

Finally Rossiter turned from Greenbaum and announced, "We need to keep one of the stones." Lagundi immediately objected, but Trevanian raised a hand to silence her.

"Why?" he said.

Greenbaum explained that he needed to show it down on the diamond bourse. "To gauge the market," Greenbaum added. "If I can't show the stone, I can't give Mr. Rossiter an indication of fair price."

"What's that, a threat?" said Trevanian.

"A statement," said Greenbaum mildly.

Trevanian eyeballed him, but Greenbaum held firm. Then Trevanian went into whispered conference with Lagundi again. It was clear she didn't want to surrender any of the stones, but eventually Trevanian seemed to talk her around.

"Okay," he said, turning back to Greenbaum. "You can have the smallest stone. But you only have it till the diamond bourse closes. When's that? Three?"

"Four-thirty."

Trevanian pointed. "Four," he said. "And if the stone's not back with us by then, I'll report it as stolen."

"Report it to whom?" said Greenbaum, and Trevanian looked so mad so suddenly that I thought for one moment he was going to plant Greenbaum through the wall. I stepped between them. Greenbaum retreated behind his desk to safety. Trevanian eyed me, surprised, almost as if he'd forgotten my presence there until that moment. At last it was Lagundi who spoke.

"I will need a receipt for the stone."

Greenbaum laughed.

"It's a few hours' loan, for chrissake," said Rossiter.

Trevanian stood toe-to-toe with me, so close I could smell the mint on his breath. "No receipt," he said, "no stone." He was watching me, keeping himself in my face. I held his look, waiting for him to move. But he didn't move. Finally Rossiter swore and reached for his pen.

CHAPTER 9

What the hell are you doing here?" said Rita the moment I stepped in and closed her office door behind me. "Well?"

"Good to see you too."

"Don't jerk me around, Ned." She dropped into her chair. "What do you want?"

I took a couple of Customs forms from my briefcase and pushed them across her desk. She glanced down. She had a careworn look, the corners of her mouth turned down. After a second, she looked up.

"What's this?"

"I thought you might sign them," I said, and she stared at me. The forms related to a small-arms deal Haplon was doing into Britain. Inconsequential. Rita seemed ready to explode. "Sign them," I added, "and I've had a reason to be here."

"You've got no damn reason to be here." She pointed. "If you want to end up like Spandos, that's your business. When I want a target pinned to my back, I'll tell you."

"You got my fax?"

"I got it," she said.

"Have you read it?"

She leaned back and pressed her hands to her face. Then she pulled some stapled pages from her desk drawer and slapped them down. I'd intended to deliver copies of the stolen paperwork to her in person, but after my unexpected late-night visitor at home, I'd decided not to wait. I'd faxed her everything instead. She'd obviously had time to give it some attention. She didn't seem thrilled. "This is an order, Ned. A done deal."

"It hasn't been signed yet."

"There is no way this slipped by you by accident. Someone did not want you to see it."

I conceded that. I said it seemed likely.

"No, not just likely. It's a fact. This is a draft contract." She indicated the fax. "It's clearly been gone over by both parties. It's been gone over by the lawyers. The only one it hasn't been gone over by is you." When I made no response, she kicked back in her chair. She bit her lip. "You know what I'm going to ask, don't you?"

"I've got a fair idea."

"Rossiter didn't start feeling guilty because he'd cut you out. He didn't just up and give this to you."

"I stole it."

She looked at me. "That easy, huh?"

I told her about Rossiter's double-locked door. She frowned. When I mentioned my late-night visitor at home, she groaned out loud.

"I'll get the papers back into his office," I said.

"You have any clue when? Or how?"

"My problem."

"It's our problem."

"I'll get them back in."

She cupped her forehead in her hand. "Either you know less about what is going on in Haplon than I do, or you're lying to me. And if you're lying to me—"

"Why would I?"

"You work for Channon, not me. How many times have I heard that from you? From you and Dimitri both. And if Channon ordered you to lie to me?"

I pointed to the fax. I told her that the first time I'd seen the originals was the previous night.

"When you stole them."

"Right," I said.

She looked out her window, turning things over. She still wasn't happy. "So tell me," she said, swiveling back. "What happens if Rossiter checks his files and finds the draft contract gone?" When I didn't answer, she flipped. "Okay, I'll tell you what happens. He'll know it's been stolen. And given that you're the guy he's tried to keep this from, I think we can assume you're going to be high on his list of suspects. He'll fire you. And that is not just your problem, Ned. Because if Rossiter decides for sure that Haplon has been under surveillance, he won't go through with this deal. And if he doesn't do that, we've got no damn case. We're screwed."

"If he doesn't go through with this deal, his bankers'll pull the plug on his California factory. He's not going to let that happen."

"You're sure of that."

"I've just come from West Forty-seventh." When she gave a sound of surprise, I nodded. "Diamonds." I said. "First time ever for Rossiter. He wants this deal." I explained that there simply wasn't time for me to go through the regular procedure and arrange a meeting with her at Grant's Tomb. Since I couldn't raise Channon, I'd had to come to her office. She grimaced, lifting a hand, brushing my belated apology aside. Then I told her about the meeting on West Forty-seventh. I mentioned Lagundi's surprising expertise, and I told her about the deal Trevanian was proposing. I offered my opinion that the diamonds might be under Lagundi's control, not Trevanian's.

While Rita was considering all that, someone buzzed her. When she took the call on her desk phone, I got up and went to the window. If I was going to keep Hawkeye alive, I needed Rita to work with me. If the deal went ahead, and Trevanian took delivery of the Haplon materiel and transported it in contravention of the embargoes, it was U.S. Customs who would prosecute. And Customs had already agreed with Channon that the deal should take its course, under our surveillance. They were even prepared to let the materiel make its way to Liberia, as Channon predicted it would, just so the illegal trail could be wound up in its entirety, corrupt African officialdom included. But to get the deal that far, Rita had to be satisfied that I was gathering evidence Customs could actually use. She had to be convinced that a smart lawyer couldn't destroy it in court. She had to be sure that I wasn't breaking the law.

When she hung up, I faced her, ready to plead my case.

"What happened to the diamonds?" she asked me abruptly.

I hesitated. "Lagundi took them back to the bank. Greenbaum kept one of them to show down on the diamond bourse."

She stood straight up. Then she invited me to accompany her on a walk down the hall.

In all my time with Hawkeye, this was the first time I'd been inside the Customs building, so when Rita led me through two corridors and down a flight of stairs, I was lost. The decor changed, the feel of the place too, it was bare and functional. We passed a few guys wearing jackets with CUSTOMS AND EXCISE stamped on the back in gold letters. The rooms off the hall had numbers instead of nameplates. It was like we'd stepped through a movie-set facade into grim reality.

Rita spoke to a guy outside one room, then led me through an unmarked door just past it. Two steps in, I balked.

"One-way glass." Rita waved me in. "Soundproof too. We used to do the taping in here." On the other side of the glass was a small, brightly lit room with a table at its center. A guy in a Customs jacket was seated at the table. Seated opposite him was Mordecai Greenbaum. I was suddenly at sea. "They're halfway through an interview," Rita explained. She flipped a switch, and immediately Greenbaum's voice came through some hidden speaker. He was recounting the meeting I'd just left at his office on West Forty-seventh. Who said what to whom. Recounting it accurately, as far as I could tell.

I looked at Rita. "Okay," I said, waiting for an explanation.

"You came here uninvited. You've got no right to be mad at me."

"I'm not mad. Not yet."

"We caught Greenbaum smuggling stones in from Antwerp last year. While we're thinking about what charges to lay, he's doing his civic duty."

"A stooge."

"An informer."

"How'd you get him into the Trevanian deal?"

"We didn't. He got us in." Rita explained that two weeks earlier, Greenbaum had told his case agent, the Customs guy at the table, about some loose talk he was hearing on the bourse. Someone in the arms trade was looking to off-load some African roughs, provenance unknown. "Our agent told him to get himself involved. Offer his services."

"And you thought I didn't need to know that?"

"Our guy thought it was bullshit. Informer overdoing it. They always do. Then yesterday Greenbaum came up with a name. Rossiter."

"When was I going to hear that?"

"Today." She looked at me, her expression blank. She was lying. I didn't know why. She asked me if I was sure Greenbaum had kept one of Trevanian's stones. When I nodded, she left the room. A minute later, the agent rose from the table behind the glass and disappeared into the hall. When he came back in, he immediately started questioning Greenbaum about the conclusion of the meeting over on West Forty-seventh. Rita rejoined me. As we listened some more, Greenbaum became evasive.

"What's so important about the stone?" I asked Rita.

"Analysis." She braced her hands on the ledge, her face up close to the glass. "We can send it out to the lab in Santa Fe. They'll put it through some tests."

"Greenbaum already confirmed they were D flawless."

"Bully for Greenbaum."

"You don't trust your own informer?"

"Not just that. The lab can tell us where it's from, whether they're conflict diamonds. Blood stones. If we know where they're from, maybe we can get ahead of the game."

"Channon's still guessing Liberia."

"They've got the war and the diamonds. But we need some corroboration."

I watched Greenbaum through the glass. "Greenbaum has to give the stone back to Trevanian by four."

"Four?"

"Half of eight."

"Shit," she said. Her face tightened in dismay, and I stepped up closer to the glass. After leaving Forty-seventh I'd walked a block, then gotten a cab down to Customs. Greenbaum must have been just minutes behind me. It wasn't possible he'd already taken the stone to the bourse. I was sure the diamond was still on him.

"Have your man search him."

Rita frowned. "Greenbaum's not stupid. He'd have to wonder how we made such an inspired guess."

"You could have bugged his office."

"Yeah. Either that, or else one of the three people he just met came scurrying back here and told us." She folded her arms and faced the glass again.

Greenbaum's interview continued. It was a polished performance, he answered each question without embellishment, and though he cast a few glances in our direction, clearly aware someone might be watching from behind the glass, he never faltered. He acted more like a colleague of the Customs agent than the unpaid informer he was. When the questions finally returned to that point at the end of the West Forty-seventh meeting, when he'd kept a stone, he was ready. There were no evasions this time. He said straight out that Lagundi had taken them all.

"Search him," I said.

Rita looked at me. I stared at Greenbaum through the glass. Rita finally shrugged and went out, and a few seconds later the agent left the interview room. Rita must have spoken to the agent out in the hall, because when he returned to the interview room, he skipped the preliminaries and asked Greenbaum if he was carrying any diamonds. When Greenbaum hesitated, the agent told him to stand up. After considering his options, Greenbaum opened his jacket, removed an envelope, and passed it to the agent. With a straight face, he told the agent that he wanted a receipt.

The agent left the room, and within moments Rita rejoined me from the hall. Greenbaum's envelope was in her hand. She opened it with two fingers, we peered in at the stone. An unremarkable pebble.

"We could send it to Santa Fe anyway," she said. "Let Greenbaum take the heat from Trevanian."

"If they don't trust Greenbaum, they'll drop him. You'll lose your source."

"We could switch the stone."

"It wouldn't get past Lagundi."

We considered the rough. It was a crystalline rock the size of a pea, something you'd sweep off your porch without a second thought. Unless it was analyzed before evening, it was, for the purposes of Rita's investigation, totally worthless.

Rita studied it, musing out loud. She returned to her first idea, sending the stone out to the government lab in Santa Fe, letting Greenbaum deal with the inevitable eruption from Jack Trevanian. She was trying to argue herself into it against her own better judgment, trying to convince herself there was actually some merit in the plan.

By that time, of course, I'd long since made up my mind. Through the glass, I watched Greenbaum rise from his chair, then stretch. He asked the agent what had happened to the rough. When the agent ignored him, Greenbaum rapped the table in an ill-advised show of impatience. He asked the agent how much longer he was going to be kept, he said that he had business to attend to at the bourse. The agent told him to shut the fuck up.

I opened a hand toward Rita. I told her to give me the stone.

CHAPTER 10

Fiona rolled the rough between her thumb and forefinger as we walked down the hall, then she dropped the stone into a plastic petri dish. "You've got a damn nerve," she said.

"This is the first time I've ever asked."

"The first time you take advantage, I'm meant to just roll with it, am I?" When I didn't answer she looked up from the dish. "Okay, so what's the deal here? Suddenly I'm meant to smooth the wheels of commerce in the arms trade."

"That's not what I told you."

We turned in to one of the labs. Two long benches divided the room, each lined with flasks and bottles and Bunsen burners. A kiln sat in one corner, wired up to a series of instruments. No one was in the lab. I stopped at the opposite side of the bench while Fiona checked an experiment book that was lying there. When I'd phoned, she'd told me that the Geometrics lab in Yonkers had the equipment to do the analysis on the stone. She'd also warned me that without a few days' notice, the analysis would be rudimentary. All we needed to know, I assured her now across the lab bench, was whether or not the rock came from Nigeria.

"Nigeria doesn't produce any diamonds worth mentioning," she informed me, inspecting the book. "What else do you want to know?"

"Can you tell if it comes from Liberia?"

"What if it is from Liberia?" she asked, closing the book. She set down the petri dish and opened it. "Don't tell me you're going to give the stone back."

"If it's from Liberia, the deal collapses. There's an arms embargo on the place. And a trade embargo on their diamonds."

"Blood stones."

"Conflict diamonds," I countered automatically, but the corporate euphemism didn't go down too well. Fiona gave me a dark look. "Listen, call them what you like," I said. "We just need the analysis."

"What if you don't get it?"

"Then we give our client the benefit of the doubt. We assume the stones are legitimate, and the deal goes through."

She considered me. "Haplon didn't volunteer to get the analysis done," she decided.

"It's at the request of Customs."

Fiona nodded, her generally low opinion of my employer's principles apparently reconfirmed. If the sole purpose of the analysis was to further Haplon's commercial interests, Fiona wouldn't have so much as considered it. Without the Customs fig leaf, I wouldn't even have bothered to ask for the favor. But presented as a possible encumbrance to the transaction, an ethical hurdle that had to be cleared, the analysis was something Fiona could contemplate with a clear conscience. She might even see it as her liberal duty. Finally she replaced the lid on the petri dish.

"It'll take two and a half hours."

I nodded. I didn't want to open my mouth and change her mind.

"It'll cost three thousand dollars," she said, and I nodded again. Rita was going to have a fit.

Then as we exited the lab, heading for Fiona's office to sign the paperwork, we saw Olympia, Dimitri's ex-wife, entering the Geometrics reception. Before Olympia could see us, Fiona grabbed my arm and hauled me back into the lab.

"Jesus," she said. "You saw her?"

"Olympia. What's she doing here?"

"We've got a lunch date," Fiona explained. "She kept calling. I couldn't put her off. She wants to talk to someone about Dimitri." I nodded sympathetically. Fiona raised her hand to her forehead. "I am up to here in work, Ned. And I am not in the mood for any kind of heart-to-heart just now. Certainly not one about husbands, ex, dead, or otherwise."

"So tell her."

"How can I?" Fiona gestured to the door. "She's driven all the way up from Queens." I volunteered to go out and make an excuse on her behalf, but Fiona dismissed the offer. Then she brightened, struck by an idea. "Look, all she really wants is to make talk about Dimitri with someone who knew him."

I saw where she was going. I raised my hands. "Hey. Olympia didn't call me."

"You've got a two-and-a-half-hour wait for the results of our analysis."

"You can phone them to me."

She held the petri dish up between us, turning it in her hand. The stone clicked softly against the sides.

"Hey," I said again.

"There's a table booked at Marco's," she told me. "I'll push the lab. We'll try and have the results ready when you get back."

"I don't want to speak to her."

"Enjoy," Fiona said.

Marco's was a tony pizza place with a polished pine floor, the local eatery for Geometrics' middle management. The tables were spaced far enough apart that you weren't obliged to hear the conversation of every fellow diner, but even so, when the waiter showed us to a table by the window, I suggested somewhere farther back for the sake of privacy. Olympia overruled me.

"I'm not going to cry, Ned. Here's fine." She dropped her purse on a chair and sat down. I took a chair opposite and hung my head over the menu.

I'd always liked Olympia a lot. She'd married Dimitri a few years before the Gulf War, and they had twins soon after, girls who were locked forever in my memory as two-year-olds, the age they were frozen at in the photo Dimitri had always kept in his wallet. Identical dark-haired, sloe-eyed creatures in bright pink pajamas.

Since divorcing Dimitri a year after his return from the Gulf, Olympia hadn't always had it easy. For years she worked as a hairdresser, every hour God gave, just keeping herself and her daughters housed and fed. Maintenance checks from Dimitri, so Fiona told me, arrived irregularly and were always light. Olympia finally opened her own salon, got herself into serious debt, and ended up marrying the accountant, Laurence Maguire, who'd saved her from the bankers. Things had gone well for a while, then Laurence was diagnosed with cancer. His health insurance didn't cover the treatment. Olympia had told me that if Laurence hadn't received some inheritance money from a long-lost relative, they would have had to remortgage their home just to keep him alive. Now Laurence was in remission, but things clearly hadn't been easy for either one of them.

But during our five-minute stroll from Geometrics to Marco's, Olympia hadn't said a word about herself. Or, more surprisingly, about Dimitri. After explaining that I had the day off work, and that I'd brought a forgotten file from home to the lab for Fiona, we just talked. From Fiona's appearance in reception, and the uncharacteristically half-assed apology, Olympia had intuited that something wasn't right. She wondered if I shouldn't maybe take Fiona on a vacation, she suggested they were working her too hard at Geometrics. I conceded that it was possible. No point telling her that the break Fiona really needed was from me. Olympia didn't raise the subject of Dimitri's death until we'd ordered.

"Fiona said you were there." Olympia snapped a bread stick as the waiter removed our menus. "You know, with Dimitri? I couldn't believe it when the police called. He had me on his passport as next of kin. It was a real hassle for them to find me."

"What have you told the girls?"

"Everything. What the police told me, that it was a stupid accident." Her eyes skittered up from the bread stick. I'd been preparing to console her, but she didn't look like she needed consolation. If anything, she seemed curious. "You're wondering why I'm not more upset," she said.

"No."

"Yes you are. The truth is, I was. When they told me, I mean, it was a shock. Four years married. Two kids. You can't just turn that stuff off, can you. I can't, anyway. Not that I haven't tried." She tilted her head. "They said there were no witnesses."

"No."

"So what happened?"

"Didn't the police go through it with you?"

"Sure they did. But I just wondered, well, you're not the police, Ned. You know what I mean?"

I collected my thoughts a moment, then I gave her the official version of what I'd seen out at Springfield. It hardly took me five minutes. She seemed disappointed that I didn't know more, so I told her that the Fettners guys might have a better picture, and I scribbled the Fettners number on my business card and gave it to her. When the waiter returned I ordered the house red, then Olympia started quizzing me about Springfield again. I excused myself and went to the rest room. If there was one person in the world who could inadvertently trip me up on the subject of Dimitri Spandos, it was Olympia.

They'd gotten married while Dimitri and I were serving in the Rangers, but by the time of their marriage they'd been together, on and off, for years. I'd known Olympia for most of my adult life, and she knew me about as well as anyone did, apart from Fiona and Brad. Of all Dimitri's buddies, it was me Olympia came to when Dimitri's gambling became a serious issue within their marriage. She told me she'd gone three months without seeing a single cent from his pay. I'd done what I could, spoken to Dimitri about it, but he hadn't been ready to face his problem, or even admit that he had one. Their marriage collapsed irretrievably before the year was out. Olympia moved away from the base, she went to New York with her kids to be close to her parents, but she and Fiona stayed in touch. When I took the job at West Point, our family friendship with Olympia was rekindled. By that time she'd remarried. When I'd told her that Dimitri had conquered his habit, that he was transferring from the Rangers to Delta Force, she'd made a wry crack, then let the subject lie. They hadn't stayed in touch, and as far as I knew, their only contact since was the secondhand news that passed through Fiona and me.

Now he was dead, and it was hard to imagine how she must have felt. Surprised, certainly. Perhaps there was some measure of regret too, but whatever she felt, I didn't want to say too much. Frankly, I had enough on my plate without having to fend off Olympia's understandable but unwelcome curiosity. After zipping up, I went to the basin, washed my hands, and splashed my face. I decided that I hadn't yet said anything out of line. I also decided that when I returned to the table, I was not going to recap on Springfield.

"How are the girls?" I slid into my chair, firing off the question before she had a chance to open her mouth. "Still cute?"

"Only in my dreams." Olympia smiled, then she told me about her daughters, adolescents now, who were causing Olympia and Laurence the usual kind of grief. "I wouldn't mind if they just once in a while confided in me," she concluded. "As it is, I'm just pathetically grateful when they even bother to tell me where they're going. Honestly. A girl hits thirteen, what happens? Some switch goes off in their brains."

"Like you were any different."

"If I'd behaved like my two at their age, my mother would have thumped me." She paused, seeming to hear what she'd just said. She hooted. "God. At their age." The wine arrived, she took a sip from her glass. "Tell you what, though. The boys they bring home? PlayStation and MTV. Doesn't anyone want to be a doctor anymore? These days I'd settle for a kid who wants to be a damn politician."

"How about a soldier?"

She pulled a face.

"Come on, Olympia. We weren't that bad."

"Maybe not you." As she took another sip of wine, I found myself thinking back to that time when she'd first told me about Dimitri's gambling habit. She'd started out joking about it, then real pain had broken through and she'd burst into tears. "When I imagine them getting married," she went on, referring to her daughters now, "I kind of hope it'll be to guys like Laurence. Nothing glamorous. Just a guy who'll look after them. Someone who's kind." She smiled glumly. "You suppose I've got any chance selling that one to my pair of hormonal crazies?"

Her problem, though she didn't say it, was that she recognized a good deal of herself in her daughters. Twenty years earlier, when she'd first alighted on Dimitri, she was something of a hormonal crazy herself. It wasn't an accident that she'd ended up with someone like him, she'd flown to him like a moth to the flame. Back then she'd loved the fact that he was a soldier, she'd loved everything about him. His uniform. Army life. His popularity with his fellow officers. His dedication to his career. Before she married Dimitri, his life probably seemed quite exotic to Olympia.

Our pizzas arrived and we ate in silence a minute, then she asked after Brad. I admit I was starting to find her conversation odd, even somewhat weirdly detached. Dimitri, her ex-husband, had been killed by a bullet through the brain, and here she was asking me how my son was doing with his Ph.D. I told her about Brad's new job. She was thoughtful awhile as she ate, and I decided to venture a question, one that was silently plaguing me.

"What do you think Fiona might say if I reenlisted?"

"The Army?"

"Yeah."

"Weapons instructor at West Point? Your old job?"

I turned my head, no. She put down her fork and pointed with her knife.

"Active service?"

"Possibly."

"Don't do it to her, Ned."

"It's just hypothetical."

"She'd kill you. Or maybe not you, but it might finish her. Jesus, I can't believe I'm hearing you. Have you forgotten what she went through? I haven't. I was there, remember. She was a nervous wreck after you came back from Kuwait. When you went to Mogadishu she spent the whole time shuttling between her shrink and the drugstore."

"Forget I asked."

"I'm trying. You wanna know what she'd say? She'd say exactly what she said to you after Mogadishu." Olympia put down her knife. "You go back on active service—divorce." I bowed my head. "Divorce instantaneous."

"I get the message."

"I hope so, Ned. I really do."

When she saw I didn't want to discuss it further she started on her pizza again. After a minute she said, "If you and Fiona divorced, how often would you see Brad?"

"Come on, Olympia."

"Hypothetically. Say you moved out of town. How often would you come back and see Brad?"

I sliced my pizza, not much caring for this turn in the conversation. As often as I could, I said. I said that I'd visit Brad as frequently as he wanted to see me. When she fell silent again, I glanced at the clock. The lab results were still a long way from being ready.

"Dimitri saw the girls six times," Olympia finally volunteered. "Four times the first year after the divorce, twice the second, then zero."

I reminded her that by then she was remarried. "Maybe Dimitri didn't want to screw up your new family," I said.

"Dimitri? Mr. Consideration? Let's stay in the real world here. I'm not saying he wasn't glad Laurence took the maintenance problem out of his hands, but listen. If Dimitri didn't come and see the girls it was because he'd written them out of his life."

"I'm sure that's not true."

"Why?" She looked at me with sudden challenge. "What makes you so sure?"

"They were his kids."

"That's it?"

"Olympia. He's dead."

Her gaze never wavered. Now I seriously wanted to get lunch over with and return to the Geometrics lab. Dimitri's death seemed to have hit her harder than I'd first thought, maybe even unbalanced her a little. This was Fiona's territory, not mine. I bowed my head over my pepperoni pizza. Olympia set down her cutlery.

"I thought I loved him, Ned. But you know what? I never even knew him. I only realized that after I married Laurence. I had a lot of good times with Dimitri, sure, but we were never close the way Laurence and I are now. Dimitri wouldn't let me get that close. He always had the goddamn Rangers to fall back on, you guys were his real family. When you told me he'd gone into Delta, it was, like, no big surprise. He was full of that whole Army bullshit, death before dishonor."

"He was probably the finest soldier I ever served with."

"He was a crappy husband and father." She shook her head. "Then when Fiona told me he'd quit Delta, that he was making this big career move, going into the private sector, selling guns—"

"I did that too."

"Yeah," she said. "And you know how Fiona felt about that." I stared at my fork. What Fiona had told me at the time was that if my decision to resign my commission was genuinely heartfelt, then she was behind me. But I knew, of course, that she was never really one hundred percent behind my move to Haplon. It was just that for Fiona, any job I took, even a job selling arms, was infinitely better than seeing me return to active service. "I'm not saying I didn't know what Dimitri was like," Olympia went on. "Hell, if it hadn't been for the gambling, I'd have stayed with him. I wouldn't have even met Laurence." She paused, then added, "Maybe if I'd stuck with him, Dimitri wouldn't have gotten involved in that other stuff either."

When I lifted my eyes, she was watching me.

"Other stuff?" I said, and she nodded. I felt my heart beat. My first thought, naturally, was Hawkeye. Was it possible that, contrary to every operational rule in the book, Dimitri had told Olympia what he was doing? But after a moment's reflection, that thought seemed crazy. He wasn't in any kind of regular contact with Olympia, and even if he had told her, she wouldn't have been able to keep it from Fiona. And Fiona wouldn't have kept it from me. "What other stuff?" I ventured at last.

She shook her head. She said it wasn't my problem.

"Olympia." I looked at her.

Sighing, she pushed aside her plate. "The IRS has frozen Dimitri's assets. His papers were lodged with this lawyer. The IRS was on to the guy the day after Dimitri died. They put a freeze on everything. Deeds to Dimitri's apartment. Stock certificates."

"This lawyer called you?"

"Dimitri left everything to the girls. He put me down as a trustee until they reach twenty-one."

The earlier part of our conversation suddenly came into perspective. This is what had been playing on her mind. "So he hadn't written them out of his life."

"His estate's worthless, Ned. At least it will be by the time the IRS is through with it. Somehow, you know, that wasn't a real big surprise. You know what Dimitri was like with money. Some bank's seized his apartment, he was way in arrears on his payments." She took a sip of water, then considered the glass. "Was it an accident?" she said.

"Did someone say that it wasn't?"

"His lawyer told me the IRS was asking questions about Dimitri's work. Like maybe that had something to do with his death."

"It was an accident," I said firmly.

She frowned at her plate. She was still holding something back, so I folded my arms and waited. She took a few seconds with herself, then finally came out with it.

"There's a trust fund. I'd never heard a damn thing about it, but it turns out Dimitri set it up after we divorced, for the girls. It's not part of his estate. The lawyer never mentioned it to the IRS. He says they can't touch it anyway. But he doesn't want any more to do with it either, so he's putting the paperwork through to make me sole trustee."

"Well, that's good, isn't it?"

She grimaced. "Was it really an accident?"

It took me a moment. "You're drawing a connection between the trust fund and Dimitri's death? That doesn't make sense."

"Doesn't it?"

I averted my gaze. Olympia read me.

"I'm not going crazy, Ned." She leaned forward, lowering her voice. "There's five hundred thousand dollars in the fund, and I don't know where Dimitri got it." I sat frozen. Stunned. Five hundred thousand? Olympia's hands bunched into fists on the table. Her knuckles were white. "If I'd known the son of a bitch had half a million dollars sitting there while I was snipping out grocery discount coupons, I'd have killed him myself."

The results were delayed, so I waited in the hall outside the Geometrics lab, where I had time to ponder Olympia's story. She wasn't going crazy. There was simply no way Dimitri could have accumulated half a million dollars from regular savings out of his monthly paycheck. Gambling? But how many gamblers have those kind of wins? The only other obvious source was some cloak-and-dagger corner of the arms trade, and after what Channon had told me, it seemed possible. Given where and how Dimitri died, Olympia's concern made a whole lot of sense. She didn't want the same kind of violence spilling over to her and her family, but equally she didn't want to relinquish the money, not to the IRS or anyone else. Laurence's illness had taken a heavy financial toll on them, and she'd told me over coffee that she wasn't sure they'd have enough savings to put the girls through college. The trust fund, if they could hold on to it, would make everything possible.

God, that would be so weird, she'd said, gazing into her cup. Dimitri dead, finally doing something right.

She wanted to send me the trust deed and the statements of account. I couldn't see what good that would do, but I didn't have the heart to refuse her. Besides, there was always a chance, a very small one, that the statements might give me a clue as to what Dimitri had been up to, and with whom, before he died. After thinking it through, I decided that for the time being, at least, there was no need to reveal the existence of the trust fund to Channon. He might feel obligated to report its existence to the IRS, and that wouldn't help Olympia at all. She deserved better from me than that.

When Fiona finally emerged from the lab, I got to my feet. She handed me the petri dish containing the stone as we headed for her office.

"What are they trying to buy from you?" she asked me.

"You don't want to know."

"Yes I do."

I tapped the container. "Liberia?"

She turned in to her office. I asked her if they'd confirmed it D flawless.

"It's a D flawless," she said, dropping the lab printout on her desk and facing me as I went in. "What are you selling them, Ned?"

"What do you think we're selling them?"

"Okay, how much are you selling them? A lot?"

"Enough." I flipped through the printout. It was full of numbers and symbols, geophysical terminology as incomprehensible to me as hieroglyphics. "So where's the stone from?"

"Enough for what?" she said. "To fight a war?"

"A small one," I admitted.

"If there's an arms embargo on the country, you can't sell them anything."

I dropped the printout on her desk. She knew me better than to believe I was going to embark on an impromptu debate on the ethics of the arms trade. She sat and dropped her head onto one hand. I asked her again if she'd gotten a fix on the stone. This time she nodded.

"Liberia?" I said.

"No."

I was surprised. I raised a brow.

When she looked up, her eyes had filmed over. "Mbuji-Mayi," she said. "The goddamn Congo."

CHAPTER 11

Up here!" Brad called after I'd shouted his name a few times. "In the loft!"

I went up the stairs to the landing, where I found the loft ladder locked into position. At the base of the ladder lay a jumbled pile of small canvas sacks. Geologists' sample bags. Another one dropped from the loft as I neared.

"Hold fire!"

"They're empty," Brad called, dropping another.

I mounted the ladder and climbed on up. Brad was seated on a crate, sorting through a trunk I hadn't seen for years, a piece of U.S. Army surplus I'd acquired somewhere along the way. Fiona had requisitioned it in the days before she rose into management. She used to store her field equipment in the trunk, occasionally she'd even taken the whole damn thing with her out to a site.

"Mom thought I might find some stuff in here." Brad rummaged in the trunk despondently. "All's it is is sample bags and rocks."

I stepped off the ladder onto the warped wooden floor. Brad asked me what I was doing home.

"I was over at Geometrics. One of our customers needed a stone looked at." I cast around for some subtle way of approaching what I had to say. "How was your dinner with Barchevsky?"

"Okay. What kind of stone?"

"I guess you told him you got your visa."

Brad nodded, hanging his head over the trunk again. Another canvas bag arced through the air past my face and plummeted down to the foot of the ladder. "Mom's already given me the routine, Dad, so save your breath. I'm not gonna change my mind." He rummaged some more, then dropped the trunk lid. Turning, he opened an old chest of drawers. "If her field kit's not in here, I give up."

"Did you discuss the situation out there with Barchevsky?"

"Oh, give me a break. Were you listening? I'm not gonna change my mind, okay?" There was a sharpness to his tone that had nothing to do with the Congo. I decided, foolishly, to tackle it head on.

"Brad. There is nothing going on between me and some other woman."

His back turned to me, he shrugged. "Whatever," he said.

I felt my hackles rise. Looking back, I can see that I'd already lost the argument, that he was going to hire himself out to Barchevsky regardless of any objection from me. And on the subject of my relationship with his mother, he'd thrown up a wall that was simply unbreachable. The one time in years when I really needed to communicate with my son, and there was absolutely no way through. I took out the petri dish.

"This is what I had Geometrics look at." When Brad looked over his shoulder, I told him, "It's a rough diamond. By all accounts, a good one."

I tossed the dish, he spun around and caught it. His professional curiosity finally got the better of him, and he rolled the rough in the dish, then popped off the lid and pushed the stone with his finger. "Did they grade it?"

"D flawless."

"Be worth somethin'," he remarked, then his glance suddenly shot up. "This isn't, like, for Mom, is it?" It took me a moment to understand his concern. When I did, I screwed up my face. Was it a gift, he meant, to assuage my guilt over the mysterious other woman. "If it is—" he said.

"It isn't." I lifted my hand. "It's nothing to do with your mother and me, all right? Someone's offering a heap of those as payment for Haplon materiel. I took it to Geometrics to see if they could tell us where it's from."

"That's a problem?"

"If they're conflict diamonds, it's a big problem."

He asked me about the End User Certificate. Living under the same roof with me, he had not completely missed the mechanics of my purported trade.

"Nigerian," I said.

He studied the stone in the dish. "So now I'm guessin' this isn't Nigerian."

"No. That's from the Congo."

Brad kept his eyes down. After a second he dipped his head, re-sealed the dish, and handed it back to me. Stepping past me, he swung himself onto the ladder and started down.

"Brad. It's from the Congo." He continued his descent. When I looked down through the opening, he was gathering up the sacks from the foot of the ladder. "Haplon won't be the only supplier they've approached," I told him. "And there's every chance that whoever's behind this has already done other deals. Someone in the Congo's rearming."

"You're guessing."

I went down the ladder fast, then faced him. "What if I am? If the shooting starts up again out there, you know what they'll be fighting over. They'll be fighting over the diamond fields. And where are you going to be?"

"Barchevsky says it's cool."

"Barchevsky's not a soldier."

"Well, neither am I. And in case you hadn't noticed, Dad, neither are you." Having delivered this low blow, he wrapped his arms around the bundle of canvas sacks and started down the stairs. When the phone in my study started ringing, he jerked back his head. "That damn thing's been going half an hour."

Ignoring the phone, I went after Brad. I caught up with him in the garage, where he dropped the sacks, then knelt on the concrete floor and began sorting through them.

"I'd like you to postpone your trip. I think your mother would too."

"Did she ask you to say that?"

"No."

"This isn't like some camping trip I'm goin' on. It's a job, not a vacation. You don't just phone in and cancel."

I asked him if he would mind me calling Barchevsky. His head rose sharply.

"Yes, I damn well do mind."

"Maybe he doesn't know—"

"For chrissake, you want it in semaphore? N. O. No. Don't speak to Barchevsky, it's none of your damn business." He eyed me a moment, then got up and kicked aside the sacks, making for the stairs to his room.

"I'm asking you not to go, Brad."

"And I'm tellin' you I'm goin'," he said.

"For your mom's sake."

He stopped and swung round. "Oh, Jesus, that is too good. For Mom's sake, like that really matters to you. Like you really care about her feelings." I stayed silent. I did not trust myself to speak. Brad took a step toward me. "I come down this mornin', I find her in the god-damn kitchen, crying. Not just a little teary, honest-to-God crying. She's got her elbows on the table, her head's in her hands, and the tears are just pouring into her Cheerios. It was like when Grandpa died. That's what I thought at first, you know. Who's died?"

"I'll talk to her."

"Don't you get it? Or is it you don't wanna get it?"

I turned for the door, there was no point staying. We were not going to have any kind of rational discussion on the security situation in the Congo. But Brad cut in front of me.

"She doesn't need you to talk to her. She wants you to stop screwin' around."

I tried to step by him, but he moved and blocked my way. We looked at each other.

"I could tell you it's none of your damn business," I said.

He nodded slowly. "So tell me," he said.

It was well and truly time for me to leave. I lifted a hand, intending to ease him out of my way, but suddenly his shoulder dipped and his fist came swinging up. My left arm rose instinctively, blocking the punch. Appalled, my arm remained frozen in the air, locked against Brad's arm.

"Son," I said.

Then he hit me with his left, a straight jab that caught me full in the mouth. I staggered back, he swung again, and I ducked, grabbed his arm, and drove my shoulder hard up under his ribs. He buckled and fell backward, slamming into the door. I kept hold of his arm as we slid to the floor. He was strong, and if I let go of his arm he would keep swinging until I was forced to really hurt him to make him stop. Pulling his thumb back to his wrist, I twisted and pushed his arm high up his back as he hit the floor. Then I jammed my other forearm down across his shoulders and pinned him with the weight of my body.

Ah, he cried. Jesus.

"Settle down, Brad, I'll let you go."

"Get off. You're breaking my fucking arm!"

He bucked, pushing with his knees, twisting his body, but I held on. I leaned some more weight on his thumb, and he cried out again and kept fighting. He cursed me.

I ran my tongue over the backs of my teeth. There was a taste of blood, but no teeth were dislodged or broken. In some ways I might have felt better if they were. My own son had slugged me. After twenty-three years, this is where we'd ended, what we'd come to. From me, ineffective good intentions riding on a wide sea of deception, and from my son, the overpowering urge to strike.

"Okay, I'm going to let go of your arm."

He went rigid, one cheek resting against the concrete, breathing hard. I gave it a moment, then I eased the pressure off his thumb. As his arm slid down his back, straightening, I lifted my weight off him, then I shuffled back on my knees and stood up. He rolled onto his back, holding his shoulder. He didn't rise.

"You okay?" I said.

He sat up, still holding his shoulder. He wouldn't look at me. My fingers went to my bottom lip, it was starting to swell, but the real hurt went a hell of a lot deeper. I felt about as bad as I'd ever felt in my entire life. The doorbell rang, a long, insistent peal. It stopped, then rang again.

"You expecting someone?" I asked Brad.

He didn't reply. He clambered to his feet, crossed to the stairs, and climbed up to his room. The door closed behind him.

I clasped my hands behind my head and looked up at the ceiling. There was not a damn thing I could say, nothing I could do, that would even begin to put things right. When the doorbell rang again, I strode out to the hall and flung open the door. Rita Durranti was standing on my doorstep, looking wild. Wild and worried.

"You too busy to answer your phone?" she said. I lifted my chin. "Greenbaum needs the diamond," she told me, holding out her hand.

"What are you doing here?"

"They're going to sign the deal."

"What the hell are you doing at my home?" I said.

She put a hand on my chest. "Trevanian's going to Rossiter's office to sign the deal. Those papers you took?" Those papers, the ones stashed upstairs in the ceiling of my study. I felt my heart lurch. "Have you got them here?" she asked me.

I nodded, momentarily dazed. When Rossiter got to his office and opened his cabinet, he would find the papers gone. She clicked her fingers, asking me for the diamond again. I took out the petri dish and gave it to her.

"I can get the stone back to Greenbaum," she said, slipping the dish into her purse. "But if you want to keep Hawkeye alive, you'll have to do something about that paperwork. They've just left Rossiter's apartment."

I didn't have the first idea what I was going to do. Rita read that in my face.

"At least get it out to your office," she suggested.

"Then what?"

Turning, she hurried down the front path, calling over her shoulder. "I don't know, Ned. But whatever it is, do it fast."

CHAPTER 12

By the time I drew up to the Haplon parking lot, I had the bare bones of a plan, but the plan required Rossiter's absence, so when I saw that his parking bay was empty I was nearly sick with relief. I scooped up my pocket flashlight, and the folder containing the paperwork, and hurried across to the Haplon lobby.

My single desperate idea had come to me as I was standing on my desk at home, reaching into the ceiling cavity for the stolen paperwork. It had seemed feasible at the time, but as I rode up in the elevator to the Haplon third floor, it was much harder to convince myself that the idea was actually going to work. I found Barbara, Rossiter's secretary, sitting in her usual place outside Rossiter's door.

"Is Milton around?" I asked, glancing at the door behind her desk.

She told me he'd phoned earlier to say that he'd be back in half an hour. She looked at her watch. "That was nearly half an hour ago. If it's urgent, I can get him on the cell phone."

Declining her offer, I made a mental note of the distance between Rossiter's office door and the hall. Then I walked down the hall, counting off the paces to my office. After locking my door, I drew the blinds, then shed my jacket and tie. My flashlight I slipped into my pocket. Climbing onto my desk, I hauled up my chair, then reached up like I had at home and popped back the ceiling tile with the heel of my hand. I got onto the chair, then straightened, my head and shoulders rising through the opening into the ceiling. When I shone my flashlight into the darkness, my heart sank like a stone. A solid wall of ducting and cables ran right down the length of the ceiling space, effectively blocking any passage to the region immediately above Rossiter's office.

I studied the layout, then I slid the tile back into place, got down, and put my chair back under my desk. I stood there a moment, hands on hips, and closed my eyes. I tried to picture the layout of the third floor. Gillian's office. Conference room. Sales office.

Service room, I thought.

Grabbing the stolen paperwork, I unlocked my door and went down the hall, counting my paces again.

Entering the service room, I turned to lock the door behind me, but there was no lock. I made sure the door was closed, then I hit the lights and looked up. A ceiling hatch was directly above me. Deep tiers of shelving rose up the wall, the shelves stacked neatly with stationery, coffee refills for the machine, and farther along, sprays and detergents. It wasn't perfect, but I didn't have the luxury of searching out a more secure point of entry. Tucking the folder beneath my shirt, I scaled the shelves, unlatched the hatch, and clambered awkwardly into the roof-space.

It was several degrees warmer up there, and the air was dusty. Crouching on a metal truss, I turned on my flashlight and lowered the hatch cover behind me. Then I pointed the lightbeam in the direction of Rossiter's office. There were no unpassable obstacles, no ducting or cables, so I took out my white handkerchief and tied it to the steel upright nearest the hatch. Next I gauged the distances I'd paced off down on the third floor. I noted the eighth steel upright, that was the one I estimated was located directly over Rossiter's office. I placed the base of the flashlight between my teeth and set off in a crouching shuffle along the narrow steel beam. I pressed my hands along the underside of the roof above me as I moved, keeping myself from toppling straight through the ceiling.

During my years of active service, even as far back as my cadet-ship at West Point, I'd carried out scores of more demanding maneuvers. I'd once slithered on my belly through mud for half a mile before clambering across a single strand of rope that spanned a hundred-foot ravine, all this with a pack and rifle strapped to my back. I'd once stepped out of a chopper a hundred feet above a U.S. destroyer at sea, with nothing to prevent me from hurtling into the pitching ship's deck but a pair of asbestos gloves, a wet rope, and the jocular advice of my instructor to hang on tight. I'd been involved in fire-fights in both the Gulf and Mogadishu, where I'd pushed myself to the point of physical collapse, and of course I got to the eighth up-right of the Haplon roof-space. But it cost me more time and effort than it should have. When I stopped, I was perspiring and my legs ached. I had to sit down on the beam to stretch and recover. The Fort Benning obstacle course that I'd completed only two years back seemed half a lifetime away.

At last I got up and squatted on the beam. I reached down, prised up the ceiling tile, and peered through the crack. Rossiter's office was right below me. After studying the office layout a second, I let the tile fall back, pressed it into place, then moved forward another two yards along the beam. This time when I lifted the tile below me, I was directly over Rossiter's filing cabinet. Leaning down, I turned my ear to the muted noises coming through from the far side of Rossiter's door. Barbara, I decided. Gassing on the phone.

I lifted the tile and slid it aside. Then bracing one hand on the beam, I gripped the truss near my shoulder, took my weight on my arms, and lowered myself carefully through the opening. When my shoes touched the metal cabinet, I eased the weight off my arms, then I let go of the beam and truss. I crouched, and my head dipped below the ceiling. My whole body was in the office now.

I could hear Barbara talking outside. But she wasn't on the phone, she was talking to someone at her desk. A male voice. My heart jumped, but the next moment I recognized the voice. Micky Baker. He wasn't coming in.

Carefully, I climbed down from the filing cabinet to the table, from there to the floor. Outside, the conversation ended, Micky drifted away. Then on the table behind me I noticed a clear black footprint. When I wiped it with my hand, the print smeared. I looked at my palm, it was black. My other palm too. With a feeling of dread, I looked down. Then I lifted my foot. There was a clear black footprint on the floor beneath. Alarmed now, I wiped my hands on my pants and saw the black stuff come off like coal dust. It must have been something they'd painted on the steel beams in the roof-space, paint that had dried and turned to powder. I stopped and made myself stand still. I thought a moment. Then I crouched and unlaced my shoes. Slipping them off, I placed them upside down on the cabinet. Then I wiped my sleeve across the footprints on the table and the cabinet. Once the prints were gone, I got down on my knees and used my other sleeve to wipe away the prints on the floor. Perspiration rolled down my neck into my collar.

At last the prints were gone, and I stood up and pulled the folder from beneath my shirt. Ever so gently, I eased open the second drawer of the cabinet. It slid smoothly, without a sound. After cleaning my right palm on my thigh, I took the papers from the folder, dropped them into the N folder in the cabinet, then closed the drawer.

I crumpled my folder, shoved it in my pocket, and inspected the cabinet for any signs of black dust. There were none. Good, I thought. Then I heard the sharp ping of the elevator outside.

I quickly climbed onto the table and looked down at the floor. No prints.

Outside, Barbara was speaking again. I climbed onto the cabinet, picked up my shoes, and pushed them into the roof-space. Then I heard laughter, unmistakably Rossiter's, and I reached for the beam and the truss.

A key went into the door, Rossiter shouted "Ned!" and all my muscles seized. But in the next moment I understood. He was shouting for me in his usual way, leaning back and yelling down the hall. Heaving, I dragged myself into the roof-space, got my ass on the beam, then pulled up my legs. As Rossiter worked at the double-locked door with his keys, I heard him tell Barbara to go get some champagne.

"Any preference, Jack?" he said.

I didn't wait to hear Trevanian's answer. Sliding the ceiling tile into position, I pressed down the edges, sealing it, then I put on my shoes. I shone my light around the trusses, located my white-handkerchief marker, then I put the flashlight between my teeth again.

As Rossiter entered his office below me, I set out on my shuffling return journey to the service room.

I'd opened the ceiling hatch cover a couple of inches before I saw that my troubles weren't yet over. A secretary and one of the junior marketing guys were leaning against the shelves, shooting the breeze, so I waited a minute. Then two minutes. Until they were done analyzing the previous night's installment of *The Simpsons,* I was not going anywhere. I was peering through the crack, wondering what to do, when someone opened the service room door.

"Have you guys seen Ned?" Gillian Streiss. When they said they hadn't, she told them, "Well, if you do, tell him Rossiter's after him. And by the way, how long's it take you two to pick up stationery?" She withdrew. Stirred into action, the pair collected some paper, exchanged a few quiet words about Gillian, then left the room.

As soon as they were gone, I clambered down to the shelves, lowering the cover behind me and securing it. When I got to the floor, I grabbed a sheet of paper and cleaned off the soles of my shoes. After trashing the paper, I put my head out, checked that the hall was clear, then walked quickly down to my office, went in, and locked the door.

Ten minutes later, I'd cleaned myself off properly and put on my jacket and tie. I unlocked my door and left it ajar so that someone like Gillian could discover me working at my desk. But it wasn't Gillian, it was Rossiter who found me. He passed by in the hall, then checked his stride and came back.

"Where the fuck you been?" he asked, coming in. "I've got Trevanian and Lagundi here. Come on down to my office, we're having a drink. They just signed for this order we been sweatin' on."

"Signed?"

"Yeah."

"Signed what?"

"The headline agreement."

"I haven't seen any agreement."

"Well, come on down to my office, you can see it now." He gave me a direct look. This wasn't something he expected me to question. Rising, I went around and closed the door. Then I faced him.

"Milton, what the hell is going on with this deal?" He didn't reply. "I thought this was my order. Then suddenly we're down on

West Forty-seventh, and I'm sitting there pretending like it isn't total news to me that we're trading arms for diamonds. Now this." I gestured to the hall. "They've signed an agreement, and I haven't even seen it."

"I'm not takin' any risks with the diamonds. We'll get our money direct from Greenbaum."

"That's not the point. How long's this agreement been under negotiation?"

"The ink's still dryin' on the signatures."

"Why wasn't I consulted over it? I'm your marketing manager for chrissake, not the damn office gofer."

"You'll get your cut of the bonus."

"I'm not concerned about the bonus."

"Offer withdrawn then." He shot me a smile, came across, and clapped my shoulder. "You wanna stand here mopin', or you comin' for a drink?"

I didn't answer. I turned to my desk.

"You're just pissed because you weren't in on it the whole way."

"I've got a right to be pissed, Milton."

"Listen," he said, his tone mollifying. "Don't make a thing about it. It wasn't just you, Trevanian didn't want anyone involved, just me. The guy is secrecy crazy. Some bad experience with his last U.S. order. Too many people involved, talking too much. Commerce ended up withholding half the export licenses, he didn't want a rerun with us."

"Then what was I doing out at Springfield? And here, down on the range, what was that, just going through the motions?"

"Lagundi had to feel part of it."

I turned that over. "She never knew it was a done deal?"

He pointed two fingers in warning. "And there's no reason for anyone to tell her. Her people are getting what they wanted. Everyone's happy."

With hindsight, of course, I can see that Rossiter's explanation did not totally add up, but since I had just broken into his office, replaced the draft agreement, and gotten away with it by the skin of my teeth, my critical faculties weren't as engaged as they might have been. I was blindsided, too, by Rossiter's belated admission of me into the inner circle of the deal. He seemed, at last, to be coming clean with me about the whole transaction. As I followed him along to the celebration in his office, I honestly thought that I was starting to get some kind of handle on what had been going on.

In his office, the atmosphere was loose and friendly. Gillian was there, Benny Skalder, the head of Design, and half a dozen other Haplon notables, everyone with a drink in hand. Trevanian and Lagundi were mingling, and Barbara was circulating around the room, refilling glasses with champagne. She gave me a glass, and a moment later I found myself standing by Lagundi. A claret red slacksuit, and a white scarf wound through her high-piled hair.

She congratulated me on winning the order. I nodded and tried to smile. I remarked that maybe the congratulations should be extended to the Nigerian army, who'd gotten some very fine weapons.

"We will see more of you, then," she said. I raised a brow. "Rossiter told us you will be handling the shipment."

I nodded again. It was news to me. "Can I ask you where you got that accent, Miss Lagundi?"

"Mission school. My teachers were Irish nuns. You can call me Cecille."

"Ned," I said, and her eyes smiled. "The nuns teach you how to shoot, Cecille?" She dropped her eyes and sipped her drink. "I don't suppose it was them who taught you how to grade diamonds either."

"I wasn't expecting to see you there this morning." She meant the meeting at Greenbaum's office. "You looked bored."

"Not my thing."

"You don't like diamonds?" When I shrugged, she touched the pendant at her throat. "You like this?"

I glanced down at the stone. Her hand rested on her cleavage. When I raised my eyes, her own dark eyes were smiling at me again.

"I'd have to ask my wife," I said, then I took a long pull at my champagne. I was like that, head back, glance sliding over Lagundi's shoulder, when I saw them, four distinct black marks on the ceiling tile directly above Rossiter's cabinet. Fingermarks. Fingermarks that I must have left when I lifted the tile. The champagne suddenly burned in my throat. My stomach churned. Swallowing hard, I turned aside and set down the glass. Before Lagundi could stop me, I excused myself and angled around her toward the door.

But Rossiter intercepted me midflight. He wrapped an arm over my shoulder and guided me across to share a celebratory drink with Trevanian. I didn't feel like a celebratory drink with Trevanian or Rossiter or anyone else. I wasn't even sure I could hold another drink down. But another glass was shoved into my hand, and I had to stand there smiling pleasantly, listening to the conversation between Trevanian and Rossiter while trying to keep my eyes from straying up to the ceiling. They kept straying there anyway. The damn fingerprints seemed gigantic, getting larger with every excruciating minute that passed. At last Trevanian started dipping into his well-worn supply of stories concerning the exploits of his private military company, the group around us began to grow, everyone leaning in for a touch of vicarious danger, and I managed to slip away.

I retreated to my office to do some real soldiering. I sat down and worried and waited. Most soldiering is waiting, something Channon first taught me. It's not about the brief flares of violent action, it's about using downtime constructively, staying ready, doing reconnaissance and planning, keeping up with the hard daily grind. While I waited in my office, the late afternoon turning to evening, I had plenty of time to reflect on how my carelessness could end up bringing Hawkeye crashing down.

My fingerprints, like the fingerprints of every Haplon employee, were kept on file, a standard security procedure that I'd never even given a second thought to. Now all Rossiter had to do was notice the marks, make the connection that they were fingermarks, and from that moment on, Hawkeye would be history. Even if he didn't notice them right away, they'd still be there the next day, and the day after that.

Sitting at my desk, I had plenty of time, too, to think about Brad. Brad and the Congo and me. I touched my lip, it was bruised and sore.

The long day waned. At 6:00 P.M., the lights went on in the parking lot. Finally the celebration in Rossiter's office broke up. People passed by my office, collected their coats, and came back down the hall and went home. I carried on waiting, watching from the window in my office. Trevanian and Lagundi left together in a Cadillac. Rossiter put his head in, told me not to feel sore, and said goodnight. I watched as he departed in his Lotus. I waited some more. An hour later, I saw the Haplon security guard take a turn around the nearly empty parking lot, and I gave it another ten minutes, then I went along to the service room. I climbed up through the manhole and got myself back into position over Rossiter's office. I lifted the marked tile, wiped off the prints with my handkerchief, then replaced it carefully. Returning to the service room, I wiped the soles of my feet, and my hands. I went back to my office and put on my jacket and tie. Down in the lobby, I said good-night to the security guard, then I crossed to my car and got in and drove out of Connecticut, over the state line into New York, where I stopped and got quietly drunk in a bar.

TWO

It was days before the materiel had all been crated, ready for trucking down to the dock in New Jersey, and I spent most of that time just going through the motions of my regular routine.

At 6:30 A.M. I would rise, work out for half an hour, then shower and have breakfast, a meal that I invariably ate alone in that period. Then I would drive up to the Haplon plant and have a meeting with Gillian Streiss and the sales team before settling down to answer my e-mail, send off a few faxes, and make some calls. Lunch was sometimes a trip down to Manhattan to schmooze a client, but more frequently a round of sandwiches at my desk before the early afternoon call along to Rossiter's office to discuss the state of play on various orders, placed and pending, after which I would go out to the main office and kick the appropriate butts. In the late afternoon I would try to get myself down to the firing range, with or without a client, and spend twenty minutes or more blazing away with the Haplon weapons.

And on the way home each evening I stopped at a phone booth, as ordered, and phoned Channon. These exchanges never varied.

Hello?

Red Hawk.

You okay?

I'm okay. Shipment schedule's unchanged.

Call again tomorrow, he'd instruct me before hanging up.

Then, the day's work finally over, when I couldn't put it off any longer, I would make my way home to Ellis Street, where it was increasingly clear I would not be truly welcome until my life changed in some fundamental way. In the meantime, I had no choice but to endure Brad's silence and Fiona's simmering anger. I'm sure Brad never mentioned our ridiculous tussle to his mother, but she seemed to pick up on the new distance between us, the natural counterpart of my continuing distance from her. I was still sleeping in the spare room.

So the morning when the materiel was finally trucked to the New Jersey docks, and I set off after it to supervise the loading, it felt like I was hitting the wall midway through an arduous and extremely painful marathon. There were six containers, and I'd fixed a cigarette-sized tracking device inside the internal frame of each one of them.

The ship was Ukrainian, its name, *Sebastopol,* and home port, Odessa, were embossed on the stern in large Cyrillic letters that were rusting. I left our truck drivers with the forklift guy and went and sat with the old stevedore by his prefab cabin to wait for Cecille Lagundi. She was supposed to oversee the loading with me. After a quarter hour, she hadn't shown, so I wandered down the dock. There was a smell of diesel and old rope in the air, the smell of every port in the world. I threw some stones in the water, watched the birds wheel, and thought about Dimitri and some of the decisions he'd made, as a soldier and as a man. I thought about some of the decisions I'd made too. I told myself that when Hawkeye was over, I would do better. When I reached the Customs post, the uniformed officers were gathered around a portable TV watching a ball game. I loitered awhile, then turned and went back. By this time the giant straddlelift had unloaded the six Haplon containers. The last truck pulled out through the gates as I watched, and was gone. I put my head in at the stevedore's cabin.

"She ain't here yet," the old guy told me. He nodded shipward, advising me to go aboard and have a word with the captain. "Speed those fellas' work, you wanna get them started now. Shore crane's ready when they are."

The clock behind him said 10:50 A.M. We were due at the bank at 4:30 P.M. I still thought we had plenty of time.

I went aboard ship, climbing the gangway to the deck. The railings were draped with dirty canvas. A bare-chested guy was kneeling over a bucket, rinsing clothes in soapy water and hanging them over the air vents to dry. Another guy lounged at the railing and peeled an orange. What had once been white paint on the bulkheads was stained a dirty cream. It wasn't the kind of scene I'd ever witnessed aboard a vessel of the U.S. Navy. When I asked to see the captain, the guy at the bucket looked me over and said something in Russian. The guy with the orange jerked his head up to the ship's bridge.

When I turned in that direction, an officer emerged on the upper deck. He looked over the rails at me.

"How soon can you get the Haplon cargo loaded?" I asked, pointing to the containers down on the dock.

"You stay," he ordered, then he withdrew into the bridge.

I leaned against the railings and watched orange peel floating on the water below, then I lifted my eyes to the Haplon containers. Once the materiel was loaded, the captain would issue me a bill of lading, and I'd return with Lagundi to meet Rossiter at the Manhattan bank where the diamonds were stored. There I'd give Trevanian the bill of lading. He, under Greenbaum's expert eye, would weigh out the diamonds in payment. Once that was done, I was out. From that point on it was up to Rita Durranti to collate the evidence, and it was up to Channon to bring down the hammer. The close of Trevanian's grubby career would coincide with the end of mine.

Someone behind me whistled, and I turned. That officer again.

"You are not consignee," he said loudly.

"No," I agreed, then I explained my position. I told him that the consignee's representative had been delayed, but that she'd be along shortly. "If you call down to the stevedore, we can get started."

He wasn't interested. He disappeared into the bridge, and another ten minutes went by. The guy along the railings from me finished his orange. The other guy with the dirty washing emptied his bucket over the side. Then the officer reappeared, he shouted down to me that the shore crane wasn't ready. He was jerking me around. I told him what the stevedore had told me, that the crane was ready whenever we needed it. I didn't actually call him a liar, but he got the idea. It didn't do me any good. He leaned on the railings, gazed over my head, and calmly informed me that we would wait for the consignee. As long as it took.

I got on my cell phone to Rossiter. After explaining the situation, I suggested he call Trevanian, get him to hurry Lagundi along. Rossiter's blood pressure had been rising all week. The news about Lagundi's tardiness didn't go down too well. He bawled me out, reconfirmed the 4:30 deadline for our meeting at the bank, then hung up.

Returning to the dock, I settled down with a newspaper by the stevedore's cabin and waited. I waited a long time. It was after 12:00 before I glanced up from the sports pages and saw Lagundi picking her way around the machinery by the warehouse. She was wearing a white slacksuit and dark glasses, and she had her trademark Gucci purse slung over her shoulder. She could not have looked more completely out of place if she'd tried. Shedding her glasses, she smiled as she neared. I rose without greeting her and went inside to tell the stevedore to get started.

After a round of calls up to the ship's captain and down to Customs, the loading finally began at 1:00 P.M. At 1:30 P.M., with just two of the six containers aboard, the ship's crew decided to break for lunch.

"For crying out loud," I said when the stevedore told me. "So when do they get going again?"

"Two. Maybe two-thirty." He shrugged like it was guesswork, then he went to speak with the crane driver.

Two containers in half an hour. There were four more to load. Assuming the stevedore's guesswork was correct, we could have it all done by 3:30 P.M. I phoned Rossiter. He made some unprintable remarks, and reminded me that the bank closed at 5:00 P.M. He told me to be there. No excuses, he said.

A single Customs officer had been overseeing the loading. Now he went back to the Customs shed, and I went with him. I'd sent Lagundi along there earlier to get the paperwork done, but now when we got there I saw her sitting on her ass, browsing through back copies of the *National Enquirer*. There was a pile of the old magazines by her chair. The Customs guy went through to the back to see his colleagues.

I asked Lagundi, "Have they signed the clearance?"

She kept her eyes down. "Not yet."

"Well, what's the holdup?"

She ignored me. I took a step in her direction, then stopped when another Customs officer emerged from out back. As he collected some files, I called across, asking him when the Haplon clearance would be through. He checked the OUT tray and shrugged. Then Lagundi suddenly got up and went over and placed our documentation on the counter. The Customs guy glanced through it.

"Give us an hour," he told me, flicking the papers. "The boss has to countersign these. He's at lunch." He retreated out back.

I turned to Lagundi, she was already flipping idly through another magazine. "What are you playing at?" I said.

"They will get done."

"You've wasted time." She flipped another page, and I said, "How long were you going to wait?"

She dropped the magazine onto the leaning pile of back copies, got up, and edged past me out the door. She headed for the johns over by the warehouse. I called after her to stay close, warning her that the loading should be done by 3:30, that I wanted to leave right after. She wiggled her fingers at me over her shoulder, then picked her way carefully around some giant coils of cable and disappeared into an avenue of oil drums and pallets.

"Client trouble?" a voice at my shoulder inquired, and I swung around. Rita.

Lowering my voice, I said, "I needed the clearance pushed through fast."

Rita looked out toward the warehouse where Lagundi had disappeared. She remarked that my client didn't seem overwhelmed with any urgency.

"You noticed."

"What's her problem?"

I shook my head. Anyone's guess. Then I asked Rita how her

own work was going. She'd wanted to record everything on the Port Authority's CCTV, from the arrival of the Haplon goods to the loading. She figured video evidence might forestall any improbable arguments from the defense lawyers about the shipped containers not being the same ones Haplon had delivered to the port.

"We won't make the Sundance Festival, but it's taped. Lawyer-proof evidence."

"No such thing."

"I'll take my chances," she said. "Now how about you get the rest of it loaded so I can get back to town. I'm going nuts staring at these little black-and-white screens." She got herself a Hershey bar from the dispenser and exited into a back room.

It was past 2:30 before the loading started again. I stood with Lagundi and the Customs guy as the crane trundled along the rails. It stopped and lowered the mechanized clamp to the container. The container rose, the crane motors whining loudly under the strain, then it crept out beneath the crane's arm and stopped over the ship's hold. Then it descended out of sight. Five minutes later, the empty clamp at the end of the crane's cables rose slowly from the hold. I checked my watch. 2:45. I thought we'd make it. Just.

Then Lagundi made her big announcement. "I must inspect those," she told the Customs guy, and she pointed to the three containers remaining on the dock. The Customs guy thought he'd misunderstood, she had to repeat the request twice. I couldn't believe my ears.

"Trevanian inspected the equipment as it was loaded," I said. "Customs inspected it too. Their goddamn seal's on the containers." She ignored me. She leaned into the stevedore's cabin, told him to radio the crane driver, stand him down for a while. "Look, call Trevanian first," I said, throwing out a hand in exasperation. "Speak to Customs. Everyone knows what's in the containers. Here." I gestured to the Customs guy standing beside me. "Show her the manifest."

He angled his clipboard for Lagundi to see. She wouldn't look.

"The red container first," she said.

The Customs guy glanced from her back to me. The container's contents remained Haplon property until the bill of lading changed hands. Until then, it was entirely my decision whether Lagundi got the requested access or not. Whether we got paid or not, of course, was entirely up to her. I got on the phone to Rossiter again, and this time he went berserk. He told me to hang up and wait for a call from Trevanian. Two minutes later I took Trevanian's call. I explained Lagundi's request, adding that if the Customs seals were broken they'd have to be replaced. More paperwork, and more time. Trevanian sounded every bit as wild as Rossiter. He told me to put Lagundi on, so I handed her my cell phone. She walked away down the dock, talking to Trevanian. I didn't hear the conversation, but she seemed calm enough. When she returned after a minute, she gave me my phone and it rang in my hand. The caller this time was Rossiter.

"Let her do the fucking inspection. Trevanian can't talk her out of it, Christ knows what's on her mind. You got two hours." He hung up before I could speak.

So that was it. When I gave the order, the stevedore arched his brow and went inside to radio the crane driver. The Customs guy went to get a tool to break the seal. Lagundi and I were left alone, standing on the potholed tarmac by the containers. She stared at the ship. She'd gotten what she wanted, but her poise and confidence seemed to have left her. Her thick lips were clamped tight.

"Something you want to tell me?" I said.

She wrapped her arms around herself, dropped her head, and walked off.

We got to the bank just after 5:00 P.M. Drawing up to the sidewalk, I wound down my window and Rossiter came over, shaking his head. We'd missed the deadline. The bank was closed.

"Jack'll take you back to your hotel," Rossiter told Lagundi as he opened the passenger door of my car to let her out. As she stepped onto the sidewalk, he added, "We'll meet here in the morning, lady. See if we can't do it right then." She gave him a cool glance, then she went to join Trevanian by the locked door of the bank. Rossiter climbed into the passenger seat beside me. "You get the bill of lading?" he asked me.

I handed it to him. He folded it into his inner jacket, then craned around to watch Trevanian and Lagundi. They seemed to be arguing.

Trevanian appeared to be giving her a piece of his mind. As we drew into the traffic, Rossiter faced the front again, we drove on a full minute before he spoke.

"What can you do about the woman?"

I looked across. I wasn't sure I knew what he meant. I wasn't sure that I wanted to know. "What do you mean, 'do'?"

He seemed to consider spelling it out for me, then he changed his mind. He lifted a hand and raked the back of his thumb against his forehead. The corners of his mouth turned down. "Go left here," he said, and I swung up the avenue. We cruised to his apartment in an uncomfortable, lowering silence.

CHAPTER 14

Saying good-bye to my son never was going to be easy, and when I heard that Barchevsky would be at the airport I almost decided not to go, just to say a private farewell at home. Fiona volunteered to run Brad down to the airport alone, but when it came to the point, I found that I couldn't let them go without me. Driving down there, Brad sat in the backseat and received his mother's last-minute advice and instructions with admirable forbearance.

While I parked, they went on ahead, I caught up with them again at the South Africa Airways check-in. Brad was talking with some bearded guy in the line. When I came up, Fiona introduced me, and that was my first meeting with Ivan Barchevsky.

"Ivan's flying out with Brad," Fiona told me. Unexpected news. She was pleased.

I asked him how far he was going.

"Mbuji," Barchevsky replied, releasing my hand. "For my sins." His smile was sardonic and dry. Folding his arms, he shoved his duffel bag toward the check-in with his foot. His beard was trimmed close, a mat of tight curls, the same silver-gray as his hair. His face was tan, it bore the lines of someone who'd been around the block a few times. He was in his mid-forties, but well weathered.

As we waited, the three of them talked about alluvial deposits and kimberlite pipes, and each time I tried turning the conversation to something that I could at least partway understand, Brad turned it right back. In his mind, my son was already out there in Mbuji-Mayi doing fieldwork, analyzing samples in some prefab bush laboratory. Finally I gave up and went to wait by myself in the cafeteria. Fiona joined me several minutes later, but we didn't have much to say to each other. She kept glancing over her shoulder at Brad while I pushed my spoon around a cup of tasteless coffee. I told her not to worry, that Brad would be fine. She asked me what I thought of Barchevsky.

"Seems okay." I'd been prepared to loathe the guy. "At least he's got the balls to go out there himself."

"What's that mean?"

"It means he seems okay. Better than I expected."

"What did you expect, an ogre? Some monster?"

I expected, I told her, the usual corporate nonentity, a bullshit MBA type in a suit.

"Well, he's not."

"Okay."

"And what gives you the goddamn right to criticize anyway?" She leaned forward, her voice low but vehement. "Have you looked at yourself lately? You talk like you're still instructing at West Point. You're a salesman, for chrissake. Someone who sells guns."

"You finished?"

"If there's a bullshit MBA type here, it's you. Get used to it, Ned. Lord knows, I've tried. I really have tried."

She pushed away from the table, got up, and walked briskly to the rest rooms. I concentrated on the froth in my coffee. Brad's imminent departure had contributed to Fiona's outburst, but I couldn't kid myself that her frustration and anger with me were anything other than real and deep. I was never going to look back on this moment and smile. The truth was, my marriage was sliding away from me with a momentum that was getting beyond my control. But midnight at J.F.K. Airport was neither the time nor place to face up to that thought squarely. I tried to put it out of my mind.

Brad and Barchevsky came over from the check-in. Barchevsky pulled up a chair. Brad dropped his hand luggage under the table, said he was going to get some tapes for his Walkman, then left us.

"He'd better get plenty," Barchevsky remarked wryly. "He'll need them."

I asked if the mining camp was really that quiet.

"Dujanka? Deadly." Barchevsky checked the plastic menu. "Half a dozen white guys you see all day long. Once you're done being amazed by the stars—somewhere around night five—all you really want to do is get back to your own room and close the door. They still serving coffee?" he wondered, getting to his feet. While Barchevsky went to the bar, I watched Brad over at the music store. He was idling at the racks, killing time. Avoiding me. After a minute, Barchevsky returned with a coffee. "Fiona was saying you're not so sure about Brad going out there."

I nodded, then braced myself for the hollow reassurances. He sat down.

"If he was my son, I'd be concerned too," he said. "The country's a disaster. Nothing works, not even the goddamn army. We're employing a private security firm to keep the peace near some of our camps. And corruption?" He made a face. "The place is the Africa of Africa. Unreconstructible."

"You mentioned that to Brad?"

"Many times."

"And Fiona?"

He took a pull at his coffee. "Look, when she asked me about work for Brad, I didn't take it that seriously. She floated the idea, I just went through the motions. Then we had someone quit from the Dujanka mine. Brad jumped at the job. What was I supposed to say to him? Sorry, no job, your mom's gotten worried? I laid the deal out for him, straight."

"You told him the country's stable."

"I told him stable compared with last year. And it is."

I looked at him. I asked him how many other geologists had applied for the job he gave Brad.

"Two. Both more experienced than Brad." In other words, Brad was replaceable. He hadn't been hired out of desperation. "Bottom line?" Barchevsky said. "It's Brad's job. I offered it to him, and he accepted. If I'd known you and Fiona weren't all right with that, I probably wouldn't have made the offer. But keep it in mind, it was Fiona who started the ball rolling."

"Am I meant to be reassured?"

"I'm trying." He smiled plaintively.

I wanted to dislike the guy, but it was hard. In his position, I probably would have done what he'd done. For sure I'd have felt less bad about it than he appeared to. After evading a couple of questions from him about my own time in Africa—Fiona had evidently mentioned my tour in Somalia—I asked him about security at the Dujanka mine.

"It doesn't need any security. It's in a safe zone, and the mine's hardly big enough to warrant anyone's attention anyway. Listen," he said, "maybe I overplayed how bad things are. I didn't want to give you any bullshit, Brad's not going five-star. But my mines generally work. We've had some incidents different times. Last year was not good, but there hasn't been any real trouble for six months. Even when things were at their worst, we never had any of our guys hurt. Broken fingers from the machinery, okay, but no one was ever attacked. Not by the rebels. Not even by the glorious Congolese army. Ever."

"You normally reassure your employees' families like this?"

He smiled. "Guys I employ, families aren't normally an issue."

Fiona came out of the rest room, she hesitated when she saw Barchevsky at the table with me. Then she pulled herself together and came over. Barchevsky finished his coffee. He touched his watch, saying it was about time for him and Brad to go through to Departures, so I went to fetch Brad. He was still in the music store.

"Time to go," I said, stepping up beside him.

He selected a last cassette from the rack, piled it onto his forearm with the other tapes, then edged by me to the checkout. He asked me what I'd been talking about with Barchevsky. "Me?" he said.

"The Dujanka mine. Security."

"Great. So now he thinks I'm a frightened jerk."

"He thinks you'll do a good job." I placed a fatherly hand on his shoulder. "I do too."

When Brad dropped the cassettes in front of the cashier and

shrugged my hand from his shoulder, my jaw went tight. The cashier scanned the goods, and I took a moment with myself. Then I stepped around and packed the cassettes and some batteries into a carry bag. Since the incident in the garage, he'd avoided me whenever he could. We hadn't eaten one meal together. He'd stopped coming down to the living room in the late evening for his usual dose of NBA on cable. My daily return home from work he took as his cue to withdraw up to the seclusion of his quarters above the garage, reemerging only after I left for work again the next morning. The truth is, all lines of communication between Brad and me were down. And now he was leaving for the Congo. I thought of all those times I'd been called away at short notice by the Army, bound for destinations unknown. Now I knew how Fiona must have felt in those days. I'd always taken her stoicism for granted, and my only excuse, looking back, is that there are some kinds of courage no young soldier is ever wise enough to understand.

"Here." I offered Brad an envelope as we went to collect his hand luggage. "Something to tide you over."

"Till what?"

"Your first paycheck."

"I don't want it, Dad."

Folding the envelope, I pushed it into the carry bag with the batteries, warning him not to make a scene and upset his mother. At the table, he turned his back on me and shoved everything into his overnight bag. Barchevsky rose, making noises about going on ahead. He clearly meant to give the three of us some time together in private to say our good-byes, but Brad wasn't going to let that happen.

"Wait up," he told Barchevsky, and zipped up his luggage. "Just a second." He went around the table to Fiona. She beamed at him, her eyes glistening. He put his arms around her shoulders and pressed his cheek against hers and whispered a few words to her. She squeezed him tight. He had to ease himself away before she let him go. Then she wrapped her empty arms around herself.

When Brad turned to me, my arms rose to embrace him, but he thrust out his hand.

"Bye, Dad."

Checked, I glanced down at his open palm. I felt Barchevsky hovering awkwardly nearby. When I lifted my eyes, Brad's gaze stayed firm. He was not going to weaken. So I took his hand.

"Bye, son."

A brief clasp, then he released my hand and turned away. A few seconds later he had his overnight bag slung over his shoulder, and he was walking with Barchevsky toward the escalators, checking his boarding card. They were laughing at something together, while Fiona and I stood silent, watching them go.

CHAPTER 15

A light rain was falling outside, so Rossiter, Greenbaum, and I waited in the bank's lobby. Rossiter was having trouble staying in his chair, he kept wandering to the glass doors, looking off down the street.

"They still on Africa time, or what?" He dropped into the seat beside me. "How far's their hotel, three blocks?"

I suggested raising Trevanian on the cell phone, but Rossiter dismissed the idea. Rossiter had deliberately gotten us to arrive ten minutes late, some childish plan he had to demonstrate who was in charge of the deal. Ten minutes after our arrival, it was we who were waiting, and it was obvious his plan hadn't worked out. Rossiter's already dark mood was worsening. Beside him, Mordecai Greenbaum, who'd been sitting patiently, made the mistake of checking his watch.

"For chrissake," Rossiter snapped in irritation. "You got somethin' more important on?"

Greenbaum shot me a glance. I smiled sympathetically, but he didn't smile back. If he hadn't been on the hook at Customs, I figured he probably would have gotten up at that moment and walked.

Trevanian finally entered the lobby five minutes later. Rossiter got up and Trevanian came straight over.

"Has Cecille been in?" Trevanian asked, tossing his head toward the counter.

"You're askin' us?" Rossiter squinted. "What's happened, she's not with you?"

"She'll be here."

"We're not damn well waitin'," said Rossiter sharply. "She knew the time. If she couldn't get her ass down here, that's not our problem." He brought out the bill of lading. "Now let's count the stones, get this done." Trevanian gave the bill a rueful look. He asked us to give him a minute, then he veered away to the counter. Rossiter turned to me, his color rising. "Go find out what the fuckin' problem is this time," he told me, waving Greenbaum back into his seat.

Trevanian had his head hanging down when I joined him. I leaned against the counter.

"You've misplaced Lagundi?"

"Temporarily," he said.

"I thought you were staying at the same hotel."

"She wasn't sleeping in my pocket." He signaled to someone behind the counter.

"At the dock yesterday, I got the impression she was screwing me around."

He turned on me. "You want the deal, I want the deal. How about you just back off for five seconds while I sort this out." Then the bank clerk arrived, and Trevanian asked him if Lagundi had been in. I pricked up my ears. The clerk said she hadn't. "Since last week?" Trevanian pressed.

The clerk tapped at his keyboard and consulted the screen. "She came in yesterday morning."

Trevanian sagged like he'd taken a punch in the kidney. He leaned on the counter for support a moment, then he turned and hurried toward the exit.

"Hey!" Rossiter shouted across the lobby.

"I'll track her down," Trevanian called over his shoulder. "I'll phone when I've got her. A few hours."

"A few fuckin' hours," shouted Rossiter, but Trevanian shouldered his way out through the door and kept going. Rossiter opened his arms in angry bewilderment and turned to me. I jogged over.

"Lagundi got independent access to the stones yesterday," I told him. "Now Trevanian's lost her."

It only took Rossiter a second. "Holy fuck. She's taken the stones?"

"You saw Trevanian."

"Holy fuck."

I looked at the door through which Trevanian had disappeared. "I think I should go down to the docks, check the cargo." When Rossiter screwed up his face, I told him, "And I think you should take the bill of lading back to your apartment. Get it put away safe."

"What are they going to do, steal it?"

"Look at it this way, Milton. We're standing here with no payment. Lagundi's gone AWOL, maybe with the diamonds. Meantime the Haplon materiel's aboard ship, ready to go. If Trevanian or Lagundi gets hold of the bill of lading, you tell me. Where are we?"

He turned it over. Then he dismissed Greenbaum with a few peremptory words and led me out, left me at my car, and went to find a cab to take him and the bill of lading back to his apartment.

The rain had stopped by the time I got to the dock. Rita Durranti was waiting for me inside the gates. I'd called from my car to tell her what was happening, she hadn't wasted any time getting out to join me. That wasn't at all what I'd intended. Now she fell in beside me, skipping around the oil-slicked puddles.

I said, "I didn't ask you to come down here."

"And I didn't ask you to come to my goddamn office."

"Go back to your car." She stayed beside me, we walked by the warehouse, then I stopped. "Rita, go back to your car. Go back to your office. When I'm done here, I'll call you."

"Not till I find out what's going on."

"I'll call you."

"Sure. After you've called Channon. And then you'll only tell me as much as he wants me to know. Well, I'm not playing that game anymore, Ned."

"Rita," I called, but she kept on walking. I jogged and caught up to her. "This isn't smart."

"Nobody's signed Lagundi in through the gates since the loading yesterday," she said.

I looked at her. She wasn't turning back. "What about Trevanian?" I asked, giving up.

"Same. But you'll like this. Trevanian's name rang a bell with the guard. He checked back for me. Trevanian was down here a few times when the *Sebastopol* first docked."

"Seeing who?"

"The *Sebastopol*'s captain."

"Why?"

"That's not in the book."

Under the terms of the sale, the "Nigerians" were buying the Haplon goods FOB, free on board, so there was no reason for Trevanian to see the ship's captain before loading. While I chewed that over, Rita quizzed me about what had gone wrong at the bank. There wasn't much I could add to what I'd told her when I'd called.

She seemed disappointed. "You never saw the strongbox?"

"No."

"So how do you know it's empty?"

"I don't."

"But you said she'd bolted with the diamonds."

"I said that's what I thought. At the time."

"At the time?"

I glanced across. Not much got past her. "Trevanian came and went before we could talk to him," I said. "Maybe it was just a performance he was putting on. If it was, he made sure he didn't have to keep it up for too long." Rita groaned at the thought of Trevanian and Lagundi playing games with us, stringing us along while they departed with the stones. If that's what was happening, the whole operation was sunk. I said, "I don't know what Trevanian's doing, Rita. Maybe he was for real. Maybe not. Either way, I'll feel a lot easier about it once we've seen in there." I nodded ahead to the *Sebastopol*. It sat lower in the water, riding the tide, but otherwise nothing had changed. Wet washing still hung over the air vents.

We collected a Customs guy, the same one who'd overseen the

loading. He told us he hadn't seen Lagundi. When I described Trevanian, he shook his head, said he hadn't seen anyone answering the description. He told us the *Sebastopol* was due to sail in forty-eight hours, then he accompanied us along the dock. As we reached the ship, Rita and I fell back a few paces and the Customs guy climbed the gangway ahead of us.

"We can't let her sail now," Rita said quietly. "If no one's paid for the weapons, they're still Haplon's."

"We could unload them."

"Then where's our case?"

I didn't answer.

"God," she said. "This is so not turning out right."

We waited at the head of the gangway while the Customs agent went in search of the captain. Ten minutes later, he returned with the ship's mate, a guy who was plainly not pleased to see me again. When I explained that we needed to see our cargo, the mate snorted dismissively.

"Any question about my rights here," I said, "these people can put you straight." I gestured to Rita and her uniformed Customs colleague.

The mate eyeballed me, I'd made an enemy, but he knew he had no choice. He finally relented and led us to the superstructure aft, then through a bulkhead door and down a steep metal ladder. The stench was appalling. In the unseen galley, someone was cooking meat, and the smell of frying fat was clogging the air in the narrow passage. Farther on, we passed several tiny cabins, there was a strong odor from the heads, an odor overlain with the acrid perfume of disinfectant. Rita, who'd been aboard more than a few ships in her time, cast me a look of frank disgust. At last, somewhere in the ship's bowels, we reached an airtight steel door. The mate spun the wheel handle, pulled the door open, and led us single file into the hold.

The hold cover was off, and natural light came flooding in from above. The diesel-laced air was quite a relief after the fetid stench of the living quarters. Rita threw back her head and breathed as if she were surfacing from the watery deeps. I asked the mate if anyone apart from the crew had been in the hold since the loading. Instead of answering me, he went across to an open area in the center of the hold. A forklift was parked there, wet from the rain. "The African lady?" I asked. "Miss Lagundi?"

He jerked his head starboard. "There it is," he informed me.

The six containers were lined up side by side, their sealed doors facing us. I beckoned the Customs guy forward. He walked down the line, checking that the Customs seals were intact, and matching the numbered tags against the details recorded on his clipboard. When he was done, he reported to Rita. Everything was in order.

"Satisfied?" she asked me.

I studied the containers. From the corner of my eye I saw the mate leaning against the forklift, watching me. Something was wrong.

"I want them opened," I said.

Incredulous, Rita lowered her voice. "The seals haven't been broken."

"Assuming they're the same seals."

"That's crazy."

"Humor me."

She consulted the Customs guy. When he told her it would take at least an hour and a half to have the containers opened, then re-sealed, plus paperwork, Rita drew me aside. We turned our backs on the others, conferring in privacy behind a pallet-load of bulging sacks. "If you seriously want to do this," she said, "I can't wait around. There's a major meeting back at the office. People who want some answers about the department's involvement in Hawkeye. When they hear the latest, the knives'll be out. Probably for me."

"They can't pull you out now."

"It won't just be me. If they pull me out, the whole department's out. Can you blame them?" She gestured around. "Look at this. You're not even sure the materiel's where you left it twenty-four hours ago. Can you imagine what they'll say if I tell them that back at the of-fice?"

"I'm covering the bases."

"You're worried as hell, Ned. Just like I am."

She was right, but I couldn't admit that to her. Maybe I couldn't even truly admit it to myself. Instead, I asked her to at least wait un-til we'd opened the containers. If everything inside was in order, I said, she'd have at least one piece of reassuring news for her superiors. After a minute's debate, she conceded reluctantly. The Customs guy went ashore and fetched a crimping machine, pliers, and six new lead seals, then he returned and set to work. By this time the *Sebastopol's* mate had brought the captain down to witness the scene. The pair of them stood back by the forklift, silently observing.

When the door of the first container swung open, I stepped up and looked inside. The Haplon crates were stacked floor-to-ceiling, apparently undisturbed. The Customs guy helped me haul a crate from the top tier, we set it down and prised it open. The smell of packing grease wafted up. I pulled back the oilcloth and confirmed with my own eyes that a partially disassembled P23 was in place, untouched, packed tight. I studied it awhile, then I climbed up the wall of crates in the container, put my head into the empty space, and checked to see that the crates went all the way back. They did. I got down and refixed the lid on the open crate and hefted it back into its slot on the top tier. The Customs guy closed the container, resealed it, then we moved on to the next.

It took about an hour to do the same check right along the line. Every container was just like that first one, the Haplon materiel in place, untouched. When I finally signaled the Customs guy forward to reseal the final container, Rita stepped up beside me.

"Don't be too pleased," she said quietly. "We still haven't got the goddamn diamonds."

The fresh paperwork took over an hour, and Rita had long since returned to her office by the time I stepped out of the Customs office dockside. Stretching, I looked over to the *Sebastopol*. The captain and his mate were leaning on the railing of the upper deck, they stopped talking together when they saw me. I lifted my chin to them but they didn't respond. They watched as I passed below them across the dock, then turned toward the gates. At the gate guardhouse, I looked back. They were gone. The only sign of life aboard the *Sebastopol* was a lone sailor, wearily painting the bridge.

I got in my car. The Ukrainian connection really bothered me. After the collapse of the USSR, the Ukraine's emergence as a major source of weaponry and munitions for the developing world was common knowledge in the intelligence community. Even back when

I was on tour in Somalia, the arrival off the coast of any vessel from the Black Sea was invariably followed by a swift escalation of hostilities as fresh supplies of Kalashnikovs and ammunition found their way to all sides in the conflict. Trevanian had specifically requested shipment aboard the *Sebastopol,* and I had no illusions he'd done it for the quality of seamanship on offer. The *Sebastopol* was a floating envoy from the world of unregulated trade, the world of seedy ports, flags of convenience, and commercial transactions that were barely distinguishable from crimes.

Though I'd known for days that the Haplon materiel was consigned to a Ukrainian vessel, it hadn't occurred to me before that that might be a problem for us. Certainly not while the ship was still in port. After the events of the morning, I wasn't so sure. I couldn't see any legitimate reason for Trevanian to have been meeting with the captain days before the loading. The Ukrainians were buyable, and Trevanian was just the kind of man who might want to buy them. It bothered me all right. But finally I gave up thinking about matters I couldn't change, I put my key in the ignition. The passenger door of my car swung open. Cecille Lagundi slid into the seat beside me. She clasped her purse in her lap, stared across the parking lot through her dark designer glasses, and asked me if I was going into town.

We'd been driving for about half a mile when I glanced across at her purse again. It was open, but I couldn't see the gun. Lagundi's hair was pulled back tight, a tortoiseshell comb fixed beneath the knotted bun at the back of her head. She kept her eyes to the front. She looked worried, like maybe she hadn't thought this through, but I figured she'd get around to what she had to say in the end, so I returned my attention to the road. A minute later she took off her dark glasses.

"I didn't go to the bank."

"We noticed."

"What did Trevanian say?"

"Not much."

"Was he angry?"

"Angry. Confused. Same as Rossiter."

"You don't seem angry."

"They're not my guns." I looked at her. "Or my diamonds."

"They're not Trevanian's either," she said, and from her tone I gathered that was some kind of issue.

"If Trevanian can't find you," I said, "won't he call his contacts in Nigerian Defense, let them know what you've done?"

"What have I done?"

"You tell me."

She reached into her purse. My right hand dropped from the wheel to rest on my knee.

"I need the bill of lading," she said.

"I don't have it."

"You can get it."

"You can get it yourself if you just give Rossiter the diamonds."

She produced a white handkerchief from the purse. "There would have to be another arrangement," she said, touching her nose with the handkerchief, and at that moment I felt the entire operation crumbling. There was not going to be another arrangement. If Rossiter didn't receive payment as agreed, he'd simply order the cargo to be unloaded. When I'd put him in the cab to his apartment, he'd been making noises about suing Trevanian for breach of contract. Reopening negotiations simply wasn't on Rossiter's agenda. When I spelled that out for Lagundi now, she went quiet for a while.

Then she said, "Trevanian was cheating us. He had a private agreement with Greenbaum. They were going to cheat us. I couldn't let him have the stones."

I pulled over into a rest stop and parked behind a snack truck that was doing business there. A couple of trucks were parked up ahead, their drivers sitting on the curb eating burgers, swigging Pepsi. I switched off the engine, then faced her. "What private agreement?" I said.

Then she told me. And while she told me, I tried not to give any sign of surprise or downright dismay. According to Lagundi, Trevanian and Greenbaum had agreed on an undervaluation of the stones. They'd agreed to split the difference between themselves after Greenbaum sold the stones on the bourse and paid Rossiter his money. Rossiter wouldn't lose, but Lagundi and Trevanian's client would be cheated.

"If it was so private," I said when she finished, "how did you find out?"

"They thought I wasn't in my room. At the hotel. They were talking."

I didn't get it. "Your room?"

"Adjoining Trevanian's room." Her eyes stayed on mine.

I thought about saying something, then decided things were complicated enough already. Instead, I asked her what she'd been doing just now at the dock.

"I knew someone from Haplon would come," she said. "You or Rossiter."

"You're lucky it was me. If you'd gotten into Rossiter's car, and told him what you just told me, he'd have torn your heart out." I hit the ignition and pulled out of the bay while she turned things over. I asked if she wanted to come and see Rossiter. She shook her head.

"You tell him," she said.

When I asked where she was headed, she told me to drop her on the corner of West Seventy-second and Central Park West. I remarked that she seemed to know her way around the city.

"Parts," she agreed.

"How often you over here?"

"Not often."

"Bit different from Monrovia."

At my mention of Liberia's capital, she glanced at me from the corner of her eye. "New York is different from anywhere," she said at last, then she put on her dark glasses again and shut me out for the rest of the drive.

Half an hour later, I stopped at her destination. "How could we get in touch?"

"You can't," she said, getting out. "I'll call you tomorrow when I get new instructions from my client."

Tomorrow was going to be too late. "Look," I said. "We're not going to be passing anything on to Trevanian."

"I'll call you tomorrow," she said, then some guy behind me leaned on his horn and she closed the door and set off down the sidewalk.

I drove away slowly, keeping one eye on the rearview mirror. I hadn't gone a hundred yards when I saw her cross the road, dodge traffic, and enter the park. I swung right, pulled up into a parking space, and grabbed Brad's old baseball jacket off the backseat. Then I shed my own jacket, pulled on Brad's, and shoved some coins in the meter before sprinting back to Central Park West. I couldn't see her. I crossed over through the traffic, jogged up toward the Seventy-second Street transverse, and within half a minute had her in sight. She was walking east, on the transverse sidewalk, not hurrying or looking back. I couldn't have followed her in my car, it was one-way traffic in the wrong direction. She'd chosen her dropping-off point well.

I could flatter myself that I did a great job tailing her, but the truth is she thought she'd lost me already, so she didn't do anything more to shake me. The sun was out, there were plenty of joggers and pedestrians in the park, it wasn't too hard for me to blend in with the human scenery. She passed Strawberry Fields, then the lake, then Bethesda Fountain, and she didn't once look back. When she reached Fifth Avenue, she crossed over and turned south. I went and stood near some kids in the park who were out with their teacher on a nature excursion, everyone with pencils and paper, sketching a tree. On the other side of Fifth, Lagundi walked down until she was directly opposite me, then she turned east again.

I hurried across Fifth, walked along the sidewalk across from her, shadowing her at fifty yards. The only time she paused was to browse in a jeweler's window, then she crossed Madison, and a minute later she stepped into the lobby of a hotel.

On the sidewalk opposite, I slowed. The Hallam Hotel, the name was carved in florid script on the stone wall by the entrance. Inside, through the glass doors, I saw Lagundi at reception, picking up her key. When she crossed to the elevators, I didn't linger, I turned on my heel, walked back to Madison, and hailed a cab to get me back to my car. Sitting in the cab, I hung my head. If I told Rossiter what Lagundi had told me, he'd terminate the deal instantly. So what was I going to tell him? That everything down at the docks was fine? That Lagundi remained out of the picture?

It never crossed my mind to tell him the truth. The truth, by this time, was no longer the default option that came to me, as it had once done, automatically. Not with Rossiter. Not with Fiona and Brad. Not even with Channon and Rita. So I sat in the cab, plotting some plausible story for Rossiter, while remaining completely blind to the fact that there was really no one left to deceive but myself.

CHAPTER 16

The doorman had phoned up ahead of me, so Rossiter was waiting at the apartment door.

"You tell me the materiel's been frigged around with," he said, "I'm gonna kill someone."

"The containers haven't been touched."

"Thank Christ." He ushered me into the apartment. The place looked like something from an interior decorating magazine, vaguely minimalist, with expensive oriental objects in strategic positions. Rossiter's wife, Eileen, got her favorite decorator in to advise on the apartment layout at least twice a year. "Trevanian'll be here in a minute," he told me, crossing to his bar. "Drink?" I shook my head. "Seems Trevanian's been on to his client," he said. "Client sent him to their bankers."

"What about Lagundi?" I asked.

"He can't find her. He's guessin' what's she's done is grabbed the stones and run. That's why he needs the damn bankers." Rossiter opened his bar fridge, took out a tonic water, and mixed himself a very large drink. Now that I knew Trevanian was trying to organize proper payment, I was even more convinced that there was no real need to tell Rossiter about my meeting with Lagundi. Not immediately. If Trevanian didn't come through, I might think about it again. "Whole fucking thing's my fault anyway," Rossiter declared, sinking into the sofa. "What was I doing saying yes to the fucking diamond thing? Just say no. Old Nancy Reagan, maybe she was on to somethin'. What the hell got into me agreeing to that?"

"We needed the deal. We still do."

"Sign of a sucker," he remarked to himself. He took a pull at his drink, then studied the glass. "How much chance you figure Trevanian's got of producing the money?"

I shrugged. I said there was no way of knowing.

Rossiter nodded to himself, then he reached across the sofa and lifted the head off a Chinese-style blue porcelain dog that sat on the side table. Digging into the dog's hollow neck, he extracted a key. "You'll need the reference numbers from the bill of lading. Call the stevedores. Tell them if they don't hear different from us, we want our containers off the *Sebastopol* by midday tomorrow."

"What if Trevanian raises the cash?"

"When we see it, we can call them again, tell them we've changed our minds." He tossed me the key, jerking his head toward the study. The phone by his sofa rang, and as he answered it I went to fetch the bill of lading. I heard him talking with Vincent, Haplon's financial controller. They were discussing whether or not to draw down Haplon's last line of credit to cover the construction bills that were continuing to mount alarmingly out in California. Rossiter was lining up the contingency plan in case Trevanian didn't come through with the money.

Rossiter's study was the one room in the apartment where the remit of his wife's decorator didn't reach. It was oak paneled, a couple of old armchairs stood to either side of the window, and Rossiter's credenza sat at an angle across one corner of the room. I opened the credenza drawer, got out the bill of lading, and rang the stevedores. They weren't overjoyed by the new instructions I gave them, our cargo had already cost them more time and paperwork than they thought reasonable. But we were paying, so they agreed to speak to the *Sebastopol*'s captain and warn him that our goods had to be unloaded before the ship's departure at noon the next day, unless they received contrary instructions from us. Then I relocked the bill of lading in the credenza and returned to the living room. Rossiter had finished his call. He was over by the front door, showing Trevanian into the apartment.

"Jack's got the okay from the bankers," Rossiter called across to me.

Trevanian balked when he saw me emerging from the study. When I nodded, he nodded back, then he turned to give Rossiter the details of his arrangement with the bank. While they talked, I dropped the credenza key into the blue porcelain dog, then replaced its head. I looked at Trevanian. He seemed uncomfortable, not quite the confident, indestructible character he'd been right up until Lagundi's disappearance. He might have been acting, but somehow I doubted it. Too proud to play that kind of part.

After hearing Trevanian out, Rossiter slumped into the sofa again and picked up the phone. Trevanian handed him a business card and told Rossiter the banker's name. Rossiter, I am a hundred percent sure, was as surprised and as suspicious as I was about how Trevanian had secured the funds at such short notice. But it didn't show. He simply took the card and dialed, asking me to fix Trevanian a drink. Trevanian shook his head, he wasn't in a drinking mood, and he went to the window to contemplate the view. Rossiter made the call.

There was more than a little tension in the room. After the screwup at the bank and the disappearance of Lagundi, we all knew that a successful conclusion to the deal hung on Rossiter's call. The strain showed on Trevanian's face. There were dark moons under his eyes, and his lips were tight. His washed-out expression did more than anything he could have said to convince me the break between him and Lagundi was real. Rossiter finally got past the secretaries, and he spoke with Trevanian's banker for several minutes. Trevanian continued to stare out the window. At last Rossiter hung up. Trevanian and I both looked at him.

Rossiter lifted his eyes from the phone and smiled. "All clear. He confirms the twelve million's available. He's faxing me the confirmation." Trevanian nodded, expressionless. Mightily relieved. Rossiter was silent a moment, then he asked Trevanian, "Why were you shoving the diamonds at us if your client had that cash?"

Trevanian jinked a shoulder. "Africans," he said, as if that explained everything.

"Nigerians?" Rossiter said.

Trevanian stepped forward. "I'll take the bill of lading with me."

"I don't think so."

"For my client."

"You'll get the bill when the money's actually been paid into the Haplon account," Rossiter told him. "Paid in, and cleared."

"That's a technicality." Trevanian pointed to the phone. "You spoke to the man. The money's there."

"It's a twelve-million-dollar technicality. We'll wait."

"Till when?"

"According to your man at the bank, tomorrow morning," said Rossiter, and at that, Trevanian put his hands on his hips, his expression pained. Rossiter rose, went around and guided Trevanian to the door. "Come up here for breakfast. When the bank confirms the money's cleared, you can have the bill of lading." He clapped Trevanian's shoulder and opened the door. "No problem."

Trevanian didn't move. He studied his feet a moment, then lifted his eyes. He was taller than Rossiter. Rossiter looked up at him. "You fuck me around like this tomorrow morning," said Trevanian quietly, "and it's going to be a big problem." He pointed at Rossiter. "Yours," he said. Then he turned and nodded to me and walked out.

Rossiter closed the door. "Fuckin' tough guy," he said, coming back to the sofa. He hauled out a phone book. "Big fuckin' tough guy." He dropped into the sofa, checked the card Trevanian had given him, then he searched the phone book.

"What can he do?" I said.

"Fuck all. That's why he's so goddamn mouthy." Rossiter found the number, picked up the phone, and dialed. "Hi," he said when someone answered. "I'm not sure I've got the right number. Trade Finance Department? Yeah. Listen, could you put me through to a Russell Fogarty? Yeah, I'll wait." It was half a minute before he spoke again. "Russell? It's Milton Rossiter from Haplon Systems. Yeah. That's me. I was just calling back to check. I think I gave you the wrong fax number." He went through the charade, having Fogarty read the number back to him, and confirming that it was in fact correct. Finally he hung up. He stared at the phone, thoughtful.

"Genuine?" I said.

"Same guy." He interlaced his fingers and twirled his thumbs. "The bank on the card's the same bank as in the book. The number's right." He glanced up. "Any thoughts?"

"Six hours ago Trevanian couldn't pay us with anything but diamonds. Now suddenly he's got real money?"

"You don't like it?"

"I don't understand it."

"I don't much like it myself." Rossiter clasped his hands together, then threw them open. "But hey, what the fuck. We gonna let the deal fall apart? If Trevanian's got the money, we'll take it, right?"

The deal was on again. I arched a brow.

"I can call the stevedores—"

"Leave it." Rossiter kicked off his shoes and swung his feet onto the sofa. He picked up his drink. "Let's not get ahead of ourselves. His money's not in our account yet. Till it is, we just leave things be."

"We just wait?"

"We just wait," he said, and drank his drink and settled his head on the cushions. He stared at me over his glass. The corners of his mouth turned down. "Fuckin' tough guy."

CHAPTER 17

Trevanian's trying to screw everyone," I told Channon. "But the only thing he's really screwing is our operation." The shadows from the cypresses cut sharp lines across the manicured lawns of West Point as we walked down the gravel path toward the parade ground. Channon had hardly spoken a word since my arrival at his office door. I'd given him most of the story across his desk, but then a meeting of the Infantry instructors convened in a neighboring room and Channon decided it might be better if he heard the rest of my story elsewhere. "So now Lagundi's got the diamonds, Rossiter's got the bill of lading, and Trevanian, if we can believe him, has got the goddamn money," I concluded.

"You could tell Rossiter about Lagundi's offer," Channon said. I shook my head. If Rossiter thought Lagundi was still involved in the deal, he'd back off fast. He simply didn't trust her anymore. Channon asked me if I'd told Rita my story yet. I explained that she was calling me at home later. Then a couple of West Point cadets walked by, they saluted Channon, he raised a hand briskly to the peak of his cap.

"If you tell Durranti what you've just told me," he said, dropping his hand, "she might decide the situation's bad enough for her to call time. She could impound the cargo before it's legally changed hands, just to cover her butt."

"She won't."

"She might. And if she does, Rossiter'll throw half a dozen lawyers at her."

The worst of all possible outcomes. Hawkeye finished without success, the true cause of Dimitri's death undiscovered, and my undercover life wound up in something like ignominy.

"I have to tell her something," I said.

"You could tell her the money's been paid. You could tell her the deal's proceeding to schedule."

I stopped and faced him. "You mean lie to her."

He nodded. I raised a brow, but my relief must have shown. Relief that he wasn't calling me in. "I'll back you up," he said, then he turned and we walked again. "You were afraid I was going to shut Hawkeye down," he remarked. When I glanced across, he smiled wryly. "I missed my chance. I should have done it the day Dimitri was killed."

We wandered along the edge of the parade ground. Cadets in dress uniform were beating the square, the sergeant major was drilling them hard. The crump of boots on the tarmac, and the mindless bellowing, brought back memories of Beast Barracks. It brought back more recent memories too, of the graduation parades that tolled out the deadening years of my instructorship at West Point, parades that invariably left me feeling depressed for weeks. I knew that I was wasting the prime years of my soldiering life. I knew it every day when I went in to work, when I drilled the cadets on the range, when I booked their weapons in and out of the armory like some uniformed office clerk. But the parades brought the brutal fact home to me in a way that nothing else could. Cadets were becoming officers, taking on real soldiering duties all around the world, while I was locked in the dreary nine-to-five of the average office-bound civilian.

It was killing me. I was dying inside. With every graduation parade, I became more certain that it couldn't go on, that I couldn't go on, that, whatever Fiona's objections to me serving as a real soldier, I had to get back to it before I lost the last shred of my self-respect. I had to get back to it before I was too old to even try. When Channon assured me that Hawkeye was strictly short-term, and covert, it had seemed to be the ideal solution to my problems. I didn't need to tell Fiona. That was a calculated risk. I figured there was no chance of her finding out I was back on active service, though, if she had, I knew our marriage could have imploded. But if Hawkeye didn't work out after six months, I told myself, I had a failsafe. I could step back then and reassess my life. Instead, six months had become two years, Fiona had become convinced I was having an affair, and Dimitri had died. In short, nothing had worked out remotely like I planned.

Now Channon and I watched the cadets wheel around the parade ground while we spent a few minutes discussing some operational matters. Channon warned me not to access the Biron account, the one the DIA had set up in Switzerland for Dimitri and me. From what the DIA accountants had seen, Dimitri hadn't been stupid enough to use the funds inappropriately, but they'd advised Channon that while the IRS was crawling all over Dimitri's financial affairs, it would be best to keep Biron inactive. I agreed. He also told me not to send him any more written reports. He said that in the future he wanted anything I discovered to be reported to him verbally. I agreed to that one too.

Then we talked about his plan for the Haplon materiel. Channon intended to trace the Haplon containers, courtesy of the bugs I'd planted, to their off-loading point in Africa. A Special Forces unit would be stationed on one of our carriers off the West African coast, and other operatives would be alerted in Liberia, Nigeria, and the Congo. He wanted the materiel to travel as far down the supply chain as he could safely let it go, after which he'd have it destroyed. Either by an air strike while the cargo was still at sea, or possibly a Special Forces raid if the materiel went inland. After that, anyone who'd been involved in the supply, anyone who'd facilitated the trade—Rossiter, Trevanian and Lagundi, the *Sebastopol*'s captain— would be arrested and brought to justice in a U.S. court. I would be required to give testimony. He really seemed to have thought it all out. And he hadn't forgotten my purported personal motive for going on with Hawkeye either, because then he asked me, "So what are you hearing about Dimitri?"

"Talk. Nothing we don't already know."

"Anyone still blaming the Springfield rangemaster?"

I turned my head, no. I told him that a couple of Fettners guys were talking like Dimitri wasn't as straight as he might have been. I'd picked this up over lunch with clients. The initial speculation over Dimitri's death had fallen away, but without a final judgment from the FBI, suspicion lingered. The sudden appearance of the IRS in Fettners' accounts department had been widely noted. Many clients preferred not to place themselves anywhere in the vicinity of a federal investigation, or the IRS, and Haplon had consequently landed some small orders that normally would have gone to Fettners. "Frankly," I told Channon, "nobody's got a damn clue."

"What's your guess?" When I shrugged, he pressed me. He said I must have given it some thought. "Your best guess? Don't tell me you haven't got one."

We passed by a podium that had been erected temporarily for some big parade. Now a team of grunts from the Engineers was dismantling the wooden frame and wisecracking about the cadets still beating the square. I waited till we were out of earshot before I gave Channon my answer.

"Rossiter or Trevanian. Maybe both."

"Any reason?"

"Trevanian's past business with Dimitri. The way they've both pushed this order. What other candidates have we got?"

"Lagundi?"

I shook my head. I'd seen her a few times now since her sharpshooting exhibition at the Haplon range, and I didn't trust her. Maybe on her home territory in Africa she might even have had it in her to kill someone. But in the U.S.? She could shoot straight enough to have done the job, but where was her motive for murdering Dimitri? I said all that to Channon.

"The Bureau guys found a bullet," he told me. "They dug it out of the Springfield tarmac. A nine-millimeter shell from a Beretta." I stopped. Lagundi's gun. "You still think she's not a candidate?" he said, straight-faced.

I asked him if he'd seen the Bureau's ballistics, or if he'd shown them ours, from Lagundi's gun.

"They haven't got any. The shell splintered, it's unreadable." He

watched the cadets. His eyelids drooped, his expression was drawn
and tired. "If we point the Bureau at Lagundi now, they'll pick her up.
When they find out she's working on a deal with Trevanian, they'll
pick him up too."

In other words, no, he hadn't shown them our ballistics. He didn't
want to imperil the Haplon deal.

"What if she killed Dimitri?"

"What if she did?" he said. "It's not our job to call in the police,
Ned. Our job is to do our job. You were the one who didn't want
Hawkeye shut down. Well, you got that. Now we're seeing it through.
If that means letting Lagundi wander around free a few more days,
then that's what it means."

"She could leave the country."

He rounded on me. "She could, and no one'd be more pissed
about that than me. Maybe Dimitri was an asshole, but I was responsible for him. He died on my watch. Hell, look at the damn
stink you made when those men of yours bought it in the Gulf. Am
I any different? No, if she killed Dimitri, she should suffer. But that's
not the priority here. The priority is to finish the job we started."

"She might decide she needs someone else dead."

"I'm not ordering you to go on with this, Ned." He turned to the
parade ground. "That's your decision. If you want to bow out now,
fine."

Out on the square the bugler blew reveille, the Stars and Stripes
came down the flagpole, fluttering, twisting around the wires. The
company of cadets stood to attention in neat, clean ranks, like a field
of toy soldiers. When the flag was ceremoniously folded, there was a
brisk exchange of salutes. The bugler snapped his bugle arm down
to his side. As the cadets marched off the parade ground, Channon
faced me again.

"I can't order you."

"I want to see it through."

"A smart soldier never volunteers," he said, and I made a face. It
was way too late to be recalling rule number one of every boot camp
in history. He clapped a hand on my arm and held it. His grip was
like iron. "Do us both a favor. Don't take Lagundi for any more un-
accompanied drives in your car."

CHAPTER 18

There was a white van parked in the drive at home. I pulled up alongside it and got out and walked around. Stenciled on the rear door was the name of a local company, Parkes Catering, the outfit Fiona usually hired to do the Christmas party at Geometrics. Parked in front of it was another car, an old blue Ford. Olympia's.

"That you, Ned?" Fiona called from the kitchen as I dropped my car keys in the tray in the hall. It had been weeks since my entry into the house had been greeted with anything other than silence, so now I loosened my tie and undid my top button as I went down the hall and into the kitchen. Fiona was seated at the breakfast bar. A young guy wearing jeans, a canary yellow T-shirt, and a wraparound white apron was dicing vegetables over by the sink.

"Hi," he said, lifting his knife. I nodded in his direction and he started dicing again. I turned to Fiona.

"From Brad," she said, holding a card out to me. Really curious now, I took it. Fiona explained that the young caterer had brought it, he'd arrived unannounced just half an hour earlier.

Dear M and D, I'll be in Kinshasa by the time you get this, and probably enjoying myself more than you are, so don't worry. Please. I wanted to get you a present before I left, but just like normal I left it to the last moment so I didn't have the time to get into town. So this is it, my present. These Parkes Catering guys are going to do you a fine meal. (They suggested the menu, don't blame me if it doesn't work out.) It's paid for, so all you have to do is enjoy it. Maybe put some candles on the table, have a glass of wine, and think of your son eating burnt beans by a campfire somewhere in Africa.

I'll call in a few days when I'm settled in. Don't worry. *Brad*

I closed the card. It said "Get Well" on the front, the words framed in red roses. Irony wasn't Brad's strong suit, my best guess was that he'd innocently fished the card from the odds-and-ends box in the pantry. I gave it back to Fiona.

"Olympia's here?"

"She's out back with Laurence. I've given them both a drink." When I raised a brow, Fiona went on, lowering her voice. "Brad called them before he left and told them to come over tonight. He told them not to tell us. Keep it a surprise."

A catered dinner at home with my wife and the Maguires. I felt like going straight upstairs and crawling into bed.

"I was going to lay the table in the dining room," Fiona said. "I thought we could change first, do it properly like Brad wants."

Dressing for dinner, in my own house, with everything else on my mind, did not hold a huge appeal. But when I grimaced, Fiona's disappointment was painful to see, the hurt registered in her eyes. For a moment we looked at each other as if from opposite sides of a chasm across which Brad had flung the first slim rope of a fragile bridge. When she made to rise, I reached quickly and placed my hand on hers. She looked down at my hand, at the wedding ring on my finger.

"I have to make a few calls," I told her. "Give me fifteen minutes. I'll change and come back down."

———

The meal went better than I'd expected. The young chef doubled as a waiter, ferrying food from the kitchen into the adjoining dining room, where the four of us sat sipping wine and talking, and behaving like civilized adults. I'd dimmed the lights. Candles flickered from the silver candelabra that we used about once every five years. Fiona had laid out the silver cutlery and the white linen napkins, and she'd put a pale lily into a glass vase on the table. It was a long time since she'd done anything like that.

We didn't talk about anything in particular. The latest movies. Mutual friends. Nobody came straight out and mentioned Dimitri, but a couple of times Fiona had to quickly steer the conversation aside when it seemed to be heading in that direction. Mostly we talked about our respective children. At the end of the meal Olympia congratulated us on Brad's thoughtfulness, the fact that it even crossed his mind to organize the dinner.

"Our two ever come up with something like this," she said, gesturing to the empty dessert plates the chef was removing, "I'll declare a national holiday."

"They're okay," said Laurence mildly.

"Sure they're okay," she told him, smiling. "They don't have to do anything yet. Wait till they're Brad's age."

Laurence glanced in my direction and raised a brow. He was bald and thin, and since the chemotherapy his face had never really looked right. His cheekbones protruded and his dark eyes seemed to have receded into their sockets. Before cancer struck, he spent his spare time working in his garden and serving on some local neighborhood committees, and though he was a good husband to Olympia and stepfather to her children, he just wasn't really my kind of guy. Olympia couldn't have picked a second husband less like Dimitri if she'd tried. He helped the chef gather up the plates now, despite Fiona's protests, and took them into the kitchen.

When he was gone, I leaned back in my chair, the knots in my shoulders easing, while Olympia and Fiona drank some more wine and got started down memory lane. Fiona was more relaxed than I'd seen her in months. How she was meant to be, I thought as I watched her. How she always was. A few times she laughed out loud, threw her head back, and palmed her eyes. Fiona had a weakness for crude jokes, the kind I brought back from West Point by the truckload. In the old days, with some drink in her, among friends, she used to retell the jokes better than I ever could, and get everyone laughing. Then the next morning, if she needed to, she could jump on a plane, fly out to the West Coast, and give an erudite lecture on metamorphic geology to a bunch of sharp young mining analysts. In those days, we'd made each other happy. Now I found myself staring at her. She was tired, but still vivacious. Eyes sparkling. Intensely alive. I stared at her and wondered why in hell I'd done what I'd done, and doubted I could ever make it right.

"Ned?" I turned and found Olympia tapping my arm and looking at me strangely. She nodded to the kitchen, from where I now heard Laurence calling for my assistance.

I went and found Laurence loading coffee cups on a tray, the young Parkes Catering guy was getting ready to leave. I slipped the Parkes guy twenty bucks, let him out, then came back to help Laurence. I got cream from the fridge and put some beans through the grinder.

"Great dinner," he said, fiddling with the cups on the tray. "Lovely evening."

"Brad's work, not mine."

"Yeah. Nice boy. You're a lucky man."

Something in his tone made me glance across. Was he implying that he wasn't so lucky? Or was I simply overreading an offhand remark? I nodded and poured the coffee powder into the percolator.

He switched on the kettle. "Olympia said she told you about this trust fund."

"Ah-ha."

"What do you make of it?"

"Truthfully?"

When he nodded, I lowered my voice. "Dimitri wasn't the total asshole Olympia makes him out to be. I'm not sure she even believes that herself."

"Oh, she believes it."

"Then how does she explain Dimitri leaving the girls the money?"

"She doesn't," Laurence said, his eyes dropping. "She can't."

I put down the percolator and faced him. He'd invited the moment. I wasn't going to let it pass. "You've never asked me about Dimitri. I understand that, I'm not saying you should have. But lis-

ten, Laurence, there are two sides to every story. And now that
Dimitri's dead, I don't think it's fair his daughters—I mean your
girls—" I said, suddenly awkward and out of my depth, "the twins,
I don't think it's fair they should go through their lives believing
their natural father was an asshole who never felt anything for
them."

"I've never told them that." He looked straight at me. Not my
kind of guy, but in his own way, absolutely decent and honorable.

"No," I said. "No, I'm sure you haven't."

"You want the truth," he said. "Dimitri's never been an issue
with the girls. I mean, they know I'm not their natural father, but
they know I'm their dad. They were so young when I came on the
scene. It was like I stepped into another guy's life. His wife. The kids.
I used to wonder how it might be when they got a little older, if
they'd want to meet him. But now ..." He shrugged, perplexed.

I went over to the kettle, we both watched it in silence till it
boiled, then I poured the water into the percolator.

"Maybe if they want to speak to someone about him when
they're older," he said suddenly, "I could send them to you." I looked
up. He was serious.

"What would Olympia think of that?"

"Olympia's not asking you," he said. "I'm asking you."

"So you don't believe he was as bad as Olympia makes out?"

"For Olympia, he was. For me ..." He pressed his lips together
and shook his head. "I mean," he said, "he gave me Olympia. The
girls. Everything."

I said I doubted that an extravagant act of generosity was actually Dimitri's intention. Laurence's expression became pained, and I
realized then that any stab at humor was completely inappropriate.
He wasn't a well man, and he was speaking to me in a way he'd
never spoken to me before, from the heart. I turned my hand over.
"I'll speak to them, okay? If that's what you want. But I won't gloss
anything. If the girls want to hear about him, I'll tell them what I
know."

"Sure."

"I think Dimitri's owed that."

He dropped his head, a brief nod.

I turned from him, picked up the percolator, and pointed to the cups on the tray. It had been a long day and I wanted it over. When we went through to the dining room Fiona was rounding off some story, Olympia hooted with laughter as Laurence arrived with the cups.

When Olympia and Laurence had finally left, I bolted the front door then went around the house, locking up. At last I returned to the living room, where Fiona had retreated. She'd put an old Kenny G tape on the player, and she was sitting in the big armchair, sipping cognac, her legs curled beneath her. A photo album lay open on the arm of the chair, I glanced down as I walked by. Scenes from the eighties. Me and Dimitri in uniform, goofing off on the roof of his Chevy. Fiona and Brad crawling over rocks, up near the shack. I crossed to the sofa and slumped down. Kicking off my shoes, I stretched back and lifted my feet onto the cushions. We listened to the music awhile. A false peace.

"You asleep?" Fiona said after a minute.

When I opened my eyes, she closed the album.

"Olympia was asking if you'd looked through the things she sent you." The paperwork relating to the trust fund. Olympia's parcel had arrived the previous day.

"I'll call her about it tomorrow."

"Is it about Dimitri?"

"He set up a trust fund for their girls. Olympia's concerned it might somehow be tied up with his death."

"Is it?"

"No." The paperwork Olympia had sent me was straight-forward. Over the previous eighteen months, Dimitri had made two payments into the trust, the first for a hundred and fifty thousand dollars, the second for two hundred and fifty. The money had been placed into a stock fund, Dimitri had gotten lucky and the fund had grown to half a million. The money, as Olympia suspected, must have come from commission payments from Fettners or kickbacks from some of his clients. But the most recent payment into the trust was six months earlier. That, and the very public nature of Dimitri's death, finally convinced me that Olympia would be safe just hanging on to the money and keeping quiet. I hadn't mentioned the trust fund to Channon. Now that I'd seen the paperwork, I'd decided that I wasn't going to. "She's got nothing to worry about," I said.

Fiona reminded me that Olympia had a husband in remission from cancer, and two tearaway daughters. Nothing-to-worry-about, she said, didn't do Olympia's situation any real justice. I eased my head into the sofa cushions and focused on a picture across the room. My mind, I admit, was already moving on from Olympia's problems. It was drifting down to the New Jersey docks, to the *Sebastopol* and its cargo. In less than twenty-four hours the ship would sail, with or without the Haplon arms. I ran through a mental checklist of everything we'd done, trying to see if anything had been overlooked.

"Ned?"

"Mm?"

"I thought this might be a good time for us to talk." When I looked up, Fiona was studying me over the rim of her glass. There was no need for me to ask what subject she had in mind.

I took a breath. The only pleasant evening we'd shared together for months was about to end. "Can we leave it just now?"

"Delaying it won't change anything. A little more time, what's that going to change?"

"I don't know."

"Nothing."

"Okay. Let's just say I'm beat."

She set down her glass. "You may not find this easy, Ned. But imagine what it's like for me." I didn't need to imagine it, it was etched on her face. It had been written there for months, an insurmountable disappointment and unhappiness. I found I couldn't hold her gaze, couldn't even look her in the eye. "I can't go on pretending everything's going to work out," she said.

"It's been a rough week."

"It's not just this week. It's been months. You know what? If we're going to be honest, it's been nearly two years since things have really been right." At that I made a face, turned my head in denial, but Fiona went on, "I'm not blaming you. But that's the truth. I've thought about it a lot, believe me I have. I'm not just saying this because of what's been happening lately. It's since you left the Army. When you joined Haplon."

"You said you supported my decision."

"I never knew what that meant. Not then. I mean, it's not like I'm saying it's been totally awful the whole time. That's not true. I'm just saying, well, something changed with you somehow. With us."

"I'm the same guy." Fiona didn't reply, a silence that was way more eloquent than words. I put down my glass. Elbows on my knees, I spread my hands. "I am the same guy."

She looked at me long and hard. "Who is she, Ned?"

"Oh, Jesus." I threw up my hands and got to my feet.

"You can't walk away from it. It'll still be there tomorrow. You have to face it sometime."

I rounded on her. "There is no 'she.' All right? Let it go. You're driving yourself crazy. You're driving me crazy."

"You're not the same guy."

"What?"

"The guy I married could have faced it."

"Fiona." I leaned over her, speaking quietly. "You show me what I've got to face, and I'll face it. Right now, you're asking me to come to grips with a goddamn mirage."

"I show you, and you'll face it."

"I'll face it."

She pointed at me, her eyes suddenly hard as stones, then she rose and left the room and I dropped onto the sofa. I'd been beat when I'd arrived home, but by this time I was finished. When Fiona returned a minute later, I raised a hand. "Let's do this tomorrow night. Let's not spoil the evening."

She produced a plastic wallet from her purse and tossed it onto the coffee table. I looked at the wallet. "So?" she said.

"So what?"

"So are you going to face it?"

I looked up at her. Her arms were folded, she was wound up tight as a steel spring. Leaving anything till later wasn't on her agenda. Reaching, I placed my hand on the wallet, tapped it with my finger a few times, then picked it up and flipped it open.

Shock. Like I'd touched a high-voltage wire. My muscles clenched, my heart momentarily seized. I stared down at the first picture in the wallet. A plastic-encased photo, in color, like a holiday snap, of me and Rita Durranti strolling around the Grant memorial plaza. Numbed, I flipped the photo over. The next one was of me and Rita too, this time seated together on the plaza bench. "You've been following me." I lifted my head. "Taking goddamn photos?"

"I used an agency."

"An agency? What agency?"

"Listen to you. What agency? Who gives a damn what agency, look at the goddamn pictures. There they are. Can you face it now?"

I dropped my head, tried to get a hold on this thing, struggled to pull myself together. I turned the photos over one by one. Me and Rita sharing a sandwich. Heads together over a file. Saying good-bye at her car. Each picture was dated, the record stretched back three months. I thought about that incident I'd reported to Channon, the feeling I'd had of being followed on my way to the 7-Eleven. I gave a soft groan.

"Who is she?" asked Fiona.

"Why don't you ask the agency?" I said tightly.

"I want to hear it from you. I want to know if you've got the guts to look at me and say her name."

"You've got this so wrong."

"You can't even say her goddamn name."

"She's a colleague."

"Durranti. Her name's Rita Durranti, and she's not your colleague, she works at Customs. Don't lie to me. I don't want any more lies."

"What else did this agency tell you?"

"What else can they tell me?"

"I work with her sometimes."

"At Grant's Tomb?"

When I hesitated, Fiona snatched the photo wallet from my hand. She located a picture of me and Rita and held it up to my face.

"Saturday," she said. "The weekend before last. Do you remember where you told me you were going?" I stayed silent. "You were going into the office. And when you came home, I asked you about it. Everything okay? Sure, you said. Fine. Some new guy screwing up, but you'd put him right. Everything A-okay." She made the sign with forefinger and thumb. "A-okay." She flung the photo wallet at my chest, it struck, then fell to the floor. Kenny G blew a bright riff on the player.

I bent and picked up the wallet. I thumbed through the photos, seeing them now as Fiona must have seen them. The photographer had chosen his moments well, Rita and I seemed to be enjoying each other's company in a way that Fiona and I hadn't for months. Finally I put the wallet aside. "I'm helping her in a Customs investigation she's running on illegal arms exports."

"No more lies."

"It's the truth."

"Look at me," she said, her voice breaking. When my head stayed down, she shouted, "Look at me!" and I lifted my eyes. Her own eyes were filling with tears. "I can't take any more."

"Hey," I said gently. I rose, reaching to put my arms around her, but she stepped back and held me off.

"I can't take any more lies. I mean it." She shook her head, then clasped her arms around herself. "Ned. I think I want a divorce."

CHAPTER 19

In the morning I lay in bed, my hands behind my head on the
pillow, and listened to Fiona in the neighboring room get herself
ready for work. The shower. The sliding door of the closet. The
hum of the electric toothbrush, then the retreat to her study before
the hurried rush out the front door. I didn't want to believe that our
marriage might be over, and the deep familiarity of her routine was
in some strange way a reassurance that behind our current troubles
there were lasting verities, bonds that couldn't be so easily broken or
changed. When the front door banged shut, I climbed out of bed and
went to the window and watched her, briefcase in hand, march
down the front path. She turned left on the sidewalk and didn't look
back.

I took a raincheck on morning excercise, and I'd showered and
dressed by the time Rossiter called. I knew it was him before I
picked up the phone. I asked him if the deal was done yet, if he'd
made the exchange.

"Nothin's done. Trevanian hasn't got the money." I was silent.

Dumbstruck. "Get yourself down to the docks." he told me. "Get our materiel unloaded."

"But he had the money yesterday. You spoke to his bank."

"We spoke, but they never sent me a fax confirming it. And they haven't transferred a dime into the Haplon account. Trevanian's calling me every ten minutes. Wait, he tells me, the money's comin'. I'm done waitin'. It's over."

I couldn't let it be over. It had cost me too much. "Lagundi wants to make the payment," I heard myself say.

There was a pause. "The fuck?" said Rossiter.

"With the diamonds."

"Jesus H. Christ. We been there already, haven't we? When did this come up? Did she call you?"

"Five minutes ago. She gave me an address downtown."

"Why?"

"I agreed to meet her." I screwed up my face. "To find out what she's playing at. Why don't I just go down there, see if she's serious, then call you." There was silence from Rossiter's end. "If it doesn't work out, I can go from there straight to the docks. The worst I can do is lose half an hour."

He thought about it. "She can't be serious."

"There's only one way to find out." I tried to keep the desperation out of my voice. Instinctively I aligned my tone to Rossiter's— pissed off, but reluctantly resigned. "Hell. What have we got to lose?"

Rossiter remarked that it was turning out to be the worst cock-sucking deal of his life. "Christ. Go down and see her," he decided. "Call me when you're done."

I hung up before he could change his mind.

Driving down to Manhattan, I had plenty of time to consider the possible outcomes, none of which had any appeal. Until this point, my role in the deal, if it came to a court case, had been secondary. Trevanian and Lagundi were unquestionably the initiators, and Rossiter had been their primary contact at Haplon. My role, basically, had been surveillance of the deal, even the most contorted lawyer's argument couldn't have twisted it into anything other than that. But if I now took it on myself to resurrect the diamond pay-ment from Lagundi, I'd become a facilitator of the deal rather than a mere observer, a change that would leave us vulnerable to a charge of entrapment. And that, of course, was assuming that Lagundi could actually be persuaded to agree to an eleventh-hour deal that was also acceptable to Rossiter.

Channon wasn't in his West Point office when I called, and as our range of code words didn't stretch to the situation, I left no message. Instead, I called Rita and gave her the bad news. It was the first time I'd ever left her at a total loss for words. But when I told her how I was going to try to salvage the deal, she immediately started talking about entrapment. I cut her off.

"It's not this or some better alternative. It's this or nothing."

"Well, let me tell you, right now *nothing* doesn't seem so bad," she said sharply.

I told her to keep her line clear, that I'd call again once I'd seen Lagundi. In the meantime I asked her to get hold of Channon and let him know what was going on. When she started in with her objec-tions, I hung up, tossed the cell phone on the passenger seat, and drove.

The lobby of the Hallam Hotel was a domed atrium with doorways leading into the restaurant and bar. When I asked for Lagundi at re-ception, I drew a blank. I told them she was a recent divorcee, that maybe she'd registered under her maiden name, which I didn't know. "She's not American," I elaborated when the guy looked skeptical. "She's West African." He arched a brow. I asked him, politely, if he could recheck the register, and while he did that, I looked around. The walls and floor were lined in pale marble. Discreet luxury was the prevailing style. The room rates weren't listed, but singles must have started at three or four hundred a night, Lagundi hadn't gone to ground in a dump. Then through an open door off the lobby, I saw her. She was in the restaurant, sitting at her table alone. As I walked across the lobby, the receptionist called me back. I told him it was okay, that I'd seen her. She didn't see me till I was almost at her table. Her fork stopped halfway to her mouth.

"Friendly visit." I slid into a chair beside her. Her glance flitted over my shoulder. "It's just me," I said.

"You followed me yesterday."

"I've talked your proposition over with Rossiter. He agrees we might have the basis for a deal."

"Who else knows I'm here? Trevanian?"

"No one."

"Rossiter."

"No one. Just me."

She put down her fork. She glanced to the far side of the restaurant where four businessmen in suits were busy polishing off a late power breakfast. "Then if I get up and walk out," she said, "there'll be no one to stop me." She made to rise, my hand shot across and gripped her wrist. "Let me go," she said.

The waiter looked over. Then he started across, and I spoke quickly.

"The weapons, your whole order, it's all set to be off-loaded from the ship. Unless we can work something out right now, your order is history. You can either play games, get mad and have me thrown out of here, or we can try and do something sensible."

The waiter arrived at our table. "Madam?"

I let go of her wrist. The way she looked at me, it wasn't too hard to imagine her shooting Dimitri down in cold blood. Finally she waved the waiter off and told me to come up to her room.

Her room turned out to be a suite somewhere near the top of the hotel, from the main window there was a view between the office buildings toward Central Park. The view alone must have cost her hundreds a night. She dropped her keys by her purse on the table. Then she turned to the mirror and pushed back a loose strand of hair. "Have you seen Trevanian?"

"He's around."

"Looking for me?"

I studied the back of her neck. Whatever was going on between her and Trevanian, it seemed pretty clear that their dispute wasn't purely professional. But I didn't want to get caught up in that. "If you'd screwed me around like you've screwed him around," I said, "I'd be looking for you."

She turned. "He was cheating us."

"All I know is, he was due to make a payment on the order this morning, and he didn't. That's why I'm here."

Her face bunched in real surprise. "But Trevanian has no money."

"Your client's money. Yesterday the bank said it was there. Today, they're not paying."

She frowned. She asked me which bank, I gave her the name, and her brow flexed down. When she went to the phone, telling me to wait, I protested, but she made her call anyway. A long number, outside the U.S. She spent five minutes being put on hold, then being transferred, before she got through to who she wanted, then she spent ten minutes holding a conversation in some African language I couldn't even recognize, let alone translate. Trevanian's name was mentioned several times, it came out of Lagundi's mouth like a curse. I checked my watch. It was past nine. She was wasting time I didn't have. Eventually the conversation ended, she put down the phone and faced me.

"Trevanian lied. He has no money. The client has not agreed to pay through that bank."

I indicated the phone. "That was his client?"

"My client. He has given the diamonds. He will not be paying more."

My heart dropped into my shoes. But then Lagundi said, "The client has instructed me to make Rossiter a final offer." She watched me carefully. I told her I was still listening. "I can sell the diamonds immediately, then pay Haplon in U.S. dollars."

Too easy. Way too easy. I said, "What's the catch?"

"To sell the diamonds quickly, they will have to be discounted."

"Greenbaum's cut?"

"Nobody's cut. And not through Greenbaum. Another trader. One my client can trust."

"I don't suppose you want to give me a name."

She turned her head. "The discount will be twenty percent."

I made a sound. That was never going to play with Rossiter.

"Negotiable," she added.

"The time for finessing is gone, Cecille. Way gone. If your client hasn't given you authority to make a better offer than that, there's no point in us wasting more breath on it. The Haplon goods are coming off the ship inside two hours." I opened a hand. "Make me your best offer. I can't guarantee Rossiter'll accept it, but if you want to stop the unloading, I need to take it to him right now."

She thought that over. Then she went back to the side table beneath the mirror and put her hand in her purse. I moved around to where I had a clear view. But it wasn't her Beretta she brought out, it was a pen and a notepad.

"The twenty percent discount is a real loss for us on the stones." She scribbled on the pad. "The best my client can do is split the loss with Rossiter fifty-fifty."

"Rossiter won't go for that."

"We get ten percent less for our diamonds. You reduce the price of the shipment by ten percent." When I screwed up my face, she finished the note, and signed it. "It is our best offer."

"I'm not sure it'll work."

"Our final offer." She came over to me, stopped uncomfortably close, and pressed the note into my hand. Her perfume was strong. "Try," she said.

When I couldn't raise Rossiter on the phone at his apartment, I called Barbara, his secretary, at the office. He wasn't there, but Barbara said she'd spoken to him ten minutes earlier. She said he'd called from his apartment and told her he'd be working there all morning, so I got in my car and drove over.

There was no answer when I knocked on his door, but I thought I heard voices inside so I knocked again, harder. Still no answer. I turned my ear to the door, there were definitely voices, but then a burst of music came through and I realized it was only the TV. I rested a hand on the door and studied my shoes. I didn't know if Rossiter would accept or reject Lagundi's final offer, but I was damn sure he wouldn't like it. Ten percent of twelve million dollars. One-point-two million. After that steep a discount, Haplon's profit would be wafer thin, under normal circumstances, unacceptable. But Rossiter needed cash badly, and ten-point-eight million dollars wasn't an amount he'd reject out of hand, not without proper consideration, no matter how aggrieved he might feel after I'd delivered Lagundi's scribbled note. My fervent hope, of course, was that he'd take the money and let the materiel sail. But he could only do that if he had the chance to consider Lagundi's offer.

"Milton!" I banged on the door with my fist, then waited. Nothing live came back from inside, only the disembodied jingle of an advertisement. It was somewhere around then that I stopped thinking about Lagundi's offer and started wondering why Rossiter wasn't where he'd told Barbara he'd be. And why, if he'd gone out, he'd left the TV going, and turned up loud. I rapped on the door again and called his name. There was no response. Pretty soon, I figured, his neighbors along the hall would be poking their heads out to find out who the jerk was making the noise. I took out my key ring. If Rossiter was inside, and the door wasn't chained, I could just say I'd pushed it and the door had opened. If he wasn't inside, he might have left some clue as to where he'd gone.

I turned the key and pushed the door. It wasn't chained.

"Milton?"

The only sound came from the TV. I let myself in and closed the door behind me. After listening a moment, I crossed the living room to the rear hall and went down there calling his name again. I pushed open his bedroom door. He wasn't there. The door to the adjoining bathroom was open, but he wasn't in there either, so I retreated up the hall, glancing in the other bedrooms. There was no sign of him anywhere, nor any sign of anything unusual. It was the same when I looked in the kitchen. Everything in place. Out in the living room again, I stopped, hands on hips, and considered what the hell to do next. While I was considering, my eyes fell on a copy of the latest *Jane's Defence* lying on the coffee table. Rossiter's reading glasses were sitting beside the magazine. Next to the glasses, a half-finished mug of coffee.

Stepping around the table, I reached down and touched the mug. It was cold. When I dipped my finger inside, the coffee was tepid. On the TV, a CNBC reporter was running through the latest news from Wall Street. I looked at the sofa, indented where he'd been sitting, and at his glasses, and the copy of *Jane's*. My gaze wandered up to the end of the sofa, and stopped. The blue porcelain dog, Chinese-style, was missing. I looked around at the other low tables near the sofa. The porcelain dog wasn't on any of them. I stepped up to the table where I was sure it had been. Then, on the floor, I noticed shiny fragments of something glinting. Crouching, I examined the fragments. Blue porcelain. I shouldered the sofa back a few inches, and lying there were the larger shards and broken pieces of the shattered porcelain dog. My throat dried.

I stood straight up and crossed to Rossiter's study, I went directly to the drawer where I'd locked the bill of lading. When I pulled on the drawer, it wasn't locked, it slid open easily. The drawer was empty. The bill of lading was gone.

CHAPTER 20

If Trevanian stole the bill of lading," said Rita, "where's Rossiter?" She sat in the passenger seat of my car, trying to make
sense of my story. My lack of ready answers wasn't doing much
to help her in the task. After leaving Rossiter's apartment I'd gone
straight down to the doorman, who'd confirmed that a guy answering Trevanian's description had gone up to Rossiter's apartment
sometime in the previous hour. At my request, the doorman checked
the security monitor for the basement garage. The space for Rossiter's Lotus was empty.

"I don't know that he stole the bill of lading," I said. "I'm just
telling you how it looked."

"What's the alternate view?"

"Maybe he and Rossiter came to some agreement."

"Then they smashed the porcelain just for kicks?" She glanced
across and saw I wasn't in the mood for wisecracks. "Okay," she
conceded. "So it looks like Trevanian stole it. I guess you must have
noticed when he stole it. Right when you were tied up, talking with
Lagundi."

"They've parted company."

"That's what they're telling you."

But I'd already considered the possibility that Trevanian and Lagundi had double-teamed me. Considered, and dismissed it. Lagundi's break with Trevanian was real. Now I told Rita to try Channon again, and she dialed on her cell phone.

"Not there," she said, holding the phone to her ear. She suggested leaving something on his voice mail, but I shook my head. Explaining how the deal had collapsed around our ears, and how we were on our way to the docks to make sure Trevanian hadn't gotten hold of the Haplon weapons—that wasn't a message to be sent over the insecure ether. Rita hung up.

If Trevanian had the bearer bill of lading, he had control of the Haplon containers aboard the *Sebastopol,* and if he had control of them, he could move them. Worse, with the compliance of the Ukrainian captain and crew, he could remove the materiel from the containers in which I'd planted the beacons, and after that we'd be chasing the weapons blind. I needed to speak with the ship's captain. If he was formally notified that proper payment for the goods hadn't been made, and that consequently legal ownership of the goods, despite Trevanian's possession of the bill of lading, remained vested in Haplon Systems, the onus would then be on the captain to unload the containers at our command. Frankly, I wasn't confident a fine point of U.S. commercial law was going to make much of an impression on the man.

We left the car in the dock parking lot and hurried over to the gates. The guard took his eyes off his portable TV just long enough to register the Customs badge Rita flashed at him. He pushed the sign-in book in our direction. Rita started asking after Trevanian, giving a description, but I cut her off.

"Leave it," I said, touching her elbow as I looked across the dock to the *Sebastopol.* "He's here."

She followed my gaze to the ship. We were eighty yards away, but the two men walking along the ship's deck were instantly recognizable. Trevanian in his tan slacks and blue blazer, and the bearded mate. They passed by the bridge, descended to the next deck, and walked along to the hold, where they stopped and looked down.

I hustled Rita around into the shadow behind the gatehouse

while the guard returned his attention to the TV. After a moment, Trevanian and the mate walked along the deck a short way, then the mate gripped some railings and climbed down out of sight. Trevanian followed him down, now the ship's decks were empty. I started out for the ship, Rita caught up with me.

"Wait up," she said. She gestured along the dock toward the Customs post. "I'll get some of our officers to come aboard with us."

"Later maybe. Not yet."

"You tell me what you're doing, Ned, or I'll go get them myself."

"Trevanian doesn't know Lagundi's made us another offer," I said, still walking.

"I'm listening."

"Rossiter hasn't heard what she's offering either."

"Ah-ha."

"If we can get this back to where it was two hours ago, maybe Rossiter might be inclined to forget whatever happened at his apartment this morning and accept Lagundi's final offer."

"This deal isn't salvageable. You don't even know where Rossiter is." She looked at me, almost jogging to keep up. "Where's Rossiter?"

The killer question, one she'd asked me several times since I'd picked her up, and just like those earlier times, I didn't answer her. After discovering that the bill of lading was missing, I'd made a thorough search of Rossiter's apartment, fearing, I admit, the worst. But the closets contained nothing except clothes, and under the beds there were only shoes and puffballs of lint. I looked in every corner of the apartment where it was possible to cram a corpse, and I found nothing. That didn't necessarily mean Rossiter was still alive, but it gave me plausible grounds for hope. Rita's harping on the question of Rossiter's whereabouts was an unwelcome reminder that hope was all I really had.

I climbed the gangway, Rita followed reluctantly. Stepping onto the deck, we paused. Rita looked up to the bridge. "There must be someone around," she said, and I signaled for her to be quiet.

Then I led her along to the hold where we'd seen Trevanian and the mate disappear. I grabbed a stanchion, leaned over, and looked down. In the hold, more goods had been loaded. An open central space remained, but now there were half a dozen containers on the port side counterbalancing those from Haplon. There was no sign of anyone down there. Rita peered over the edge.

"I wouldn't trust this bucket to get me to Staten Island," she remarked. "Maybe it'll just sink, save us all a year in court."

I pointed into the hold. "What's that?"

"Where?"

"Between the second and third container. On the floor."

She located it. "A bin liner? Or a bag or something?"

A bag or something. I chewed my lip. Then I went around to the metal ladder on the far side of the hold. Rita trailed after me. It was like a fireman's ladder, designed to be played out in retractable sections, with a winch on deck to haul it up and down. It must have been raised the day we'd trekked through the living quarters to the hold. Raised, or maybe more likely on the *Sebastopol,* temporarily out of order. But now that it was down, it must have been used by Trevanian and the mate. I grabbed the uprights, swung myself around, and started to clamber down the rungs into the hold.

"That counts as trespass," said Rita.

Reminding her that I was with an officer of U.S. Customs, I continued my descent. When I stepped off the last rung, the deep humming vibration of the ship's engines rose through my feet. Preparing myself for the worst, I crossed to the portside containers, to the gap between the second and third container in line. It doesn't matter how many body bags you've seen, when the zip falls open and a lifeless human being flops out, it's always the first time. I walked between the containers, stopped and looked down. It wasn't Rossiter. It wasn't anybody, it was just a sleeping bag. When I crouched and pulled it aside I found a workman's tool bag underneath. Wrenches, a hammer and a flashlight, pliers, and a jumble of other stuff. I stood up and tilted back my head and breathed.

"What is it?"

Swinging around, I found Rita standing behind me, craning around me to see what was lying at my feet. "Nothing," I told her, coming out from between the containers. "A sleeping bag."

"What did you think it was?"

I shook my head, but she grabbed my arm.

"I thought it might be a body," I admitted, then removing her hand, I walked aft.

"Jesus Christ," she said. "You thought it was Rossiter?"

I went toward the door through which Trevanian and the mate must have exited, but as I passed by the newly stowed containers, I noticed they had the same special Customs seals as the Haplon containers. I paused, curious, and read one of the tags.

"You never said you thought he'd been killed," Rita said angrily, coming after me.

I looked from the tag to the containers on the starboard side. The Haplon containers. I cocked my head.

"Are you listening to me?" she said. "If you'd told me that's what you thought, I wouldn't have left my goddamn office. I would have gotten hold of Channon and called this whole thing off. That's why you didn't tell me, isn't it?"

I tapped the container tag beside me. "Look at this."

"Am I talking to myself here?"

I drew her over and made her look. When she saw the tag and the seal, she did what I'd done. She glanced across the hold at the Haplon containers. "They've moved them?"

I took the tag in my hand. It identified the container as being part of the Haplon consignment, according to the tag, a consignment bound for Nigeria. I pushed the tag along the tie-wire and showed Rita where the wire had been cut and clumsily rejoined. Then we inspected the Customs seal. A similarly careless job had been carried out there too, the lead seal had been broken and reglued, the split was visible to the naked eye.

Rita's mouth opened in surprise.

I crossed the hold to check the real Haplon containers. They had new tags on them, and their Customs seals had been removed. According to the new tags, the real Haplon containers held refrigerators, video recorders, and air conditioners, and they were bound for the Democratic Republic of the Congo. Rita came over.

"They've switched the seals and tags," I said.

It was clear now why Trevanian had been so keen to get his hands on the bill of lading. He needed to prevent Rossiter from unloading the Haplon-tagged containers and discovering the carelessly premature switch. If the Customs guys dockside ever got to see the clumsy handiwork, the entire ship's crew would have been detained, the *Sebastopol* wouldn't have been sailing anywhere for months.

"Can you believe these guys?" Rita said, amazed. "They didn't even wait till they were at sea. How dumb is that?"

I held a tag between my thumb and forefinger and stared at it. The Democratic Republic of the Congo. After the analysis at her lab, I'd told Fiona that the rough diamond was just a piece of African currency, that it had probably passed through many hands and several countries before appearing in Greenbaum's office on West Forty-seventh. I'd told her that the Haplon weapons could conceivably be bound for anywhere between the Cape of Good Hope and Cairo. I'd known that was wrong. Now here the evidence was on the tag, irrefutable. The Democratic Republic of the Congo. The weapons were destined for the same place Brad had chosen to launch his professional career.

I gestured toward the portside containers, at the switched tags and seals. "Is there enough here to nail Trevanian?"

"Maybe. Unless he pleads ignorance and blames the crew."

Turning from the containers, I headed for the closed door.

"You're not going to confront him," said Rita, alarmed. "Promise me."

I grabbed the wheel handle and pulled, but it was stiff and wouldn't turn, so I leaned more weight on it. Then there was a sudden metallic clanking noise back in the hold, and I froze. When I looked at Rita she was standing stock-still. Releasing the wheel, I gestured for her not to speak. All we heard for a moment was the deep thrumming of the engines, then the clanking suddenly sounded again. Rita's brow furrowed. Someone else in the hold? Beckoning her back, I stepped cautiously toward the open space in the hold's center. I looked to port, taking in the shadows between the containers and along the narrow aisles between the loaded pallets. There was no shortage of places to hide. I stood still. I couldn't see any movement. Then I heard that noise again, and I swiveled and looked across the hold. The retractable ladder down which we'd climbed was rising. It was already out of reach. My eyes shot up. There was no one up there I could see.

"Hey!" Stepping into the open center-hold, I cupped my hands to my mouth and shouted up, "Hey, you got U.S. Customs down here. Hold the ladder!"

The winch-motor drowned out my voice, the ladder went up and up. Rita came over, we both hollered till finally the ladder retracted completely, sliding over the edge of the hold. The winch-motor cut out. I cupped my hands to my mouth and tried again.

"Hey! Up on deck!"

"Hey!" shouted Rita.

High above, white clouds drifted beneath a brilliant blue sky, a picture framed by the dark steel square of the hold. Our cries drifted up and were lost. It was silent up there. I returned to the bulkhead door. I grabbed the wheel handle with both hands and hauled hard. The damn thing didn't budge, not even a quarter inch.

Another whining noise came from a motor up on deck. At first I thought it was the ladder being lowered, that someone had seen or heard us, but then Rita said, "Holy shit," and I leaned back and looked up.

The sky was shrinking. A clear shadow-line moved steadily across the hold opening as the hold cover was rolled noisily into place. I put my shoulder to the door and yanked at the handle. "Holler!" I shouted at Rita.

She hollered. But the hold cover moved on regardless, grinding across the dwindling patch of sky, and the darkness in the hold gathered fast. I let go of the door and started searching for the electrics, for an alarm or a light. All I could see were pipes, so after a few moments I gave up the search.

"Rita! Over here!" I ran to the container nearest the bulkhead door. The light was almost gone now, and I stood with my back to the container and looked around the hold, fixing the scene in my mind. Containers to port and starboard. Crates and pallets aft. Aisles leading off the four corners of open space. Rita knocked into me, she stopped hollering. We tipped back our heads as the last piece of sky shrank to a sliver way above us. Then it suddenly disappeared.

CHAPTER 21

It was totally dark. The ship's engines throbbed through the steel vault. "Fucking hell," said Rita.

I took out my cell phone, switched it on. The soft luminescent glow lit up, and I dialed, miskeying the numbers twice before I got it right.

"Channon?" asked Rita, hearing me dial.

"Stevedores." I'd been calling them daily the past week, arranging the shipment, I had their number by heart. And unlike Channon, the stevedores were dockside, they were sitting in an office not two hundred yards from where we were standing. But when I put the phone to my ear all I got was an electronic message. No service in my area. When I got Rita to try her phone, the result was the same. Entombed in a steel hull and calling from a hold beneath the waterline, we were cut off as effectively as if we'd been dropped down a mine shaft.

"Sit down," I said.

"What?"

Reaching, I touched her jacket and tugged it lightly. "Put your back against the container. Don't go moving around."

"Move around? I can't even see my goddamn hands."

Once she was seated on the hold floor, I rested my own back against the container and tried to remember the hold, picture it as I'd seen it in the fading light.

"Ned?"

"Right here."

"You think it was an accident, or what? Jesus, I screamed loud enough, didn't I? They must have heard me."

"The motor's controls might be back on the bridge."

"Someone must have seen us come down here."

"Don't move," I said, then I held my arms out in front of me and walked gingerly across the hold, lifting my feet high, placing them down carefully. The pitch dark added yards to the distance. I started moving my arms wider, groping, then I finally touched the first port-side container.

"Ned?"

"Hang on."

"Shall I scream?"

"No one'll hear you."

"There must be air coming in somewhere."

Feeling my way along the first container, I reached the edge, then took a step and stretched out and touched the second container. I let go of the first, shuffled across, and groped my way along the door of the second container in line. When I reached that one, I turned down the aisle separating it from the third container. Probing with my feet, I shuffled forward another couple of yards until I felt something, then I stopped and crouched down and felt with my hands. The tool bag was open. Something sharp pricked my palm, and I swore. I tried again, cautiously, and I made out the hammer, then the pliers.

"That's you, isn't it?" said Rita warily, hearing me jostle the tools.

"Ah-ha."

"What are you doing?"

My hand touched the flashlight. I picked it up, pressed the button, and there was light. I grabbed the tool bag and retraced my steps across the hold.

"Ned?" When the beam swept over her, Rita twisted aside, raising a hand to shield her eyes. She scrambled to her feet. "Can we get out?"

"I don't know."

I led her to the bulkhead door and put down the tool bag. Then I shone the light on the door. There were no fancy locks or catches, just the one big wheel handle dead center. Handing Rita the flashlight, I grabbed the wheel, braced my legs, and heaved. The damn thing wouldn't move.

"Shine the light in the tool bag."

"Is the door jammed?" she asked me.

"It's either jammed or locked. Let's pray it's just jammed."

"If it's locked, can't you break it?"

"It's solid steel. It weighs a goddamn ton." I reached into the tool bag and grabbed a crowbar. It was clawed at one end, about two feet long, and I stuck it between the spokes of the wheel handle, hooking the claw over a steel lug that was welded to the door. "Stand back."

She stood back. I hauled on the bar. I hauled so hard, I just about gave myself a hernia, then something gave way and the bar flew out of my hands.

"Is that it?" said Rita, moving in with the flash. I pulled on the wheel. It didn't move. Then I ran my hand over the door where she shone the light, feeling for the steel lug, but it was gone. "Did that do it?" she said. "Did it turn?"

I shook my head. I'd levered so hard, the weld had broken and the lug had come clean away.

"Try again," she urged.

"It's not jammed. It's locked."

"Shit."

I found the crowbar and handed it to her. "Bang this against the door. Don't hit the wheel, just the door. Maybe someone in the crew's quarters might hear." I took the flashlight.

"Like this?" She whacked the door. There was a solid thud, a sound that immediately died beneath the deep hum of the engines. She looked at me despairingly.

"Keep trying," I told her, then I went to take a look around the hold. The containers were the largest items of cargo, but both fore and aft there were pallets loaded with cartons and sacks of grain, stacked deep. I made a circuit of the hold looking for another exit, a door or a hatch, but there wasn't one. At last I clambered up on some grain sacks, and from there I hauled myself onto a container. I shone the flashlight upward. I was still some twenty feet from the hold cover. Even if I could get myself up there, I'd be no nearer to getting us out. I took out my cell phone and tried again. No signal.

From over by the door, I heard a dull and hopeless thudding. Rita, still swinging the crowbar. I got myself off the container and rejoined her.

"Any luck?" she said.

I gave her the flashlight and took the iron bar and beat on the door for all I was worth.

"Someone'll miss us," Rita decided.

We were sitting with our backs against the steel door, the crowbar lying on the hold's floor between us. We'd been taking it in turns, ten minutes from me, five minutes from Rita, but after half an hour we had to face up to it. Our position was hopeless. We were wasting our time. We'd switched off the flash to conserve the battery, so the darkness around us now was solid again.

"Who'll miss us?" I said.

"Heaps of people." She paused. "Everyone at your office."

"They'll assume I'm with Rossiter."

"Channon?"

"I'm not due to report to him till this evening."

"When he misses your call, he'll call me. When he finds I've been gone all day, he'll know something's not right."

"Unless he's telepathic, Rita, he won't know where the hell we are."

"He's bound to check the docks here. When he sees our names in the book at the gate, he'll know we never left." A brief glimmer of hope. But when I remarked that I hadn't seen her sign us in, Rita said, "I didn't. You did." I didn't respond. "Oh fuck," she said.

I laughed grimly.

"If it comes to it," she asked, "couldn't we bust open a container and blast through the door with a mortar?"

"They're not armor piercing. Fire anything in here, and the only thing we'll get is burst eardrums. That's if we live through the hail of shrapnel."

"Well, I'm out of ideas."

"Quiet," I told her, cocking my head. Then I placed both my hands on the steel-plate floor.

The next second it was unmistakable, the ship's engines were cranking up. The background hum rose, the vibration strengthened through the floor, the sound and vibration reached a new pitch, then leveled off. I grabbed the iron bar, stood up, and hammered on the door again.

Rita called out to me, "Why'd they do that with the engines?"

I whacked the door once more, then staggered as the floor seemed to move, I just managed to stay on my feet. Behind me Rita moaned, I dropped the bar and got the flashlight out of my pocket. When I shone it around, I found her sprawled on the floor, I went over and helped her up.

"I'm all right." She rubbed her leg. "I'm okay." She dusted herself off, then rubbed her elbow too. "What the hell happened?"

She wasn't hurt badly, just frightened and bruised. I went back and picked up the bar and swung it at the door with everything I had now, my hands and my arms jarring painfully with each dull strike. It wasn't going to do us much good, but I had to hit something or I was going to burst, I was furious. With Trevanian. And with me.

After five or six strikes I dropped the bar and reached down and grabbed the wheel handle and pulled, a cry rose from deep in my chest, it was like the cry of some caged animal. It was no damn good. Finally I let go of the handle and turned and slumped back against the door. My chest heaved. The muscles of my arms were locked tight. Somewhere above the sound of the blood in my ears, the ship's engines sang, while the vibrations rose through the floor and into my feet, numbing them. My whole body trembled. We were moving. We were slipping away from the dock, nosing our way out into the Hudson, and soon we'd be cruising along the New Jersey shoreline.

"Ned," said Rita. She gripped my arm. "Ned?"

She knew it too, we were moving. Trapped, we were headed for the Atlantic. Entombed in the ship's hold with the Haplon materiel, we were on our way to Africa.

THREE

CHAPTER 22

In those first few hours after the ship sailed, I made several
more excursions around the hold to satisfy myself that my initial
assessment was correct. It was. We weren't getting out. Rita, to
her credit, didn't blame me for the position we were in. She didn't
voice the accusation at least, but she must have known I blamed myself. She hadn't wanted to go aboard without another Customs officer, I'd pushed her into it, and now she found herself trapped with
me, without food or water, on an unscheduled and lightless voyage
to Africa.

"Will you quit saying that," she said after I'd said, yet again, that
there had to be a light. She'd taken the flashlight from me, she was
crawling along by the wall near the door. She stopped suddenly and
made a sound.

"Rats?" I said.

"Close your eyes."

I didn't listen. I was watching her silhouetted when she hit the
switch. Light pierced my eyes, I flinched, banging my head on the
door.

"How's that?" she said.

Holding the back of my head, I got up and let my eyes adjust to the glare. After hours of darkness it was like being reconnected to the world. Rita rose from her knees and dusted herself off. She saw me staring at the covered switch on the wall down by her ankle. "You'd tried everywhere else," she said, referring to my increasingly desperate attempts to locate the damn switch. "It had to be somewhere."

I walked out to the middle of the hold. The lights were set into a steel flange and angled upward, that's why I hadn't been able to locate them with the flash. Now that my eyes had adjusted, the lights didn't seem so bright, they threw a dull, uneven glow across the containers and the rest of the cargo. For the first time since the hold cover shut, I felt a glimmer of hope.

I looked around the Haplon containers while Rita checked out the other end of the hold. The sacks of grain I'd climbed on earlier were stamped AgAid, the tag on one pallet said the sacks contained genetically modified seed, and that they were bound for some farming project out in Ghana. The other pallets were stacked with crates, mostly liquor destined for various ports along the West African coast. It seemed to be a cargo of goods that the main shipping lines had rejected as too small, or simply not worth the hassle. Returning to the hold door, I found Rita there already, slashing a screwdriver through the top carton of a stacked pallet. She peeled the carton open and pulled out a glass jar.

CHERRIES, said the label. BEST QUALITY.

She unscrewed the lid, popped a cherry in her mouth, then sat down and propped herself against the stacked cartons. I grabbed a jar and sat down beside her and we ate the cherries and drank the sweet cherry syrup. The discovery of the light switch, and the cherries, buoyed us. Rita, to take her mind off our dire situation, began to tell me some stupid jokes she'd learned from her father. We laughed hard. Slightly hysterically. The jokes were only funny because they weren't funny at all.

I went and took a leak at the back of the hold, over to the right. When I returned, Rita went back there, over to the left.

"God," she said, tucking her shirt in as she came back. "If my dad could see me now. You know what he said when I told him I was joining Customs?"

"Don't do it?"

"He didn't say a damn thing. He just gave me this look he's got and walked out."

"Overwhelmed."

She laughed. "Yeah. He was so overwhelmed that Mom had to withdraw conjugal rights before he'd speak to me again. Real overwhelmed he was. He wanted to know what kind of guy was going to marry a girl in Customs." When I smiled at that, she said, "Can you believe it? The man is Jurassic. But I think about it sometimes, you know. I mean, look at me. Was he right?"

"You'll find someone."

"That's what all my married friends say."

I glanced at her. "For what it's worth, my wife thinks maybe you already found him."

Rita looked at me curiously. Then I told her. I hadn't intended to, but the moment just seemed to have presented itself.

"You and me?" she said, aghast.

"You and me."

"That's crazy."

"Don't tell me."

"Well, where'd she get the idea? She doesn't even know me."

"She had me followed. She knows I've been lying to her about something. She just drew the wrong conclusion." I swigged the cherry syrup. "The guy she had tailing me took some pictures of you and me down at Grant's Tomb."

Rita turned that over. Then she laughed.

"It ain't funny."

"Oh, come on," she said. "You've got to admit, it's got its funny side. We're doing the cloak-and-dagger thing, and some guy's off in the bushes taking photos of us for your wife?"

"Fiona's not laughing. Last night she was talking about a divorce."

Rita studied me. "You're serious."

Looking down, I rescrewed the lid on my jar. I remarked that shooting the breeze wasn't doing much to get us out of the hold. Then I got the flashlight and climbed up on a container and shone the beam up over my head till I finally saw what I was looking for. An air vent. It was no bigger than a hand. I half strode, half jumped onto the next container, then on again to the next. At the fourth container, I stopped and pointed the flash straight up. The vent was right above me.

"Harry Houdini couldn't do it," called Rita when she saw the vent. "Come back down and finish your lunch."

From the top of the container to the vent was about twenty-five feet.

I switched off the flash and clambered down. I went across and slapped the boxes she was resting against, my glance flickering back to the container. "Feeling strong?"

"You want to stack them?" She was appalled. "And then what, climb up?"

"That's what I want."

She shook her head and ate another cherry. I could see she was thinking about mentioning Fiona again, but she didn't, and the moment passed. "Never happen," she said, referring to my suggestion about the boxes.

"If we can make a platform up there, five or six feet high, the vent's reachable."

"With a very long broomstick, maybe. What are you going to do, act like an irate neighbor, bang on the ceiling, hope someone hears?"

I got the sack of tools, explaining that the vents must open onto the deck. "If we could get something up through the vent, someone up on deck might see it."

"Something like what?"

"Cloth. Material. Anything bright." I tugged the metal straps binding the boxes to the pallet. "We can use these to feed the cloth up through the vent." Rita looked at me skeptically. "It's either that," I said, "or sit on our butts till we get to Africa."

"This is assuming they don't already know we're down here."

I screwed up my face. We'd been through this a score of times. If the crew knew we were down in the hold, any effort we made to get out was going to be a waste of time. We looked at each other, then Rita finally got to her feet. She warned me that if she put her back out, she was going to sue me down to my shorts.

The container was too high to heft the boxes onto directly, so first I built a small step-platform of boxes on the floor beside it. Once I'd done that, I gave Rita a leg up onto the container, then I started carting boxes over from the pallets. I stepped up onto the platform, jerked the boxes onto my shoulder, then heaved them up onto the container, where Rita built them into a stepped tower rising toward the vent. The work was killing, after twenty minutes my arms felt like lead, but we kept going till Rita finally said, "Last one." She grunted as she picked up the box.

I climbed up and watched her haul the last box up the tower. She positioned it carefully at the apex, then turned and trudged down and sat and buried her face in her hands. She was perspiring and her cheeks were bright red. I went and squeezed her shoulder.

"The last last one," she muttered.

I climbed the tower behind her. Stopping on the second-highest tier, my legs straddling the apex, I looked up at the vent. Then I lifted my hand and stretched. The vent was about eight feet from the tips of my fingers. Then I suddenly overbalanced, my arm swung out, snatching air, and my knees buckled and I came down hard on my butt. It took me a few seconds to steady myself. When I glanced down, Rita was staring up at me.

"Don't do that again," she said quietly.

I came down, bracing my hands against the boxes as I descended. Over by the door, I found the crowbar, and I busted two metal straps off the pallets. I crimped the two straps end-to-end with the pliers, a total length of around forty feet. Rita found some red tape, we tore it into short lengths and tied them into something that looked like a giant fishing-fly. We used the last piece of tape to tie the fly to one end of my forty-foot-long metal strap.

Next I tested it. I lifted the strap and fed it into the air, but each time, the fly rose only three or four feet before the strap buckled and fell.

"A pole?" Rita suggested.

After searching the hold, she found something better than a pole, it was a long length of polyethylene pipe. I pushed the fly into the pipe, then fed the metal strap up after it. A second later, the fly popped out the other end.

I climbed onto the container. Rita handed the contraption up to me, and I made my way up the tower of boxes and sat on the apex and raised the pipe toward the vent. It was way short. I stood on the second-top tier and fed the metal strap up the pipe. Rita was standing on the container by this time, shining the flash up at the fly and the vent.

"Two more feet," she said.

I pushed more strap up the base of the pipe, and saw the strap emerge from the top of the pipe and begin to buckle. I pulled it down and tried again. Again it buckled.

I lowered the pipe. The ship was rolling gently, I looked at the top box on the tower. Rita saw what I was thinking.

"Don't," she said.

"Shine the flash up there at the vent. Direct me."

I climbed onto the top box. When I felt balanced, I stood upright, then raised the pipe with my left hand. With my right hand, I fed the strap up into the pipe and saw the red-tape fly bob out a few inches beneath the vent.

"A little more," Rita said. "And toward me."

Stretching, I pushed on the strap. High above, the fly touched the steel plate. I moved the pole left, overshot the vent, then dragged it back.

"There!" she called. "There!"

I shoved the strap hard, the fly shot up and straight into the vent. Rita whooped.

"Okay," I told her. "Come up here. Push some more of this strap through the pipe before I fall and kill myself."

She stopped just below me and fed the strap through. "How much before the tape's out on deck?"

"Keep feeding."

"Hey," she said after a while. She grinned, surprised. "It feels easier. Like maybe it's out there?"

I told her to feed through another few feet, then to jiggle the strap. She did that.

"What if it's come out where no one can see it?" she said, but there was nothing we could do about that, so I didn't answer, just told her to keep jiggling the strap. I craned back, arms extended, then I suddenly overbalanced again. This time when I jerked upright, recovering my balance, Rita swore. "Get the hell down from there," she ordered.

I got down. She jiggled the strap fiercely.

My neck was sore. I rubbed it and turned my head. I was aching and tired, but pleased to have done something. Then a movement caught my eye away to the right. I peered into the shadows.

"Rita," I said after a moment, but she kept working the strap. I reached and touched her shoulder. When she finally looked at me, I nodded to the shadows on our right. She turned that way, and I jiggled the pipe in my hand. In the shadows, something fluttered. Rita peered at it hard. Then, tentatively, she jiggled the strap. In the shadows, there was an answering flutter. She turned to me slowly. We'd been working for at least an hour, working hard. We were totally shattered. And what did we have to show for all our labor and ingenuity? A tower of boxes going nowhere, and a metal strap passing through a vent twenty feet above us and emerging, pointlessly, from another vent fifteen feet to our right.

Rita jerked the strap, the tape-fly danced, and she gave a sound like a sob. "Oh, Jesus."

"We could try another vent."

She flung aside the strap and flopped back, spent.

We were not going to get out. Not unless the Ukrainians let us out. I looked around at the steel hull, our prison, then I climbed down off the tower and the container and went over and busted open a crate of bourbon. I needed something to wash away the sweet taste of cherries.

It was past ten before we decided to try to get some sleep, I hauled some sacks of grain to over near the door by the light switch, then I built them into two makeshift mattresses, six sacks apiece, a couple of yards apart.

When Rita came back from the far side of the hold and saw what I'd done, she held out the torn sleeping bag, the one I'd mistaken for a body bag when we first came aboard.

"It's yours," I said.

"Push the sacks together," she suggested. "I'll unzip the bag, we can use it like a blanket."

I told her I had my jacket, I could pull that over me if I got cold.

"Toss you for it," she said.

"Go to bed." I sat on my sacks of grain and unlaced my shoes.

She dropped the sleeping bag on her sacks, then she fetched the open cherry jars left over from supper and the half-empty bottle of bourbon. She put these on the floor between us, then stood up and unbuttoned her blouse. I turned and stretched out on my dusty bed.

"You want the light off or on?" she said.

"Off."

"What if there's rats?"

"Leave it on if you want."

"I'll get the flash." I heard her fetch it, then place it on the floor between us. "It's by the cherries if you need it," she said. There was a pause. "A nightcap might help us sleep."

"I'll sleep fine if you just turn off the goddamn light."

I heard her slither into the sleeping bag and pull up the zip. A second later, the light went out. The sudden dark seemed to chill the air.

"Ned?"

"What?"

"I'm sorry about your wife."

I didn't reply. She gave it a moment, then she said good-night, and I said good-night. I lay still for twenty minutes, my cheek cupped in my hand, then I said her name. Rita didn't answer. She was asleep.

I rolled onto my back, staring into the dark, wide awake. When I was done thinking about Fiona, I thought about the electronic beacons I'd planted in the Haplon containers. They were already transmitting to the Defense Department's mid-Atlantic satellite. They were powerful transmitters, beaming over Defense spectrum, and their signals, unlike our cell phones', would get through. Channon would know by now that the Haplon materiel was on its way, cruising toward whatever form of destruction he determined appropriate. What he didn't know was that Rita and I were lying alongside the materiel, helpless.

In the solid darkness of the hold, I could imagine everything very clearly. Navy jets speeding like bullets, screaming over the waves. A radio warning to the captain and crew. Guidance systems locking on to us as the ship was abandoned. Smart bombs lasering death from the sky.

CHAPTER 23

I **dreamed I was in a silo full of wheat. A chute opened above** me and tons of grain came pouring down until I was drowning in it, fighting for air, and I thrashed upward, burst through to the surface, and opened my eyes. Rita was there, sitting up, watching the door. I coughed and picked up the cherry jar and tipped some syrup down my throat. I covered my eyes.

"What time is it?"

"Listen," she said.

I listened. All I could hear were the engines.

"There was another noise," she insisted. "It's gone now, but I'm sure someone was trying the door." I shook myself awake, went over and put my ear to the door. Humming engines. When I glanced back at Rita, she said, "I'm sure I did." She unzipped the sleeping bag and reached for her skirt and blouse.

I put my ear to the door again. Nothing.

"They'll be back," she said.

"Maybe it was a sound from the engine room."

"It was the door." When I looked doubtful, she got mad. "Do I look crazy? It was the goddamn door."

I wandered over to the Haplon containers. Rita buttoned her blouse, then went and watched the door handle. I withdrew behind the Haplon containers and took a leak. "Any inspiration strike in the night?" I called, zipping up.

"Hush!"

As I stepped out from behind the container, Rita turned sharply. She made a face and pointed to the door. The wheel handle turned a few degrees, then the lights suddenly went out.

"Ned?" said Rita.

"Stay still."

I peered into the dark. The door hadn't opened. I figured there must have been a switch outside. Then a slim frame of light appeared as the door slowly opened, and I stepped back behind the container. There were voices, some talk in Ukrainian, then the hold lights came on again. I could see Rita from where I was, but not the door. When the Ukrainian voices died away, she spread her arms. No holster. No pistol.

"Yeah, you locked me in this goddamn hold, you morons. I'm a U.S. Customs officer, and I want to see your captain."

"How are you here?" I recognized the gruff voice, it was the ship's mate.

"I'm here because you locked me in here. Now get me out of here, and take me to the captain."

"You are illegal."

"Listen, bozo. You take me to your captain or I'll make sure this ship and every member of its crew are prohibited reentry into U.S. waters. How do you think the captain'll like that?"

There was more talk in Ukrainian, then the mate asked, "Where is the other?"

"What other?" Rita said, but I'd heard enough.

I stepped out from between the containers, my arms spread wide. The mate had four crewmen with him. "You knew there were two of us," I said.

He looked from me up to the tower of cherry boxes on the container behind me, then one of the crewmen pointed to the broken loads on the pallets. They started talking angrily, it was going to cost them plenty of hard work to put the cargo right. At last the mate looked down at the sacks of grain near his feet, and the sleeping bag.

"Two beds," he said, looking up at me. "Two beds, two people."

"Bullshit," I said. "You knew there were two of us before you opened the door."

He shrugged like he didn't give a damn. He ordered two of the crew on ahead, and gestured for Rita and me to follow.

Under escort, we passed through the living quarters and up onto the deck. The morning sun was dazzling, the light sparkling like diamonds on the sea, and I squinted and covered my eyes. Sea in every direction. We were out of the hold, but we were still in plenty of trouble. If the captain decided we were a problem he didn't need, there wasn't much to stop him from doing whatever he liked with us. I stayed close to Rita as the mate led us up to the bridge.

The bridge floor was laid with ridged rubber, worn near the doorways. Wood paneling, cracked and faded by the sun, ran around the bridge waist-high. There was one guy at the wheel. Behind him, a smaller guy locked some scrolled charts into a cabinet.

"Our stowaways," said the smaller guy, pocketing his key as he turned to face us. The captain.

"My name's Durranti," said Rita, stepping forward. "I'm a U.S. Customs officer."

"You have no permission to be on my ship."

"Getting permission's a tad difficult when I've been trapped in your hold."

He asked to see her papers. Rita flashed her ID, but when she returned the wallet to her pocket, the captain extended his hand. She gave him the wallet reluctantly. "You?" he said, lifting his chin in my direction. I gave him my wallet, explaining that I wasn't from Customs, that I was a representative for the consignee of some of his cargo.

"Officer Durranti came aboard at my request," I told him.

"Your request." He studied my Amex card, then lifted his eyes to me. "Are you the captain now?"

"I was concerned about our cargo."

"Did you contact the stevedore?"

"You knew we were in that damn hold when you sailed."

Rita raised her hand, then addressed the captain. "Nobody's blaming anyone. An error's been made, okay? Now I just need to contact my colleagues. After that you can put into the nearest U.S. port, we'll get off your ship."

"Our next port is in West Africa."

"The Coast Guard can fetch us."

"We are outside U.S. waters."

"I don't care if we're halfway to the South Pole. I want to use your radio. If you deny me that, I guarantee you will never sail a vessel into a U.S. port ever again. Are we communicating here, Captain?"

The threat didn't faze him. He considered it a moment, then spoke to the mate for a minute in Ukrainian. When he next spoke to Rita, the captain's tone was more conciliatory. He agreed that a terrible error seemed to have been made.

"Our communications officer is using the radio. In one hour, he is free." He gestured to the mate. "Mr. Bosnitch will take you to a cabin. If you are hungry, there is food. Also a shower." He returned our wallets, then finally introduced himself. "Gregor Damienenko." He shook Rita's hand, then mine.

"We can use the radio?" Rita asked, not sure she'd understood.

He told her yes, that she could use the radio in an hour. Then he dismissed us.

The mate, Bosnitch, showed us down to a cabin. It wasn't much of a cabin. It was a cubicle with an upper and lower bunk, and floor space of about eight by three. Bosnitch pointed out the shower and the heads along the passage. The galley and mess room, he told us, were one flight down. When he left us, I put my head out the door and watched him disappear aft. Then I closed the door.

"Do you get this?" Rita frowned. "They knew we were down there. Those guys Bosnitch brought down with him, they were there in case we made trouble. Now we're out, and suddenly we can use the radio?"

"You threatened him," I said. "Maybe that did it."

She didn't buy that. She went to the porthole and looked out at the endless expanse of blue. "I don't get it."

"Maybe he thinks we're in the wrong."

She spun around. "Is that a joke? We spent a night in their stinking hold. Damienenko says we're not even in U.S. waters anymore. We've been shanghaied, for crying out loud."

"All Damienenko did was close the hold, then sail."

"He knew we were down there."

"We can't prove that."

"Then he just lets us out and suddenly we can use the radio?"

Like Rita, I could see that it didn't add up. "Trevanian?" I suggested.

She made a face. "You didn't actually see Trevanian at Rossiter's apartment, and you only thought you saw him on the ship. You've got Trevanian on the brain."

"I saw him."

"Okay. So why did Trevanian tell Damienenko to let us out?"

"No idea."

"Right. And why didn't you mention to Damienenko that he's freighting stolen property?"

"Because he might not know that," I said. "And I'm not going to tell him what he doesn't know. He's a gunrunner, but I don't think he'd knowingly get involved in a heist from a U.S. company. Not when he's driving the slowest getaway vehicle on record." I told her my guess hadn't changed. Trevanian stole the bill of lading and presented it as his own. Damienenko shipped out with us in the hold because of the switched tags.

"But I can report the switch now, on the radio," she said.

"You never said anything about it just now up on the bridge. Maybe he's betting you didn't notice the switch."

"Oh, come on."

"Say he listens in to your call. When he hears something he doesn't like, he can just shut you down."

Rita sat on the bottom bunk and buried her head in her hands. At last she said, "You don't have the faintest idea what's going on with this deal." I made a sound. She looked up. "It wasn't a criticism. You don't know why Dimitri was killed either, do you?" It sounded like she'd only just figured that out. I looked at her curiously. She pushed her fingers up through her dark hair. "At least we've learned something useful from this fiasco."

"You've lost me."

"I'm talking about you. You and Dimitri. This whole damn deal.

I'm talking about not totally believing you and Channon. Not since Dimitri started jerking me around."

"I'm not Dimitri."

"You're the other half of the same operation. You were brother officers. Let's just say I found it a little hard to believe you were as ignorant about what he was up to as you claimed."

"You didn't trust me?"

"I didn't trust what you were telling me."

I turned that over. I felt a sudden chill in my spine.

"Have you tapped into any of my private conversations?"

"No."

"Any of my conversations?"

"I don't want to discuss this."

"Rita." I stepped forward. "Whatever you did, it was a professional call. I'm a grown-up. So tell me. What did you do when you figured you couldn't trust me?"

She lowered her eyes, and touched her forehead. "It wasn't just you. We did it with Dimitri too." I waited. Finally she dropped her hand and looked at me. "We got undercover Customs agents into Fettners and Haplon." I reeled back. I asked her who. "Does it matter?" she said. I stared at her. "Baker," she said finally.

"Micky Baker?" Our new marketing grad. I couldn't believe it.

"We owe you an apology too. That break-in out at your house."

I missed a beat. "You?"

"Micky Baker. Going a million miles over the line. For which he was severely reprimanded." I was speechless with surprise and, after a moment's thought, with real anger. I was suddenly unsure of my place in the intrigue. Fiona had employed someone to spy on me. And so, I now learned, had Rita. She opened her hands in apology. "Like you said," she told me. "It was a professional call."

I nodded, my jaw clenched tight. Then I snatched a towel off the top bunk and walked out.

By the time the communications officer came, I'd showered, had a breakfast of toast and salted pork, and generally simmered down. Rita had returned from the ship's mess with two clean white shirts from the ship's laundry, courtesy of the cook, she'd given one of them to me as a peace offering. Though I'd accepted it, the atmosphere in our cabin remained somewhat frosty.

"Rourke?" said the officer, looking into our cabin. "Your call is connected."

"What call?"

"You will come?"

I looked from him to Rita, who shrugged. Then I got off my bunk and went to the door. When Rita tried to follow, the guy told her to wait in the cabin. The communications room, he said, was too small for all of us.

Small was generous. The room, when I got there, was tiny, not much more than a large cabinet leading off the bridge. On the way up, I'd asked several times what the call was about, who it was from, but the officer hadn't answered. Now he sat on his stool in front of a narrow wall of electronics and passed me the handset. The door was latched open, Captain Damienenko was standing within earshot on the bridge.

"Rourke," I said, lifting the handset. There was static down the line. "This is Ned Rourke speaking."

"What in the name of Christ are you doing on that goddamn ship?"

"Who is this?"

"You a grown-up sales manager or a fucking crazy kid? I'm tryin' to run a business back here."

I was dumbstruck. "Milton?"

"I've had Customs all over me, they've lost some woman. Now Trevanian tells me she's with you." Milton Rossiter was alive, and somewhere out there on the far side of irate. "How soon can you get your ass back here?"

"Are you okay?"

" 'Course I'm okay, except for losing my fucking sales manager."

I missed a beat. "Trevanian told you I was on the ship?"

"He contacted the captain—delivery of the materiel or somethin'. The captain mentioned you and the woman, so Trevanian called me." He paused. "So when are you back here?"

I was lost. Not only was Rossiter alive, he was talking with Trevanian. I turned my back on the communications officer, away from the open door to the bridge. I lowered my voice. "How about you tell me what's going on, Milton. Because the way I read this, Trevanian stole the bill of lading. The materiel's not his."

"It's his, okay? The man's paid the money."

"That's not how it looked at your apartment yesterday."

"Well, here's the bulletin. That's how it looks this mornin'."

"Milton—"

"I don't wanna hear history, Ned. The money's in our account. Let it alone and I might even forget that you broke into my apartment."

"I was trying to save your ass."

"When I need it saved, I'll tell you."

"Where'd Trevanian get the money?"

"Maybe they sold the diamonds. Maybe his client coughed up." Rossiter hesitated. "Hey, are you alone there?"

"No."

"Well, let's terminate this subject right here. So. Where can you get yourself off the ship? You got plastic, or you need me to wire you some money?"

He wasn't thrilled when I told him it looked like I'd be going all the way to Africa. We talked some more, and in a rare moment of sympathy he volunteered to call Fiona. After thinking about it, I declined the offer. With access to the ship's radio, I could call her myself. There were a whole lot of questions I wanted to ask Rossiter, but he wasn't keen to continue the conversation. He fended off a few questions, then said he was going to hang up, but before he could, I asked, "Did you get hurt yesterday?"

He hesitated. "I got a bump."

"A bump."

"You deaf?"

"But you're okay now."

"I'm plenty okay enough to kick your ass when you get back here. Call me if anything changes. Otherwise, you're on unpaid leave till I see you in my office." He hung up.

Next, the communications officer placed a call to my home for me, but Fiona wasn't in, so I left a message, telling her I was fine, saying that it was a long story, that I'd call again later. I didn't mention where I was, or that my cabinmate was Rita Durranti.

Back down in the cabin, I recounted my conversation with Rossiter to Rita. She hit the roof.

"You told me Trevanian had no money," she said in disbelief.

"That's what I thought."

"He stole the bill of lading. That's what you said. God. If you hadn't told me that, I wouldn't have gone to the docks with you. I wouldn't be here."

"That's what he did. He must have. That's what Rossiter meant about getting a bump. Trevanian must have sapped him."

"Then he paid Rossiter twelve million dollars?"

I went through it again. "Yesterday the materiel was aboard ship, set to go. But Trevanian knew Rossiter would unload it unless the money came through. Once it was unloaded, even if Trevanian produced the money later, he'd have been tied up with Customs paperwork for days. The stevedores might take weeks to find another carrier." I pointed. "And if the stuff was unloaded, Customs would have seen the switched tags."

"It doesn't make sense."

"It does if Trevanian always intended to pay the money. If he knew the money was coming through, what risk was he taking stealing the bill, maybe holding on to Rossiter for a while? When the money came through, it was a safe bet Rossiter wouldn't give a damn about the bill of lading."

"But if Rossiter got sapped—"

"Twelve million bucks has cured his headache."

"Rossiter never struck me as a forgive-and-forget kind of guy."

We were still chewing it over when the communications officer came and called Rita away for her turn at the radio. When she was gone, I climbed onto the upper bunk and lay down and wondered about the money. I didn't understand how Trevanian had gotten his hands on it so fast. If it was always available, why get involved with the diamonds? The Greenbaum side deal? Maybe. But would Trevanian really have risked the whole Haplon deal just for the sake of that? I decided that Rossiter was right. Either Lagundi had sold the diamonds and then given Trevanian the twelve million dollars, or the money had been stumped up by the real end user of the materiel, Trevanian and Lagundi's client.

I studied the rusting rivets in the ceiling. I put the first possibility, the diamond sale, aside for the moment. The second possibility, money from the client, seemed more straightforward. The materiel was going to the Congo. The end user had to be either the Congolese government or one of the rebel groups opposed to the government. Either side could have been using diamonds to make the purchase, so that didn't help me, but the money had been transferred extremely fast when Trevanian really needed it. That suggested some well-established chain of command, which in turn suggested a government. The Congolese? But then I recalled that the rebel groups were supported by other governments in the region, the likes of Zimbabwe and Rwanda, so I was back to square one. I was no further on when Rita returned fifteen minutes later.

She climbed into the lower bunk without saying a word. I hung my head over the side of my bunk.

"Well?"

"Well what?"

"Can they get us off?"

"No."

"Why not?"

She screwed up her face. "Let's just say they weren't feeling in much of a mood to help us out."

I asked her if they understood how important it was to get word to Channon.

"They're not stupid," she said.

"Care to tell me what they said?"

"They didn't say much. They know the line's not secure."

"You're pissed off."

She looked at me. "I have to report to the nearest U.S. consulate when we put in at the first port. Somebody mentioned disciplinary action."

"Against you? That's ridiculous."

"My job is on the line now, Ned. And if you don't mind, I don't feel like discussing it just now. Not with you."

She rolled over and faced the wall. When I said her name, she didn't move and I watched her awhile, thought of speaking again, then checked myself. What could I say that was going to make her feel any better? Or me? It was as if the operation was cursed, blighting the lives of all who came too near. Dimitri was dead, my marriage was foundering, and now Rita's career seemed to be holed beneath the waterline. It had been way too long since anything even partly connected with Hawkeye had come out right. At last I withdrew my head and rested it on the pillow and felt the ship's engines thrumming steadily.

It wasn't the time to mention that I'd figured out the cause of Damienenko's unexpected gesture, the access he'd given us to the ship's radio. Basically, the public gesture of goodwill was raising a useful smoke screen between him and the U.S. authorities, or anyone else who came looking. It was an open signal of his honorable intentions toward Rita and me, something he could hide behind should the need arise to pitch us over the side.

CHAPTER 24

The voyage stretched our nerves tighter each day, both of
us kept waiting for something to happen, the ax to fall. But
Damienenko didn't seem to be in any great hurry to deal with
his stowaways. As we sailed southeast into the warmer weather, our
faces and arms turned red and then tan. The crew generally ignored
us. The only English speakers aboard, apart from Rita and me, were
Captain Damienenko, the mate, Bosnitch, and the communications
officer, whose name I never knew.

Each morning Rita and I had access to the communications
room. After failing to raise Fiona at home two days running, I finally
got through to her secretary at Geometrics. Fiona, the secretary told
me, had left for Johannesburg. He gave me the Geometrics number
down there, but when I called Johannesburg she hadn't arrived yet,
and when I called twenty-four hours later, they said she'd already
left. Someone thought she'd gone with some geologists from Anglo-
American out to a game park; someone else thought she'd hopped
on a plane to Botswana. General confusion. Eventually I gave up
and left a message on the answering machine back at Ellis Street, ba-

sically telling her that I was okay, that I was traveling, and that when we both got home I was going to give her an explanation for all the things that had been going wrong in our lives. Damienenko was listening in, so I left it at that.

I called Rossiter again too, but he made it very clear he had nothing to say to me until I got back, and when I asked him how I could contact Trevanian, he bawled me out, then hung up.

Rita's superiors, meantime, weren't even taking her calls. Four days into our voyage, we both started skipping our morning visits to the communications room and lingered over breakfast instead.

A day at sea can be a very long time. Damienenko gave us some old paperbacks he'd found in his trunk, and after the crew complained to Bosnitch that Rita was monopolizing the TV in the rec room, the communications officer dug up a shortwave radio that she could listen to back in our cabin. I took to spending a few hours at the stern rail each morning, fishing and watching, then retiring to our cabin during the heat of the day. Around 4:00 P.M. I'd reemerge to put in some more time on deck, playing at fishing while watching the bridge and the crew.

I was badly unnerved by Damienenko's manner toward us throughout, he was way too accommodating and polite. And Bosnitch, though he had the manners of a pig, was obviously under orders to put himself out for us. When my fishing chair broke the third day at sea, Bosnitch had a crewman repair it for me while he watched the whole operation in glowering silence from the bridge. There was a flagrant falseness about their whole attitude that kept me on edge, on my guard, and it wasn't just me, Rita felt it too. One time she went up to the bridge uninvited and surprised Damienenko and Bosnitch in whispered conference. She said they acted like red-handed thieves when they saw her. Like they were planning something, she said. Something, apparently, that the rest of the crew weren't in on.

Every night I bolted our cabin door. Our helpless vulnerability kept me awake, I found myself turning in late and rising early. But during the days, at least, we could escape the suffocating confines of the cabin. A week into the voyage, with the sun going down and Bosnitch keeping half an eye on me from the bridge, Rita came out and joined me at the stern. She leaned against the rail and watched me play out my fishing line. The white cotton shirt the cook had given her was miles too big, now it billowed out in front of her like a sail. When her hair whipped across her face, she took out a hair clip, coiled her hair, and clipped it back. Then she said suddenly, "Why'd you do that?"

I glanced from her to the bridge, then played out more line.

"You looked at your watch," she said.

"Nearly packing-up time."

She considered the other lines I had tied to the stern rail. Then looked at me and turned her head. I glanced over my shoulder. We were alone.

"I've notched the lines," I told her.

She turned that over. "You're working out our speed?"

"Eighteen knots."

"That doesn't tell us where we are."

"He's been holding a steady eighteen knots the whole time. We're a week out of New York. Our latitude's roughly two degrees south." When Rita eyed me skeptically, I tapped my watch. "Noon yesterday, the sun was a touch south. Noon today, a shade north."

She laughed. "You do card tricks?"

"Old-fashioned Army training."

"So where are we?"

I told her I'd show her when we got back to the cabin.

She considered that. "It doesn't really help us any, does it."

"It will if Damienenko drops us in a lifeboat mid ocean. Or if we have to get in one ourselves."

She looked at me. She seemed to decide not to ask if I was joking. She leaned on the stern rail again and looked back at the wake. It was a minute before she spoke. "Do you know how many times I've dreamed about taking a cruise? Even when I was in college. I used to think about it, you know, like a fantasy. All my friends kept on about trips to Europe, I'd sit on my bed studying brochures for cruises in the Caribbean or up to Alaska."

"Beware what you wish for."

"This?" She turned and clasped the rail behind her. "It was meant to be days by the pool and nights on the dance floor. Exotic locations. Shore excursions. A Latin lover buying me heaps of trashy souvenirs." She gestured around. "This ain't it."

"Trashy souvenirs?"

"Don't be a wet blanket. It was a dream."

I remarked that she must have had plenty of opportunities since college.

"Either I've had a vacation but no man, or vice versa. My timing's lousy." She looked astern to where clouds were banking on the horizon, the sun's rays slanting up through the clouds like splayed fingers. When I started reeling in a line, she said, "What will you do when Hawkeye's over?"

"Haven't thought."

"Liar."

I concentrated on the line. "Okay. I don't want to think about it."

"Would your wife really leave you?"

I hauled in the last of the line and corked the hook. Then I leaned forward and grabbed the next line.

"I shouldn't have asked that," she said.

"No reason why not." I put my feet on the rail and wound the line around a plastic reel. "The truth is, I honestly don't know."

"What would you do?"

"If she left me?"

"Yeah."

I shrugged. It wasn't something I had the courage to face directly. The possibility that the past two years had screwed up my marriage was something I really couldn't bring myself to look at. So I made a joke of it. "Go fishing?" I said, but Rita didn't smile. She looked astern again.

"If you needed me to explain to her," she said. "You know. Grant's Tomb. Whatever."

I nodded, my lips clamped tight.

"One thing I never figured myself for," she said. "A marriage breaker."

I looked at her, but she kept her gaze fixed astern. The light was going fast now, the clouds on the horizon turning purple, then red. At that moment I longed for Fiona. Too late, but I needed to explain everything that had happened. I wanted to get Brad back from the Congo, bring him home where the three of us could be a family again. I wanted what I could not have. Everything I'd destroyed.

Bosnitch came out from the bridge and called out, ordering us back belowdecks. I hauled in the lines. Rita stood waiting for me, her back turned on Bosnitch. When he shouted something in Ukrainian at her, she muttered in Italian beneath her breath. The sun set in a bright slick of gold.

"We're still here, then," said Rita when she woke in her bunk and saw me unbolting our cabin door. I asked what she was expecting, a port? "Either that," she said, "or forty fathoms under."

I let myself out. I went and dropped my lines over the stern, then played them out and timed them. Eighteen knots. After tying the lines to the rail, I took a turn around the deck. It was good to feel the cool morning air on my face. I nodded to the few crewmen I saw, they acknowledged me with neutral grunts, they always kept their distance from me and Rita, like those were their orders. Then I went belowdecks, where I found our cabin empty. Rita had gone to the showers and left the radio on. We'd gotten into the routine of listening to the news on BBC World Service before going along to the mess for breakfast, now I fiddled with the tuner till the buttoned-down English voices came in clearly. Then I pulled a school atlas from under my mattress and opened it on my bunk. I'd found the atlas among some old 78 records in the rec room. No one was going to miss it. It was an out-of-date French publication, but the place names were mostly recognizable.

I lined up a ruler on the course I'd been plotting—the daily inch of movement across the map as the ship plowed at a steady eighteen knots across the Atlantic—then I sketched the night's movement in with pencil. The weather had been kind, we'd made good time, and now we were closing in fast on the West African coast. According to my rudimentary navigational calculations, we were somewhere just north of the Congo.

Hearing a sound in the passage, I shoved the atlas under the mattress.

"Only me." Rita came in and closed the door. She was dressed in baggy khaki pants and matching shirt, another outfit salvaged from the laundry by the cook. She opened the porthole and toweled off her wet hair. "Tell me we're nearly there. Another plate of fatty mince for breakfast, they won't have to kill me, I'll die."

"Nearly there."

She let the towel fall on her shoulders. I pulled the atlas from beneath my mattress, and she came over to see. I placed a finger on our estimated position.

"How many days to go?" she asked me. When I said I'd be guessing, she told me to go ahead and guess.

"A night and a day." I shrugged. "Maybe two days, one night."

She beamed, and then in an instant of relief and delight, she kissed me. It happened suddenly, she aimed for my cheek, but when I turned in surprise she caught the corner of my mouth. Her lips were warm and soft, and she let them stay on mine a little too long, then she drew away and looked at me. I dropped my eyes before it could get worse, then I turned away and closed the atlas and slipped it under the mattress.

"I could be way off," I told her. "And don't assume Damienenko's just going to let us disembark."

"If he was going to do anything to us, he would have done it by now."

I didn't say anything. I climbed onto my bunk and stretched out and took care not to catch her eye. I wasn't sure what had just happened. I knew I didn't want it to happen again. She moved back to the porthole. She dried her hair with the towel, then set to work combing, a procedure that took at least five minutes. It got us past the moment.

"He has to let us off," she said at last.

"He doesn't have to do anything."

The time beeps sounded on the radio. Rita reached over and cranked up the volume for the news. She grabbed another strand of hair and raked fiercely.

Seven A.M. Greenwich Mean Time. The BBC guy read us the headlines. Big move to the right in some European parliamentary elections. The U.S. President and Congress deadlocked in budgetary negotiations. Unconfirmed reports of a coup in the Democratic Republic of the Congo.

Rita swung around, openmouthed. I signaled for her to be quiet, and the announcer finished the headlines, then read the news in full. When he reached the item on the Congo, it was clear that there wasn't much more information than what we'd already heard. Within the last hour the BBC had picked up reports of fighting in Kinshasa. They were seeking corroboration, the announcer said, and further updates would be broadcast in later bulletins.

He moved on to the next item. I got down and flicked through the radio channels, searching for more news.

"This is not good," said Rita, alarmed. "This is so not good."

"Unconfirmed reports."

"From the BBC? If they say it's happening, Ned, it's happening."

Failing to find another English-language service, I switched back to the BBC. The news was over. I turned off the radio.

"They have an hourly bulletin?" Rita wondered.

I stood up. "If the BBC has heard, so has Trevanian. And Trevanian's first thought's going to be those Haplon containers."

"You think he'll contact Damienenko?"

"He'll try." I thought a moment. "Your people definitely got word to Channon."

"Sure."

"Definitely? They actually told you that?"

"Of course not, the line's not secure. But they know I'm here and you're here. I told them everyone should be informed."

I couldn't speak for a second. Until this point we'd been aboard a ship that was about to break an international arms embargo. Now, suddenly, we were aboard a vessel that was running guns into a war zone. Not only that, but U.S. Customs and the DIA had been complicit in the shipment. When Channon heard what was happening in the Congo, his duty would be absolutely clear.

"Get up to the communications room," I told Rita. "Call your people. Don't worry about the insecure line, just say it straight out. Get word to Channon. Make sure one hundred percent he knows we're on this goddamn ship."

"I'm sure he knows."

"You're assuming he knows. Do you want to risk him launching an air strike on the Haplon weapons, or do you want to get up to the bridge and make sure your people have told him we're here?"

Someone came hurrying along the passage, the door opened, and Bosnitch thrust his head in. He looked angry. He demanded to know if we'd seen the communications officer. When we said no, he withdrew and hurried away.

"They've heard," she said.

"Get moving." I slipped the radio into the pocket of my baggy pants. I told Rita that once she'd finished in the communications room, I'd meet her down at the stern.

There was a row of unused tool lockers beneath the stern lifeboat. I went back there and pulled at a locker door. The handle was jammed so I tried the next one, and when it opened I put the radio inside. Someone shouted at me. When I turned, I saw one of the crewmen, he shouted again and waved me over. I stood, pushed the locker door closed with my foot, and stepped away.

Back at the stern rail, the crewman kept calling me. Warily, I went across. I was almost beside him before I saw what he was pointing at. It had nothing to do with the radio. He pointed astern, and a flash of silver broke through the wake seventy yards back. A huge fish had taken the hook on one of my lines. The crewman spread his arms. *"Grosso,"* he said. *"Grosso. Grosso."*

The line was as tight as a bowstring. The crewman ignored my suggestion to cut the line, he went and fetched some gloves from a bucket. He pulled on one pair, made me put on the other pair, then together we started hauling in the line. I'd caught several big fish in the preceding days, but this was something else. God knows how the line didn't break. We hauled, but the line kept slipping through our gloves, we hauled again and the line jerked out of our hands, then finally we gave up and dragged the line over to the hand winch mounted on the rail. The crewman braced his foot on the stern rail and heaved in enough line for me to get a couple of turns around the winch barrel. When he eased off, the line went taut, and I cranked the winch handle. A dozen turns, then I locked the ratchet and let the crewman step up. While he worked the winch, I looked up to the bridge. There was no sign of Rita.

After a minute, I was back on the winch, wasting my strength on a goddamn fish. We kept it up awhile longer, taking turns, then the line suddenly stopped moving back and forth across the ship's wake. It stayed taut. I locked the ratchet and stood up.

"It's dead." The crewman gazed astern. "Dead," I said, pointing back. *"Morte."*

He kept staring astern, and now I saw he wasn't looking at the line, he was gazing much farther back, to the horizon. When I followed his gaze, I made out a dark shape above the horizon. As we watched, it got closer, then it split into three dark shapes. Jets. They climbed, then banked in close formation as they arced south of the ship. A second later, the deafening thunderclap of the sonic boom struck us, and the jets arrowed eastward.

F16s. I recognized the profiles. A plane that our military-industrial complex has never yet been quite crazy or greedy enough to sell to any nation in West Africa. Their carrier was probably astern of us, below the horizon. They must have been dispatched on a recce over the Congo—either that, or they were taking a dummy run over us, confirming our identity before returning to blow us apart. For several seconds, I couldn't move. I stood rock still and listened, straining to hear. An irrational instinct. I knew listening wouldn't help anyone if they'd already chosen to take us out. We wouldn't hear anything except the explosion that killed us. Maybe not even that.

I looked up to the bridge. No Rita.

The crewman turned from the eastern horizon where the jets had disappeared. He looked up to the bridge, then at me. Finally, with a bloody-minded peasant stubbornness, he went and found another winch handle. He inserted it in the far side of the barrel and impatiently called me back to work on the fish. I dragged my eyes away from the sky. I grabbed the handle, my arm cranked around, and after a minute the hauling got easier. I glanced skyward several times, then finally the dead fish broke through the water just astern. It was a swordfish, its body about six feet long, with another three or four feet of sword. We strained at the winch, hauling hard, craning the weight up the stern of the ship, till at last the sword tip appeared at the rail near our feet. We locked the winch and the crewman went and fetched a gaff. He hooked the gills and we manhandled the swordfish over the rails onto the deck, then we stood over it, our chests heaving.

"*Grosso,*" he said, and I clasped my hands behind my head and leaned back, looking skyward, breathing hard. The sky was blue. Not a jet in sight.

"What in the name of Christ are you doing?" Rita. I turned to find her approaching from over near the lifeboat. Her brow was creased, she was looking at my chest. I glanced down. My shirt was smeared with fish blood. When I gestured to the swordfish lying silken-wet on the deck, Rita looked at me as if I'd gone crazy. "Didn't you see those jets?"

I nodded.

"So you went fishing?" she said.

I took her arm and drew her away from the stern rail. I asked her if she'd gotten through to Customs.

"No chance. I had a stand-up shouting match with Damienenko. He wouldn't let me near the radio."

"Trevanian must have contacted him."

"Damienenko just about wrenched his neck getting a look at those jets. They must have something to do with this coup."

"They're F16s. The only force out here with F16s is us."

"The Navy? Our guys?"

I nodded, looking skyward. Our guys. But did they know we were their guys?

Bosnitch suddenly appeared, shouting. The jets seemed to have struck the fear of God into him. He stalked past the derricks, shouting to the crewman who was prodding the swordfish with the gaff. The crewman answered in Ukrainian, he seemed to explain to Bosnitch about the catch. Bosnitch raised his fist, but the crewman quickly pointed back to the lifeboat and the row of lockers. Bosnitch shot me a menacing look as he heard the crewman out, then the crewman led Bosnitch over to the lockers. All I could do was watch.

Crouching, Bosnitch jerked open the disused lockers, starting from the left and working his way along. In the fourth locker, he hit the jackpot. He reached in and brought out the radio. When Rita saw it, she groaned.

Pocketing the radio, Bosnitch came back to us. "You will go to your cabin."

"We want the radio," Rita told him.

They eyeballed one another, then suddenly a dull rumble like distant thunder rolled across the sea. We all turned. Just above the horizon, a single F16 sped like a black bullet toward the Congo. In moments, the jet disappeared, and the rumble died. Bosnitch faced us again. He didn't say anything this time. He didn't have to. I touched Rita's arm, and we beat a retreat to our cabin.

CHAPTER 25

They can't keep us down here."

"They can do what they like," I said. I was sitting in the upper bunk, studying the atlas spread open on my knees. Rita was staring out the porthole, searching for jets. We hadn't been locked in the cabin, just confined belowdecks, a restriction any captain might impose from time to time on non-crewmembers. Even now, Damienenko seemed determined to play it by the book. He'd done that since we first emerged from the hold, he was no dummy. If Rita and I got out of this alive, and his conduct was ever exposed to official scrutiny, he could plausibly claim the restriction on our movements was necessary for reasons of safety.

We'd been to the rec room and found that the TV had been removed. In the mess, the crew kept themselves well apart from us, but their previous indifference had turned to a brooding hostility. News of the coup in the Congo had obviously percolated down the ship's chain of command, and the crew must have known about the contents of the containers belowdecks. The pass of the U.S. jets had rattled them. We were not a welcome presence.

"Why do you keep looking at that goddamn atlas?" Rita said, turning from the porthole. "Put it down. Figure out how we keep from getting bombed."

"I think we're safe."

She put her hands on her hips. "That makes me feel so much better, Ned, I just can't tell you."

"There've been three flights go over. There's high-altitude surveillance too. If they were going to do anything, they would have done it by now."

"If? Jesus."

I reburied my head in the atlas, my attention divided between our likely location at sea and Brad's camp at Dujanka in the Congolese interior, near Mbuji-Mayi. I prayed Barchevsky had the sense to get Brad out.

"Remember I said two days, two nights to the Congo?"

"Ah-ha."

"I was wrong. We're closer." I turned the atlas around and placed my finger on a point near the West African coast. "I reckon we're around here." When she saw where I was pointing, she snorted in surprise. "My guess at our latitude must have been off," I told her. "We swung south in the night."

"If we're that close, wouldn't we see land?"

I climbed off the bunk and went to the porthole. "What do you see?"

"Nothing." She looked out. "The ocean. Some clouds."

"Seen any other clouds like that since we've been on the ship?" She thought a moment, then turned her head, no. "Long and low," I said. "Sea air meeting land air."

She peered out. "That's the Congo?"

We went back to the atlas. The national boundaries on that part of the coast were irregular. A slim finger of the Democratic Republic of the Congo jutted out to the coast, giving the country access to the sea, but to the north and south of it the territory was Angolan. We were cruising, on my new reckoning, southward along the north Angolan section. I pointed. "We should reach the Congo sometime tonight."

"We have to get off this damn ship."

I closed the atlas, my fingers drummed on the spine. "The only thing stopping Channon from taking this ship out," I said, "is us."

"So?"

"Rita. If Trevanian's client gets his hands on the Haplon materiel, a lot of people are going to get killed."

She looked at me. "Oh, no," she said after a moment, shaking her head. "No, no."

"No what?"

"No to whatever you're thinking."

"We're partly responsible, aren't we?"

"Whatever you're thinking, I'm not going to help you."

"Help me what?"

"I don't know. Destroy the Haplon materiel? Our responsibilities don't extend to getting ourselves killed. My only responsibility is to get myself off this ship in one piece."

"We're freighting an arsenal into a war zone."

"We?"

"This ship."

"This ship isn't us. I'm not the engineer and you are not the captain. God, yesterday you were fishing."

"There wasn't a coup in the Congo yesterday. Yesterday I didn't see F16s tearing across the sky."

"I'm not having this argument, okay? If the Haplon materiel ends up in a war zone, I'm sorry. I'm really sorry, but there's nothing anyone could expect me to do about that." She folded her arms. I slung the atlas onto my bunk and climbed up. "I'm not going to feel guilty about this," she said as I opened an old Mario Puzo and pretended to read. She went to the porthole, looked out, then came back. "If I'd just used my common sense and said no to you in New York, I wouldn't be standing here wondering if I'm still going to be alive in ten minutes, or blown to pieces." I turned a page. "Don't do that," she said, and I put the book down. I lay down with my hands behind my head on the pillow. "And don't sulk," she told me.

Rolling onto my side, I cocked my arm, resting my cheek on my fist. "You want me to leave the cabin?"

She slumped back against the wall and slid down till her ass touched the floor. She bowed her head onto her knees, silent.

I let her be. I knew I was never going to convince her to help me, but there was an outside chance she might convince herself.

"There's nothing we could do anyway," she said, after a minute. When I didn't reply, she looked up at me. "That's right, isn't it?"

"We can't destroy the materiel."

"Right."

"But we can get ourselves off the ship."

"Why am I listening to this?"

"When we get near the port," I said, "Damienenko'll have to wait for a pilot to take the ship in. We'll be anchored within sight of land. If we can get ourselves off the ship, get to land—"

"Swim?"

"We'll take a lifeboat."

"The last time I listened to you I ended up stacking cherries till I nearly died." When I didn't reply, she pushed her hands up through her hair. "You ever read that book, *Why Do Bad Things Happen to Good People?*"

"No."

"Me neither," she said. "I'm starting to think I should have." I watched her but said nothing. Finally she gestured despairingly. "So tell me about the fucking lifeboat," she said.

In the hours before nightfall we wandered belowdecks, not spending more than twenty minutes in any one place, getting the crew used to the idea that we weren't always in our cabin. We moved from the rec room to the mess, and along the passage to the heads. I even went below to the engine room for ten minutes till the chief engineer came down and chased me out.

After the first hour or so, Bosnitch stopped traipsing down from the bridge to check on us and bawl us out. At supper in the mess, the crew talked among themselves in Ukrainian, we didn't have to understand the language to feel the tension. They were like grunts about to enter the front line, guys who knew their lives were moving beyond their control. Rita and I ate quickly, then left.

I went to the rec room and stuck my head in a book. The cook and some other guy were playing chess, distracting themselves from the reality about to break over them. They'd been playing for a quarter hour, barely exchanging a word, when the cook suddenly lifted his head. I looked up. The other guy lifted his head too, then I felt it. The ship's engines were throttling back. They abandoned their game and went out. I crossed to the porthole, looked out, and saw nothing but black sea and dark sky. While I was standing there, the pitch of the engines changed again, the ship juddered and perceptibly slowed. I cupped my hands against the porthole glass and strained to see something more than darkness. When I couldn't, I gave up and went back to the cabin. Rita was waiting for me.

"Did you feel it?"

"We've dropped anchor," I told her. I looked out the porthole. I figured we had to be somewhere inside the mouth of the Congo. If we'd dropped anchor, we were also somewhere near a dock. But there were no lights out there, and no sign of land. I left the cabin and went along to the heads on the starboard side. When I looked out the starboard porthole, my heart leapt. A string of yellow lights, a mile or two away across the water.

Rita looked over my shoulder. "Is that it?" she said. I nodded, then she grabbed my arm and pointed to the right. "What's that?"

To the right of the dock, and a little higher, a bright white light drifted down through the darkness. A flare. It drifted slowly, then two staccato lines of broken light appeared from high on the right, streaming into the docks. Four bursts, five seconds apiece, then the flare went out and night-darkness came down again.

"Tracers." I stared out toward the yellow lights of the dock. "The first one was a flare. Someone trying to get a fix on someone else's position."

"Like a battle?"

"A skirmish." We waited, but there were no more flares or tracers. "If Damienenko saw that, he'll be wary."

"Should we be reconsidering? I mean, is out there any safer than here?"

"Out there we can take our own chances. If we stay here, what happens to us is up to Damienenko and Bosnitch." I turned to her. "You want to stay?"

She grimaced, then shook her head.

I decided on the lifeboat near the stern. Up on the bridge, all eyes would be turned away from us, landward. We could lower the stern lifeboat on the seaward side and make a wide looping run astern of the ship.

Back in our cabin, I explained the plan to Rita. "Give me five minutes," I told her finally, "then come up and go straight back to the lifeboat. If anyone sees you, you just went up on deck for some air. Don't fight it. If you're not with me inside ten minutes, I'll come back down, we'll forget the whole thing." I went to the doorway, then looked back. "You're really okay with this?"

"Just go," she said. "Before I change my tiny mind."

I went along toward the heads, then mounted the first ladder I came to and climbed up, emerging by several deep piles of folded tarpaulins. There were coils of rope nearby, and barrels of paint, and row after row of steel lockers. It was a storage room with a door out to the deck, the place smelled of tar. I stayed low and peered through the windows aft. The deck was clear. I went out, crouching as I made my way to the stern. Outside, it was warm and still. There was a smell of vegetation and mud in the air, the fresh saltiness of the sea was gone. I moved from a derrick to an air vent, then across the open deck to the lifeboat. I went around between the lifeboat and the railing, then set to work on the lifeboat gantry. The only light came from the sliver of moon directly overhead, but it was enough to work by. It took me a minute to release the chain holding the first swinging arm in place, then I moved up to the bow of the lifeboat and started on the other arm.

I hit trouble immediately. There was a padlock on the holding chain. I stared at the padlock, momentarily chilled by the sudden wild thought that the padlock had been fixed there to stop us from getting off the ship. But the padlock, when I touched it, was rusty. Someone had simply snapped it on, against every safety regulation in the book, to hold the lifeboat secure. I glanced up the deck toward the other lifeboats. They were too close to the bridge for me to even consider. It was the stern lifeboat or nothing.

I made a crouching dash back to the storage room. After searching awhile, I found a hammer and a bolt. I was crossing back to the door when I heard footsteps on the ladder behind me, and I spun around with the hammer raised. Another step, then Rita's head appeared. She gave a start when she saw me. I lowered my arm and beckoned her up.

"Couldn't you get out?" she whispered. "What went wrong?"

I told her about the padlock. There were voices from below, and we fell quiet till the voices passed on. I beckoned her on, and Rita followed me onto the deck and back to the lifeboat.

I positioned the chain and padlock again, then I held the bolt against the padlock barrel and drove the bolt hard, like a nail, with the hammer. The chain slipped, there was a loud jangle. We stood absolutely still, the noise echoing in our ears. Finally I reached down for the padlock. It remained securely fastened. I repositioned the chain, lined up the bolt, and swung the hammer again. Instant re-play. The slipped chain, the noise, and the padlock that remained se-curely fastened to the goddamn chain. I twisted the chain back into place to try again.

Then Rita reached over, grabbed the chain in one hand, and held the padlock in position with her thumb and forefinger. I looked at her. If I missed, her finger or her thumb would be crushed.

"Just do it," she said.

"Hold still."

I gave it one sharp blow. There was a single retort, no jangle of a slipped chain, but the padlock held. I repositioned the bolt, then looked at her. When she nodded, I struck again. The padlock broke open this time. Rita's head dropped in relief.

Uncoiling the chain, I pushed the gantry arm, and the lifeboat swung out. I climbed up on the ship's rail, leaned across the lifeboat gunnel, and released the rubber ties holding the canvas canopy in place. After flicking open the canopy, I got down.

"I'm going to swing it out and lower it. Once it's down to the ship's rails, I'll get in. You wait till I run it down another few feet, then you get in."

She glanced over the side, at the long drop to the water. "I could get in now."

"Not till I've checked the winches." I reached under the lifeboat, grabbed the keel, and pulled. The boat swung smoothly, I ducked as it passed over my head then out over the ship's rail. Once it was out there, I locked the arms in place.

Rita whispered my name. When I turned, she was pointing land-ward. Halfway between us and the docks, a boat was coming our way. A small red light shone from its cabin.

"The pilot?" said Rita.

I grabbed the control line to the lifeboat pulleys with my right hand. With my left, I got hold of the rope-brake. I eased off the brake and played the rope out slowly as the lifeboat started down. Then the bow pulley snagged. I got Rita to reach over the rails and give the lifeboat keel a shove. She did that, and the thing moved again. When the lifeboat gunnel reached the ship's top rail, I secured the brake on the control rope. I passed the rope to Rita, then climbed up and scrambled into the lifeboat's stern. I loosed a few more rubber ties, pulled the canopy right open, then signaled for Rita to pass me the control rope and brake. As she handed them across, the lifeboat swayed sickeningly beneath me.

When the lifeboat steadied again, I eased off the rope-brake. Nothing happened. I looked above me, at the pulleys, stern and bow. They were both snagged. I jerked the rope-brake, but still nothing happened.

"Give it a shove," I told Rita.

She reached over and pushed the gunnel, and the lifeboat swung out, then back. I tugged at the control rope. Nothing.

"This probably isn't the time, Ned, but that pilot boat's getting awfully close."

Soon, someone would come out to throw a ladder over the ship's side. I looked up at the snagged ropes, and then, stupidly, I jumped. It wasn't a big jump, barely six inches, a frustrated attempt to shock everything free. But when my feet landed, the rope-brake shot out of my hands, and the lifeboat gave way beneath me. I fell, snatching for a handhold, and caught the ship's bottom rail as the lifeboat jerked to a halt. I was suspended, on tiptoe in the slewed lifeboat, my hands gripping the ship's rail.

Twisting, I looked up. The rope-brake was caught in the tangle of ropes and pulleys overhead. If the tangle slipped or came free, the lifeboat would plummet into the sea, taking me with it.

"Hang on, for chrissake." Rita got down on her knees and looked at me through the rails. "Don't let go. I'll get someone."

"No."

"Well, what can I do?" she whispered urgently.

I shuffled my feet along the tilted lifeboat gunnel toward the highest point, the bow. At the same time I moved my hands along the ship's rail, trying to keep my weight on my arms. As I inched along, I felt sweat break out on my palms.

"You're nearly there," said Rita. "Come on."

When my chest came level with the ship's bottom rail, I grabbed the next rail up. Then I glanced down. There was a shimmer of moonlight on the black sea.

"Tell me what to do," she said.

"Keep back."

My arms were weakening fast, and the longer I waited, the worse it was going to get. So I fixed my eyes on my hands. I grabbed a steel upright and took a firm hold, then I shoved off the lifeboat hard, hauling with my arms. The lifeboat lurched, I swung my leg and got my right knee cocked over the ship's lowest rail. My left leg flailed against the hull. I hauled and scrabbled, finally got myself level with the deck, then I got my head through the rails, then my chest. Rita grabbed me under the arm and hauled, and I dragged myself through the railings, rolled onto the deck, and just lay there. I saw the moon and the clouds. Rita's face.

"I'm okay." I gasped for air.

"Okay? I don't care if you're okay. You try that again, I'll murder you."

When I got my breath back, I sat up and flexed my arms and looked over the side at the dangling lifeboat. It wasn't going to take anyone anywhere.

Voices came from up near the bridge, then two figures appeared on the upper deck. Damienenko and Bosnitch.

I got up. Crouching, Rita and I crept back across the deck and into the storage room. We dived down the stairs and made it back to our cabin without passing anyone. I shut the door behind us, slumped back against it, and we looked at each other. The Haplon weapons were going to dock. Our plan had failed.

A short while later, Bosnitch flung open the door and saw us lying on our bunks. I peered at him around the edge of my paperback. He looked from me down to Rita without saying a word, then withdrew, closing the door. We listened to his footsteps recede.

"They've found the lifeboat," said Rita.

I'd figured on that. And I'd also figured that if we stayed put, Damienenko was going to have a hard time guessing exactly what had occurred out there at the stern. He had a crew full of guys who'd been skirting trouble all their lives, men whose only real loyalty was to themselves. After seeing the flare and tracers, any one of them could have decided this wasn't the best time to be aboard a ship running guns into the Congo.

I dropped my paperback, reached under the mattress, and pulled out the atlas. Mbuji-Mayi.

"He'll be fine," said Rita. I paused, then looked over the edge of my bunk. She had her own book lying open on her arm. "Your son," she said. "Studying the atlas isn't going to help him much anyway."

"Are you a mind reader now?"

"We've already arrived in the Congo. What else could you be looking at in the atlas?" After a moment, she reached up and touched my hand. "He'll be fine," she said. There was a knock at the door, and she let her hand fall.

When the door opened, the guy standing outside wasn't one of the crew. He was an African, dressed in a dark green uniform. He had a holstered pistol on his hip and a green cap on his head. He took off the cap as he came in. I sat up. Rita got out of her bunk, and the guy smiled at her.

"Mademoiselle Durranti. Welcome to the Democratic Republic of the Congo." He shook her hand. He was young, early thirties, but self-assured. Someone used to getting his way. He told her his African name, which was unpronounceable, then advised her to call him Henri. "I will take you to your embassy," he said.

Rita shot me a glance. It seemed too good to be true. "The embassy sent you?" she said, facing him again. "Did you come out with the pilot boat?"

"I have my own boat." He looked up at me, extending his hand. "*Bon soir,* Monsieur Rourke." I reached down from my bunk. Then as I took his hand, I noticed the name tag on his breast pocket. Captain Henri something unpronounceable. Sécurité. My hand went rigid in his. "*Oui,*" he said, grinning when he saw that I'd seen it. "Monsieur Rourke, you are under arrest."

CHAPTER 26

Twenty minutes later, the ship docked and I walked down the gangway with my hands cuffed in front of me, Rita and Internal Security Henri following behind. He hadn't been aggressive and he hadn't explained the nature of my supposed crime. It was an official concern, he told us, he hadn't been informed of the charge. His orders had come through to him that morning from Kinshasa, he said, his job was to get us transported to the capital, Rita to the U.S. Embassy and me to his superior officers who, presumably, would know what to do with me.

There'd been an argument about the handcuffs, but I'd eventually relented when Henri pointed out the soldiers loitering on the dimly lit docks, cradling AK47s. It wasn't so much a threat, more an attempt by Henri to open my eyes to the reality of my situation. He meant to carry out his orders, with or without my cooperation. Damienenko and Bosnitch came out from the bridge and watched us descend to the dock, they didn't say a word.

The dock smelled bad. It wasn't just an odor, it was a stench like rotten mango. As I stepped onto the dock, a great spurt of raw sewage shot from a pipe near the gangway and dropped into the water by the ship. Henri didn't even notice. He nodded me toward a prefab single-story concrete office block by the nearest warehouse, where a faded sign said BUREAU DE L'IMMIGRATION.

Henri hadn't been pleased to discover that we weren't carrying passports, and now as we crossed to the Immigration office he asked if we had any money. I exchanged a glance with Rita. He asked us again.

"Twenty dollars," I said.

"You?" he asked Rita.

"Nothing," she said, and he smiled.

That smile of his was starting to get to me. He told me he needed my twenty bucks for Immigration, so I stopped and hitched up my hip. Rita fished out my wallet, removed a twenty, and gave it to him. Then she flashed the empty wallet at Henri before shoving it back in my pocket. Welcome to Africa.

Inside the Immigration office there was an empty waiting area and three large tables at the rear. On the wall hung a photo portrait of the latest Congolese President, in military uniform, with lots of medals and bars on his chest. At the farthest table, two guys were eating a late supper, spooning stew from their bowls. When one of them scuttled away, Henri took the vacated seat. Then a soldier strolled in, his forearms resting on the AK47 he had slung from a strap over his shoulder. He put one foot up on a chair and chatted with Henri.

"How long's this going to take?" I called across.

Henri flicked a hand imperiously. He continued shooting the breeze with his buddy, so I sat down on the bench beside Rita.

"What happened to the other twenty?" I asked her quietly.

"I palmed it."

"Which leaves us?"

"About a hundred and twenty."

"Somewhere safe?"

"I damn well hope so." She glanced down to her cleavage.

I told her that if we got separated, I wanted her to get hold of Channon, have him call in a strike on the containers.

"They're not going to separate us," she said.

"And contact Brad," I told her. "Get whatever help you can at the embassy. Make sure he's safe. Pull whatever strings you can."

"Is this before or after I find out what our friend Henri here's done with you?" Her glance slid by me. "Don't look now, but I think the boss just arrived."

I looked. A guy built like a refrigerator was standing in the doorway. He was wearing a blue uniform, there was a tag on his breast pocket saying IMMIGRATION and something else I couldn't read. His eyes were red, like he'd been sleeping, and he didn't look too happy about being called from his bed. Over at the table, the soldier stood up. The other guy started digging in a drawer, while Henri got to his feet.

The big guy went across, had a brief talk with Henri, then finally settled himself behind the main table. Some forms were produced. The big guy looked over and crooked a finger at Rita. I rose to go with her, but he wagged his finger at me and clucked his tongue.

For the next fifteen minutes Henri acted as translator between Rita and the Immigration boss, a totally bizarre session in which Rita was asked everything from the color of her eyes to the number of previous visits she'd made to each one of the Congo's neighboring states. The junior official copied Rita's answers down onto forms as if they actually mattered. Rita kept her cool. She answered the absurd questions and signed each form as it was completed.

While this was going on, I became aware of machinery moving outside on the docks. I stood and looked out a window and saw the derricks up on the *Sebastopol* working. I went to the door. Outside, three low-loaders were parked near the ship, the first truck was already loaded with two Haplon containers. The unloading from the ship was being carried out under military supervision, there were guys in fatigues everywhere, and officers bawling orders. I noticed that the containers hadn't been opened. As long as they stayed that way, Channon wouldn't have any trouble taking them out.

"Ned," said Rita quietly behind me.

I turned. She wasn't looking at me, she was looking at the soldier who was sighting down the barrel of his AK47 at my head. I opened my cuffed hands. "Hey," I said. I looked toward Henri, the gun stayed trained on me. "Tell him to stop pointing his gun."

"He saw you near the door," said Henri.

"I don't care where he saw me. Tell him to put the thing down."

"Will you run?"

I couldn't believe the question. Run? I was handcuffed, there were soldiers everywhere, and I was in the Democratic Republic of the Congo. Where the hell was I going to run to?

"Tell him to put it down."

Finally it was the Immigration boss who gave the order. Disappointed, the soldier lowered his gun. Then the Immigration boss beckoned me over. I went and braced my hands on his table.

"I'm five-eleven," I said. "I weigh a hundred and seventy pounds. I've never been to this hellhole before, and from what I've seen in the past half hour, I doubt that I'll be back."

The guy eyeballed me lazily. Henri gave him a letter, presumably the orders about me from Kinshasa. The Immigration guy ran his eyes over the letter and passed it back. There was a discussion, then Henri got up and went to the door. When I glanced over, he was folding my twenty bucks into the letter. Returning to the table, Henri passed the letter to the Immigration guy, who took it and turned his back. The performance was utterly childish, everyone in the room knew what was going on. At last the big guy dug a rubber stamp from his drawer. He banged the stamp down on the letter, tossed the letter at Henri, then walked out.

Rita leaned across to me. "You've arrived."

Henri waved us curtly to the door.

Outside, another Haplon container had been off-loaded from the ship and transferred to a truck. The Congolese army wasn't wasting any time. As we trailed Henri past the trucks, Rita nudged me, nodding to the first truck in line. A white guy in military fatigues was busy giving orders to the Congolese soldiers. When he saw us, he turned and watched us go by. He made no attempt to hide. Then something about the loading caught his attention and he forgot about us and yelled at the soldiers again. "Hey, is that gonna bloody do it? How many fucking times have I told you?" He went to fix the problem.

"Brit?" said Rita quietly. I nodded. I'd been on joint maneuvers with the British army many times, even fought alongside some of them in the Gulf. Good soldiers. Poorly equipped, but tough. "What's he doing here?" she said.

"Mercenary."

Her head swung around, she looked back at the guy. I wondered how long it would take her to make the connection. A few steps farther on, she got it. "One of Trevanian's?"

"Has to be."

"He was giving the local soldiers orders."

Lifting my chin toward Henri just in front of us, I shook my head. Not the time to talk. Rita shot another backward glance at the trucks, then we passed behind a warehouse.

A vehicle was waiting for us there, a jungle-green Toyota. Rita and I were bundled into the backseat by the armed soldier standing guard, then an unarmed soldier emerged from the shadows and got into the driver's seat. Henri got in beside him, then the guard with the AK47 climbed into the back behind Rita and me. We turned a hundred and eighty degrees and cruised back along the docks, passing the trucks, then the ship. Up on deck, Damienenko was supervising the unloading of another Haplon container. Near the stern, Bosnitch, the mate, was trying to get the dangling lifeboat back to its station.

Looking up at them, Rita mused, "Now where'd you rather be?"

I leaned forward and asked Henri where we were going.

"Kinshasa," he said.

The driver was middle-aged and gaunt, one of the thinnest men I'd ever seen. He banged the steering wheel with his palm, and repeated it, "Kinshasa, Kinshasa," and grinned.

Soldiers were positioned behind sandbags outside the dock gates, their weapons pointing down the road toward the local town. A sergeant came out from the gatehouse and looked in at us warily, but when Henri snapped two sharp words at him, the sergeant couldn't get the gates opened fast enough. He actually saluted as we drove out. I exchanged a glance with Rita. The sergeant was clearly petrified of Henri.

After a hundred yards we turned onto a sidetrack. I leaned forward again.

"We heard there's been fighting here." No response. "In fact, we saw it," I said. "Flares. Maybe some tracers."

"No fighting."

"It sure looked like fighting."

Henri waved a hand like he didn't want to hear any more about it. When Rita asked how long it would take us to get to Kinshasa, he told her we'd arrive the following morning. She groaned. But I was far more concerned about the nocturnal gauntlet we were about to run.

"Does your man in back know what he's doing?" I asked Henri.

Henri spoke to the soldier in French. The soldier dropped the tailgate, shuffled onto it, then stood up and faced forward. We must have been doing nearly sixty. Henri pointed to a road sign ahead, and as our headlights lit the sign up, it disintegrated in a shower of bullets from our guard's AK47. Inside the cab, the noise was deafening. The guy kept blasting when we were long past the road sign, in the end Henri shouted and thumped his hand on the roof. The guy still wouldn't stop shooting, so Henri gave the hand brake a jerk. The Toyota jolted, there was a loud bang on the roof, and the blasting stopped dead. A second later, the guy shuffled back inside sheepishly and closed the tailgate. Rita dropped her head into her hand.

A few miles farther on, two soldiers suddenly appeared out of the darkness in front of us, waving us down. We stopped, and a third soldier came out of the bush. He shone his flashlight in at us, flourishing a pistol and shouting. Our guard in back did nothing.

Henri turned in his seat. "This man want money."

"You already took it."

"Tell him to screw off," said Rita.

Henri seemed remarkably unconcerned about the pistol waving by his ear. When he warned us that the guy would make trouble, I said, "If you can't get us five miles past the goddamn port, Henri, how do you expect to get us to Kinshasa?"

"Hundred dollars," said Henri, and I shook my head and he spoke to the soldier again. Then he turned back to me. "Fifty."

"For crying out loud," said Rita.

"Fifty dollars." Henri held out his hand. The guy with the pistol stuck his head in, he looked with bloodshot eyes at Rita and me. Mainly at Rita.

When I shook my head again, Rita said, "You know what you're doing, right?"

I nodded. I wasn't sure that I did.

The guy with the pistol suddenly pushed a hand in toward Rita. She hunched her shoulders and cried out, but the next moment there was a rattle of gunfire from the darkness real close. The bloodshot eyes widened in surprise, then the guy spun around and ran. In back, our guard dropped the tailgate and opened fire indiscriminately. I grabbed Rita and shoved her down. The smell of burnt powder filled the cab, my eyes stung. Henri shouted in panic, the driver hit the gas, and we lurched forward and accelerated down the track.

I sat up and looked back. There were powder flashes off in the bush, Henri's buddies who'd tried to shake us down were finally returning fire at their ambushers. We sped on up the road, took a bend, and the flashes disappeared behind us. Henri looked over his shoulder, his eyes wide.

"No fighting?" I said. "That's what you call no fighting?" I held up my cuffs and told him, "Take them off." Henri shouted past me to the soldier in back. I thrust my hands forward between him and the driver. "Take these damn things off!"

Henri shouted to the soldier again. Rita shouted, "Ned!" and then there was an explosion of pain in my shoulder and I cried out and slumped against the door. My hand clutched my shoulder. Our guard's gun butt hovered over me, Rita screamed at him, then Henri barked an order and the gun butt withdrew into the back.

"Ned. Oh, shit. Are you okay?" said Rita. "Oh, shit."

I nodded grimly. It hurt like hell, but it was just the muscle, not the bone, nothing was broken. Rita started abusing Henri then, and after a minute I hauled myself upright and pulled her back into the seat. She kept on at him. I let my head fall back and closed my eyes and tried to forget the pain. We were in no position to dictate terms, but Rita couldn't help herself, she was letting off a week's worth of fury. Henri growled a couple of times but his heart wasn't in it. It didn't matter anyway. However much she screamed at him, my cuffs were staying on.

Sometime in the night, we stopped for gas. About twenty trucks were parked at the ramshackle gas station, it seemed most of the drivers weren't eager to brave the road alone at night with a coup going on. Congolese army vehicles were parked there too, and soldiers wandered around, being careful not to stray too far beyond the dim yellow light near the gas pumps. The night air was warm, the sounds of insects and larger animals out in the darkness pulsed loud. We sat in the corrugated-iron diner with Henri and our guard and ate a meal of sweet potatoes and grilled goat while our driver organized the refueling. It took him the best part of an hour. A couple of hookers were working the gas station, Rita kept herself entertained counting the minutes they gave each client around behind the diner. Nobody got more than ten. One guy only got three.

Soon after we started out again, Rita dropped off to sleep. Henri levered back his seat, and soon he was out too. I didn't want to sleep, but when the driver had the guard give me his jacket, I pillowed it between my head and the door. I couldn't fight the tiredness forever, and the last thing I saw before I went out was the clock on the dash. Two A.M.

When I woke, it was just past 5:00 A.M. and we were still moving. I lifted my arm and felt the dull pain in my shoulder. The driver smiled at me in the rearview mirror. In back, our guard was sleeping like a baby. Rita's head was cradled on my thigh, she felt me move and slowly came around. Morning time, I told her, and she sat up, massaging her neck.

After fifteen minutes the sky started to gray as dawn came on, and the driver nudged Henri awake. Henri rubbed his eyes, then cranked up his seat and turned to look at Rita.

"*Ça va?*" Okay?

Rita rolled her eyes.

In the dim morning light I could make out the tin huts by the roadside, women carrying sticks for their fires, and children pumping water. Sometimes a skinny goat ran from the roadside into the undergrowth, and we passed several cows tethered outside huts, beneath sheltering trees. Smoke rose from many of the huts, and soon the horizon opened out in front of us, a clear African daybreak, a mother-of-pearl sky. In other circumstances, it would have been glorious.

Another fifteen minutes and we came to a roadblock. The soldiers manning it weren't like the shakedown artists who'd stopped us outside the port the previous night, they were professional army. Henri sat up straight as he presented his papers to the senior officer. The guy looked in at Rita and me, then inspected the paperwork as he spoke to Henri in French. Henri looked disconcerted by what the guy told him. So did the driver. In back, our guard dropped the tailgate and lifted his gun. Finally satisfied, the soldier returned Henri's papers and waved us on. Once we were on our way, I leaned forward.

"What's up?"

"Kinshasa," said Henri, nodding ahead. There was no real sign of the city yet, though the tin huts by the roadside were becoming more numerous. The outskirts of one of the city's shantytowns.

"So what's happening in Kinshasa?" I said.

Henri waved me back into my seat. The driver hunched over his wheel, his eyes darting left and right. The tarmac road widened, and as we swung north we saw several pillars of smoke rising ahead. Ten minutes later, we heard the first gunfire.

"Jesus Christ," said Rita, pressing back in her seat. We were passing buildings now, mostly concrete shells, with plenty of rusty reinforced steel poking out of unfinished walls and floors. Then a column of women and children went by, walking away from the city. The women were fully laden, with babies on their backs and hips, and bundles of possessions piled high on their heads. It was a mini exodus. "You take us straight to the embassy," Rita demanded firmly. "And you take us there now."

Henri paid no attention. The gunfire outside was intensifying, getting louder the closer we got to the center. Henri unholstered his pistol and wound down his window. The driver took the small golden crucifix dangling from a chain around his neck and put it between his lips. He kept it there as he drove.

"Huddle down," I told Rita, and we pressed down in the seat. I kept my eyes just high enough to look out.

It wasn't like Mogadishu. There, the locals had gotten used to the fighting by the time our Ranger units arrived, the different clans had occupied different parts of the small city, and everyone knew where they could and couldn't venture. Kinshasa was way different. It was more of an urban sprawl, and the fighting, from what I could see, wasn't concentrated. We passed long stretches where everything looked normal except that there was no one around, but a hundred yards farther on, every shop was burned out. After a while Rita put her head up, but then she saw charred bodies lying at the roadside and she hunkered down again and covered her eyes.

I tried to get a fix on some landmarks, but it was nearly impossible. The concrete office blocks were featureless, almost indistinguishable, and we turned too often for me to have a clear idea of our direction at any given time. Our driver slowed down frequently to put his head out and listen for gunfire. It wasn't high-tech, but it worked. He kept us clear of the fighting until at last we turned into a street and found ourselves confronted by a unit of the Congolese army. Half the unit was aiming weapons in our direction.

Our driver hit the brakes. Henri, his nerves stretched to breaking point, screamed at our guard in back, who immediately lowered his gun. Then Henri jumped out, waving his paperwork and talking fast. The officer of the unit came over, his men still sighting at us down their guns. Our driver, lips clamped on his golden crucifix, began to moan. But after a brief discussion with Henri and a check on the papers, the officer waved us through. We drove on two hundred yards, then stopped outside a nondescript low-rise office block. The sign outside was peeling. SÉCURITÉ, RÉPUBLIQUE DÉMOCRATIQUE DU CONGO.

Henri came around and opened my door.

"Take us to the U.S. Embassy," said Rita. "Both of us."

Henri pointed his pistol casually at Rita. "You stay." Then to me, he said, "You come."

I faced Rita. "Brad's at the Dujanka mine. Remember that. Dujanka."

"Barchevsky Mining," she said, repeating what I'd told her.

"Find Brad and get him out." When Henri waved his pistol, Rita grabbed my arm. "Dujanka," I said. "Barchevsky Mining."

"Ned," she said quietly, staring right past me.

I followed her gaze. Slumped against the gatehouse beside us was the body of a young white guy, he couldn't have been more than thirty years old. He was wearing jeans and a sweatshirt with the words *AfricAid* stenciled across the chest. Flies had settled on his open eyes, and on the blood that had dried on his mouth and in his wispy beard. Henri jabbed at me with his pistol.

"Find Brad," I told Rita, dry-mouthed. "Get him out of here."
Then I prised Rita's fingers off my arm and climbed out. The Toyota
door slammed closed, and Henri yanked on my cuffs and hauled me
away. Rita stared out, her horrified gaze still fixed on the body. Both
the kid's arms were missing, severed like ripe fruit, clean at the
shoulders.

CHAPTER 27

Henri took me down to the cells in the basement, the warder's room was at the bottom of the stairs. Cell doors lined either side of a long corridor, the concrete floor was wet. While Henri signed some paperwork, I told him I wanted my cuffs removed. He gave the warder my cuff keys, the prick dropped them into his desk drawer. The paperwork all signed, Henri turned to leave.

"Have I been charged with something?" I called after him.

"It is not my affair."

"It was your affair when you arrested me and brought me to this stinking hole."

He turned up the stairs, past a slouching guard, and disappeared.

"Allez." The warder waved his keys toward the corridor.

I made a gesture, tipping my cuffed hands to my lips. Water, I said.

He came around his desk, calling to the guard on the stairs, and the guard hurried in, brandishing his AK47 like he wanted to use it.

I raised my hands. "Okay. Take it easy."

I edged into the corridor. Three doors along, on the right, the warder opened an empty cell and shoved me in and locked the door. The cell was about six feet by twelve, the floor, walls, and ceiling were bare concrete. The only objects in there were a bucket in one corner and a naked lightbulb dangling from the center of the ceiling. There was a barred opening in the door, six inches by six, and I found I could see the three cell doors immediately across the corridor. I called for water a few times but nobody answered. Something stank. I looked in the bucket. It was full of urine and feces. Retreating to the far corner, I sat down.

The body of that young AfricAid guy, the severed arms, had shaken me. All the normal barriers of human restraint were clearly down, raw violence had bulldozed aside the fragile civil order of the country, forces were loose that had nothing to do with politics. Being a white man was no protection. Until the army or the rebels gained the upper hand, there'd be no safe place in the city for anyone. Out in the diamond fields it would be the same, maybe even worse.

I tried to cast my mind back to some courses I attended at Fort Bragg, instruction meant to prepare officers for the rigors of captivity. After several minutes' reflection I regretfully concluded that most of it didn't apply. I was a civilian, not a soldier, my value for the purposes of propaganda was virtually zero. There was no credible threat of retaliation against my captors if I was mistreated or harmed. I was merely John Doe, arms dealer, and as far as my fellow citizens were concerned, if they knew, probably getting what I deserved.

"Hey," someone called, and I lifted my head. "Hey. You speak English?"

I got up and went to the peephole.

"Hey." From the peephole opposite, two eyes looked out at me. A black face. "Hi. You speak English?"

"I can try."

"Oh Jesus, man. You American?"

I strained to see along to the warder's room. I couldn't see a damn thing. "Yeah. You?"

"Detroit, man. Lovely, beautiful Detroit. Never gonna leave it again, long as I live."

"How long you been in here?"

"Two days."

I asked him his name.

"Jay."

"How old are you, Jay?"

"Twenny-eight. They ain't gonna let us out. These people, I swear, they ain't like us, man. They're killin' people."

"You alone?"

"Yeah."

"Anyone outside know you're in here?"

"No. That's bad, ain't it. That's real bad."

I asked him his surname.

"Jones."

"Jay Jones."

"Right."

"Birthday?" I said, but he didn't respond. "Jay?"

"What kinda stupid question's that, man? Shit. I look like I be throwin' a party?"

"When I get out, I'll give your name and date of birth to the embassy. It'll give them a fix on you. It might just save your ass."

He thought that over a moment, then finally told me his date of birth. I repeated it back to him, and he confirmed I had it right. Then I told him my name. I kept straining to see the warder, I could hear people talking down at his office. I asked Jay what he knew about the coup.

"Man, like against the government? That what they sayin'?"

"You didn't know that?"

"Shit no. They bust in and arrested us like they was mad about somethin'. No one tol' us for what."

"I thought you said you were alone."

"I am. They took Johnny somewheres else."

"Johnny."

"Johnny. The guy I brung the Bibles to at AfricAid. Hey," he said, suddenly thinking of something. "You don't s'pose they holdin' us 'cause we Christians. What religion they all got here, anyways?"

Johnny. At AfricAid.

I asked Jay if this guy Johnny was a friend, but before he could answer we heard the warder coming from his office, and Jay backed away from his peephole, murmuring, "Duck and cover, man. Duck and cover."

My cell door opened. The warder beckoned me out and I got up and followed him. At the foot of the stairs we stepped aside, and three manacled men were led down past us. They'd been beaten. Their faces were swollen and bruised, and their lips were bloody. The soldier pushing them along suddenly struck them with a wooden truncheon as he shoved them into a cell. The warder barked a command at another soldier by the stairs, who responded by jabbing his AK47 into my ribs. Halfway up the stairs, I heard one of the prisoners below give a scream like the cry of a mortally wounded animal, and the hairs on my neck stood rigid.

"I want to see Trevanian. Jack Trevanian. Take me to one of your officers."

The warder ignored me. Up on the ground floor, there were more guys in manacles, about twenty of them with their hands cuffed behind their backs, seated on the floor. Internal Security men wandered among them delivering indiscriminate kicks and blows, which the prisoners took like abject cattle.

We went past into a rear foyer, then on outside, where there was a dirt yard with basketball hoops at either end and a twelve-foot-high stone wall all around, topped with broken glass and razor wire. There was a steel door in the wall, and an armed guard slouching on a chair. He eyed me as we neared, but didn't bother to rise. He unhooked a large key from his belt and handed it to the warder. The warder opened the steel door and beckoned me. I balked. I had a bad feeling.

He beckoned again. *"Allez."*

"What's in there?"

"Allez, allez."

Now the guard roused himself from his chair and cocked his gun. *"Bon,"* he said, grinning. My bad feeling wasn't getting any better. He put the barrel against my spine and his mouth up near my ear. "America dollar, *oui?*"

"Fuck off."

The warder yanked on my cuffs and hauled me through the open doorway. I stumbled, and the steel door slammed shut behind me. I got up off my knees, waiting for the bullet, but when it didn't come I looked back and saw that the guard had remained on the far side of the wall. The warder let go of my cuffs, then disappeared behind some banana palms up ahead, and that's when I realized I was in a garden. An African version of a garden, trodden red earth instead of grass, but definitely a garden. There were banana palms, heavy-fronded greenery, and creepers going up frames of wrought iron and wood. A pungent sweet scent came from a stand of white flowers that looked like African cousins of the lily. I looked around me. The steel door was closed, and no gun barrels pointed down at me from the wall. I crouched, scanning beneath the nearby shrubs and bushes, but there was nothing. My uneasiness grew, I stood and walked on, brushing through the line of banana palms, calling to the warder, "You bring me out here for some reason, or you just getting your kicks?"

"They said you were thirsty."

I stopped in my tracks. Ten yards in front of me was a garden bench nestled in a shaded arbor. On the bench, a pitcher and two glasses of water. Beside the glasses, Cecille Lagundi.

CHAPTER 28

She was dressed African-style, her hair wrapped in a high turquoise turban, swathes of the same shimmering material were draped over her shoulder and twined around her body. She picked up a glass. "I also do not like the heat," she said. "Like New York in August, but all the year."

I said nothing.

She gestured to the far end of the bench. I held up my cuffed hands and she spoke to the warder. He uncuffed me, then stepped back to his place outside the arbor. I rubbed my chafed wrists. Lagundi held out the glass, and I took it and drank the cold water. On the higher ground behind her, obscured by the arbor and the foliage, I glimpsed a large colonial house.

"You have not been to my country before," she said. I poured myself another water, drank it, then set the glass down on the bench. "You have not chosen the best time," she added, smiling.

"Did you engineer my arrest?"

"You arrived here illegally."

"I want to see Trevanian."

"I, also, would like to see him. Unfortunately, he is busy."

I picked up the pitcher and swung it against the steel frame of the arbor. The pitcher shattered, the startled warder stepped forward, but when Lagundi cursed him in French, he retreated like a beaten dog. I dropped the pitcher handle at her feet.

"You are tired," she said.

"I'm not tired."

"If your cell is not comfortable—"

"If you can't get me to Trevanian, get me to the U.S. Embassy."

She turned aside, smiling again.

"Stop playing stupid games," I said. "Tell me why I'm here. And while you're at it, maybe you can tell me why you're here too."

She rose, stepped around the pieces of broken pitcher, and left the arbor. I had a powerful sense of displacement. The last time I'd seen her she'd been wearing a designer outfit, we'd been up in her suite at the Hallam Hotel in Manhattan.

"I'm a U.S. citizen. I'm being wrongfully detained and I want to contact my embassy."

She stopped and looked back. "Why were you on that ship?"

"Because I'm a fool."

"The woman was a Customs officer."

"There was a query over the shipment. I went aboard with her to check the ship's manifest." When Lagundi looked skeptical, I said, "Listen. The Internal Security guy who picked us up, Henri, he spoke with the captain. Go ask him."

"The captain said you were on board illegally. Accidentally trapped?"

I tilted my head. "Who are you working for?"

"You never asked me that in New York."

"In New York it wasn't necessarily in my interest to know."

"I am working with Trevanian."

"Who's Trevanian working for?"

There was a sound of distant gunfire, then the crump of a small explosion, maybe a grenade. Though she glanced in that direction, it really didn't seem to worry her.

"You don't seem too concerned," I said.

"I'm not." She faced me. "Are you going to be cooperative?"

"Not until I know who you're working for."

She considered me a moment, then turned, smoothing a fold of material over her thighs. When she went up through the garden toward the house, the warder squatted on his haunches, waving me on after her, and I went. The house was two stories high, with a sweeping stone staircase leading up from the garden to the ground floor. An armed soldier sat on the bottom step. Parts of the decorative stonework had fallen away, but the place looked pretty much as it must have when the last Belgian colonial master packed his bags and left for home, a piece of European architectural history slowly decaying beneath the African sun.

She led me up the steps, then across the wide covered porch that ran the entire breadth of the house. The room we entered was large, high-ceilinged, with a polished stone floor. The tall windows were shuttered, and in the center of the room a suite of outsized cane furniture sat beneath a slowly revolving fan. It felt cool.

I stopped beside Lagundi. She pointed to some framed photos on the wall.

"My father."

I didn't get it at first. I went over to the photos for a closer look.

"The big man with white hair," she said.

There were a few big men with white hair, but only one who appeared in every photo. Standing in a lineup of suited colleagues. In African dress, shaking Nelson Mandela's hand. An official pose alongside white guys in suits, vaguely recognizable figures from the past two or three U.S. administrations. Seated beside the current Congolese President.

"Your father," I said, and she nodded. "Lot of friends."

"The Minister for Police is always a popular man."

There was an involuntary spasm in my gut. My arrest. This house next door to Internal Security HQ. Thoughts tumbled, I grabbed at one of them.

"Back in New York," I said. "That call you made from the Hallam."

"To my father," she confirmed, retreating out to the porch. "Are you surprised?"

Surprise did not cover it. I took another look at the photos, then went out to join her. She was seated in one of those cane chairs whose backrest flares like a peacock tail. The soldier had come up from the bottom step, he was slouching against the porch balustrade.

"You remember the final offer I made you at the Hallam?" Lagundi said, and when I nodded, she asked, "What happened?"

"You got what you wanted."

"You never came back to me with an answer."

"You got the materiel."

"I think you lied to me."

"To you? We thought we'd sold the materiel to Nigeria. Now it turns out we were dealing with the Congolese government."

"You never believed it was going to Nigeria."

"It was their End User Certificate."

She brushed that aside with the contempt it probably deserved. "Why did you come to see me at the Hallam?" she asked.

I didn't answer. I wasn't sure what she was after.

"Had Trevanian already paid you?"

"It was confused," I said.

"It is not possible to be confused about twelve million dollars."

"I couldn't get hold of Rossiter. The way you and Trevanian were behaving didn't make it any easier for me." I extended a hand. "Look, who's this for? Your father? Get one of your men to drop me off at the embassy, I'll send you a statement."

"Did you take my offer to Rossiter?"

"Why am I being held?"

"I need to know what happened."

"That's not a charge."

"You are charged with importing arms. Illegally."

"That's bullshit." I pointed. "That's pure bullshit."

"A capital offense."

"You imported the arms. You and Trevanian. And you just told me you did it with the full knowledge of your father. What the hell are you talking about, capital offense?"

"What happened in New York?"

"Who cares? Your weapons are here. You got what you wanted."

There was another explosion in the distance, I turned and looked out across the garden. The flat roof of the Internal Security block jutted above the banana palms. Way beyond, several black pillars of smoke were rising. On the streets of Kinshasa, out past the invisible protective boundary that surrounded us, people were dying.

"You are nervous," she said somewhat mockingly.

I faced her. "Where's Trevanian?"

"I don't know."

I tossed my head toward the smoke pillars. I asked her if this was going on right across the country.

"Mainly here. Also in Katanga. Mbuji."

"Mbuji-Mayi?"

She nodded and I hung my head. Where else would they be fighting? There wasn't a damn thing in the country worth fighting over except the wealth in the ground. I had to find Brad. Get him out.

"If I tell you what you want to know, can I go?"

"If you don't tell me, the charge against you will become official."

"The charge is bullshit." She didn't respond. She didn't have to. Finally I dropped into a cane armchair, facing her. I leaned forward, elbows on my knees. "What happened in New York."

"Please," she said.

So I told her. I told her about what I'd found at Rossiter's apartment after leaving her at the Hallam, and about my suspicion that Trevanian, with or without her connivance, had stolen the bill of lading. After that, of course, I lied. Rita Durranti, I said, had informed me that she was going down to the ship, and fearing that the deal was about to collapse, I'd gone with her. "Once we got stuck in the hold, I played stupid. She knows nothing about what's really been going on. Soon as we got out of the hold, I radioed Rossiter. He told me the deal was clean, that he'd been paid."

"Who paid?"

"Trevanian. You." I threw up my hands. "Your old man, for all I know. I've been sitting on a goddamn ship since then. That, or walking around in handcuffs. How do I know who paid? Ask Trevanian." She regarded me closely. The huge mess of the transaction had followed me all the way to Africa. "Call Rossiter and ask him. If you want more from me, you're out of luck. I don't know any more."

"If the bill of lading was stolen, Rossiter would have told the stevedores."

"Like I said, you'll have to call him."

She suggested he might still be awaiting payment.

"Rossiter?" I managed a smile. "If he hadn't been paid, he would have been here dockside with a bazooka and a lawyer when the *Sebastopol* arrived." In truth, her suggestion had raised a sudden doubt in me. Was there a connection I hadn't seen, something going on between Rossiter and Trevanian? An insurance scam, maybe, on the materiel? "Haplon's been paid," I told her firmly. "The screwups in the payment—the diamonds, all that crap—that was down to you guys. Trevanian and Greenbaum." She studied me. I asked her, "Have you had this kind of trouble with Trevanian before?"

She thought about that, then turned her head.

"Good at his job," I said.

"He understands guns."

"Why'd he choose the Haplon materiel over Fettners'?" When she squinted, I said, "Fettners. The company Dimitri Spandos was with." She looked at me, puzzled. I repeated his name, it still didn't register, so I said, "The salesman who got shot at the Springfield fair."

"Why didn't Trevanian buy their weapons?" She opened her hands and shrugged as if it was none of her business. The name Fettners clearly meant nothing to her. Dimitri's name, likewise. I was watching her eyes the whole time and I knew that she wasn't deceiving me, she wasn't even aware that maybe she should be deceiving me. The ground moved beneath me. She hadn't killed Dimitri.

She called to the soldier in French. He went down the steps into the garden, then she looked at me again and I held her look. The rule of law. In my entire life that phrase has never meant to me what it meant in those few moments. Cecille Lagundi was judging me. The realization went through me like an arrow, fixing me to the chair. Unelected by any democratic authority, unappointed by any legitimate judiciary, yet she was sitting in judgment over my story about the payment and there would be no court of appeal. She hadn't killed Dimitri, but she might yet kill me. She was the daughter of the Minister for Police and I was no one, an American arms salesman, adrift in a strange land. I did not move a muscle.

At last she rose and went to speak with the warder, who was coming up the steps. I got to my feet. My shirt, clammy with perspiration, clung to my back.

"What now?" I said.

"He will take you," she told me over her shoulder.

"To the embassy?"

"I have told him not to handcuff you."

"Where am I going, to the embassy?"

She spoke to the warder again. I was not going to the embassy.

"I've got nothing more to tell you," I said. "There's nothing more I know."

She faced me. "I will have a statement prepared. If you sign it, you will be taken to your embassy."

"Give me a pen and paper and I'll write it now."

"It will be prepared for you."

I asked what the statement would say. When she smiled, I got the idea. "Okay, I don't care what it says. When will I have it?"

She gathered up a swathe of blue material that was slipping, then pushed it back over her shoulder.

"When?" I said.

She nodded to me gracefully and disappeared inside.

CHAPTER 29

The warder took me back through the garden to the Internal Security HQ, and as I passed through the upstairs hall I took a good look around. There were uniformed guys everywhere, regular soldiers and Internal Security. Some were roughing up their manacled prisoners, others strutted around with weapons slung from their shoulders, spoiling for a fight. Apart from the dismembered AfricAid guy, I hadn't seen one white face.

When the cell door closed behind me, I sat down with my back to the wall. She hadn't killed Dimitri. Something wasn't right about the payment for the Haplon materiel. There was fighting where Brad was working at Mbuji-Mayi.

"Hey, Ned. Ned, that you, man? They brung you back?"

I got up and went to the peephole just as the warder shouted and came running. He unlocked Jay's cell and went in, swinging a wood truncheon. Jay screamed.

"Hey!" I yelled. "Leave the kid alone!" I banged the door with the heel of my hand, helpless. "Hey, you! Over here!"

I heard the truncheon hit hard, and Jay crying "No!"

I kicked my door in fury and frustration. He hit the kid again, and I rolled around, my back against the door, and closed my eyes. Jay was wailing now, the blows thudding into him like the warder was banging on a drum. One hit on the wrong place, on his head or neck, and the kid was dead. I listened to it and listened to it, then I suddenly spun around and shouted through the peephole, "Lagundi! Lagundi!"

Jay went on wailing, I shouted the name again, and the beating slowed, then stopped. I looked through the peephole. The warder came to Jay's door, perspiring. He stared across at me, his eyes bloodshot with exertion.

"That's right, you bastard! You hit him once more, Cecille Lagundi's going to hear about it. And her father. Old man Lagundi. Papa Lagundi."

The warder pointed the truncheon at me and shouted in French. He didn't understand what I was saying, but he understood the name Lagundi. The name rattled him. He'd seen me with Cecille. He knew I had some kind of access.

"Papa Lagundi! You don't like that, do you, you cowardly prick. Papa Lagundi!"

He shouted at me again, took a last swipe at Jay, then exited the cell and relocked the door.

"Minister for Police," I called. "He'd squash you like a bug." He waved his truncheon, I shouted, "Papa Lagundi!" and he whacked the truncheon against my cell door and retreated along the passage to his office.

"Jay!" I called across. There was no answer, so after a few moments I called again. "Jay! He's gone. You okay?" Still no answer. I didn't know if he was hurt bad, or just too frightened to speak. "He won't hit you again," I said. "But best you stay quiet now, anyway. When I get out, I'll give your details to the embassy. Just hang in there." No face appeared at his peephole. There was absolute silence from his cell. "Hang in there," I said, then I stepped back and slumped down by the wall.

Time passed slowly. Prisoners were led to their cells past my door and others were taken away, the basement cells seemed to be a holding area, a staging post on the way to another part of the compound where the full nightmare occurred.

Minutes turned to hours. The first warder went off duty. His place was taken by an older and bigger man who took regular tours of inspection along the passage, looking in at the peepholes. I asked this second warder for water, I mimed a drinking action, and he went away and brought back a canteen. I had to hold out a cupped hand to catch the water as he poured it through the peephole. When I'd had my fill, I gestured for him to give some to Jay, who I still hadn't seen or heard since his beating. The warder corked the canteen and went back to his room.

As time went on, it got harder to believe that Rita had reached the embassy, or that Lagundi was going to collect my signature then let me go free. Other grim possibilities went through my mind like poisoned darts, sapping my energy, wearing me down.

At times I lay on the concrete floor, I even slept for a while, but the sleep was shallow, broken by the low moans of prisoners and keys turning in locks. Mostly I just sat up and stared at the wall. From time to time I got to my feet and walked around the cell, pausing by the door to look out through the peephole.

Nobody threatened me. No soldiers appeared at my door with electric cattle prods. No one waved a machete in my face. But I'd seen enough by then to imagine all that, and I did imagine it, and more. In my worst moments I imagined Brad. Brad at the Dujanka mine, stumbling over rocks toward me, eyes rolling, both his arms severed, lying behind him on the ground.

After an eternity my cell door opened. As I got up, some prisoner was shoved in. He collapsed on the floor, then the door closed and the lock turned. I went to the peephole. Jay's cell door was open, and five manacled prisoners were being shoved in there.

"Jay!" No answer. The guy on my floor was moaning. "Jay!" I called through the peephole. "You okay?"

"I'm fuckin' dyin'." The guy on my floor rolled over, I turned and looked at him. Jay? His right eye was swollen shut, and there was a deep cut on his cheek. He held a hand to his ribs, clearly in pain, and examined me with his left eye. "I'm fuckin' dyin', man."

I knelt by him. When I lifted his arm off his chest, he winced, then I opened his shirt. There were three livid welts across his chest and one across his stomach. None were bleeding.

"Where's it hurt worst?"

His hand went to the lowest welt on his rib cage, then he couldn't help it, tears rolled down his cheeks. "Shit, man. Shit."

"You bringing up any blood?"

He shook his head.

"Passing blood?" I said, and he shook his head again. I pressed gently on his top rib, then on down. When I pressed on the second-to-last rib, his head jerked up, he opened his mouth in silent agony.

"It's okay." I put my hand behind his head, eased it back to the floor. "Anywhere else bad?"

"Everywhere."

"But that's the worst."

He made a face and tipped his head a fraction, yes. I sat back on my haunches, and he put a hand over his eyes and wiped the tears. "You a doctor?"

"No."

"I don't wanna die in this fuckin' place."

"You've busted a rib. You're not going to die."

He turned his one good eye on me, mistrustful yet desperate to believe. It was a look I'd seen on the face of every new black recruit I'd dealt with in the Army. This time, against the evidence of his entire life, a bruised hope that the white world might not let him down. I squeezed his shoulder, then went to the peephole and hollered for water until it came.

Jay was sleeping when the statement arrived. The warder opened the door, dropped the stapled pages, and a pen, on the floor, then withdrew. I scrambled to my feet and looked out the peephole but there was no one in the passage.

"Cecille!" I called. "Cecille Lagundi! I know you're there."

Nobody answered. Jay twitched in his sleep then lay still.

I picked up the stapled paper. Six pages, in English. A three-page statement in duplicate, each copy with my name typed in bold at the end and two blank spaces for me to sign. I sat down by the wall and read the damn thing.

It was my account, supposedly, of the twists and turns the Haplon deal had taken in New York. I read it once, then after some consideration, read it again. The blend of fact and fiction was seamless, I read it a third time before I could fully unravel the strands. When I'd done that, I sat down on the bare, cold concrete and thought it over. It took me a good few minutes to figure it out. When I did, I hung my head. Then I got up and went to the peephole. "Cecille?" I didn't raise my voice. "Cecille, I won't be signing this before I speak to you. So do you want to speak to me now, or do you want to wait?"

Then I waited. At last she came into my line of sight, wearing a different outfit than she'd had on in the garden. African-style again, but bright red, with a white shawl. Was it nighttime?

"I'm not going to speak to you through this goddamn door."

The warder opened the door at her signal, she came and stood in the open doorway. We faced each other across the cell. She glanced at Jay, curled in sleep on the floor, then back to me. I held up the statement.

"This isn't accurate."

"Oh?"

"It isn't meant to be accurate, is it?"

"You said you would sign it."

"Things like when you sat in my car and told me Greenbaum and Trevanian were cooking up a private side deal. You told me they were ripping you off." I flicked the statement. "Here it's the other way around, you're not telling me, I'm telling you. That's not how it happened."

"Sign it, then you can go."

"And the first time at the bank. According to this statement, Trevanian never showed up. How I remember it is, it was you who never showed up." She stared at my pointing finger. "You know what I think?"

"I don't care what you think, Mr. Rourke."

"I think you're stitching Trevanian up. I think you're making it look like he was the one screwing things up in New York. Like he was trying to hang on to the diamonds. That story you spun me about Greenbaum and Trevanian doing a private deal, that was bullshit. Just like this." I slapped the statement.

"Are you going to sign it?"

"There's only one reason I can figure you'd want to do all that. Maybe Trevanian wanted to hang on to the diamonds, but if he did, he wasn't the only one, was he, Cecille? You wanted those diamonds too. You personally."

She spoke to the warder over her shoulder, he stepped around her.

"Knocking me around isn't going to do it," I said. "Unless that's how you get your kicks, Cecille, you'll be wasting your time."

"You will get nothing."

I took a moment with that. "You think I want to be cut in? You honestly think I'm that stupid?"

"I think you want to get out of here."

"What I want is to know why I'm here in the first place. I've been shipped halfway around the world, then dropped into a Congolese jail cell, for chrissake. Now you're telling me to put my signature to a pack of goddamn lies."

Her eyelids drooped, her anger poorly concealed by the feigned show of boredom.

"This statement's for the Congolese government," I said. "That's how I read it. It's something for your father to show the President. You and your father have got the country's diamonds in a strongbox in New York. The Congolese government's lost them, and they've had to pay twelve million dollars to Haplon. When the guns stop firing, you're going to point the finger at Trevanian. He's your scapegoat. You'll say he took the diamonds. And this"—I flicked the statement—"this is the independent corroboration for your story." We looked at each other. Then she turned sharply on her heel. "Wait," I said, and she stopped and looked back.

I had hit the target. Maybe not the bull's-eye, but close enough to shake her, and pushing her further wasn't going to help my cause. I stooped and picked up the pen. I knew that if I signed it, she still might decide it was safer to have me executed on the arms importation charge than to let me go free. But if I didn't sign, I certainly wouldn't get out, and if I didn't get out, then Brad was on his own in Mbuji-Mayi.

I rested the statement on my knee, and signed.

CHAPTER 30

Jay groaned. I went over and crouched by him.

"You need water?"

He made a sound and I bent my head closer.

"Up," he said, and I put an arm around his shoulders and eased him up against the wall. He winced and clutched his chest.

"Any better?"

He sucked in air through clenched teeth. "Man," he said. "Oh, man."

"You've been sleeping."

"I been dyin'."

I looked at his eyes, they were clear. Then I shuffled around and sat beside him with my back to the wall. His head fell back, he closed his eyes.

"Feel like some mother run me down with his motherfuckin' truck." After a second he opened his eyes and looked at me. "They didn' do nothin' to you."

"I'm waiting my turn."

One corner of his mouth turned up, then he clutched my arm and squeezed it tight, his face suddenly bunched in pain. The air hissed through his teeth as he breathed. He moved, got himself into a position that didn't hurt so much, then let go of my arm. There were deep scars on his knuckles. Old scars. He saw that I'd seen them.

"You wonderin' about them Bibles?"

"No."

"Whatchoo doin' here, anyways?"

"I'm a geologist."

"Like mines, that shit?"

"Yeah."

"Smart," he said.

"You don't have to talk."

"Like you got somepin' better to do."

I told him I was thinking about his injured rib.

He put his hand inside his shirt, then winced. " 'S'okay. Not gettin' any worse." Perspiration trickled down his face and neck. He was in pain but holding it back, trying to distract himself by talking. That wasn't going to work for very long. "I ever get a hold'a that Johnny, man," he said. Johnny. The dead white kid with the severed arms and the AfricAid sweatshirt. I didn't say anything. "Got some mouth, the fuck. Talked us in here, now probly talked his ass out'a here already, an' gone."

I asked why he and Johnny had been arrested.

" 'Coz we was rubes, man. 'Coz Johnny keeps his brains in his butt an' his mouth."

When I asked if Johnny lived in Kinshasa, Jay made a face.

"Detroit. He ain't never seen this shithole till last week, same as me." Then Jay dropped a hand to his ribs and rocked forward. I offered to call the warder, but he rolled his eyes at me and shook his head. After a few seconds the pain seemed to ease, he rested back against the wall and let his breathing settle. After a minute, he spoke again. "I get back home, might just as well reenlist." At that, I gave him a sideways look, more than just a little curious now. He lifted his chin at the walls. "U.S. Army, man. Safer'n this fuckin' place."

I turned that over. "Your friend Johnny ex-Army too?"

"Corporal. Meant to have some fuckin' brains."

I asked how long they'd been out.

A year, Jay said.

A year. For most grunts who leave the Army, the first six months aren't usually too bad, everyone seems to cope short-term. But after a year they've generally split into three classes. Guys who are going to make it in civilian life, guys who are reenlisting, and guys who are just about ready to do something extremely stupid. Jay and his dead friend Johnny seemed to be straight out of class number three.

I said, "So now I am getting to wonder about those Bibles."

"You an' me both, man," he muttered.

"Who was Johnny working for? Some Christian aid agency?"

Jay snorted. "Tol' people he did."

"But he didn't."

Jay faced me. "What's it to you, motherfucker?"

Jailed in the Congo midcoup. Ex–U.S. Army grunt. I was pretty sure by then, but I decided I might just as well ask him anyway. "You a mercenary, Jay?"

He held my look a few seconds, but finally gave up and turned away.

"Jay?"

"Freelance security."

"Working for who?" He didn't answer, so I prompted him. "Trevanian?"

"You-all a geologist? Kiss my ass."

"Trevanian's men do security at our mines."

He looked at me again. "No shit," he said. When I shook my head, he spent a few seconds thinking things over. Then he said, "We just signed up and got flown out here an' stuck in a hotel. We been sittin' on our butts, waitin' till some brother come pick us up, tell us what to do. Hell. Maybe was your mine we was meant to be going to. Mbuji?"

"Mbuji-Mayi."

"Hey."

"That's not a mine, it's a town."

"It's big fuckin' trouble. This whole shitfight started out there."

My gut lurched. "You sure?"

"Sure I'm sure. Guy meant to pick us up, he couldn't make it. Too busy with the bust-up in Mbuji, that's what they tol' us. Sit tight. So we do. Nex' mornin' five crazy fuckers kick our door in, haul our asses down here. Johnny keeps tryin' to talk to them, like tryin' to be reasonable. Shit. Reasonable? I tol' him to shut his big fuckin' mouth. But man—talkin's like his thing." Jay paused. "Shit. Talk hisself out'a any damn thing. Talk me right into any damn thing too." Then he moved, not much, but the rib seemed to do something inside him. He cried out and pressed back against the wall.

"Stay still," I said, crouching beside him. But when I rose and turned toward the peephole, Jay clutched at my leg. I looked back down at him, his lips were pressed tight together, his eyes were wide in pain and desperation and he was shaking his head. He couldn't take another beating. I bent and prised his fingers off my pants. "I'll try to get us some food. Some more water."

Amazingly, I managed it. The warder seemed to be acting on new instructions from Lagundi. When I finally got him to the peephole, communicated what I wanted, he disappeared for fifteen minutes, then returned and unbolted the door. He pushed the door open and I stood up and he waved me to the rear of the cell. As I went back there, he ordered Jay to follow me. Jay tried to stand but couldn't. He slumped down groaning and clutched his ribs. Even the warder could see it wasn't an act. He came in and put a canteen on the floor, and a small plastic bucket, then withdrew, rebolting the door.

In the canteen, there was water. In the plastic bucket, several pieces of tropical fruit that had started to turn. Overripe mangoes, blackening bananas, and a few other things I could barely recognize, let alone name. I put the bucket between me and Jay and we went through the fruit, peeling it, scraping off the worst parts, and dividing the rest. Between mouthfuls, we swigged the water from the canteen.

Brad was somewhere out near the fighting in Mbuji-Mayi while I was stuck in a jail cell in Kinshasa, eating rotten fruit and waiting for Lagundi to decide what to do with me. I hadn't felt so physically helpless, so totally frustrated, for years, not since I was lying half-dead in some hovel in the Mogadishu backstreets, weaponless, watching the blood ooze from my stomach into my shirt and pants, and listening to the Somalis raining fire down on two trapped Rangers across the street. Neither one of them made it, but they probably saved my life. Now I chewed the pulpy mango and drank the brackish water and found my memories of Mogadishu turning to Dimitri. He'd seen the worst of the Mogadishu firefight, yet he'd gone through the whole thing unscathed. He'd gone through his Delta career the same way too, right up till he took the shot down in Colombia that shunted him out of Delta and into Hawkeye. Being trapped in a Congolese Internal Security jail cell was the kind of thing they trained you for in Delta—Dimitri's kind of action, not mine—it was something I'd never remotely expected to face. When I signed up for Hawkeye, I wanted simply to serve again. Instead, a trapdoor had suddenly opened beneath my feet and dropped me into a nightmare world I knew nothing about.

When we'd finished the fruit I shoved the bucket into the corner. Jay held out the canteen and shook it. A mouthful.

"Yours," I said, and he drank it straight down.

Then he dropped the canteen by his side. "Hey, whatchoo in here for anyway?"

"Same as you," I said, and when he grunted, I quickly elaborated. "For nothing. Nothing at all."

"Ain't that the truth."

Now that he wasn't pretending to be a Bible peddler, he didn't need to play the ignorant innocent abroad. I figured he might actually know something about the coup and the fighting outside. But when I asked him if he could remember anything from before he was arrested, any more about the fighting out in Mbuji-Mayi, he turned his head.

"Wasn' payin' it no mind. Johnny tol' me it was gonna be okay, couple a days keepin' our heads down in the hotel, we was gonna be picked up for sure. Me, I jus' chilled out, got some z's. You wanna know 'bout that strategy shit, you akse Johnny."

For a long time I stared at the floor between my feet. Internal Security had arrested two of Trevanian's new recruits and murdered one of them. The split between Lagundi and Trevanian had turned lethal, and I was caught right between them. Finally I got up and went over to the bucket in the corner and unzipped to take a leak. The door bolt clunked back. As I looked over my shoulder, the door flew open and three guards and the warder rushed in. I zipped up and turned just in time to take a rifle butt in the gut. I crashed back into the wall, then dropped to the floor, winded. I lay there, curled up, trying to breathe. One guard stood over me. I saw the warder and the two other guards beating Jay, and shouting. Jay screamed, raised a hand to ward off the blows, then one guard swung his boot into Jay's rib cage. There was a deep thud, a faint cracking sound, and Jay toppled onto his side, his face smacking hard against the floor. A moment later, blood came bubbling out of his mouth.

I tried to get up, tried to breathe, but I couldn't. They kept kicking Jay, driving their rifle butts into him. Then one blow caught his temple and the bone crunched. Jay's body went momentarily rigid, then his arms flopped, his face dropped onto the floor again, and his tongue lolled out of his blood-soaked mouth.

After a few moments they stopped hitting him. One guard grabbed Jay's lifeless arm. Finally I got air into my lungs, I pushed myself up, but the guard kicked me in the gut and I went straight down again. I rolled and covered myself as they dragged Jay's body from the cell. The door crashed closed and the bolt slammed.

When they were gone, I rolled onto my front. At last I got myself up onto my hands and knees. I'd seen men die, too many, but never like that. I'd never seen any creature on God's earth die like Jay. I crawled a few feet, braced one hand against the wall, then dropped my head and threw up hard.

I **hadn't had time to get myself properly together when I heard** the warder returning ten minutes later. I retreated to the rear of the cell and set my back against the wall. I wasn't ready to die. My son needed me. I had to see my wife. But if Lagundi had delivered the verdict against me, these guys would carry it out, I knew that now. I fixed my eyes on the door. I found myself praying beneath my breath, calling on God to watch over my wife and son, to deliver my soul.

The door finally opened, I crouched and braced myself. I saw the warder. Then the door opened a little farther, and there—there was Rita Durranti.

"Jesus Christ, Ned." I stared at her. The warder smiled, and if I could have gotten to him in that moment I would have killed him. Rita seemed to sense that. She stepped in and took hold of my arm. "You're out, Ned. You're getting out." She looked over her shoulder, and, pushing past the warder, Alex Channon stepped into view. He wasn't in uniform. He held a hand toward me, I was stunned.

"Alex?"

"Move," he told me with his usual quiet authority. "Or you won't be getting out, ever."

Rita led me out, then Alex placed a hand on my back and turned me down the passage. There the warder passed us on to an armed Congolese soldier who escorted us upstairs. I started telling Channon about Jay, the split between Trevanian and Congolese Internal Security, but Channon told me to shut my mouth. The large reception hall was empty, the soldiers and the prisoners I'd seen earlier had all gone. Alex and Rita kept me sandwiched between them, we followed the soldier to a desk where a lone Internal Security officer was waiting for us. He turned a big ledger around, then opened it to a blank page and made all three of us sign. The mindless bureaucracy of a madhouse. The formality completed, he insisted on shaking Channon's hand. After that, the soldier escorted us out through the forecourt and onto the street, where a Ford off-roader with diplomatic plates was parked. Another soldier stood guard over it. The body of Jay's friend Johnny had been removed from its place by the guardhouse. While Channon handed over a fistful of U.S. dollars to the two soldiers, Rita and I got in the back of the Ford. Then Channon got into the driver's seat.

"There's a gun in the side pocket," he told me, hitting the ignition. "It's loaded."

I took it out. I asked him who I should shoot.

"Anyone who tries to stop us." He reached beneath his jacket and took out his own pistol as we pulled away from Internal Security HQ. Then he placed it on the seat beside him and looked at me in the rearview mirror. "How are you feeling?"

"Alive."

He gave a tight smile. I turned, bewildered, to thank Rita.

"Thank Alex," she said. "If he hadn't shown up, I wouldn't have gotten you out. Are you hurt?"

Bruised, I told her. Nothing serious.

"Lucky man," murmured Channon.

I asked him what in the world he was doing in Kinshasa. "Shouldn't you be in Washington?"

"There's a U.S. aircraft carrier lying off the coast here. I flew out to join them, see if they could track down the *Sebastopol*. Now the carrier's taking evacuees. Americans and Europeans. Some UN people. Choppers have been flying out there from the embassy all day long. Everyone wants out."

I looked at Rita, then back to Channon. "Why'd you need to track the *Sebastopol*? The beacons—"

"The transmitters never worked," he said. "Complete fucking disaster. They gave out before you left the Hudson."

"So where's the Haplon materiel?" I asked. Channon was silent, he stared straight ahead. "We haven't lost it," I said.

"We never had it." He looked pained. "After the *Sebastopol* sailed, we weren't picking up any signals. It took me three days to convince the Navy we needed some help. Best they could do was get me to a carrier in the area, monitor the sea traffic." He gestured around the eerily empty streets. "Then this goddamn coup."

"Jesus Christ."

"I'm trying to find the stuff."

"We've just shipped six containers of U.S. equipment into a civil war."

His voice rose. "I'm not over the moon about it myself, Ned. All right?"

I slumped back in my seat. I could not believe it. As I was digesting the awful news, I became aware of the burned-out buildings we were passing, and the bodies lying in the street. I turned to Rita.

"Where's Brad? Did you find him, did you get him out?"

"I couldn't trace him. His name's not on any of the evacuee lists."

A cold chill ran up my spine, but I forced the fear down. There was nothing I could do about Brad just then.

"I saw Cecille Lagundi in the jail. You'll never guess what her father does for a living."

"He's the Minister for Police," said Channon, and I looked at him in the rearview mirror. "Our ambassador told me," he explained ruefully. Apparently Channon had been present when the ambassador contacted Cecille's father with a warning to keep the Congolese police clear of the embassy. Marines from the carrier had flown into Kinshasa and laid down a secure perimeter around the embassy. If the Congolese police crossed the line they were liable to be shot. "Lagundi," Channon finished. "I nearly died when I heard the name."

"Oh, this is great." I held my forehead. "Our ambassador knows the guy?"

"They're not drinking buddies."

"No one mentioned that to us back in New York. You were chasing background on Cecille for two weeks. Our spooks didn't match the names?"

"Evidently not."

"Oh, for chrissakes."

"Get down!" he shouted, then he jerked on the wheel. I was flung sideways into Rita, then there was a roar of automatic gunfire, we hunkered down in the seat. Channon threw the vehicle left then right. There was a bang and a spray of shattered glass, Channon turned sharp left and accelerated, there was a loud popping sound, then the gunfire faded behind us.

"Rita?" said Channon. She lifted her head off the seat and brushed the glass from her hair. "You hit?"

"No," she said.

"Ned?"

"I'm fine." I sat up, shaking off the shattered glass.

The rear window and the one to my left had imploded. Up front, Channon raised his hand and fingered two bullet holes that had appeared in the roof about eighteen inches from his head. "Twelve-year-old with a damn AK47."

I asked him if he knew where we were going.

"Embassy." He dropped his hand. "I want you two on the next bird out."

Every shop front we passed now was smashed, some were still burning, smoke billowing upward, grim markers over the destruction. There were bodies too, lying by the buildings, and some farther out in the street. When a flock of crows flapped into the air then resettled on a body as we passed, nobody talked for a while. Then Channon pointed over to the east. A chopper rising into the sky just a mile away. Channon picked up the radio handset.

"Oscar five nine, Oscar five nine, this is Charlie six, do you copy me, over?"

"We read you, Charlie six."

"I'm approaching the ex–fill site from the south. One vehicle. You should have visual."

"Negative, Charlie six." We drove for another minute, then

turned a corner. The radio crackled into life. "Okay, Charlie six, we've got you. Come on in."

Channon went straight up the long avenue and past a nest of sandbags. A Marine darted out, I turned and watched him drag a coil of razor wire across the road behind us.

The park in front of the embassy was really just an open space of bare earth, a few token eucalyptus were planted around the edges for shade. Channon parked beneath one of the trees and we got out. There must have been two hundred people there, but everything seemed remarkably calm. The Marines were running the evacuation like clockwork.

The evacuees had been formed into chalks, lines of around twenty people apiece, they were all waiting their turn to be ferried out. Not just men, there were women too, and some children. Now that they'd made it inside the protective line of razor wire and into the care of the Marines, you could read the relief on their faces.

Channon took us across to the Marine captain organizing the chalks. The captain didn't hesitate when Channon requested our immediate departure. He simply deleted two people from his list, then asked us our names. He entered them, and pointed us to the rear end of the chalk. "Stand back there. When the helicopter lands, wait. When I call you forward, proceed in an orderly fashion, single file, to the open door. You may be assisted aboard." He nodded to Channon, then walked away.

"Just do like he says," Channon told us, leading us to the first chalk. "I have to see the ambassador, I'll be out to the ship later."

"What about Brad?"

Channon backed away. "Tell them on the carrier. My bet is, he's out there waiting for you." He raised his hand, half salute, half wave, then he turned and jogged across to the embassy. I watched until he'd entered through the gates.

"Hey," said Rita when I left the chalk. When I didn't answer, she came after me. "We'll lose our places."

I found the Marine captain giving instructions to his men. I asked him if he had access to the names of everyone who'd already been evacuated. He did.

"B. Rourke," I said, and I spelled it for him. "Can you try that for me?" He entered the name into his organizer. It drew a blank. "Try Barchevsky," I said. He tried it, but that drew a blank too. I explained that they'd come from another part of the country. "Mbuji-Mayi. The diamond area. Geologists. Has anyone come through from there?"

"Miners?"

"Yeah, miners. Anyone."

"There was a bunch of miners went through first thing, but they're all in here." He tapped his organizer. Then he pointed. "Along on chalk four, there's some more. But they're all in here too."

The buzz of talk all around suddenly grew, people craned back, some of them pointing off to the west. I looked that way and saw a small black dot in the sky. A chopper. The Marine captain ordered Rita and me back to our chalk, and we went. Rita stopped at the chalk, but I kept going.

She skipped after me. "Hey, this is us." She pointed to the chopper. "That's our lift out."

I passed the rear of chalk three and saw the miners in chalk four immediately. Half a dozen unshaven guys in their thirties, their faces baked brown by the sun. I went straight up to them.

"Anyone here just come from Mbuji-Mayi?"

Three of them had.

"The Dujanka mine?"

None of them.

"I'm looking for a Bradley Rourke. He's a geologist."

Nobody knew the name.

"He was working for Ivan Barchevsky."

There was silence. My heart sank. Then one of the three from Mbuji-Mayi said, "Why you looking for this guy Rourke?"

"He's my son."

The miner looked at me, thinking it over. Then he said, "I was working on one of Barchevsky's mines. He shut them all down. We flew back in with him this morning." When I asked if he knew whether Barchevsky had been evacuated, he shrugged. "I guess. Last I saw him was at the airport." He gestured vaguely. "He had a car waiting. The rest of us piled in a bus."

"Did anyone go with him?"

He shrugged again. He didn't know. Maybe, he said.

"A guy in his early twenties. Wiry. Looked a little like me."

He turned his head, apologetic. He really hadn't noticed.

"Ned," said Rita, tugging my sleeve, looking up at the nearing chopper.

Then the miner volunteered, "I think Barchevsky was going to his office first. Maybe he didn't make it here."

"His office."

"He's got an apartment there." He pulled out his wallet and gave me Barchevsky's business card. He suggested I try calling.

Then someone shouted, "You two!" and everyone turned. The Marine captain was pointing at Rita and me. "Get back in your chalk. You miss this bird, you go to the end of the line."

Rita grabbed my arm, she hauled me around behind chalks three and two. The chopper was close enough to hear now. As it neared, flares shot out to either side of it, decoys for any ground-based missiles. I turned Barchevsky's business card through my fingers. "When we get to that damned carrier," Rita said, watching the chopper, "I swear I'm going to get down on my knees and kiss the deck."

"I'm staying here."

She faced me. She shook her head. "Don't be crazy. You heard Channon. Brad's probably out there already."

"His name's not on the list."

"So they've made a mistake."

"If his name's not on the Marine list, he hasn't made it out."

"There's nothing you can do about that."

I looked at the embassy gates. I squinted as the descending chopper stirred up a swirling dust cloud.

"You're really not coming," Rita said, raising her voice over the chopper engines.

"Chalk one!" bellowed the Marine captain over a megaphone.

"I'll get the next one."

"I can stay," she shouted.

I shook my head, grabbed her arm, and put my mouth to her ear. "Go! Go on!" The others in the chalk were moving forward, I pushed Rita firmly after them. She looked back over her shoulder and I waved her on, then I turned and headed for the embassy. There were no guards on the gates. I guess with the Marine perimeter stretching around the block, they thought the place was already secure. A lone

Marine was posted at the door of the building. I told him I needed to see Channon, but when he discovered I had no ID he pointed me back to the park.

"Look, just tell him I'm here, okay? Rourke. Ned Rourke."

He finally went to pass the message. When I turned and looked across the park, chalk one was climbing aboard the chopper. Rita was the last in. The doors closed behind her, then the captain gave the pilot the thumbs-up, and the chopper lifted, tilting into the air.

"Mister." A white woman wearing horn-rimmed glasses leaned out the plate-glass door. "Can you give me a hand in here? I need some furniture shoved, it's heavy."

The chopper passed directly overhead and I followed the woman inside.

The front desk had been abandoned. She led me a short way down the hall, and I saw people, local and American, scooting in and out of offices, their arms piled high with paperwork and files. There was some shouting too, an atmosphere of urgency and re-strained hysteria. Turning in to her office, the woman pointed to the three filing cabinets in the corner. She explained that she'd cleared out the first two, now she needed to get to the one at the rear. I went and shoved the front cabinets out of her way, it didn't take me a minute. She opened the third cabinet, asking me if I could take some files along to the shredder. Before I could reply, she was piling the files on my arms. When I was loaded, she nodded me to the door, and I didn't linger, I went out and found someone else loaded with paperwork, then followed him down the hall. The hall passed right through the embassy, opening onto an enclosed porch at the rear. A shredding machine had been set up there. Through the windows out back I could see a U.S. government–issue incinerator, gas-fed, being loaded with shredded paper. The paperwork and files were piled high around the shredder, the operation had some way to go. I dumped my files on the heap, then slipped past a couple of locals in white shirtsleeves and went up the back stairs.

Locating the evacuation operations room wasn't difficult. Three doors along, phones were pealing and voices were being raised. I went in and found a large African American lady at the front desk, she was clearly the one running the room. A map of the country was on the wall to her left. On her right, a map of Kinshasa. Behind her, a half dozen or more staffers were manning the phones, making and taking calls, jotting notes, and yelling at each other. I went up to the front desk. I told the woman I was looking for two U.S. citizens, Brad Rourke and Ivan Barchevsky. She leaned back and shouted the names to her colleagues behind. They consulted their lists. The names weren't there.

"Nope," she said, looking up. "Friends?"

"One's my son."

She pursed her lips in sympathy. "Lotta people lyin' low. Could be he's doin' that," she offered. "We've got embassy people we still ain't heard from. There's different ones callin' in or showin' up all the time."

I asked if I could use her phone. She pushed it across the desk to me and I took out Barchevsky's card and dialed his office. The line was dead. Then I dialed his apartment. That was dead too.

"Where is this place?" she said, and I read her the address on the card. She frowned and rose from her desk and went to the map of Kinshasa. She placed a plump finger on the major arterial road into the city from the east. "Out near the airport," she declared. "We ain't heard from anyone out there for a while." I saw her exchange a glance with one of her colleagues. I raised a brow. "There was some heavy fightin' out that way earlier," she told me finally. "All those lines are down."

I looked at the map. The arterial road came almost all the way to the embassy, which was marked in green. Barchevsky's office, the place she'd pointed to on the map, was on a street corner just past a bridge. I asked her how far it was. Five or six miles, she said.

"You wouldn't have a spare map?" I said. She regarded me curiously. "A small one. Like a street map of the city."

"You plannin' a tour?"

"Not exactly."

"You a fool."

"I'm a father."

"Hmph," she said, and went back to her desk and sat down. She moved some paper around the desk.

"He's my only child."

"You want a map."

"Yes."

"An' that's all."

I nodded, aware that she was keeping her voice down now so that her colleagues couldn't overhear. Finally she puffed out her cheeks and blew. She rummaged in her desk drawer, took out a pocket guide to the city, and slid it across her desk. I picked it up.

"You a fool," she said again, and I nodded and walked out the door.

Out the door, and almost straight into Channon. He was standing just along the hall with a dapper, silver-haired guy in a suit. They had their backs to me, their heads together, conferring over some papers. I turned sharp left and went down the stairs to the rear porch. I hoisted a trash can full of shredded paper onto my shoulder and carried it outside to the incinerator and dropped it by the other trash cans and kept walking. A minute later, I was out front in the park. I walked on through the chalks of evacuees like I knew what I was doing, like I might be on embassy business, and no one stopped me. Channon's Ford was still parked under the eucalyptus. I got in and flipped down the visor and the keys fell in my lap.

I checked the map, then I drove over to the razor-wire barrier on the eastern perimeter. A young Marine emerged from the machine-gun nest to see where I thought I was headed.

"Airport." I sliced my hand purposefully forward.

"You got orders?"

"I'm with the embassy."

"You still gotta have orders, sir."

"Channon wants me out there." The name didn't register. I sensed the kid wavering, wondering if the easiest thing might be to turn me back. "Channon," I said forcefully. "Charlie six. Now do I get through the goddamn wire, or do I go get your captain?"

He thought about it a second, then decided he really didn't need the hassle. He pulled back the razor wire, waved me brusquely through, and I drove on past him, out into the city.

CHAPTER 32

I **drove due east for half a mile, one eye on my map, then I** turned south. I hit the arterial road almost immediately, then turned east again and stepped on the gas. After a few hundred yards I had to back off fast, two burned-out trucks lay abandoned in the middle of the road. I slowed to a crawl, got my pistol ready, and eased my way between the trucks, eyes peeled. I was almost through when someone darted out from behind the second truck. I swung my pistol, pointed it out my side window, my finger on the trigger. Then I saw. It was a woman. She had a basket resting on her hip, it was piled high with blackened bananas she'd scavenged from one of the abandoned trucks. She stopped when she saw the pistol leveled at her. We looked at each other. Then she simply raised the basket onto her head and turned her back on me and walked away.

Sweat trickled down my neck. I dropped the pistol on the seat beside me, and drove.

A few miles up ahead, there was a thick wall of black smoke, it wasn't like the other plumes rising from the burned-out shops in the city. I checked the map again. Heavy fighting, that's what the embassy woman had said. I figured the dense smoke was coming from the airport. Barchevsky's office was well short of there, maybe a mile and a half.

After another minute I was nearing the wall of smoke and still hadn't crossed the bridge. Off in the side streets there was sporadic gunfire, but the only guys with guns I saw were standing guard by a pile of looted TVs. They gave me the eye but didn't shoot, maybe they thought I'd shoot back and damage their merchandise. Finally I saw the bridge. I peered into the smoky haze beyond it, searching for Barchevsky's building, then a pothole appeared in front of me and I swerved too late and hit it hard.

There was an explosion, the Ford tipped violently left, balanced on two wheels for a few yards, then smashed down on its side. I held tight to the wheel, pressing my ass against the door as the vehicle slewed along the road on its side, metal screaming, the scoured tarmac skimming past my shoulder. It was over too fast to think. The Ford juddered to a stop and I got myself upright. Claymore, I thought. In the pothole, someone had planted a goddamn mine.

I found the pistol down by my feet, used the butt to smash a hole through the shattered windshield, then I kicked out the glass and scrambled through. I crouched a moment, got myself reoriented. I was fifty yards short of the bridge. There was a three-story building on a street corner on the far side. Barchevsky's. I went around to the exposed underside of the Ford. The front right wheel had taken the mine's full blast, the tire was shredded and the wheel was twisted at an angle to the axle.

I knew I couldn't hang around. I turned and jogged toward the bridge.

It was a humpbacked thing, purely functional, spanning a river that was about twenty yards wide. From the high midpoint of the bridge, I could see out to the airport, the control tower and the hangars, and nearer than that, a refinery with thick black smoke pouring from one of its four huge storage tanks. As I jogged down the other side of the bridge, I noticed a body lying down by the water. It was a Congolese soldier in battle gear, he must have been taking cover when he was hit. I went down there, scrambled down the bank, and picked up his AK47 and a few magazines of ammo. There was shooting from the far side of the bridge, I clambered up the bank fast and took cover by a small pumping station.

They weren't shooting at me. There was some shouting, then I saw six men come wandering up the road toward the wrecked Ford, they took shots at it as they neared. They spread out, half circled it, then approached cautiously. Maybe they were hoping to find themselves a prisoner, someone they could rob and then shoot. When they found nobody inside the cab, one of them crawled in and ripped out the cassette player. A couple of kids, maybe eight or nine years old, arrived on the scene, hefting jerry cans. The kids siphoned the gas out of the tank while the men stood around, smoking.

If I made a dash for the rear of Barchevsky's building and they saw me, I was finished. It was their territory, not mine, and there'd be plenty more to arrive if any real shooting started. I'd seen that a dozen times in Mogadishu. We'd drop a platoon into an empty street, and next thing, the guys with guns would suddenly swarm.

So I stayed by the pumping station and waited. It was late afternoon, and hot, the cloud of smoke from the refinery hung like a stifling blanket over everything. I waited a long time. A soldier's labor, that's what Channon used to call it. Waiting. Sitting on your butt for hours, sometimes days, before you got the order to move. This time it wasn't so bad. The kids finally got their jerry cans full, then the men torched the Ford, and they all wandered back west.

I checked the ammo in my pockets, and the pistol in the waistband at my back. Then I picked up the Kalashnikov, poked my head out, and rechecked. No one. I got up and ran, sprinting across the potholed road and into the colonnaded arcade of the building. It hadn't been torched but it was badly shot up, there was broken glass everywhere. The concrete facade was pitted with holes the size of fists where bullets had come spraying in from the street.

There were nameplates by the main entrance, the ground floor was occupied by an airline company, and the floor above was Barchevsky Mining. The floor above that was designated simply PRIVATE.

I went into the lobby. There was more glass, and what looked like a dried slick of blood on the floor. As I crossed to the stairs, I stepped past the open doorway of the airline office, and a zip of hot air and a concussive pop flicked past my right ear. I spun around and dropped against the wall. Someone had almost killed me. I waited for the next shot, but when nothing came, I moved, creeping along the wall to the rear of the lobby. Another door back there led into the airline office, where the shot had come from. The door was ajar. I crouched, then carefully, quickly, put my head around the corner, snatched a look, then withdrew.

It was a girl. Some Congolese kid of seventeen or eighteen, dressed like an office worker, green skirt and white blouse. She was holding a pistol in both hands, aiming at the first door. I snatched another look. Not a rebel or a soldier, just a kid, maybe she worked in the place, I couldn't just shoot her. But I couldn't let her shoot me either. I pressed my back against the wall.

"You speak English?"

Two shots came—bap, bap—hitting the wall inside. Then a third shot splintered the door beside me. I fired a short burst from the Kalashnikov into the rear wall of the lobby. Silence followed.

"I'm going to count to three," I called, "—*un, deux, trois*—and then I'm coming in there." She didn't answer. I fired another burst into the rear wall, then waited again. More silence. *"Un!"* I shouted. *"Deux!"*

She ran. I heard movement and snatched a glimpse around the door. She bounced around a couple of desks, then exited through a side doorway out into the street. When I crossed the big open-plan office and looked out, she was gone.

Then I saw movement on the far side of the bridge. The gang that had torched the Ford were returning, stalking now, their weapons raised. They must have heard the shots, but they hadn't seen the girl, they seemed to be checking out the bridge.

I retreated across the office to the lobby, pointed the Kalashnikov up the stairwell, and climbed warily. Files lay scattered on the landing, paperwork spilling out everywhere. There were more bullet holes in the landing wall. I went on up to where a door with the Barchevsky Mining nameplate hung askew, on one hinge. I listened. There was no sound from inside, so I darted a look around the door, then withdrew.

The place had been ransacked. PC monitors smashed, filing cabinets tipped over and trashed, windows broken. No one in there.

I edged past the hanging door. It was a big space, like the airline office downstairs, but it had once been divided into sections by a series of high plywood screens. A few of the screens remained standing, but most lay toppled and broken across the desks and on the floor. Up on the wall, geological maps had been torn and left hanging. Bullet holes peppered the ceiling.

I picked my way through the wreckage, cautiously.

Toward the rear of the office there was a door marked PRIVATE, and beside it an intercom that was smashed and left dangling from wires in the wall. The door lock had been shot up, but when I put my shoulder to the door and pushed hard, the lock held firm. I went across to the radio set on the table nearby. It was a big set, they must have used it to keep contact with the mines, but it was wrecked, pieces of metal and electronics hanging out from all sides. Then I saw a list taped to the table. It was a list of mines, and beside each name a frequency and a scheduled contact time. Dujanka was on the list. I tore the list off the table and shoved it in my pocket. I turned and headed for the stairs, and one of the divider screens moved beneath my feet. I jumped off it.

When I looked down, my heart stopped.

There was a body lying facedown beneath me. The upper torso, the arms and the head, were hidden under the screen, but the twisted legs in denim jeans, and the large white sneakers, were visible beneath the scattered papers.

Denim jeans, white sneakers.

Please God, I thought, no.

Crouching, I lifted the screen. It slid off the body, and there was blood everywhere, congealed and dark, I could hardly breathe. I turned my head away, but my eyes stayed on the body. I took hold of the shoulder and rolled it, then I stood straight up and swallowed air.

Barchevsky. He'd taken shots in the gut and throat, his beard was stained crimson, and his face was gray. He was dead. Shock. Relief. I stood there, breathing, then finally I dragged my eyes off him and picked my way back through the wreckage, checking now beneath the other toppled screens. I didn't find anything. When I got out to the stairs, I went up, careful and slow.

The door to Barchevsky's apartment was open. I listened, heard nothing, then went in. The place was trashed. A sofa and two arm-chairs had been upended, books were scattered across the living room floor. Stepping around the devastation, I looked in at the kitchen. Broken crockery. Open cupboards, and a refrigerator lying on its back on the floor. There were two bedrooms farther along, the mattresses in both rooms were slashed and tipped off the beds. Clothes lay everywhere. In the bathroom, the shards of a broken mirror had fallen on the tiles and into the bath. The busted sink hissed quietly.

Returning to the living room, I looked through the last open door. It was an internal staircase leading down to Barchevsky's of-fice. There were pieces blasted out of the concrete stairs and the floor below, as if someone had opened fire from where I was stand-ing. I withdrew my head, turned and faced the apartment.

Barchevsky was dead. He was dead, and Brad might be any-where, and I was stranded on foot, miles from the safety of the embassy and the Marines. A nightmare tactics lesson from West Point. Okay, Rourke. What now?

Then I heard a sound on the internal staircase. I didn't move my feet, I simply let my shoulders fall back against the wall, then froze. The sink hissed. Half a minute went by. When no other sound came, I wondered if I'd imagined it the first time, but then I did hear an-other sound, one I hadn't imagined. A click. Down on the internal staircase, someone had just cocked a gun.

I raised my left hand. With my right I cradled the AK47 across my stomach, the barrel sighted on the doorway. Then male voices came up from the lobby, African voices. The armed gang had ar-rived. I blinked the sweat out of my eyes. My heart pounded hard and high in my chest. Someone was definitely coming up the internal staircase, I heard tentative footsteps.

Down in the lobby, glass smashed and voices rose in anger, like the gang were arguing over some trophy.

The footsteps on the staircase quickened. I crouched and put down the Kalashnikov. I slipped my pistol from my belt. With the gang right there, I did not want to shoot.

Then a pair of legs suddenly appeared, I swung my left arm, hit the knees, and the legs buckled. A gun came up, I hit the hand with my pistol, the hand opened, the gun flew clear, and I leaped on the fallen body, grabbed a handful of hair, and pressed my pistol barrel against the white neck.

I bent and whispered, "Speak and you're dead."

The head turned, the terrified eyes rolled. Fiona. My wife.

CHAPTER 33

Fiona's mouth opened, I covered it with my left hand. "Don't speak." Her eyes were wide-open in fear. "Are you hurt?" She shook her head. "If they hear us downstairs, we're dead. You understand?" After a second she nodded, and I eased my hand off her mouth. We stared at each other. Then she wriggled, tried to get up, she elbowed me in the thigh. I got off her, and she sat up and rubbed her right hand. I went and got the gun that I'd knocked out of her hand and gave it back to her. I picked up the AK47.

She whispered, "What in the name of Christ—"

I raised a hand to quiet her. Then I nodded toward the internal staircase. "Is there somewhere safe we can hide down there?"

"No."

"Any way out?"

She told me there was a fire escape outside the window of the main bedroom.

"Okay, we'll wait in there. Anyone comes up, we're out."

"I think Ivan's hiding down in the office. He was radioing Dujanka, talking to Brad, when the shooting started."

"Brad's still at the mine?"

She nodded. Bad news. Extremely bad. I turned for the bedroom, but Fiona grabbed my arm. "What about Ivan?" she whispered.

"He'll have to find his own way."

"We can't just leave him."

"Barchevsky's dead."

Fiona looked at me. Then I heard the gang start moving up the main stairs, they shouted to each other as they came on up, and I hauled Fiona after me into the main bedroom, crossed to the window, and checked the fire escape outside. It was a rusty iron staircase bolted to the exterior wall. Across the bridge, the torched Ford was now a charred and smoldering heap. Guys with guns and RPG-7s, rocket-propelled grenade launchers, were wandering past the Ford and taking up positions by the bridge. I drew my head in quickly, swearing beneath my breath.

"There were a lot of soldiers at the airport," Fiona volunteered. She was looking right through me, dazed. "Some white soldiers too."

Congolese government troops, and Brits from Trevanian's private military company. They were probably using the airport as an operational base. If we could get ourselves out there, we'd be safe. I asked her if Barchevsky had a car. She took some keys from her pocket, then crossed to the rear window and pointed down to a garage, a concrete shell with steel security doors that remained shut and intact. Suddenly there were noises right below our feet. The gang had entered Barchevsky's office.

I put my mouth to her ear. "Okay," I whispered. "We're leaving." I guided her back to the fire escape window. I pointed out to her the armed men on the bridge. "They might not see us, but even if they do, whatever you hear or see, just keep going down. Don't stop for anything. Straight down, then around to the garage. Back there you'll be out of their line of fire. Anyone around there shoots at you, shoot back. Any questions?"

She turned from the window to the door. "My passport."

"Forget it." I told her to check the keys, make sure she had the right ones. She checked. Her eyes glistened.

"Are you sure?" she said. "About Ivan?"

When I nodded, her hand played over her mouth. She stifled a sound in her throat. I took her by the shoulders and she looked up at me. I kissed her forehead, then turned her toward the window. "I'll be right behind you." I helped her out onto the fire escape. "Straight down," I whispered, but when I let her go, she went rigid. "Go!" I whispered, my heart in my mouth. She gave me a startled look, then turned and moved like a cat across the rusted plate and on down the steps, and I went out after her.

We were halfway down before the guys on the bridge saw us. They started shouting, but Fiona kept moving and I stayed close on her tail. We were almost down before they got off their first shot. Fiona ducked and hit the ground running. I leaped off the bottom step and went after her, and the bullets smacked into the wall high above me, and we were around the back and out of sight before they could adjust their fire.

While Fiona opened the garage, I trained the Kalashnikov on the upper floors of Barchevsky's building. The garage doors clattered open, Fiona went in, and right then a face appeared in the rear window of Barchevsky's bedroom. He saw us, I fired a quick burst, and he ducked as the shots sprayed up the wall.

"Let's go!" I shouted.

The engine kicked into life, revved high, and a battered Jeep shot out of the garage. It slowed beside me, I fired another burst up at the window, then I clambered into the Jeep, and Fiona jammed her foot on the accelerator. We swerved out onto the street and turned south for a block, speeding away from Barchevsky's building, then east. Behind us, the gunfire died away.

"Where now?" Fiona gripped the wheel tight.

"Airport. Go another couple of blocks before you turn back onto the main drag."

"Why?"

"Because I say so."

She threw me a scorching look.

"Those guys back on the bridge have got RPGs," I told her. "If we get back on the main drag too early, we'll be in range." My eyes swept the buildings up front for any sign of men with guns, and the potholed tarmac for any sign of land mines. "Are you okay?"

"No!" she shouted.

Ahead, a bus moved slowly out from a side street, I glimpsed a man with guns taking cover behind it.

"Left!" I yelled, and when she didn't react, I shouted, "Left!" again and grabbed the wheel and swung left just as the guy stepped out from behind the bus and fired. Bullets fizzed through the air and smacked harmlessly into a nearby building.

"Oh, Jesus," she said. "Oh, Christ."

"Go right at the T."

She swung the Jeep around the corner. We were on the main drag now, the airport road, and I got up, braced my knee on the seat, and looked back toward the bridge.

"Are we clear?" she called up.

We weren't. Way back on the bridge, a guy with an RPG on his shoulder had seen us. He went down on one knee.

"Keep going!" The smoke from the refinery fire was thickening around us. I clutched Fiona's shoulder. "Faster!"

She accelerated. "I can't see."

The guy with the RPG took aim.

"Faster, for chrissake!"

"I'm doing sixty, blind!"

He fired. There was a rush of air, and the shell missed us, just to the right. A moment later there was an explosion somewhere way up ahead in the smoke.

"Jesus Christ," Fiona said, shaken.

The bridge behind us disappeared behind the veil of black smoke, I dropped into my seat and told Fiona to slow down. She slowed the Jeep immediately, her hands trembling on the wheel, and we cruised up the center of the road, guided by the broken white lines. For a minute she was silent, then she said, "What in hell are you doing here?"

"Me?"

"You just disappeared."

I peered ahead through the thinning smoke. I patted the air. "Slow down."

The control tower came into view, then the hangars. We were passing through no-man's-land, then a half mile ahead I saw a tank, part of the perimeter the Congolese army had established around the airport. I reached into the backseat and grabbed a pair of white overalls lying there, then I opened my window and flapped the overalls up and down. The AK47 was down by my feet, out of sight.

"Slower," I said, and Fiona eased right back off the gas and we crawled up the road and finally stopped ten yards short of the tank. A Centurion. British army surplus.

I opened my door and swung out, standing on the footboard. The tank's cannon swiveled fractionally right, but the turret stayed shut.

"We're Americans."

"Is that a recommendation around here?" Fiona wondered aloud.

"We got caught in town. There's just the two of us, we'd like to come in if we can."

There was no response.

"Tell them we've been shot at," said Fiona, but before I could say anything, a Congolese soldier appeared from the rear of the tank. He walked once around the Jeep, then came closer and looked in. He saw the Kalashnikov at my feet and reached in and took it, then he went around to the back and climbed in. When he signaled for Fiona to drive on, she glanced at me. I nodded, and she eased the Jeep around the tank. We crawled slowly up the road, passing several sandbagged machine-gun nests before we finally entered through the airport gates.

There were two fighter jets parked out on the runway, and a chopper on the helipad and another one nearer the terminal. Old tanks of various European makes were positioned every few hundred yards around the airport perimeter. Sandbagged machine-gun nests and mortar emplacements had been set up between the tanks. Soldiers came and went from the terminal, but there was a real sense of order to the place, it wasn't anything like the Internal Security HQ. This was a fully functioning and purposeful outfit.

We parked by the dozen other civilian vehicles near the first hangar. Our escort pointed to the white civilians sitting in the shade of the hangar and indicated that we should join them. Then he got out and crossed to the terminal. A white guy in uniform came out toward him.

Fiona rested her forearms on the steering wheel, her head slumped on her arms. I got out and watched our escort talking with the white soldier, then I went around and opened Fiona's door. I remarked that we seemed to have gotten through the worst, that I thought we'd be safe now.

"Safe?" She turned on me. "It's a goddamn war. And what about Brad? How safe is he?" She got out, pushing past me, and slammed the door. She stepped away from me, then turned back. "Why didn't you tell me you were coming here? You just disappeared, not even a note."

"I called as soon as I got the chance."

"Were you with that Durranti woman?"

"Oh, come on."

"You were, weren't you." When I hesitated, her look turned icy. "I could kill you, Ned. I could damn well kill you."

"Don't you want to listen to me?"

The white soldier walked toward us, Fiona flung up a hand and stalked away from me toward the hangar. I was debating with myself whether to go after her when the white soldier called out to me, asking if I was the one who'd just come in. He was a Brit. Pink-faced and clean shaven. I nodded.

"We heard some heavy ordnance out there." He pointed west, the way we'd come.

I told him about the gang on the bridge. When I mentioned the RPG-7s, he raised a brow skeptically.

"I'm ex–U.S. Army," I said. "They were RPGs."

He reconsidered me a moment, then told me to accompany him to the terminal. He said he thought the colonel would probably want to see me. I glanced over my shoulder, but Fiona had already disappeared into the hangar, so I went with the Brit. As we neared the terminal entrance, I slowed, my head swiveling toward the service block. Beside the service block, six containers sat in a line. I'd seen them loaded, and I'd seen them shipped, there was no mistaking them. The Haplon six. Their doors hung open, the containers were empty.

My face burned. I'd chaperoned tons of materiel from New York into a war zone, and now it was out on the field of battle, destroying lives. People were being killed because we had screwed up.

"In here," said the Brit, guiding me into the terminal.

Inside, a large communications suite had been set up on the

mezzanine, looking out over the runway. A white guy in fatigues and several Congolese soldiers were manning the radios. Other Congolese soldiers were taking scribbled messages from the radiomen and delivering them upstairs.

The Brit took me on up past the radios to the next level, where another big area of floor space overlooked the runway. Here a giant map of the Congo was spread out on a huge central table. Smaller detailed maps were pinned to the wall. Older Congolese soldiers were moving between the maps, receiving messages from downstairs, and talking. There were colored ribbons on every pocket, and on every shoulder, epaulettes braided in silver and gold. It was clearly a command center. The temporary war room of the Congolese government. A couple of these officers glanced at me, then immediately returned to poring over the maps.

My Brit escort led me to a desk where an epauletted colonel had his back to us, he was talking into a phone. My escort stepped around the desk, caught the colonel's eye, then tossed his head in my direction. The colonel swiveled in his chair.

Trevanian. We stared at each other a moment, then he hung up the phone.

CHAPTER 34

Colonel?" I said.

"Honorary. And don't get clever." Trevanian led me along the hall, away from the war room. He asked me what I could tell him about what I'd seen in town.

"It's not my fight," I told him.

"Then why'm I wasting my time talking to you?"

"I guess because you'd like to know if I noticed the Haplon containers you've got parked outside."

We stopped by a drinks dispenser, he inserted some coins and got himself a Coke. He inserted some more coins, then, finger poised over the buttons, he asked me what I wanted.

"I want to know what's happening in Mbuji-Mayi."

He glanced at me. "Thought it wasn't your fight."

"My son's out there."

"Bullshit."

"He's a geologist at one of the diamond mines. Dujanka."

Trevanian cocked his head, still not sure. Then he hit the dispenser button, another can of Coke rolled out and he handed it to me. He popped his own can, took a swig, then led me across to the room he'd made his office. A linoleum floor, a desk, and a phone. There was another map of the Congo on the wall, he went over and put his finger on Mbuji-Mayi. After studying the area a second, his finger moved. "Dujanka," he said, his eyebrows rising. I went over and looked at the name on the map. It lay southeast of Mbuji-Mayi. Trevanian dropped into his chair, rocking as he swigged at his Coke. "The miners out that way were evacuated."

"My son didn't get out."

"You sound like you think I can do something about that."

"Can you?"

"Hard to say. Your friend from U.S. Customs still with you?" When I told him Rita had been flown out to the carrier, he nodded. "If she wants to make an issue of anything," he said, "there's a ton of paperwork says the Haplon containers got shipped to Nigeria."

"We saw them unloaded from the *Sebastopol*."

"So? You saw six containers unloaded."

I jerked my thumb over my shoulder. "The same six containers you've got outside."

"A lawyer might dispute that."

"You broke the goddamn embargo. Unless you help me get my son out, you'll be arrested the moment you set foot on U.S. territory. Or any other country where there's an extradition treaty. That includes Britain, right?"

He studied me. "My information was, you got arrested by Internal Security."

"Your order?"

"Nothing to do with me." He squinted. "How'd you get out?"

"I had a chat with Cecille."

He looked at me, but said nothing.

"She told me about the side deal you had going with Greenbaum on the diamonds."

He screwed up his face. "What?"

"She said you were trying to scam Rossiter and your client at the same time. Taking a piece for yourself out of the middle."

"Oh, for fucksake." He was shocked.

"Not true?"

"You crazy?" He pushed back his chair, then stood up. "A piece out of the middle, what's that worth? Am I really going to try to rip them off, then come back here and have one of old man Lagundi's goons shoot me through the head? Jesus. A piece out of the middle. She said that?"

I nodded. He hitched his belt, then pushed both hands up through his hair. He stared out the window, stunned. He wasn't pretending. Cecille Lagundi's claim was a total, and very unwelcome, surprise.

"Cecille's setting you up to take a fall for the theft of the diamonds," I said.

He swung around. "I hardly saw the bloody things."

"You took them to New York."

"We didn't take them. They were already there in the bank vault. Christ, I wish I'd never heard of the damn stones. She told you I stole them? She actually said that?" When I nodded again he shook his head in disbelief. Then a thought struck him. "Why'd she tell you that?"

"Because she thought I might corroborate her story."

"Her story's crazy." We looked at each other a moment, then his face fell. "You didn't," he said.

"I was a prisoner in her father's jail."

"Oh, shit." He closed his eyes, then opened them. "You didn't put anything in writing, did you?" He read the answer in my face. "Christ Almighty."

"You help me get my son out of Dujanka, and I'll retract the statement."

"She stole the fucking diamonds."

"That's not really my problem. All I want is to get my son out." We looked at each other.

"You might be lying to me now." He pointed. "You might have dreamed this up just to blackmail me into helping you get your son."

"I didn't dream up those empty Haplon containers."

He waved that off. He didn't seem to care that I knew he'd broken the arms embargo. What concerned him was the statement I'd given Cecille Lagundi, and the possibility that the goons from Internal Security might be ordered to put a bullet through his head. He knew I wasn't lying.

At last he turned and studied the map on the wall. He could see what I couldn't, the positions of the Congolese army units in the field, and the broad outlines of the major battles under way across the country. He considered the map a long time.

"You go back to the hangar," he finally decided. "Don't try coming back in here till I send for you." When I asked him what he intended to do, he faced me. "I'm going to figure out whether I should let myself be blackmailed," he said. "Or whether it might not be easier just to shoot you."

I started out in the direction of the hangar, then drifted left toward the service block. Nobody stopped me. A minute later, I was walking along the line of Haplon containers, looking in. They were absolutely bare. Not one loose round of ammo, not one spare part, remained. I glanced around. None of the soldiers back by the terminal were watching me. I stepped into the last container, pulling the steel doors half-closed behind me. At the rear of the container, I knelt and put two fingers into the open end of the triangular steel tube that formed part of the corner brace. The electronic homing device I'd planted back in Connecticut was still in place. Using my fingers like tweezers, I pincered the beacon and pulled it free of the battery beneath, then extracted it. It was the size and shape of a fountain pen. I slipped it into my pocket and went back to the doors, and right then a Congolese soldier put his head in. I pushed open one door and stepped out. When he said something in French, I shook my head and spread my hands in a show of ignorance. Then I turned toward the hangar and walked. He shouted, but when I didn't respond he seemed to give up. After fifty yards, I glanced over my shoulder and he was walking down the line of containers, closing doors.

Fiona wasn't in the hangar. I wandered through, past the bunk beds and the trestle tables. There were twenty or thirty European and American civilians in there, people who hadn't made it to the embassy. They sat around in small groups, talking, some playing cards, a few lying alone on their bunks, reading. When I'd passed through,

I saw a door out back and went over and looked out. There was a stack of worn and discarded aircraft tires dumped fifty yards away by some palm trees. Fiona was sitting on the edge of the stack. Her arms were folded. She was staring at her feet. I walked across and stopped five yards short of her. She didn't lift her head.

"I've spoken to someone about Brad. This guy might be able to help us."

She didn't reply.

"Look," I said. "I'm really trying here."

"Can he get to Brad?"

"I don't know."

She looked up. "I killed Ivan." When I made a sound, she went on. "I wouldn't leave when he wanted to get to the embassy. When the shooting started, it was too late to try."

"That's not your fault."

"Isn't it?"

I moved around and settled my butt against a tire. I asked her what she was doing in the Congo anyway. "Your office told me you were in Johannesburg."

"I was. But you'd disappeared. I was worried about Brad." She shrugged. "I called Ivan."

I asked if she hadn't picked up the message I'd left for her at home.

"On the voice mail?" She made a face. "It didn't tell me a damn thing. As usual. Ivan got me on a planeload of mining analysts coming up here from Joburg. Day after I got in, the trouble started. That was two days ago."

"You saw Brad?"

She shook her head. She said they'd spoken on the radio.

"How was he?"

"Worried. He and three other guys missed the evacuation, they'd been working out in the bush. Last night they were talking about abandoning the mine, driving out." She looked at me. "That god-damn diamond you had me analyze, that's got something to do with why you're here, hasn't it."

"Partly."

"What's the other part? Making sure your clients can use the guns properly? Maximum kill rate, or whatever you call it?" I hung my head. "Or did you come out to see what else they might need?" she said bitterly. "Rossiter must be loving this."

"I don't work for Rossiter."

"Don't you dare tell me you do your job for Brad and me. Don't you dare tell me that. That you do it for us."

I didn't see much sense in holding back now. I didn't want to hold back. So I repeated it, the only thing that might finally reach her. "I don't work for Rossiter." I lifted my head. "I don't work for Haplon."

She took a second. "You've what, resigned?"

"I haven't resigned. I never did work for Rossiter." I found I couldn't face her.

"Don't do that." She pulled me around. "I don't need any head games here, Ned, not right now. What are you saying to me? You don't work for Rossiter? What kind of cryptic bullshit is that? Who's the guy who drives up to Connecticut each morning. That's you, isn't it?"

I looked her in the eye. It was one of the hardest things I've ever done. "My job at Haplon's a cover. I'm working for Defense Intelligence. I've been working for them since I quit West Point." She didn't speak, she just stared at me. I'd had nearly two years to prepare for the moment. At times I'd even kidded myself that I was prepared. But when Fiona kept staring at me without speaking I felt my world cracking like a brittle shell.

"Defense Intelligence," she said at last.

"It wasn't safe for you to know."

"You quit West Point two years ago."

"Twenty-two months."

"Two years," she said.

"It was an intelligence-gathering operation. I thought it was something I had to do."

Her brow creased. She looked away from me, then back. It still hadn't quite sunken in.

"Guys like Rossiter were breaking the law," I said. "I lost men in the Gulf because of that. The DIA gave me a chance to do something about it. I took it."

"You're not going to tell me this is a morality thing." She slipped down from the tire, walked away a few paces, then turned. "You've been risking your life for this?"

"I've been gathering intelligence on Haplon."

"You're on active service?"

"It's not like I've been working for an enemy state. It's not something I'm ashamed of."

"Oh, Jesus."

"And I wasn't cheating on you."

"What?"

"The so-called affair. That woman in the photos, Durranti, she's a Customs officer, like I told you. She was my contact. That's who I was passing the intelligence to."

Fiona tilted her head. She regarded me closely, then seemed to recognize that I was telling the truth. There was a brief flicker of something other than anger in her eyes, but the next moment it was gone. "I think I'll skip the champagne," she said. "You've been on active service for two years. And you've been lying to me about it for two fucking years."

"I was protecting you."

"You were deceiving me. You deceived me because you knew how I felt about all that. You knew if you'd told me the truth I would have divorced you. That's it, isn't it. You didn't have the guts to tell me."

"You're pissed off because I didn't want to destroy our marriage?"

"If you didn't want to do that, all you had to do was stay at West Point."

"That job was killing me. Did you really expect me to spend the rest of my days teaching kids about breechblocks? Was I meant to watch them all go on to be soldiers while I sat around greasing guns for next year's intake?"

"You were in the Army. That's what you wanted."

"I was wasting my goddamn life."

"You're not saying this is my fault." She gestured around. "That we're caught up in this because of me?"

"I didn't say that."

"No, but you're thinking it. You're thinking that if I hadn't been so unreasonable, if I hadn't wanted you off active service, if I hadn't wanted a husband all in one piece, we wouldn't be here now. Maybe Brad wouldn't be here."

"Okay." My heart was pounding and my chest was tight. "Let's say I am. You don't think that's part of it?"

She jabbed a finger at me. "I told you to your face. I told you I couldn't take it, I wasn't proud of that, Ned. I was ashamed of it. I was ashamed of myself. I married a soldier, I should have known what I was in for, but I didn't. Christ. When they told me you'd been shot in Mogadishu I cried for two days, do you think I'm proud of that? But at least when I figured it out, I faced up to it. And I told you to your face. I didn't lie to you." Tears stood in her eyes, tears of anger and pain. She swiped them away.

"Fiona—"

"Don't 'Fiona' me. What's wrong with you? I'm your wife. For two years I haven't known a thing about you."

"That's not true."

"That Durranti woman. She knew."

"She was a professional contact."

"She knew what you were doing. She knew all about you. She knew about me too, didn't she. She must have."

"This has nothing to do with Rita."

"Oh," she said. "Rita."

"Be serious."

"I am serious. What do you want me to say, that I don't care? Two years, for chrissake."

"I get the message."

"No you don't. You don't even start to get it. I believed you, Ned. I believed in you." She wrapped her arms around herself, defensive. Furious. "Now I don't want to even look at you." I stepped toward her, and she lifted her eyes and stopped me dead. She did not want me anywhere near her. I looked at her a long moment, then finally turned on my heel and retreated to the hangar.

f Internal Security gets hold of me," Trevanian concluded, "I'm a dead man." It was an hour before daybreak, and I'd been fetched from my bunk over at the hangar by the pink-faced Brit soldier and taken to Trevanian's office in the terminal. Trevanian had just spent ten minutes alone with me, explaining the problems he'd had checking out my story. What had finally convinced him, it seemed, was a rumor he'd picked up from a highly placed source in the Congolese government. The rumor was that Cecille Lagundi's father was talking about offering his Internal Security goons a bounty on Trevanian's head once the rebels were suppressed. "Does that make you happy?" Trevanian said.

I studied the map on the wall. The colored pins around Mbuji-Mayi had been drastically rearranged. "I didn't sign the statement in order to get you killed. I signed it to get myself out of jail." I faced him. "You help me get my son out of Dujanka, and I'll retract it."

"That won't be enough to save me."

I lifted a shoulder. A retraction was the only thing I had to offer. He got up and came around to the wall map and pointed. "The rebels have almost been pushed out of Mbuji in the last few hours," he said. I glanced at him. The only way an operational success like that could have been achieved was with infantry. Trained infantry, using U.S. night-vision equipment. He felt my glance, but let it ride. "By lunchtime, the place should be secure."

"So?"

"When they lose Mbuji, the rebels won't retreat east, they'll come this way." Trevanian swept his hand southeast of Mbuji, straight over Dujanka. My stomach turned over. "They'll grab what they can and destroy the rest as they go."

"You can't stop them?"

"They'll be spread out for miles through the bush. Moving like that, they're not a target anyone can hit."

I asked him what kind of defense existed out at the mines.

"The bigger places have got private security arrangements. Mostly with me."

"Dujanka?"

He turned his head, no.

I looked at the map. Brad was out there, stranded and vulnerable. He didn't know it, but within hours he was going to become part of the front line. I asked Trevanian about getting a chopper out there, airlifting Brad and his colleagues back to Kinshasa. He waved my suggestion aside.

"Here's the deal. I've got a chopper leaving in twenty minutes. It's going out past Dujanka to Zanda." He placed his finger on a large mine southeast of Dujanka, near the Angolan border. "It'll resupply the security team at Zanda, then fly back to Mbuji to join the cleanup."

"It could land at Dujanka on the way out."

"That's the option. I could get your son out to Zanda."

I asked him about security there.

"I've got a team there, ex–British army. Once they're resupplied, they won't be overrun."

I turned it over. "The government's paying you to help them fight the rebels."

"That's right."

"And the mining companies are paying you to defend their mines."

"What's this got to do with your son?"

"Nothing."

"Right."

We looked at each other.

"Okay," I said. "Get Brad out to Zanda, and I give you my word, I'll retract the statement."

"I don't need your word. You and your wife are coming with me." When my forehead creased, he said, "That's the condition. Either you two come with me, or your son stays where he is."

"What's this got to do with my wife? If you want me to go, okay. But leave my wife out of it."

"Both of you, or no deal."

"You want to tell me why?"

"Sure." He turned from the map and dropped into the chair behind his desk. He looked up at me. "You signed my death warrant. Until it's unsigned, you and your family are going to stay close to me. Close enough for me to reach. Do we understand one another?"

We understood one another. I didn't like it one little bit.

When I returned to the hangar, there were the first signs of people stirring before sunup. Fiona was already out of her bunk and dressed, I found her sitting by herself at one end of a trestle table, near a lamp, drinking coffee. When I slid onto the bench beside her, she made as if to rise. I placed a hand firmly on her arm.

"This is about Brad."

She darted an uncertain glance at me, then slowly sank back down. I quickly explained the situation out at Mbuji-Mayi to her just as Trevanian had explained it to me. Then I told her about the chopper. "It's leaving in fifteen minutes. We've got seats if we want them."

"We can get to Brad?"

A guy wandered from his bunk to the coffee machine. I lowered my voice. "This guy providing the chopper, his name's Trevanian. He's the one I was dealing with in New York. The one who bought the Haplon shipment, the one with the diamond you analyzed?" Fiona nodded. "Well, there were other diamonds. They got stolen, probably by the daughter of the Congolese Minister for Police. The daughter's trying to get me to blame Trevanian for the theft." Fiona cocked her head, not sure where this was leading. "Trevanian wants to keep me close, he needs some time to figure out how to deal with the daughter. If he gets me to this mine at Zanda, that's perfect. His people there can hold me as long as he likes. Problem is, he wants you and Brad there too."

"Why?"

"Leverage against me."

She gave me a sideways look. "What's our alternative?"

"We don't go."

"And Brad?"

"He stays in Dujanka and takes his chances."

"That's not an alternative."

I didn't respond.

"Are you trying to scare me or something? Don't you want us to go?"

"I'm trying to be honest with you."

"Well, you're two years too late."

The guy from the coffee machine came and sat opposite us. I gave him the eye and he shuffled away from us down the table. I faced Fiona again. She was staring at the steam rising from her mug.

"This isn't about us," I said. "This is about Brad."

She got up. "Let's go before we miss the goddamn chopper."

The first thing I saw as we climbed aboard the chopper were the Haplon boxes, about a dozen of them, each one containing a set of four-thousand-dollar-apiece night-sights. Underneath these were cases of ammo, then, down toward the tail, unlabeled crates that I recognized as another part of the Haplon shipment, mortars and shells. At the back, more crates of P23s.

The pilot was a Brit, one of Trevanian's men, dressed in fatigues. He nodded to us as we clambered into our seats, then turned to speak with Trevanian, who'd slid into the empty copilot's chair beside him. The engines were already fired up, the rotors whup-whupping as they turned. I saw Fiona having trouble buckling herself into the seat harness, so I stepped across, crouching, and helped her. She pointed to the boxes, the Haplon labels.

"Night-sights," I told her, raising my voice over the engines. She jerked her head back toward the crates. "Weapons and ammo," I said. I snapped the harness buckle closed, then reached up over her head and flipped open the locker. I pulled out a headset and mike. I plugged the cord into its socket then handed her the unit. She shook her head. "Put it on and keep it on," I told her firmly. When she'd put it on, I showed her how to work the mike button. "Just do what the pilot says. Stay buckled up. If you see anything the pilot should know about, hit the mike button and let him know."

"Anything like what?"

"Like someone on the ground trying to shoot us down."

Her eyes stayed on mine. When she saw I wasn't joking, her jaw went tight. I squeezed her shoulder. She turned and stared out the window. Trevanian waved me back to my seat, and I sat and buckled up and put on my headset.

We lifted off smoothly, the chopper tilting forward, swinging north and then east, in moments we were passing over the airport perimeter. In the east, the gray sky was starting to color, the faintest whisper of pink. We could make out the outlines of the refinery and the storage tanks, the noxious black smoke was still billowing, blowing west over the city. As we climbed, we saw the lights of Brazzaville and Kinshasa, separated by a dark belt of water. The great river was a thick dark smudge snaking away from us into the interior, a colossal aquatic highway inland. We slowly veered southeast, and within minutes we were beyond the outer edges of the city and passing over open country. As the sun rose, we could make out the pattern of the land passing beneath us, the bare red earth, the scrub, and the rocks and trees.

After fifteen minutes, the pilot reached across and touched Trevanian's shoulder, then pointed to a road a few miles up ahead. Through my headset, I heard him tell Trevanian, "We stay just south of that road most of the way to Mbuji." When Trevanian nodded, the pilot pointed again. Farther up the road, there was a column of vehicles, as we got nearer we could make out trucks and armored personnel carriers. The pilot dropped a few hundred feet to give Trevanian a closer look. The open-back trucks were crammed with Congolese soldiers, they waved at us, laughing and shouting as we swept over them. Farther on, the pilot fired a test burst from the Haplon minigun mounted on the right skid of his chopper. The bullets flicked a line of dust up the side of the dirt road and disappeared into a stand of trees. Satisfied, the pilot pulled the chopper back up to cruising height.

I glanced across at Fiona. She had taken off her headset and dropped it on the floor, now she stared out the window. Rocks and red earth. Moments later, she rested her head against the glass and closed her eyes.

CHAPTER 36

We flew for more than an hour, stopping once at an army base in the bush to refuel. Dirt tracks crisscrossed the country at wide intervals. We passed no major towns, just the occasional small village, generally a collection of huts huddled together in the middle of nothing and nowhere. The few people we saw took cover when they heard the chopper, their goats and cattle scattering as we thundered across the sky. The sun was well up when I took off my headset and went across and sat next to Fiona. She stared out the window.

"What can you see?"

"Nothing."

"It won't be long now."

She dipped her head. She continued staring out the window.

I wasn't going to reconnect with her that easily, I knew my wife better than that. The white heat of her anger was passing, but now that she'd had time to think over what I'd told her about my work at Haplon, the fading heat was leaving behind a deposit like cooling lava. Untouchable. Fast becoming solid and immovable.

"I want to tell Brad myself," I said. "About my work." She didn't respond, so I touched her arm. "I'd like to tell him myself."

"I heard you."

"You're not making this easy."

"No," she agreed, facing me. "But if it makes you feel better, fine. You tell Brad, okay?"

I held my tongue. It wasn't easy. Then Trevanian turned and signaled me back to my seat, he gestured for me to put my headset on, and Fiona turned away from me. I went back to my seat. When I'd put my headset on, Trevanian pointed.

"Over there, eleven o'clock."

On a dirt track through the scrub, there was a column of vehicles that wasn't throwing up any dust.

"Stationary," the pilot remarked as we got closer. He scoured the country farther up ahead, then pointed to a horseshoe-shaped range fifteen or twenty miles away. *"Dujanka."* He glanced over his shoulder to be sure that I'd seen it. I nodded, then reached across and tapped Fiona on the thigh.

"Dujanka." I pointed the range out to her. This time when I told her to put on the headset, she did. Then I pointed out to her the line of stationary vehicles.

"Is that a drilling rig?" the pilot wondered aloud.

After a moment, Fiona hit her mike button. *"It's a rig. It's definitely a rig."*

The pilot nodded. *"Only place it could come from's Dujanka."*

I exchanged a glance with Fiona. I could see that she remembered it too, what she'd told me about her last radio contact with Brad. He'd mentioned the possibility of abandoning the mine. I asked the pilot if we could go down for a closer look. Trevanian okayed it, and the chopper slowed and gently dipped.

We got down to about three hundred feet, then circled. The truck that was pulling the drilling rig had its hood up. A couple of Congolese guys were standing on the truck's front tires, inspecting or repairing the engine, they craned around to look up at us. Trevanian trained a pair of binoculars on the convoy. After a minute, he shook his head. *"No white men."* He handed the binoculars to me.

I focused on the truck and rig, then the trio of four-wheel-drives. The logo of Barchevsky Mining was visible on two of the doors. The black guys who'd been lounging in the shade were on their feet now, waving to us. But Trevanian was right. No white guys.

I hit the mike button. *"They're definitely from the mine. Can we land?"*

"Can you see your son?"

I shook my head. *"If he's not down there, they'll know where he is."*

Trevanian turned that over. *"Okay,"* he conceded. *"But we can't put down too close or we'll have twenty of the buggers trying to get on board."* Then he told us how he wanted to work it. We'd land a few hundred yards from the convoy, and the pilot would keep the rotors turning. Trevanian and Fiona would stay with the pilot in the chopper, while I went and fetched Brad, or at least found out where he was.

When we had the plan straight, the pilot took the chopper down. We landed on the dirt track a few hundred yards east of the convoy. I took off my headset, and unbuckled my harness. Trevanian jumped out and came around and opened the rear door.

"Mind the rotors!" he shouted, patting his head in warning. "Keep down!" When I jumped down, he grabbed my arm and shouted in my ear. "If they stampede this way, we'll have to take off! Make sure you're on board before we do!"

I nodded, and he released my arm. I bent low, got myself well out past the rotors, then stood upright and walked back down the track. The track elbowed a hundred yards in front of me, the vehicles were farther on, hidden by the scrub.

It was already hot, but I walked fast, the dust rising around my ankles, perspiration rolling down my neck. I was almost at the bend before I really paid any attention to the tire tracks I'd been walking on for some while. The reason I finally noticed them was that they suddenly started zigzagging crazily, left, right, then left again. I slowed, my gaze following the tire tracks to where they slewed off the road and stopped. Then I stopped. I looked back to the chopper and saw Trevanian waving his arm at me, urging me to get on and find Brad. I almost did, but those tire marks bothered me, so I stepped off the track first to give the marks a closer inspection. I squatted on my haunches and considered the zigzag trail. Too controlled for a blowout. No nearby potholes. A puzzle.

Then I saw the other marks in the sand. Bootprints. I looked around, farther off the road, and saw bootprints everywhere. I stood up. I dropped my head to one side and looked ahead to the elbow in the track, listening. The only sound came from the chopper way behind me. Then I noticed something glinting in the sand beneath a nearby bush, and I went over. I crouched down. It was an empty magazine case from an AK47. The hairs prickled up my spine.

Then I lifted my eyes and flinched. A body lay not three yards away, behind the bush. An African, shot to pieces, there were flies but no smell, the blood was fresh.

I got up and backed away. When I hit the track I turned and walked toward the chopper, looking back over my shoulder, then I jogged. I didn't know what I was jogging from at first, but then fifty yards short of the chopper I glimpsed men with guns moving through the bush behind me. Then I ran.

Trevanian jumped out of the chopper, dropped on one knee, and raised a gun to his shoulder. As the chopper engine picked up revs, Trevanian fired. I heard the bullets flick through the bushes away to my left, then someone behind me fired and dirt kicked up on my right. I ducked under the rotor blades, kept running, and leaped through the open door. Trevanian scrambled in after me, shouting, "Go! Go!" and a second later the chopper lifted off.

Behind us, the guys with guns were coming onto the track, trying to get a clear shot at the chopper. A bullet pinged off the rotor blades, but the chopper stayed low, skimming trees. Trevanian fired a burst out the door, then he yanked the door shut, and in moments we were clear, out of effective range. The pilot was already on his radio, relaying the news back to the nearest army base. He told them that there was rebel movement southeast of Mbuji-Mayi, a small convoy from the Dujanka mine appeared to have been ambushed twenty miles northwest of the mine, number of casualties unknown. He hung up the handset.

I slumped into my seat and looked at Fiona. She was already looking at me, her face ashen. Number of casualties unknown. I wiped the sweat from my eyes and unbuttoned my shirt. Then from his place back on the crates, Trevanian called out to us, asking if we still wanted to see Dujanka. I turned in my seat to face him. I didn't have to speak. He got up and clambered past, instructing the pilot to fly us on to Dujanka.

The mine came up fast. We circled high overhead while Trevanian worked the binoculars, making sure, this time, about what we were getting into. The camp consisted of fewer than a dozen prefab buildings with corrugated iron roofs, all located within a short valley formed by a V-shaped range. The only track ran northwest from the camp, out of the valley, and on toward where we'd just left the stationary convoy.

"*Deserted,*" Trevanian decided, handing me the binoculars.

The pilot dropped lower, did a circuit about a hundred feet above the range. I peered through the binoculars. There was no sign of life. If the camp was deserted, then everyone had been with the convoy. Everyone.

"*Let's go down,*" I said. "*I want to take a look around.*"

"*Both of us,*" Fiona cut in. She'd put on the headset. She had her forehead pressed to the window as she stared down at the camp.

The pilot looked to Trevanian, who finally nodded. It was clear he thought we were wasting our time.

The chopper made a fast, low pass over the camp, and when no one emerged from the buildings, we swept up the southern arm of the V, and the pilot put the chopper down near the crest. From there we could see down into the camp and out along the track to the northwest. The pilot throttled back the engines, and as the rotors idled down, Trevanian climbed back to us.

"What do you need, twenty minutes?"

"Give us half an hour."

He checked his watch. "Maximum," he said. "I'll come down too." He consulted the pilot. They decided the pilot would fire one shot if he wanted us back at the chopper, if maybe he'd heard something over the radio. Two shots if he saw vehicles approaching along the track. Trevanian clapped him on the shoulder, then the three of us got out.

The ground was rocky, we picked our way around the boulders. Then we reached a bare patch and scrambled down the slope, skidding crablike, but after a couple of minutes we hit a goat track and the walking got easier. Below us, the camp looked abandoned. The only sound from down there was the occasional popping of the iron roofs as they expanded in the heat. Behind us, the chopper engines finally died. The goat track petered out at the foot of the ridge, near a stack of fuel drums. We passed the fuel drums, walked into the dusty square in front of the buildings, and stopped. Silence.

Fiona suddenly called, "Brad!" Her voice broke, she called again, louder. The sound drifted over the camp and into the hill behind. Trevanian looked at me from the corner of his eye. Then Fiona strode toward the first building, and we followed.

The first building was the office block. Everything looked intact, there was no disorder, it seemed that the miners had taken their time, packed up what they needed, then left. Trevanian stayed in the office while Fiona and I went on to the mess hall. Six tables, benches down either side, and a kitchen out back. Empty. We went out, and across a dirt alley was a long building raised off the ground and mounted, like the office block, on steel stumps. There was a run of about a dozen identical red doors. A long porch, the railings draped with various items of laundry. It was the living quarters. Fiona went across.

"Brad!" she called, and her voice bounced off the building and drifted away.

"Leave it," I said. "There's no one here."

She went up the steps, crossed to the first door, and tried the handle. It was locked, she shoved it with her shoulder but it wouldn't move. She tried again, twice, and I finally gave up and went over.

"Stand back," I said.

She stood back, and I stepped up and kicked the door hard. It cracked and flew open. There was a single bed inside, a side table and lamp, and a built-in closet. The bed hadn't been made, and there was an old *Newsweek* on the floor. The room could have belonged to anyone. Fiona opened the closet door, passed a hand over the clothes on the hangers, then turned on her heel and walked out. She tried the next door, it was locked too, so she stepped back and waited for me to kick it in. I obliged, then while she went inside, I walked down the porch, kicking in the remaining doors, and once I'd finished I sat down on the steps to wait for her to get done.

She came right along, room by room, then she went into the second-to-last room and didn't come out. I gave her a minute, then I got up and dragged myself across to the door. She was sitting on the unmade bed. The built-in closet was open, and she had an old frayed denim shirt of Brad's clutched in her lap. Her thumb rubbed the shirt like she was actually touching him, like she had his skin beneath her hand.

I went inside. There was a faint smell of aftershave, I closed my eyes, then opened them again. On his bedside table lay a paperback. I flipped it over, and my heart lurched. *Black Hawk Down,* the story of the Mogadishu disaster. Brad, before he left the camp, had been reading about me.

Then from outside, up on the hill, came a single rifle shot, a retort that echoed and sank into silence. I sat down on the bed. Fiona raised Brad's shirt and pressed it to her face and rocked forward. There was nothing for either of us to say. I let her cry for a while, then I put my arm around her, and she held Brad's shirt against her eyes.

"We have to go back to that convoy," she said.

I said nothing. I knew there was no chance in the world Trevanian was going to risk losing the chopper by flying back there. I got her up onto her feet and out on the porch, and she let go of my arm and held the railing. She said she was okay. She still had hold of Brad's shirt.

Trevanian called to us from the door of the office block, telling us to head back to the chopper, that he'd be a couple of minutes behind. Then he went back inside.

I hung my head. I went down the steps and Fiona came after me and we walked back through the deserted camp without speaking. The heat seemed oppressive now, almost unbearably heavy. We passed the fuel dump and turned up the goat track, trudging upward. After several minutes, just short of the crest, I stopped and shielded my eyes against the sun. The chopper stood silhouetted against the blue sky. I couldn't see the pilot, and the chopper engines were silent. Fiona stopped, put her hands on her hips, and bent to catch her breath.

I touched her arm as I went by. "Wait here."

"What?"

"Wait," I said, and walked on. The cockpit, I saw when I got closer, was empty. But a few steps farther, and I saw the pilot, he was lying in the shade beneath the chopper's tail. I went over. I didn't have long to convince him to return us to the convoy, Trevanian was already halfway up the hill behind us.

"Deserted," I said, and I stopped just short of the chopper. The pilot didn't move. His eyes stared up at the undercarriage. Then I noticed the dark stain on his shirt, and I went in closer, crouched and touched his face. It was cold. I tore open his shirt, and there was a bullet wound just beneath his sternum. I rolled him and checked the exit wound. It was enormous.

"Ned?" Fiona called.

"Stay down there!"

"Where's the pilot?"

"He's been shot." I eased him onto his back again, then I inspected the chopper, looking for a spray of blood or a bullet hole, anything that might tell me where the shot had come from. There was nothing.

"Can I do something?" Fiona called up.

"No. Just stay down!"

"Is he all right?"

I ducked under the chopper tail and climbed in through the open rear door. Busting open a crate, I grabbed a P23, then fixed a magazine. I went forward, leaned into the cockpit, reaching for the binoculars, and the glass side screen suddenly imploded. Shattered glass showered me, I snatched up the binoculars, then scrambled back to the rear door.

"Ned!"

"Take cover!" I leaped out and ran, low and fast, down the slope. Fiona had taken cover behind a boulder, I dropped down beside her. "You see where the shot came from?"

She shook her head. "Where's the pilot?"

I edged along the boulder, raised the binoculars, and looked along the ridge. The sniper had almost taken me. He had to be inside two hundred yards.

Trevanian scrambled up from below and dropped behind the protective cover of the boulder. He looked at me, breathing hard.

"The pilot's dead," I told him.

"Dead?" said Fiona.

"Fuck," said Trevanian, glancing up to the chopper. "Either one of you fly?" When I shook my head, he swore.

I showed him where I thought the shot had come from. A pile of boulders a hundred and fifty yards away. He took the binoculars.

"How many'd you see?"

"Haven't seen anyone."

He inspected the boulders. "There'll just be one," he decided. "Two or more, and they'd be spraying us by now." He handed the binoculars to Fiona, then indicated the P23. "Can you use that?"

I nodded.

"We could get back down to the camp this way," Fiona suggested, pointing behind. She didn't realize that turning tail was more dangerous than taking the sniper on.

I put a hand on her shoulder. "Stay here. Keep your head down." Then Trevanian and I shuffled around one side of the boulder. I told him I thought I could get near enough along the top ridge for a shot. "If you stay low," I said, "you'll get him if he runs."

"You know what you're doing?"

"I used to."

"Jesus," he said.

I broke cover. I scrambled up the scree, dropping behind some rocks just in front of the chopper. When I looked back, Trevanian was moving along the ridge lower down. The sniper fired. Dirt kicked up in front of Trevanian, I got up and ran. I made twenty yards, then dropped again just as a shot went singing over my head. I lifted my chest, he fired again, and a spray of splintered rock peppered my cheek and I dropped down. Forty yards below me, Trevanian was still moving forward. Then he dived, the sniper fired, and I flicked to automatic and got up and ran, firing from the hip, raking the boulders where the sniper was hidden. When I'd burned through the clip, I dropped and got myself wedged down in a gully, and a second later the return fire rattled over me. The sniper wasn't fooling with single shots now, dirt and rocks showered over me like torrential rain, when he finally eased off the trigger, the noise of gunfire still rung in my ears.

I put in a fresh clip. I crawled on my belly about twenty yards along the gully, every few seconds there was another burst from the sniper, but now he was just spraying and hoping, he'd lost me. I couldn't see Trevanian. When I reached the end of the gully I stopped. There was silence.

I counted to three beneath my breath, then I snapped my head up, snatched a look, then withdrew. No gunfire. I was less than a hundred yards from the boulders, but it was all open ground, I'd gotten as far as I was going to get. I flicked the P23 to single-fire and waited. I seemed to wait a long time, but it was probably only a minute, then I heard Trevanian fire. The sniper fired back, Trevanian returned fire, and I put my head up and saw the sniper between the boulders. He thought the rocks had him shielded. He was wrong. I eased the rifle butt into my shoulder, took slow, careful aim, then squeezed the trigger.

It took him in the chest, beneath his arm. He rose, his arms swinging up, his gun flying free and cartwheeling through the air, then he dropped and lay still and I knew he was dead.

"He's down!" I kept an eye on the body. I flicked to automatic, then got up. Trevanian climbed warily up the slope while I did a quick recce of the area. By the time I'd gotten to the boulders, Trevanian was crouched over the sniper's dead body. He dug in the guy's bloodied pocket, found some ID, and handed it up to me. The guy had been a Barchevsky Mining employee, a foreman at Dujanka.

"Rebel," Trevanian declared. "Waiting for his friends." He stood up, scuffing aside the limp arm with his boot. He considered the bloodied chest a moment, then cocked his head and raised his eyes to me. "Nice shot."

I dropped the ID on the body, turned my back on Trevanian, and went to find Fiona.

CHAPTER 37

Only one vehicle remained in the camp, a truck that was parked in the maintenance shed. As we approached along the track, we saw that the hood was up and that a canvas sheet had been spread on the concrete floor beneath the engine. Fiona stopped at the open double-bay doors of the shed while I went in with Trevanian. He jumped onto the bumper and peered in at the engine, then he got down on the canvas sheet and hauled himself under the truck.

"No battery," I remarked.

He said he'd seen one on the workbench, connected to a charger. He shuffled farther under the truck. I asked him if he knew what he was looking at.

"Ah-ha," he said.

I looked in the cab. "The keys are in it."

He dragged himself out, then stood up, wiping his hands together. He crossed to the workbench, which ran along the right wall, the length of the shed. The bench was littered with tools and old parts, he started sorting through them. I suggested we drop the battery in, turn the key, and see what happened.

"Fuck-all's gonna happen." He moved down the workbench, searching. "The starter motor's missing."

Fiona caught my eye, she tossed her head toward the mess, saying that she could go get us some food and something to drink. When I nodded, she went. Trevanian continued his search, and I went and joined him. In an open locker above the bench, there was a two-way radio. I switched it on, there was a quiet hiss of static, and I reached for the dial.

"Leave it," Trevanian said, and I looked at him. "It's probably tuned to the same frequency as that convoy. If they start talking to each other, I want to hear it."

My hand fell. I considered what he'd said. "You worried they might come here?"

"I'm worried, period." He reached the end of the workbench without finding the part he needed. He turned on the spot, looking around, then disappeared behind the truck. "Bingo," he said.

When I joined him, he was sorting through dozens of red and white boxes, new parts, stacked against the corrugated iron wall. His fingers flicked over the labels, he nodded me to the far end of the pile. As we searched, I said, "I get the feeling you've done this kind of thing before."

"Previous life."

"Transport division?"

"Something like that." Another minute and he found it, he tore the box open. "Okay. Now all we gotta do is fit the bloody thing." He collected some wrenches from the bench, and took them with the new starter motor over to the truck. He asked me to find him a flashlight.

I scoured the bench. "How long ago did you leave the Army?"

"Ten years."

"No regrets."

"Not till lately."

I asked him how many guys he had working for him.

"Seventy, seventy-five." He cocked his head. "You're not thinking about a career change?"

I found a flashlight and gave it to him. He lowered himself onto his back on the canvas, then hauled himself under the truck.

"What's the pay?" I said.

"Seven thousand U.S. a month."

"Not much for a man to get himself killed."

"I've only lost two men."

"This week."

"Ever. And one of them's that pilot up on the ridge." I wasn't sure that I believed him. And it wasn't the time to mention Jay and Johnny, the dead AfricAid guys. I listened to him working a wrench for a while, then he said, "The secret is, keep out of the politics. Stick to the mining company contracts."

"That's not how it looked back in Kinshasa." I crouched and peered under the engine. "Colonel."

He grunted, straining at the wrench. Then he stretched out a hand to me, a small bolt rested in his palm. He said he needed three more, the same size, so I took the bolt and went to search the workbench. He spoke to me from under the truck.

"Since when can an arms salesman look down his nose at anyone?"

"Just a remark."

"For what it's worth, I'm not too keen on it myself. But I have to protect my contracts."

"You're fighting a war."

He dragged himself out and sat up. He wiped the sweat from his forehead, a greasy streak appeared over his left eye. "I'm helping the legitimate goverment of the country suppress a rebellion. At least, I was until you showed up. And the reason I was doing it was to protect my contracts."

"You telling me the government's not paying you for your assistance?"

He studied me, then he held out his hand. His eyes never wavered. He told me to shut my mouth and give him the bolts.

"Is it fixed?" Fiona asked me when I walked into the kitchen at the end of the mess. She was standing at the sink, rinsing out some plastic containers. The kitchen was large, industrial, the ovens and benches were made of stainless steel. I went to one of the refrigerators and took out a bottle of water.

"No," I said. I told her Trevanian thought he might have it done in half an hour. I uncapped the bottle and drank. I was hot. Just walking over from the maintenance shed had brought on a huge sweat.

Fiona dried off the containers and waved a hand over a plateful of sandwiches. She told me to take what I wanted, for me and Trevanian both, she said she was going to pack the rest to take. I grabbed a sandwich, tomato, then I pulled up a stool and sat down and ate. Fiona went along to the pantry and fetched some tins of sardines, then she came back and picked up a knife and started spreading butter on slices of bread. Over our heads, the iron roof made cracking sounds as it warped beneath the sun. I finished my sandwich and started on another. I drank some more water from the bottle.

"Which one of you shot that man up there?" Her back turned to me, she gestured with her knife up the ridge.

"Does that matter?"

She lifted a shoulder and returned to scooping sardines onto the bread. The silence between us now was heavy.

"I shot him," I said.

She nodded to herself and went on working. "That wasn't so hard now, was it?"

My sandwich was halfway to my mouth. I put it down. "What do you want from me? Do you want me to know that you think I screwed up? Okay. I know it. And I know that beating my breast over it's not going to turn back the clock, so whatever you've got to say, just say it, Fiona." She kept her back turned to me. She started slicing. "Just say it," I said.

"What?"

"Whatever you want to say."

"Would you like that?"

"Oh, for chrissake, just get it off your chest."

She didn't respond, but she was wound up so tight, she had to put down the knife. She braced her hands on the bench.

"Look, I'm sorry," I said. "I didn't expect it to go on for two years, nobody did. I always thought the end was just around the corner." I waited. When she didn't respond this time, I gave up. "At least I wasn't having an affair," I muttered, taking a bite from my sandwich. "Give me some credit."

I chewed intently, feeling rotten. My wife couldn't say one civil word to me. My son was lost. Then Fiona's head drooped. After a second, her shoulders started to shake.

"Fiona?"

She was crying. I put down my sandwich and went across and rested my hands on her shoulders. She shrugged my hands off, turned away and dropped onto a stool. She put her elbows on the bench and buried her face in her hands.

"We'll find Brad," I said. "I promise you."

Her head shook. She looked up at me, wretched, and when I stepped toward her, she held out a hand, fending me off.

"We'll find him."

"I slept with Barchevsky," she said.

We stared at each other. I was transfixed to the spot. At last she got up and pushed past me to the sink, she turned on the tap and splashed water onto her face. Then she wiped her face and tried to stop crying, and I watched her, unable to speak. It was not real. There were no words to cover it. Barchevsky, a guy I'd seen only twice. Alive, at the airport in New York. Dead, in his office. Barchevsky.

Finally I said, "I don't believe that." She turned, her face bunched. I shook my head. "You wouldn't have."

"I did." Her voice was so choked, it was barely a whisper. It was true. I knew it was true.

"No," I said.

"When you disappeared." She swallowed down the lump in her throat. "I knew you'd gone with that woman."

"I hadn't. Not like that."

"I knew you were lying to me. I knew it, Ned. Where else could you be?"

"I never touched her."

"What good's that now?" Her shoulders sagged. She dropped her forehead onto the heel of one hand. "If I'd known that, do you think I'd be here?"

It took me a second. "You came up from Johannesburg to see Barchevsky?"

She nodded.

"Not Brad?"

"I didn't know all this was going to happen." She looked up at me, tearful but defiant now. "I didn't know you'd finally get around to being honest with me."

I couldn't move. Or speak. I stood there in front of her, completely stricken.

Then Trevanian put his head in at the rear door, shouting, "Rourke!" I turned to him, dazed. His glance flitted between us. "You'd both better come. It's about your son." Fiona rose, her face turning white. Trevanian turned back toward the maintenance shed, he called over his shoulder, "Hurry, and you might hear him. He's on the radio."

CHAPTER 38

That's not him," said Fiona. We were in the maintenance shed, leaning over the radio, straining to hear the voice above the static. The voice was speaking French. "That's not him," she repeated despairingly.

Trevanian cocked his head and listened. After a few moments the voice cut out, then there was only static. Trevanian stared at the radio.

Fiona said. "Are you sure it was him earlier?"

"They said his name. It was him."

I nodded at the radio. I asked Trevanian who'd just spoken.

"Rebel." Trevanian faced me. "Someone from the convoy that attacked us. They've got your son and some other whites from the mine."

"He's in that convoy?"

Trevanian nodded and turned toward the truck. I grabbed his arm.

"Is he okay?" said Fiona. "Did he sound all right?"

"Why'd they let Brad speak?" I said.

Trevanian pulled his arm free. "They all spoke, all the white men. Just a few words to confirm they're alive."

"Why?"

"Because the rebels want to trade." Trevanian turned back to the radio. He scratched a mark by the tuner dial so he could find the convoy's signal again later, then he started to retune. He told us he might be able to pick up a signal from the army in Mbuji-Mayi.

"They want to trade Brad?" said Fiona, referring to the rebel convoy.

"They want to trade all the white men they've captured," said Trevanian. He concentrated on the dial, listening for a break in the static. "Seems like the army captured some rebel leaders in Mbuji, the rebels in the convoy want to get their leaders back."

"Oh Jesus." Fiona put a hand on the workbench, then sat down on a drum of kerosene.

"Will the army go for that?" I said.

Trevanian shook his head. Then he found a signal and raised a finger to silence us. The signal was faint, he wound up the volume and put his ear up close to the speaker. "Army," he decided.

I watched him, I didn't look at Fiona. I needed to keep a hold on myself. After a minute, Trevanian's head came up fast.

"Get up to the chopper," he told me sharply. "Unload the night-sights and as much gear as you can carry. Wait up there and keep a lookout."

"Who for?"

He returned to the rebel channel, cranked up the volume, then walked over to the truck. "The army are on their way from Mbuji," he said. "The rebels are running in this direction. We can't hang around." He lowered himself onto the canvas. "If you see the convoy, fire a shot to warn me, then get back down here fast. If I get this heap going, I'll fire a shot, you two carry down what you can."

"What about Brad?" said Fiona.

Trevanian looked up at her. "What about us?" he said. He dropped onto his back and hauled himself under the truck.

We can't just leave," Fiona said. I jerked my head toward the southern ridge, and she hurried after me. "Brad's alive," she said, and she kept on protesting.

I waited till we were past the fuel dump, out of earshot of the maintenance shed, then I rounded on her. "I've got Trevanian to deal with. I've got the rebels to deal with. I don't need to be fighting my own goddamn wife." I turned on my heel and set off up the ridge.

She followed, silent, till we were almost at the chopper, then she asked me what I was going to do. I didn't know what I was going to do. I handed her the binoculars, then climbed into the chopper. I tossed out two boxes of night-sights and shoved a small crate of ammo over to the door. Outside, Fiona had the binoculars trained on the track to the northwest.

"Can you see anything?" I called.

She shook her head, so I went back to the rear of the chopper and dug around among the crates and boxes, opening them, checking inside. After a minute, I found something I could use.

"What's that?" Fiona said, leaning in through the door.

"You're supposed to be keeping a lookout," I told her, then I dragged the crate of grenades I'd found into the light. She started talking about the captured rebel leaders, she seemed to be trying to convince herself that there was a realistic prospect Brad might simply be traded from captivity into freedom. "Listen." I raised a hand. "The only chance Brad's got is us. Now, you're blocking my light."

She shuffled aside and I inspected the grenades. They were packed in rows of six, prearmed and ready for use, with a safety bar locked against the pins. I busted open the side of the crate, removed one grenade, then I climbed out and went around to the pilot's door. Fiona asked me again what I was doing.

"Trying to save our son." I got into the pilot's seat. I examined the internal door handle.

"I don't care if you're mad," she said.

"Mad doesn't come close." I yanked out the cord to the headphones, then I pulled on either end of the cord, testing it for strength.

"Well, I don't care," she repeated. "If you hadn't told me so many goddamn lies—"

I glanced up, I was about to say something cutting. Then I saw her face, and I stopped. She didn't look as though she didn't care. She looked just like I felt, as if she was breaking inside, but struggling, for Brad's sake, to hold herself together.

I dropped my head again, tied one end of the cord to the internal door handle. I warned Fiona not to touch the door, then I pulled the door closed. She studied me a moment through the window, her fingers played over the binoculars hanging from her neck. Then she went back to her lookout on a rock. I reached across, locked the passenger-side door, then sat back in the seat and took a few steadying breaths.

One thing, I thought. One thing at a time.

Leaning down, I wedged the grenade out of sight behind the radio bracket. I looped the loose end of the cord through the safety pin and knotted it tight. Now the cord stretched taut between the grenade and the door, it was set. I climbed carefully over the backseat and let myself out the rear door, locking it behind me.

I thought about moving the pilot's body from beneath the fuselage, but in the end I left it there. From a distance, he'd look like he'd looked to me, as if he were resting in the shade. When I walked over to Fiona, she was sitting on the rock, staring at the ground. The binoculars sat on the rock beside her.

"If Trevanian gets that truck started," she said, "he might take off and leave us here."

"He might." I leaned against a boulder opposite. I wiped a handkerchief over my face and neck. "Then again, he might just wait, like he said."

"I don't trust him."

"You want to go with him if he leaves?"

She turned her head firmly. She asked me what I'd done to the chopper.

"Booby trap."

"Why?"

"Because I couldn't think of anything smarter. And because we're going to need every bit of help we can get."

"Do you think it was really Brad he heard?"

"I don't know."

I looked down at the camp. If the rebel convoy came, the best place for us to be was somewhere low on the other ridge, above the office block. From there, we'd have the drop on their vehicles. Some of the rebels were sure to climb the ridge to check out the chopper, but it was useless to try to dream up any plan. The best we could do was take every chance that came. I wasn't hopeful.

Fiona peered through the binoculars out over the plain, then she lowered them.

"I didn't tell you about Laurence." Laurence Maguire. That wasn't really what was on her mind, but when I ignored her, she went on, "It seems Dimitri paid for Laurence's cancer treatment." I turned my head slowly and looked at her. She nodded. "Laurence only told Olympia about it a few days after they came over to our place."

"Dimitri paid for Laurence's treatment? He didn't even know Laurence."

"He'd been in contact with Laurence for years, apparently. Something you said to Laurence made him want to come clean about it." I was dumbstruck. She toyed with the binoculars around her neck. "Seems when Dimitri joined Delta he decided it was best if he stayed right out of Olympia's life. And the girls'. He wanted to give Laurence a clean run, he contacted Laurence and told him. After that, Laurence and Dimitri met once or twice a year, Laurence says Dimitri just wanted to be reassured that the girls were okay, Laurence used to give him photos, stuff like that."

"And Dimitri gave him money?"

"Only when he found out Laurence had cancer. Cancer, and no way of paying for proper treatment."

I turned it over. Finally the financial mess at the center of Dimitri's affairs made some kind of sense. Dimitri had dug himself into a deep financial hole in order to keep Laurence alive and the Maguire family—the ex-Spandos family—solvent. It wasn't a gambling debt he'd needed to pay. It was a debt he'd taken on his own shoulders for his estranged family's sake. A debt of honor. I hung my head, appalled.

"Laurence swears it was only after Dimitri died that he realized Dimitri had remortgaged his own apartment to cover the payments on the treatment," Fiona said. "He swears Dimitri promised him he could afford it with no problems."

"Jesus Christ." I squeezed my eyes, then looked out over the plain, but my vision was blurred. I was hurting bad at that moment, and not, I admit, just for Dimitri. After a minute, Fiona spoke again. This time she said what was really on her mind.

"You can't despise me as much as I hate myself," she said.

"I don't despise you." I faced her, then froze. I stared over her shoulder.

"Ned?"

Striding across, I grabbed the binoculars and focused on the track northwest. A dust cloud was moving down the track in the direction of Dujanka. I grabbed my gun and we started down the ridge.

When we reached the fuel dump, I pointed to the boulders, low on the northern ridge above the office block, and told Fiona to get up there. She veered away, looking over her shoulder down the track toward the dust cloud. It was clearly visible now, and closing fast. I ran to the maintenance shed.

"Trevanian!" He spun around, startled. "Convoy!" I said.

He got up on the bumper and leaned over the engine. "Just have to connect the fucking battery."

I jumped up on the footboard and pulled the keys from the ignition. Then I got down and headed for the door.

"Hey!" he shouted, and I turned. His glance slid to where his holster rested on the workbench. He looked back at me threateningly, and right then we heard the engines of the approaching convoy. I nodded to the holster.

"Bring it," I said.

He swore at me, but he got the holster and pistol and followed me as I ran from the shed.

The convoy wasn't in sight yet, but it was close. Close enough for us to hear the gears grinding on one of the trucks as we scrambled up to the cover of the boulders above the office block. Trevanian was raging. He asked me why I hadn't fired a warning shot, and when I ignored that, he asked me if the convoy was the one we'd seen, the one that attacked us. When I told him we couldn't make it out, he swore again.

Twenty yards farther up the scree, we dropped behind the pile of boulders where Fiona was already hiding. She was kneeling, peering down the track through the binoculars. Trevanian snatched them from her hands.

"Out of the light, for fucksake." He dropped back in the shade and turned the binoculars down the track.

Fiona looked to me, startled, and I signaled her to move along, and when she did, I went and crouched beside her. "Stay down. Keep out of Trevanian's way."

"What do we do if they've got Brad?"

"Sticking your head up won't help him." I touched her shoulder and she sat down and I went back to Trevanian. For a minute I watched him watching the track. We could still hear the vehicles, but the dust cloud was gone. "Are they coming?" I asked him.

"They're holding the vehicles back."

"What can you see?"

"Two scouts, on foot."

"Army scouts?"

"Rebels."

I eased my head a few inches to the left and looked through a gap in the boulders. To either side of the track, back past the fuel dump, I saw them, two guys in old jeans and sweatshirts with guns, crouching as they came on. Then they saw the chopper on the far ridge and they stopped and signaled behind to the vehicles, which remained out of sight. My heart stood still for a moment. If they retreated into the bush, they'd be taking Brad with them. Probably for good.

"I might be able to get around to the trucks," I said.

Trevanian lowered the glasses. He took his pistol from the holster. "Try anything smart like that, I'll shoot you."

The engines revved, finally the convoy came on slowly down the track, trundling into view. A canopied truck and three off-roaders with the Barchevsky Mining stencils on the doors, it was the same convoy that had attacked us, only the drilling rig had been abandoned somewhere along the way. The off-roaders stopped at the fuel dump, several rebels got out and started up the ridge toward the chopper with their AK47s held ready. One guy stayed behind at the dump, he walked around kicking drums, searching for diesel. The canopied truck drove right up and parked in front of the office block below us. The driver got out, then two rebels clambered out the back. I took the binoculars from Trevanian and he put a hand on my shoulder.

"I wasn't kidding," he said.

I brushed his hand off and crawled across to Fiona.

"If Brad's anywhere, he's in the truck," I told her quietly.

"What can we do?"

"You can't do anything." When she looked at me, I turned my back on Trevanian, five yards away, and slid my finger over my lips. Fiona glanced over my shoulder. Then she nodded, she'd gotten the message. "Whatever happens," I whispered, "stay with Trevanian. And keep down."

The rebels from the off-roaders were moving quickly up the southern ridge. Down in the camp, one rebel sat on the office-block steps while his two companions went inside. There was no way I could get near the truck without being seen. I raised the glasses to the southern ridge and watched the rebels climb, then I turned the glasses on the truck below us. After a while, I thought I glimpsed movement in the dark shadow beneath the canopy.

"There's someone in the back of the truck."

"Brad?"

"I can't see."

"Oh Jesus," Fiona said, closing her eyes. "Please God."

I strained but I still couldn't see, then I scanned the slope immediately below us. We were thirty or forty yards from a drainage ditch that encircled the camp. I turned the glasses up the ridge again. Minutes later, the rebels fanned out as they neared the crest. From the corner of my eye, I saw Trevanian signaling me to give him the glasses. Then we heard firing, a burst from an AK47 up near the chopper. I swept the glasses over the scene. Dust kicked up beneath the chopper tail, and a moment later we heard the matching burst of gunfire.

"What's up?" Trevanian whispered. "What the hell's happening?"

"They've seen the pilot."

"Give me the glasses."

I hung on to them. I watched the rebels close on the chopper, they fired several more bursts before they were satisfied that the pilot was dead. Then I looked down to the camp. The three rebels had left the office block, they moved out past the truck and looked up the southern ridge. The guy at the fuel dump was looking up there too.

"Give me the bloody glasses," Trevanian said.

I swung them up the ridge. The rebels were moving in cautiously on the chopper. One guy went forward and tried the rear door. A moment later, another guy went and tried the passenger door. I passed the glasses to Fiona and told her to give them to Trevanian. But then, as she moved, I reached out and touched her hand. The touch stopped her, she looked up at me, and our eyes held for a moment.

"Glasses," hissed Trevanian.

And then the chopper blew.

CHAPTER 39

What the fuck?" Trevanian crawled to the edge of the boulder and looked out.

Machine-gun fire started up near the chopper. I shot a glance around my end of the boulder. In the camp, the rebels rushed out to see what was happening, they moved toward the fuel dump, looking up the ridge. I squeezed Fiona's arm, then scurried out from cover and went down the slope. Behind me, I heard Trevanian calling me back angrily, but I kept going. I was in the open for about fifteen seconds, it seemed like forever, then I dropped into the drainage ditch by the office block.

Machine-gun fire still hammered hard near the chopper. I put my head up from the ditch and saw the truck about twenty-five yards from me. The three rebels over by the fuel dump had stopped. When they turned and came back toward camp, I ducked down.

I slung my gun across my back and crawled along the sandy drainage ditch till I was within five yards of the office block. I heard the rebels walking up the steps at the front, and I slithered out of the ditch and crawled under the office block. Two rebels were inside.

The third one was standing on the steps, I could see his boots and, ten yards beyond his boots, the canopied truck.

I dragged myself forward on my forearms, then one of the rebels stomped on the floor over my head, and I froze. One of the rebels inside shouted and came out. I watched his boots go down the steps and across to the truck, and he climbed in the back. There was more shouting, then he jumped down, dragging someone down after him. This other guy fell and hit the ground hard. A white guy. An older guy, I glimpsed his face, it was battered and bloody. The rebel dragged him onto his feet, then across to the steps and up into the office above me.

I looked up at the flexing floor over my right shoulder.

"Open!" shouted the rebel.

"Water." It was the white guy. "Give me some goddamn water." There was the sound of a strike, then a thump on the floor. The white guy had been hit and gone down. "Jesus. Jesus Christ, you dumb bastard."

"Open!"

"There's nothing in there, for chrissake. I don't have the combination."

A gun was cocked, the white guy shouted, "No!" and then the gun fired, bam, bam, bam, each shot drilling a hole through the floor two feet from my head, I went rigid. There was silence. The rebel went out to the truck again.

My chest was tight, sweat broke out on my back, and I squeezed myself up closer to the steps. I dragged my gun off my back and leveled it at a point just behind the truck. There was shouting in the truck, then a shot, then a body toppled from the back of the truck and hit the ground, lifeless. Another white guy. My heart turned to stone.

A white arm, dark hair like Brad's, but the face was turned away from me. While I was focused on the body, the rebel jumped down from the truck and dragged another guy after him. I just saw the sneakers and jeans as this guy was dragged up the steps into the office.

"Holy shit." He'd seen the body.

"Open!"

"Holy fucking shit." Brad? I strained to hear through the floor. There was a strike, a cry of pain, then another shouted order to open the safe. "Don't you hit me again, you fuckin' prick." Brad. It was Brad. I almost threw up.

The rebel hit him again, and he went down, moaning.

"Open!"

"Oh, Jesus. Oh, shit. Let me get up, for chrissake."

I squirmed around to the side of the steps. One rebel remained standing there. I could take him out, but the pair inside would hear it and kill Brad.

There was movement in the office above me, then Brad's voice again.

"Don't crowd me." They hit him. He cried out, then shouted, "You're blocking the goddamn light! I can't see the numbers. Look. The fuckin' numbers. No light, I can't see them!"

The guy on the steps turned and went inside, and I knew that was it, the only chance I was going to get. I crawled into the open, flicked the P23 from automatic to single fire, and moved.

Up the steps and across the empty porch, and when the first guy inside turned, I fired, and he smashed into the wall. I swung left, shot the second guy in the face, and the third guy raised his gun and got it tangled in the strap, and he looked at me with childlike surprise. I shot him in the chest but he stayed on his feet so I shot him again and he went down.

Brad stared at me, dazed. He was unshaven. His face was bruised and swollen, there was a deep gash over his right eye. "Dad?" Amazement. Shock.

I checked each body, made sure they were dead. Then I clasped Brad's arm. He surveyed the carnage. He couldn't speak.

"Any more of your guys in the truck?"

He shook his head.

I put my free arm around his shoulders, hugged him, then stepped back. "Let's go." I shook his arm and went to the door. When I turned back, he was looking at the bodies. "Brad!" His head came up. "If we don't get out of here, we'll be dead too." Bewildered, he came over. "Can you hold a gun?" I said, and when he nodded, I picked up one of the rebel's AK47s and gave it to him. "It's loaded. Just point and shoot." I looked out, and up the southern ridge. The rebels who'd survived the booby trap were coming down, they'd almost reached the fuel dump, and when they saw me, they fired.

Bullets ripped into the office walls, I threw myself back inside, knocking Brad off his feet. I dragged him over behind the safe as gunfire sprayed the office block. We hunkered down. After half a minute, it stopped, and I eased my head around the safe and looked out.

There were three of them, they'd passed the fuel dump, now they were loping down the track toward us, guns at their hips. I pushed myself out into the shadows of the office, took aim at the middle one and fired. He dropped like he'd been poleaxed. The other two ran for cover, shooting wildly. I rolled back behind the safe. Brad was sitting with his back to the safe, the AK47 cradled in his lap.

"You okay?" I said, and he nodded. Then I noticed the blood on his shirt. I bent closer. Then I took the gun out of his hands. "You've been hit."

He looked down and saw the blood. "Oh, Jesus." His face twisted. "Jesus fucking Christ."

I pushed down on his shoulder, lifting his shirt. "Sit still." It was on his left side, between his hip and his ribs, I wiped the exit wound with my sleeve. A small hole, and clean. I found the entry just two inches away, and when I wiped it, the blood seeped back slowly. The arteries were intact, the bullet seemed to have cauterized the wound. "It doesn't look too bad."

"I can't feel it. I can't fuckin' feel it."

The only organ the bullet might have hit was his left kidney. I couldn't be sure, but it looked to me like the bullet had missed. I told him that.

"You wouldn't bullshit me, Dad."

"I wouldn't bullshit you. It's gone straight through you. It's a flesh wound, you're okay."

He blinked back tears. I tore a piece off my shirt and made him hold the material against the wounds. Then I went back to the door. The rebel I'd dropped on the track hadn't moved. When the other two saw movement in the office, they fired, but they ceased fire the moment I pulled my head in. They were conserving their ammo.

I returned to Brad. He was breathing hard.

"I'm feelin' it now," he said between clenched teeth.

"You'll be okay."

"What are you doing here?"

"That can wait."

Then from outside, up the hill, we heard Fiona shout, "Ned!"

I swore. If we could hear her, so could the two rebels.

Brad screwed up his face. "Mom?"

"Ned!" she shouted. "There's one in the ditch behind you!"

"Mom's here?" said Brad in disbelief, but I was already up and moving to the rear window. I looked out and saw the guy immediately. Distracted by Fiona's shout, he was looking up the ridge in her direction. I climbed onto a chair, took careful aim, and fired. The window popped, cracks webbing out from the central bullet hole. I lowered my gun and saw the guy spread-eagled, facedown, on the far bank of the ditch. The rebels out front fired again, and I jumped down from the chair.

Crawling over to the door, I looked out. Two rebels had crossed to the northern side of the track, they were moving up the ridge toward Fiona and Trevanian.

"Trevanian!" I shouted, and instantly a hail of bullets came streaming in from the track out front. I rolled onto my back and lay still. When the gunfire stopped, I rolled across to Brad.

"What the hell's happenin'?" he said. "Why's Mom here?"

I got up and went to the rear window. No one out there, just the dead guy in the ditch. I returned to the door. They'd left one guy out front near the track to keep me and Brad pinned down. The other two were moving in on Fiona and Trevanian fast.

"Trevanian! They're coming up at you from your right!"

Bullets hammered into the office walls from out front, and when they stopped, Trevanian shouted, "How many?"

"Two!"

I crawled across to Brad. I told him to stay behind the safe.

"Where are you goin'?"

"Stay here." I put the AK47 in his lap, then I went to the rear window and smacked the gun butt into the aluminum frame. The glass showered down, and I tore the frame free, then slung the gun across my back and climbed out. I dropped to the ground and leaped into the ditch. The rebel out front let fly a few loose rounds beneath the office block, but in the ditch I was safe. I crawled fifteen yards, then quickly lifted my head. The rebel out front was waiting.

He fired, the dirt near my face exploded, and I ducked, then reversed five yards up the ditch, and when I cautiously lifted my head this time, I was shielded by the steel corner support of the office block.

I looked up the ridge and my heart jumped into my throat. Two rebels were just yards beneath where Fiona and Trevanian were hidden. I swung my gun up, but before I could fire there were two pistol shots in quick succession, bap, bap. The two rebels on the hill went down and stayed down. A moment later, Trevanian and Fiona came shuffling around the boulder to where I could see them. Trevanian had the pistol ready.

"Any more?" he shouted down to me.

"One!" I called up. "Out by the track near the fuel dump!"

"Can't you take him?" he hollered, and at that moment, the last rebel directed a burst at the ditch, and dirt and stones kicked up all around me. I dropped onto my butt, switched to automatic, then raised my gun up over my head, arms at full extension, and fired a burst toward the rebel. When I ceased fire, there was silence.

"Rourke?" called Trevanian.

"Still here."

"Did you hit him?"

"I don't know." I lifted my head warily. Then I saw that the rebel had fallen out from behind the earth ramp where he'd been hidden. "Maybe," I said.

Trevanian rose and looked over the boulder. "I think you did."

I crouched and switched to single-fire. I wasn't getting out of the ditch until I'd made sure. Suddenly I heard Fiona call, "Brad?"

I lifted my head. To my horror I saw Brad's sneakers on the front steps of the office block. And then, out near the fuel dump, I saw the rebel rise onto his elbows, his gun at his shoulder, taking aim.

"Mom?"

"Get inside!" I shouted, and I stood, stepped around the side of the office block, and lifted my gun, but then there was a single shot, bap, and for a moment my whole world seemed to freeze. Then I looked to the steps. Brad stood there swaying, holding his side, then he grabbed the steel banister and eased himself down to sit on the porch. I turned to the rebel. He stayed up a second longer, then his arms crumpled, and his face dropped hard into the dirt. Finally I looked up the ridge. Trevanian was leaning against the boulder, both his arms resting on top of it, his pistol gripped firm in both hands. He was still sighting down the pistol at the rebel.

I put my gun to my shoulder, walked across the open ground to the rebel, keeping him in my sights. Then I bent down. The back of his head was pulped. I rolled him over. Trevanian's shot had gone through the left eye. I studied the dead face awhile, then I stood and looked up to the ridge. About eighty yards. Fiona was stumbling down toward the office block, calling to Brad, who sat on the steps, dazed. Trevanian finished checking the two bodies up by the boulder, then he started down. It took him a minute, I watched him the whole way, he stopped on the other side of the body at my feet. He glanced down, then back up to me.

"Nice shot," I said.

He jerked his head toward the truck. He said he wanted to get moving.

"My son's wounded," I told him. "We're not going anywhere."

"The army'll be here any minute."

"The army doesn't want me or my family."

His eyes narrowed. When I raised my gun, leveled it at his chest, he tossed his head toward Fiona and Brad. "You going to murder me right in front of them?"

"What chance did you give Dimitri?"

"Dimitri," he said, and he looked down at the dead rebel between us. After everything else that had happened, I guess he hadn't expected that. But he didn't bother to deny it. "Dimitri brought it on himself. Ask your boss."

"Rossiter knew less about it than I did."

He looked up. "You came out here to get your son," he said after a moment. "So now you've got him. He's alive because of me."

"It's because of you he's here."

Trevanian screwed up his face, then held out his hand. "I need the keys," he said. "For the truck."

He had killed Dimitri, I was sure of that now. And he'd also imprisoned me in the *Sebastopol*'s hold, freighted me to the Congo, and broken the arms embargo, a list of offenses that, proven, could put him in jail for decades. Against that, he'd gotten me to Dujanka and saved Brad's life, and I didn't know how I was meant to weigh all that in the scales of justice, or whether I should even try.

Then over Trevanian's shoulder I saw a dust cloud moving toward us. The army. I looked from the dust cloud back to him. He hadn't heard the distant engines yet. I took the keys from my pocket. I considered them a second, then tossed them to him, and he caught them and smiled.

"You going to write me that retraction now, or you want to send it to me?"

"I think I'll send it," I said, then I nodded over his shoulder and he turned. The dust cloud was closing in fast. When he spun back to me, I had my finger on the trigger, I was sighting down the barrel at his heart. "You've still got a chance."

"You fucking prick."

"That's more than you gave Dimitri."

We could both hear the engines now. He wanted to kill me, I could see that. He wanted to, but he knew I'd kill him first, so in the end he just swore and turned heel and ran for the truck. I kept him in my sights the whole way. He connected the battery, then dropped the hood and scrambled into the cab. He hit the ignition, pumped the pedal, and hit the ignition again. Three times the engine turned over then died, but the fourth time it caught, the engine screamed, and the first Congolese army vehicle appeared on the track at the mouth of the valley.

Trevanian hadn't seen it, he hauled on the steering wheel, one eye on me, I still had my gun trained on him. Then he swung his truck onto the track. He must have seen the convoy then, they were dead ahead of him, a hundred yards. The lead army truck stopped, an officer got out and raised his hand, signaling for Trevanian to stop too. But Trevanian must have seen what I'd seen, the Internal Security vehicle right behind the officer. If Trevanian stopped, Lagundi would have him. It was too late to turn back. He hit the accelerator and hunkered down.

The officer didn't hesitate, he shouted to his men and they jumped out and opened fire.

I dropped to my belly. "Get inside!" I shouted to Fiona and Brad. She had her arm around his waist, they shuffled off the porch, inside.

Trevanian's truck was racing down the track now, the firing became a barrage. Bullets thudded into the truck, smashing the windshield, tearing the metal, and loose shots zipped over my head and clanged against the corrugated iron of the camp buildings.

Trevanian's truck left the track. It hit the dirt embankment, jolted, and ran on thirty yards, then smashed head-on into a tree, and stalled. The firing from the soldiers died away. As one group of soldiers ran to the truck, another followed the officer, who was walking down the track toward me. I pushed my gun aside and got slowly to my feet, my hands raised.

I watched the soldiers put another few rounds into the cab of Trevanian's truck, then they went up to it and opened the door. Trevanian's body flopped out, they pulled on one arm, and the body dropped like a crumpled rag to the ground.

Then behind me Brad shouted, "Dad!" and I looked around. He was standing in the office-block doorway with Fiona, their arms around each other's waist. I glanced at the advancing officer and his men, then walked over to the office block, keeping my hands up. When I got closer I saw the look on Brad's face, my heart lurched. Fiona staggered, I ran up the steps and grabbed her and helped Brad ease her down onto the porch.

"Oh, God," said Brad. "Oh God, oh Jesus."

Blood was seeping through Fiona's shirt, just beneath her right breast, it wasn't a flesh wound like Brad's. When she was propped against the porch rail, I withdrew my arm from her back, and my arm was bloody. Her face was turning white. Her mouth was open, she was trying to speak, but nothing was coming.

"Mom?" said Brad.

I leaned in close to her face. Her eyes were glazing over. "Hang on, Fiona. I'll get a medic for you. Just hang on." Her head seemed to dip. "Keep talking to her," I told Brad, then I got up and went down the steps, and the officer and his men raised their guns at me.

"Medic!" I gestured to the blood on my arm, pointed behind to where Fiona was lying. I made frantic hand signals, and kept talking at the officer, and after a few moments he got it. He ordered the men to lower their guns, then he took me back to one of the vehicles in his convoy. He reached in by the driver, unstrapped a small metal box with a red cross painted on its lid, and gave it to me. I flipped the box open. Bandages and unmarked bottles of medicines and pills.

"Don't you have a medic?" I asked in despair. He looked blank. "Doctor? *Monsieur le docteur, ici?*"

"*Non,*" he said, and shrugged.

I put the box under my arm and ran.

She wasn't propped against the porch rail now, she was lying on her back, and Brad was kneeling beside her, holding her hand. I leaped up the steps, opening the box, grabbing at the bandages.

"We can stop the bleeding. Undo her shirt," I told Brad. "Come on!"

He lifted his face to me, it was contorted with pain, and he looked down at his mother again. Then I looked down at her. Her eyes were wide open and lifeless, and her face was white and still. I slumped against the porch rail. Brad held both her hands in his, and wept. She was gone. The metal box fell from my hand. I lifted my eyes and stared at the sun.

CHAPTER 40

My memories of what followed are blurred, but I know we were taken back to Mbuji-Mayi by the Congolese army. From there, contact was made with the U.S. Embassy, and a few hours later a U.S. Navy chopper arrived, it ferried Brad and me, and Fiona's body, out to the carrier where Channon was waiting. I stayed close to Brad the whole journey. He was in shock, like me, but I forced myself to talk to him, told him to stay focused on himself, assured him that the Navy doctors would take care of him. In truth, neither of us was really there. We were still where we would be for months, years, or maybe even the rest of our lives, back on the porch at Dujanka, with Fiona, dead, lying at our feet.

Her death overwhelmed everything.

When the surgeon aboard the carrier took Brad into the operating theater, Channon showed me to a private cabin. He asked me if I wanted him to stay, I told him no, so he left me. Without Brad to tend to, I had nothing to hold it off any longer. I dropped into my bunk and felt the consuming wave of grief rise up and break over me. Fiona was gone. I had lost my wife. Brad had lost his mother. The why of it wasn't anything like clear to me, but I'd played some part in putting her in front of the bullet, I knew that.

I pressed my forehead hard against the steel bulkhead till the pressure burned. She was gone for all eternity. Inside me, my soul began to shrivel up and die.

"We don't have to do this now," said Alex Channon when I appeared at his cabin door with a five-page handwritten report. It had been nearly twenty-four hours since I arrived on the ship. In that time I'd grieved till exhaustion overcame me, then I'd slept. On waking, I'd gone down to check on Brad. He was still sleeping after minor surgery on his wound, but the doctors assured me he was fine, so I'd returned to my cabin. There my mind began circling, spiraling inward. I kept having thoughts I couldn't control. To distract myself, and break the cycle, I sat down and played it just like a soldier returning from a mission. I wrote my own debrief, scribbling it out on a few loose pages. Just the facts, from the *Sebastopol*'s departure from New Jersey, to Trevanian's death. It was a kind of shallow therapy, a way of seeing what had happened while keeping my feelings at bay. But when it was done, my mind immediately started circling again, so I gathered the pages up and brought them to Channon. Now he swiveled around in his chair, spreading his hands. "Leave it till we get home. You've got plenty enough to deal with."

I stepped across the small cabin and dropped the pages on his fold-down desk. I told him that it was done. I said that he might as well read it.

He fingered the pages. "Anything I don't already know?"

I shrugged a shoulder. Probably not.

"Okay." He pushed the pages to one side of his desk. "I'll take a look at it tonight. Now, how about you go back and do like I said, get some rest."

I started to nod, then everything seemed to disconnect and I touched my fingers to my forehead. My eyes clouded over, I shook my head.

"You want some water?"

I shook my head again, no.

"Something stronger?"

"Just give me a second."

"Sure." He nodded to his bunk, and I sat down. He gave me a minute. "How's Brad doing?" he asked finally.

"He's still down in the infirmary. He's okay."

"His wound wasn't too bad. In a year, he'll be bragging about it."

I looked up. "How in hell did I let it happen?"

"Hey."

"I was standing right there."

"Don't start down the blame road. You've got nothing to blame yourself for."

I made a sound.

"I mean it," he said. "Look at it this way. If you weren't there, you'd have lost Brad too."

"I lied to her."

"You were protecting her."

"If it was all about protecting her, how come she's dead?"

Alex pursed his lips together. He knew I was really talking to myself, not to him. He stayed silent, gave me a minute to collect myself. Finally I hauled myself up from the bunk.

"The ship's chaplain dropped by," Alex said. "He thought you might want him to call in on you later." When I turned my head, no, Alex said, "I'll let him down easy."

I lifted my chin to the report on his desk. I suggested I might come by in the morning to talk it through.

"If you feel up to it. Sure we can."

"I've made Rita a copy."

He made a face. "Really, Ned. This stuff can wait."

I looked at him, expressionless. Suddenly disconnected again.

"Ned?"

"Sure," I said, nodding, but not knowing why. I told him I'd come by in the morning.

Just past Channon's cabin the passage led onto a few square yards of steel plate that were railed like a balcony, I went and stood at the rail. The wind was getting up, and the waves were building like maybe a storm was coming in from farther out at sea. The ship rose and dipped, an oil drum floated past in a wide pool of slick, and I stood silent and watched the endlessly rolling water. Somewhere down in the bowels of the ship, in the mortuary, Fiona's body rose and fell with the waves.

CHAPTER 41

I **moved your son across to the IC unit," the ship's chief surgeon**
told me, then he saw my alarm and added hastily, "Nothing
wrong. Just quieter over there, I thought he could do with the
privacy."

He led me out of the general ward, where half a dozen civilian
evacuees were being treated for minor injuries or shock. He assured
me again, just as he'd assured me when he finished operating on
Brad, that the only long-term effect of the wound would be the external scars. "Neat holes," he remarked to himself. "He was lucky."

A few yards down the passage, he shouldered open the door to
the Intensive Care unit. Propped on his pillows, Brad was watching
a TV that sat on a trolley at the end of his bed. When he saw us, he
hit the remote, the sound on the TV died.

"CNN," Brad said tiredly. "They're saying the coup's over." He
dropped the remote on the bedside locker, and winced. The doctor
asked if he needed more painkillers, but Brad shook his head and
shuffled himself a little more upright against the pillows. Then the
doctor asked him some questions about how he felt. Any dizziness?

None, Brad said. Any internal pain? Brad told him there was just a dull ache in the immediate region of the wound. Satisfied, the doctor said someone would be along shortly to check the dressing, then he bobbed his head to me and withdrew.

I looked at Brad's face. His expression was vacant, totally washed out, like he'd hit bottom and stayed there, like grief had finally numbed him. He picked up the remote and seemed to stare past the TV at the empty IC beds. There were cardiac and respiratory monitors on the trolleys, and on the arms of the trolleys, opaque liquid inside clear plastic sacs. Everything had a spotlessly clean stainless-steel gleam.

"You see this?" said Brad. He pointed to the TV with the remote, turning up the sound. "Listen to this jerk."

It was still CNN, more news from the Congo. According to the journalist, life in Kinshasa was returning to normal. Reports from the east of the country confirmed that the rebels had either fled or been defeated. The government was firmly in control again. Western evacuees had begun returning to the city.

"He's makin' it sound like nothin' happened," said Brad in disgust.

We watched the rest of the report in silence. There was the inevitable mention of diamonds and cobalt, the mineral wealth of the country, then a brief interview with the U.S. ambassador. The ambassador explained that he was in close contact with the Congolese government, he indicated that the Congolese President had requested assistance to help maintain peace in the country. The ambassador had apparently promised the services of several hundred U.S. Marines who would enter the country under the UN flag just as soon as the appropriate resolution was passed by the UN Security Council. He confirmed that the coup was over. The rebellion, he said, had been quashed.

Brad hit the remote and the TV screen went blank. His head fell back into the pillows.

"Gotten any sleep?" I asked him.

"Some. Not much."

I told him it was the best thing, if he could manage it.

His head rolled, he looked at me. "How about you?"

"Sleep?"

"Yeah."

"A few hours. Enough to keep me going."

He faced the blank TV screen. "I keep seein' her," he said. "I keep seein' Mom back at Dujanka." I couldn't look at him, I faced the TV too. "It's like in a crummy movie or something. I close my eyes, she's right there." He fell silent. When I glanced back at him, tears stood in his eyes. "Christ. And that jerk, talkin' like nothin' happened." He threw the remote, it cracked against the corner of the TV and went clattering across the floor. I put a hand on his shoulder. "It should have been me," he said. "If it wasn't for me, she'd never have been there."

"That's crazy."

"If I hadn't taken the job—you didn't want me to take it."

"You can't hold that against yourself. Nobody can."

"Mom didn't want me to come out here either."

"She got you the offer."

"Yeah. But I knew she had second thoughts, and I came anyway." He looked up at me. "You know why I came, Dad?"

I lifted my hand from his shoulder. I suggested we leave this for another time.

"I came because of you," he said. "Because I knew you didn't want me to come. I came because I thought that might piss you off, because I thought you were hurtin' Mom."

"It doesn't matter."

"Yes it does. You weren't even havin' an affair, that was bullshit, right? You're still in the Army. You were just doin' your job all along. Every damn thing you said about the Congo, what you warned me about, it was all true. Everything. It was just like you said." He pushed his head back into the pillows and looked past me. "If I'd listened to you, none of this would have happened."

I sat down on the edge of his bed. I thought a moment, then I said, "I gave up the right to be listened to by anyone the day I left West Point."

"You were doing your duty."

My duty. I bowed my head and waited for the wave of shame to subside.

"Mom would never have stopped you doin' anything you wanted," he said.

"I know."

"She hated it when you joined Haplon. I could see she really hated it. I bet she never told you that."

"No," I agreed.

"She kept that kinda stuff to herself." When I nodded, I felt him studying me. Then he said, "How did Barchevsky die?" I faced him. "Mom told me," he said. "She was tellin' me how you got out of Kinshasa. She said he was trapped or somethin'. She said you found him."

I nodded, wary.

"Rebels?" he said.

"Yeah."

"Was he shot?"

"Head and throat."

"Was he dead when you found him?"

When I nodded again, his eyes stayed on me. I told him the fighting in that area had been fierce. He lifted his chin.

"I was kinda surprised when she radioed me from his place."

"She hitched a ride up from Johannesburg."

We looked at each other. My willful misinterpretation had not gotten past him. My heart thumped hard. He suspected. Talk at the mine? Pieces he'd seen and heard, then put together? Somewhere along the way, Brad had picked up on the possibility of a relationship between Barchevsky and his mother. But he couldn't say that to me. Then I glimpsed another thought lurking way back.

"He was dead when I found him," I said.

Brad considered that, then nodded. Of course. He'd never thought any different.

But this was territory we were never going to revisit, and even if we couldn't talk openly, I didn't want to leave it now quite so equivocally, with Brad feeling that Fiona had in any way tarnished her life with me, or that I nursed any rancor or grievance. That wasn't what I believed. That wasn't what I truly felt.

I put my hand on his arm. "If you knew a month back what you know now, Brad, you would have made some different choices, wouldn't you?" He looked from my hand up to me. He cocked his head. "Wouldn't you?" I asked him.

"Thousands."

"Me too," I said. "And if Fiona was here, I like to think maybe she might have said the same."

He looked at me in that same piercing way his mother had. Piercing. Down deep. Then he put his hand on my hand. "She would never have done anything to hurt you, Dad," he said, and at that moment I felt my heart gently break.

CHAPTER 42

Mind if I join you?"

I looked up. Rita sat down opposite me, and I hung my head over my plate, and toyed with my food. Rita had been with Channon, waiting for us, when we were choppered onto the ship. I'd spoken with her briefly when I dropped off a copy of my report, and ever since then, she told me now, she'd been holed up in the Communications Room. She looked around the mess in some surprise. Marines in blue UN berets were passing among the diners, remnants of the civilian evacuees, women and children, about thirty of them, with packed bags by their chairs, waiting for the call to the helipad and the return flight to their homes in Kinshasa. Some looked ready to go, but others were discussing flight schedules between Kinshasa and various European cities. Rita smiled at one or two of the women, then returned her attention to me. She produced the five-page copy of my report from her purse.

I made a face, and she looked apologetic. "I'd put it off if I could, Ned."

"If I think of something to add, I'll tell you."

She placed the report on the table between us and started talking, telling me which of her superiors she wanted me to speak with. At last she paused and waited for my response. I looked up from my plate.

"Rita. Hawkeye is finished."

"Finished?" She reared back in disbelief. "This is so not finished."

"Trevanian's dead."

"Hawkeye wasn't about Trevanian."

I stirred my fork through the cold beans and made no comment.

"It never was. It's about the materiel. Everyone in the chain."

I remarked that I didn't expect the Congolese Minister for Police to hand his daughter over to us anytime soon.

"It wasn't just Lagundi," she protested. "What about Rossiter? The Congolese government. Damienenko. Greenbaum—"

"Okay."

"This is so not finished."

"Maybe not for you." I dropped my eyes and concentrated on my cutlery. I was too physically drained and emotionally wrung, I didn't want a debate, but she went on talking. And as I listened, it occurred to me that what Rita had seen on the streets of Kinshasa had energized her. It was as if her usual diligence and application had received a sharp and unexpected ethical spur. Before, she'd wanted Hawkeye wrapped up because that was her job, but now I detected a more distinctly moral note. She'd seen what the likes of the Haplon weapons were doing in the world, and now she wanted Hawkeye pursued to a successful conclusion—personal prosecutions, a tightening up of export procedures—because she believed that was just and right.

She leaned forward. "I know this isn't easy for you, Ned. I can't even imagine what it's like, what you're going through right now. But when you gave me this"—she put a hand on my report—"I thought you wanted, you know, to get back into it."

"Maybe I did."

"But now you don't?"

"Now I don't."

"You can't just drop the ball."

"No one's dropping the ball."

"Excuse me?"

"Rita. I'm tired."

She regarded me a moment. Then frustration got the better of her sympathy. "Well, how tired do you think I was when you hauled me down to the New Jersey docks? And when we were stuck in the *Sebastopol*? I'm not comparing that with what you've been through— I'm not crazy—but listen. You are not the only one who wishes this whole damn thing was over."

I glanced across the mess to where some Marines in UN berets were moving among the civilian evacuees, reading names from a printed list. As their names were called, the women rose and collected their belongings, then led their children out. I faced Rita again.

"You think my report's trustworthy?"

She gave me a surprised look. Say what?

"Me," I said. "I'm the guy your people were spying on, re-member?"

"Oh, give me a break."

I put my knife and fork together and pushed aside my plate.

"Don't be so damn childish," she said. "If we get into pointing fingers, we could be here all week. There've been enough screwups to go around twice since this started, and then some. Not all of them mine."

I slumped back in my chair. I raised my hands. She studied me a moment, and the aggression seemed to drain out of her. She leaned back.

"I'm sorry, Ned. This really isn't the right time."

"No."

"I'm just so fed up with being one step behind. I guess it's making me ratty." When I nodded, she smiled wanly. "I wasn't asking for your agreement." In a reciprocal gesture of contrition, I confessed that my jibe about being spied on was cheap and petty. She waved that aside. Then she scooped up my report and returned it to her purse. "We'll call this a postponement," she said. She looked around at the departing evacuees and Marines, they swayed as they walked, and Rita wondered aloud if the high seas they'd been talking about up in the Communications Room had arrived. When she turned back to me, I could see she had something to say. Not business.

"Channon said you told your wife about Hawkeye." When I nodded, she said, "She understood that? That you weren't an arms salesman?"

"Yeah."

"And you told her about you and me. She knew that we weren't—"

"Yeah."

She lifted her head. "Good," she said.

I didn't say anything.

"And Brad knows about Hawkeye?"

"Most of it."

"He won't blame you."

"He doesn't have to."

"You're the same man."

I turned aside. I didn't want to talk about it. Not with Rita. Not with anyone.

She said, "It's changed everything for you, hasn't it." When I faced her again, her eyes shone. "It has, hasn't it. Everything."

I nodded.

"After my mom died," she said, "I went kind of loopy. It was my dad who got me through it. He gave me about the only decent advice he's given me in my whole life."

"What was that?"

"He told me not to turn my grief into a shrine."

We looked at each other. Then she stood up, telling me she had to get back to her cabin. I offered to walk her, and we left the mess together.

We walked in silence for a while, then Rita said, "You know, I don't know if this is presumptuous or not, but if there's anything I can do." She gestured vaguely. I thanked her for the thought, but we both knew there was nothing anyone could do. She hugged her purse to her chest as we climbed the stairs to the next deck. She asked about Brad. I told her what the doctors had told me, that the only reason they were keeping him down in the IC unit was to make sure he rested. In a few days they expected him to be walking around.

"Give him these," she said, reaching into her purse and producing two CDs. They were still in their wrappers, purchased from the shop aboard the carrier. She looked apologetic. "I thought he might appreciate the distraction."

The thoughtfulness was unexpected, and touching. I asked if maybe she didn't want to come down and give them to Brad herself.

"Strangers bearing presents and sympathy?" She arched a brow. "I know how that feels. When my mom died, we had half the neighborhood calling. No thanks." She held the CDs out to me. A thought darted through my mind, she read it on my face. "I'm not trying to be pushy, Ned. If you'd rather I keep them—"

"No."

"Really?"

I took the CDs. Gangsta rap and heavy metal. Brad was going to loathe them. I thanked her again. We moved down the gangway, swaying on our feet, then finally reached her cabin.

"Something you can do for me," she said, searching in her purse for her key. "Get Channon to see me before he goes."

"Goes?"

"Departs. Before he leaves the ship." She found her key and closed her purse. "He's flying with the Marines into Kinshasa."

"Why?" I screwed up my face. "When's this?"

"He's the Pentagon's man on this peacekeeping thing. Seems they needed a senior officer, he's here, so he's it, at least till they get someone out from Washington."

I asked Rita why she couldn't go see him herself.

"I've tried. A million times. Hawkeye's disappeared clean off his radar. The way things are going," she remarked dismally, "I'll have to buy my own ticket to Zug."

Some evacuees and their Marine escort came along the gangway, we stepped aside and let them file past.

"Zug, Switzerland?" I said.

"Ah-ha."

The Marine led the evacuees up to the next deck, they were asking if the pitching ship was going to cause problems with the chopper. He told them not to worry, and they disappeared out of sight. Rita put her key in the door. I grabbed her arm.

"What do you have to do in Zug?"

"Aren't you the guy who just told me Hawkeye was finished?"

When I gave her a look, she pulled her arm free. "We've traced Trevanian's late payment."

"For the Haplon materiel?"

She nodded, smiling now. "We threatened Rossiter with a subpoena if he didn't give us access to his banking records. We told him we were checking some other deal Haplon did last month. There it was. A transfer of twelve million dollars."

"You know who it came from?"

She nodded. "Now all we have to do is get the canton of Zug to rewrite its entire statute book so that we can find out who's behind Biron."

"Biron," I said.

"The company that made the payment."

My head reeled. I dropped my eyes to hide my confusion.

She opened her door, offering to show me the paperwork, all the e-mails that had gone back and forth between her and Customs in New York. When she looked back at me, my head was still bowed. "You okay?" she said, suddenly concerned.

I raised my head slowly. I gestured in the direction of my own cabin, telling her that the ship's movement was starting to get to me, that maybe I'd come and see the paperwork later, that right then I just needed to lie down. She nodded, sympathetic, and I walked away, numbed.

CHAPTER 43

Come!" Channon called when I knocked on his cabin door, and I hesitated a second, then went in. He had his back to me. He was in uniform, seated at a small desk top that folded down from the wall. He went on writing as I closed the door. "Just take the bag," he said without turning. "The rest can stay." On his bunk was a suitcase, zipped up and buckled. Beside the suitcase, a light blue UN beret. He continued writing, so I picked up the beret and inspected the badge. Olive-leaf garland of peace, wrapped around planet Earth. Finally Channon sensed something amiss, he glanced over his shoulder.

"Ned." Surprise.

"Am I interrupting?"

"No." He capped his pen and closed his pad. "No, just running through my diary. I've had a tap on the shoulder from home." He indicated the beret in my hands. By home, he meant Washington. The Pentagon.

"I heard." When he raised a brow, I said, "Rita told me a couple of hours ago. She cornered me down in the mess."

"She getting on your case?"

I shook my head, no.

"If she is, I'll have her taken back to Kinshasa. You don't have to put up with it, Ned. This isn't the time for her to be doing her bureaucratic bullshit no-stone-unturned act."

"She just wants to see Hawkeye through."

Channon made a face. "Didn't we all." He flipped up the desktop and locked it, then he crossed to his bunk and opened the suitcase. I remarked that he made it sound like Hawkeye was over. "It is over," he said. He slipped his diary into the suitcase. "How's your son?"

"Did you look at my report?"

He nodded, then paused in thought. At last he faced me. "Why didn't you tell me Brad was out here in the Congo?"

"It wasn't relevant to the operation."

"Reading between the lines of your report, I'd have to say that wasn't strictly true." He smiled, but there was no warmth in it.

"I didn't ask to be shipped out here."

"No. But once we'd gotten you out of jail, you could have boarded the Navy chopper, like I told you."

"The Haplon materiel was still out there."

"So was Brad."

I didn't say anything.

He pulled the straps tight on the suitcase and rebuckled it. "You make some pretty big assumptions about Trevanian too," he remarked.

"He killed Dimitri."

"Maybe. Maybe not."

"He did it."

"Motive?"

"He said Dimitri threatened him."

"With what?"

"He didn't say."

Channon made a face. He told me that did not sound like evidence.

"Trevanian wasn't up for a jury trial."

"Well, you made sure of that, Ned, didn't you. You made real sure of that." I cocked my head. He grimaced. "Without the evidence Trevanian could have given us, we're nowhere. You wonder why I'm talking like Hawkeye's over. It's over because Trevanian's dead."

"You want me to feel sorry for that?"

He raised a hand. "I'm just telling you why Hawkeye's over."

I studied him closely. Even knowing what I did, I couldn't detect one single sign that he was being anything but straight with me. I turned his UN beret through my hands, then tossed it on the bunk by his holstered pistol. I asked him what I should do with the beacon, the one I'd retrieved from the container at the airport.

He shrugged. "Hit it with a hammer. Drop it over the side."

I reached into my pocket and took it out. I held it up between my thumb and forefinger, and he stared at it a moment, then held out his hand.

"Here. I'll have it tested, see what went wrong."

"I already had it tested."

He looked at me. He didn't speak.

"I took it along to the engineers in Communications and Signals. They opened it up. Checked out the electronics. They even got another carrier up in the North Atlantic to see if it could pick up the beacon's signal. Guess what."

He squinted. "It's working?"

I nodded.

"Jesus Christ." He laughed grimly. "Now it works."

"It's never stopped working. Not since the day I picked it up from the DIA engineers."

"Bullshit."

"Every pulse this thing pumps out is recorded inside it. According to the engineers upstairs, it's been working like a charm."

He threw up a hand. "What do they know? They weren't there when the signals weren't coming through. They weren't. I was."

"Were you, Alex?"

"What the hell's that supposed to mean?"

I could drag it out, or I could just say it. I'd had enough of the horsing around so I just said it. "I know who paid for the Haplon materiel."

"Trevanian."

"Don't fuck me around, Alex." His eyes narrowed. "Biron paid," I said. "Biron, registered in Zug, Switzerland." He bowed his head, one hand covered his eyes. "As I recall, Biron was set up by the DIA to fund Hawkeye." Channon stepped across to his bunk and sat down. Now both hands covered his face. "God," I said. "God, I could fucking kill you." His hands fell, he stared at his feet. "You were never going to tell me, were you. You were just going to close the book on Hawkeye, let me go on believing the whole disaster was my doing."

He look up angrily. "Well, whose fault do you think it was? Who asked you to get yourself shipped out here? Who asked you to go jerking around the country in the middle of a goddamn coup?"

"My wife's dead. Don't play games with me."

"That had nothing to do with Hawkeye."

"That had plenty to do with Hawkeye. She was out here—Brad was out here—because of me. Because of what I've been doing with the past two years of my life. And what I've been doing is Hawkeye. Only now I'm not so sure I know what that is."

"Who told you about Biron?"

"Rita."

"Holy shit."

"All she's got's the name. She doesn't know Biron's a DIA front. Not yet."

He looked up. "I'm assuming that's not a threat."

"You're assuming wrong. You tell me what Hawkeye was really about, or I'll blow the goddamn whistle loud and strong. When Customs finds out Biron belongs to the DIA, they're not going to let it go. Before it's over, you'll be in Washington giving sworn testimony to a Senate commission. It'll be Iran-Contra all over again, only this time the star won't be Ollie North, it'll be you." The color drained from Channon's face. "You tell me what was going on with Hawkeye," I said, "or you're history."

We eyeballed each other. At last he turned aside and swore.

I pointed. "You lied to me."

He got up, turned his back on me, and rested his arms on the top bunk. He shook his head.

"You lied to me for two fucking years."

"Who was it dreamed Hawkeye up, me or you?" he said.

"I dreamed up a surveillance operation."

"Yeah," he said bitterly, turning on me. "Then you convinced me to bring Dimitri on board. Dimitri, your old buddy. Action man from Delta Force."

"Dimitri's not the issue."

"He's very much the goddamn issue. If it wasn't for Dimitri, do you think we'd be standing here? We'd be sitting on our butts at home, supervising a surveillance operation like we planned." Channon saw that he'd lost me. He turned left and right, but there was no way out for him. "Look," he said finally, spreading his hands. "Dimitri didn't come to us clean."

"He wasn't gambling."

"That's not what I meant." He took a breath, then blew. "He wasn't working for us. Even after I signed him up for Hawkeye, he wasn't answering to me." I squinted. Say what? "He was already signed up elsewhere," said Channon.

"He'd left Delta."

"Sure, he'd left Delta. He'd left Delta and joined the fucking CIA." When I turned my head in bewildered disbelief, Channon went on, "Oh yes he had. When you tried to recruit him, he passed your offer up the CIA's chain of command. Word came back to him that he should take the job with us, so he did. From that point on, Hawkeye was compromised. It wasn't strictly a surveillance operation anymore."

I looked at him askance. "Crap," I said. I said the CIA didn't operate on U.S. territory.

"Right after 9/11 they did. Probably still do." He nodded his head, slow but firm. My heart sank. I recalled now what Dimitri had told me that summer before 9/11. That he'd offered his services to the CIA. I hadn't even come close to guessing that they'd actually accepted his offer. Dimitri hadn't dropped so much as a whisper.

"Why didn't you tell me that?"

"I didn't know myself," he said. "For the first year, he seemed to be doing the job just like you. Regular contact with Durranti at Customs, monthly reports to me. Then one day Durranti comes knocking at my door. She's got it into her head that Dimitri's not giving her the full picture on some deal he's put through at Fettners. When I confronted Dimitri, he denied it. I dropped it, but she kept on at him about it. He finally told his CIA superiors, next thing I'm called into a meeting with some jackass from the Central Africa desk at the CIA." I made a sound. "These are the guys he's been reporting to all along," Channon said in disgust. "That's how I found out what the bastard was up to."

I stayed silent. I could hardly take in what I was hearing.

"I hit the fucking roof," said Channon. "Much fucking good it did me. Turned out they'd already had Dimitri shepherd a deal through the export system. Nothing major. Ordnance. Resupply of friendlies out in Africa. Middleman, Jack Trevanian."

"Jesus Christ."

"It was taken out of my hands. The big brass from both agencies, DIA and CIA, they butted heads for a while, then they cut a deal. Dimitri stayed. I was ordered to let Hawkeye run."

I leaned back against the cabin door. It felt like I'd been sapped.

"By the time he put the second deal through," Channon said, "we were too far down the line to turn back."

"Second deal?"

"You're not cleared."

I looked at him. He couldn't face me, he dropped onto his bunk and buried his head in his hands. I asked him again, and he lowered his hands.

"Second deal, same operation. More Fettners materiel. It went through Trevanian to the Congolese army under a Nigerian End User Certificate. Bigger than the first shipment, enough for training, but not enough to launch a strike."

I recalled the two payments made into Dimitri's daughters' trust fund. One the year before, then one in the spring. I asked Channon when the deals had taken place.

Last November, he told me. The second one in April. "Then in August I got that call from Dimitri telling me to meet him in L.A. Him and his friends from Internal Revenue. He was in debt up to here." Channon raised a hand over his head. "It was pretty clear we had a problem. The CIA didn't want Dimitri involved in deal three. They wanted him cut out."

"Cut out," I said.

Channon caught my tone, he screwed up his face. "Christ, not that. He was in a financial mess, no one trusted him. But he knew there was a third and final deal coming up. He got fixated on it, like if he just got that right, everything would come good for him."

I turned that over. I said, "So you switched deal three to Haplon. It was meant to be Fettners' order, but you switched it to Haplon."

Channon nodded. "The Congolese soldiers had been trained by Trevanian's men on the Fettners weapons. The Haplon materiel was the only stuff compatible."

"And you didn't tell me?"

He got up, agitated. "You were Dimitri's friend, for chrissake. And you didn't need to know anyway. Trevanian had opened up a direct line to Rossiter. If Rossiter could have just shepherded the deal through quietly, that would have been it. I'm not saying I liked it, Ned. All I wanted, frankly, was to get it over with, then shut Hawkeye down. The whole operation had turned into a big fucking mess. Then Lagundi insisted on going out to Springfield. Up jumps Dimitri like some demented jack-in-a-box."

"So Trevanian shot him dead."

Channon's glance slid away. "Dimitri threatened him. That's what I was told."

"You already knew Dimitri was dead when I called you that day. You already knew Trevanian had killed him."

"No I didn't. I got off the phone from you and called the Central Africa ringmaster at the CIA. I floated the idea that maybe Trevanian was responsible, and I was advised to drop it. Death by misadventure, that's the official line."

"Unofficially?"

He chewed his lip. "Unofficially, Dimitri made some stupid threat. Depending who you listen to, either Trevanian took things into his own hands, or he called and reported the threat up the line, then got told what to do."

"He used Lagundi's gun."

"He must have," Channon agreed. "That threw me too."

I had a flashback to that day at Springfield. Dimitri in front of me, hands braced on the table, leaning forward with a wild look in his eye. My order, he'd said. The order that he was counting on. For the financial kickback that would get him out of a deep financial hole. For the chance to salvage his reputation with the Agency. The order he needed to resurrect his life. Looking back, it seemed only too likely now that Dimitri would have gone on to threaten Trevanian. Dimitri had pushed his luck one final time, and lost everything.

"So the Haplon deal," I said. "Start to finish, it wasn't anything to do with surveillance. It was us rearming the Congolese government. That's what we were doing all along. Giving them the firepower to take out the rebels."

"The country was turning into a nightmare. A failed state in the heart of Africa. Another goddamn Afghanistan."

"So we sent them more guns?"

"I didn't dream up the policy."

"You implemented it, Alex. You implemented it by using me."

"Using you? I did everything I could to keep you out of it. If you hadn't gotten on board the damn *Sebastopol*—"

"You could have closed Hawkeye down."

"You begged me not to. Remember?"

I didn't buy that. I turned it over. "You needed me to keep you informed of what was happening with the deal. You didn't trust Trevanian, not after Springfield, you needed him watched. That's what I was doing."

Channon turned away from me. He picked up the UN beret and turned it through his hands. "After Springfield, there was a lot of pressure. When Lagundi started screwing around with those fucking diamonds, just trying to piece together what was happening was hard enough. She was telling her father and his cronies back in the Congo that Trevanian had the diamonds. Trevanian was telling us that she had them. Rossiter started threatening to recall the Haplon materiel. Meanwhile, the rebels were getting ready to strike Kinshasa. The Haplon materiel had to sail."

I said that I still didn't see why Trevanian had to steal the bill of lading.

"Bureaucracy." Channon gave a bitter smile. "Butt-covering by the CIA. They had to be able to put their hands on their hearts and swear they didn't have an operation under way on U.S. territory. They had to transfer money into a DIA account."

"Biron."

He nodded. "The transfer took time."

I asked why the CIA hadn't simply given the funds to Trevanian, and let him pay Rossiter.

"After what happened with the diamonds?" Channon shook his

head emphatically. "We figured so long as Rossiter got paid, he wasn't going to make a problem about losing the bill of lading a little early, or about being held out of town for twenty-four hours. The CIA could get a reimbursement from the Congolese government later, after the rebels were put down, and after we had figured out where those damn diamonds went."

"But now Rita knows about Biron."

Channon studied me. "The only thing Durranti's got is the name. The Swiss lawyers will make sure that's all she ever gets."

I dropped my head. Two years. Two years buried in a deceit that cost Fiona her life. And Dimitri's.

"Ned?"

I looked up. "If you think I'm just going to let bygones be bygones, you're insane."

"Listen—"

"You used me." I stabbed a finger at the air. "You lied to me, and you used me. Now you're going to chopper into Kinshasa, become a big fucking peacekeeping hero? I'm supposed to go home and tend the flowers on Fiona's grave?" He stepped toward me, opening his hands in a placatory gesture. I jabbed my finger into his chest. "That is not going to happen. You implemented the policy. Now let's see if you're man enough to take the goddamn consequences."

"You're not thinking straight."

"It's the first time I've been thinking straight in two years."

"I'm ordering you not to tell her."

I reached to open the cabin door.

"Ned!" he shouted, and I turned. He'd grabbed the Beretta from the holster on his bunk. He wasn't pointing it, he was holding it up near his waist. I looked from the gun up to him. Once, I'd taken orders from the man. Once, I'd genuinely respected him. We stared at each other for several seconds, finally his shoulders dropped and he tossed the gun back onto the bunk. When he stepped toward me this time I shoved him, and he stumbled back and struck his head on the bunk. He touched his head, then he turned and flew at me, he dropped his shoulder into my chest and pinned me back against the wall. I reached over his back and hammered my fist into his left kidney. He cried out and released me, twisting away, clutching his back.

I turned and stepped out the door. Suddenly he grabbed me from behind and tried to haul me back into the cabin. I gripped the door frame and braced my legs. When he couldn't budge me, he wrapped an arm around my neck, I crouched and heaved his weight onto my back. We stumbled into the gangway. I clawed his arm, he squeezed tighter, so I pushed back, slamming him into the wall, then I staggered a few paces and we fell, sprawling onto the wet steel plate by the service area. His arm was still around my throat. Through the railings I glimpsed the rain lashing down on the sea.

"We can talk," he said, breathless. "If I let go, we can talk. We can work something out."

I clawed along his forearm, got hold of his thumb, and yanked it back against his wrist. He gave a choked cry, his arm went limp, and I held on to his thumb and scrambled to my knees. Then as I got up, he swept his other arm against my legs, and I went down again, and he pulled his thumb free.

He rose, cradling his right hand. His chest heaved. "You can't tell her. For chrissake, what good would it do?" I got to my feet. "You'd just be buying yourself a whole lot of grief."

"Grief?"

"We could get you recommissioned. We could get you back into West Point."

"West Point's not the goddamn Promised Land."

"Well, what do you want, Ned? You tell me. What do you want?"

The ship rolled, I swayed on my feet. The steel plate was slippery, the wind swept a gust of rain into us. We looked at each other. We both knew what I wanted. The one thing that no power on earth could give me back. At last I turned away, took a step across the wet steel. He grabbed at me again. I spun around and took a swing, my fist glanced off his jaw, and he lurched back, clinging to my left arm. We stumbled against the railings, I slipped and went down on my knees. He grabbed me by the hair, shoved my throat up against the middle rail, then he released my hair and I felt his forearm slide onto the back of my neck. He pressed down hard. I started to choke. My throat was on fire, I struggled, tried to push away from the railings, but now he had his knee on my back, and when the ship rolled, I saw the gray sea beneath me, then it darkened, and black spots burst in front of my eyes.

I twisted, strained till I finally got one foot planted under me, then I reached up over my head and clutched his left arm. His left hand was holding the rail. Then I powered up, straightening my leg and heaving my shoulders into his chest, dragging his left arm down. His feet lifted off the steel plate, his weight swung forward onto my shoulders as I rose. I could have stopped, but I didn't, I kept driving up, hauling on his arm. He tried to wrap his other arm around my throat again, but I kept my chin tight against my chest, and he twisted and I stumbled against the rail. His weight suddenly slid from my shoulders, I let go of his left arm, shoved his right arm off my face, and he hit the top rail on his side, and fell outward. His arms slapped frantically against the rails as he grabbed at them in his fall, then he was gone. I leaned over the rail and saw him turning. One second. Two seconds. He hit the water hard, flat on his back.

The dark shape of him was like a dolphin just beneath the water. The shape slid back along the hull toward the propellers, then went down, disappearing into the churned foam, and I watched astern but nothing resurfaced, and I turned and slumped against the bulkhead. I stayed like that for maybe half a minute, then I finally moved, sliding into automatic.

I went back to Channon's cabin. I checked that nothing in the cabin had been overturned by our tussle. I wiped my handkerchief over the doorknobs, inside and out, then I closed the door and retreated to my cabin. I changed my clothes and lay down on my bunk. I breathed. My senses were shredded. My heart went on beating, beating, an incessant rhythm that wouldn't let me forget, and at last I surrendered to the sound of it, closed my eyes, and listened to the pulse in my ears. Drumming. Remorseless. The undeniable murmur of continuing existence. The insistent whisper of unended life.

EPILOGUE

After it was over, I came up to the mountains. It is spring now, the sugar maples are coming into leaf. Most mornings I rise early and walk from the shack down through the woods to the river where my father used to fish with me as a boy. Once there, I bait my line, then crouch and study the clear river awhile. Finally I plant my feet on the dappled riverbank, make my first cast, and wait hopefully for some kind of peace.

No trace of Channon's body was ever found. He wasn't missed till more than an hour after I saw him go under, and it was another half hour, after an increasingly alarmed search, that the captain decided Channon was lost overboard. The carrier turned back to retrace its course. Choppers were sent skimming over the sea in all directions, but night came on fast. The search continued through the darkness and into the following morning, it was Rita who came to my cabin around midday with the news that the captain had at last called an end to it. Once one of the Marine officers was appointed to lead the peacekeepers in Channon's place, the choppers were reassigned from the search to start ferrying the Marines into Kinshasa.

Some CIA spook came out to the carrier on a return flight, he collected Channon's suitcase and spent a couple of hours with me finding out what I knew. I stuck by the five-page summary he'd found in Channon's suitcase, he seemed satisfied with that. He flew back to Kinshasa and I never saw him again.

The next day, Rita was on a military flight back to America. Brad and I followed several days later, after the doctors had given him the all-clear. We declined the captain's embarrassed offer to bury Fiona at sea, and took her body home. She was cremated in Yonkers. We carried her ashes to a high rocky outcrop above our shack in the mountains, a place she liked to climb to in the fall. I opened the urn, then found that I could not do it. I gave the urn to Brad and he said a prayer, then scattered his mother's ashes on the wind.

The first two weeks I stayed with Brad down on Ellis Street, receiving calls and cards of condolence, and being debriefed by a pair of agents from the DIA who were closing the file on Hawkeye. They weren't bad men, but having them in my home so often, being compelled to deal with them on a daily basis, I couldn't help but see that they were just soldiers dressed in suits, with all the soldier's clarity of commanded purpose and narrowness of sight. Instruments of the institution they served, they worked methodically through my story, stripping it down, as they said, to the essentials. In the end, they reduced it to a recitation of events that had apparently occurred without the intervention of any human motive beyond what might be found in a Superman comic or a presidential speech. Good guys and bad guys. White hats and black hats. Us versus them.

From various remarks they made, it was clear to me that they had no idea of the real nature of Hawkeye. I took care not to enlighten them.

Rita Durranti, on her return to work, found that her zeal to pursue into court those behind the illegal shipment was not shared by her superiors or colleagues. Hawkeye, down at Customs, had become a byword for operational disaster. Rita's intimate association with it had lowered her standing in the department and somewhat tarnished the bright silver star of her career. As Channon had anticipated, all her inquiries into the principals behind Biron came to nothing. The Swiss authorities were uncooperative at best, sometimes actively hostile, and after a month knocking her head against *a legal brick wall, she was ordered by her superiors to stop trying. She sent a note to me at the shack, explaining what had happened. To that one, I never replied.*

I left Haplon, of course. The day after my return to New York, I drove up to the plant in Connecticut to offer my resignation. I intended to collect from my office any paperwork that Customs might find useful, but I was a week too late. Gillian Streiss had already been promoted to my chair. Rossiter sat me down for half an hour and after explaining the necessary rearrangement of Haplon's business that had left me unemployed, he gave me a check for fifteen thousand dollars to tide me over. I banked the check without a qualm. I assumed, at the time, that Rossiter simply wanted to put some distance between himself and the Trevanian deal, and letting me go achieved that. Since then, however, I've learned from Rita that Micky Baker resigned his job at Customs while we were in the Congo, informing them that after the mandatory six-month break he would be returning to Haplon as a bona fide employee, Gillian Streiss's assistant, in fact. What Micky did or did not tell Rossiter about me, I can only guess. That something was said seems more than likely.

With my career as an arms salesman ended, the DIA offered me a no-brain desk job down in Washington, which I declined, and there was an approach from West Point indicating that an instructorship might be offered me if I wanted it. That, too, I turned down. After all that has happened, I can't return now to the world of snappy salutes and freshly pressed uniforms, of young men offering unquestioning obedience, and old men issuing commands. Somehow that would not be right. In her note to me, Rita suggested I had a range of skills and knowledge that Customs would gladly pay for, and maybe, in time, there will be a niche there in which I can turn my training and experience to good effect and yet still be able to face myself in the mirror each morning. But I am not ready. For now, I have decided to let it lie.

With Brad my relationship has changed fundamentally. He's still at home back on Ellis Street, but making noises, recently, about a move up to some diamond mine in Canada. I think he should go, but I keep my own counsel. He's not a boy, looking for my approval, or an adolescent, seeking reasons for dissent. We seem to be able to accept each other, these days, in a way we never managed before. Fiona's death has given us our own personal ground zero, a time and place beyond which the usual concerns and everyday battles of life are so diminished as to no longer be of any real account. If I have a hope for him, it's that he will learn from what has been the greatest misjudgment, regret, and sorrow of my life, and be sure not to follow me. I pray that he never lends or surrenders his conscience to any man, woman, or institution, and that he recognizes early those duties higher than any owed to the world. That he holds faith with himself. That he stays true to his own.

He has recovered completely from his flesh wound, the naval surgeon did a fine job. The other wound goes deeper. Deeper, I know, than he will ever let me see.

For my part, I've gone through many staging posts of grief, and each stage, at the time, has seemed to me the final one, the point at which my emotional compass would stay fixed forever. But even in the mountains, time passes. Even the quietest of lives has a way of moving the lodestone. Yet if I was asked to swear that what I feel now will remain with me, I could do that, because what I feel now I have felt since the moment of Fiona's death. I feel a burden of sorrow. I feel inexpressible remorse and regret.

She was my wife. To Fiona I swore vows that I did not keep, and that is a cold, hard truth that I will carry with me to the grave.

Today, Brad is coming up to the shack to see me. He has come up every weekend this past month, he tells me he has finally decided he wants to learn how to fish. I know it's just his way of reaching out to me, but with each hour he spends by the river I can see him becoming quietly entranced. We tend not to speak much, even during meals at the shack, but the silence between us these days is comfortable. Last weekend, over breakfast, he suggested that it might be time for me to return home. He said it lightly, just an aside, but I know Brad, and he must have given it plenty of thought, and I can't pretend that I haven't thought about it too.

I can't go on like this forever, I know that. At some point, I'll have to take up the reins of my life again, and I will. Maybe someday soon. But for now I want to remain here, just where I am. In a few hours, I'll do what I've done every weekend this past month. I'll cast my line into the river, and watch Brad, on the far bank, cast his. Then we'll wait, and watch the river flowing past us down the mountain, sweeping over the stones, whispering.

A sparkle of sunlight on the water. A turning leaf. Time passing.

Imperfect peace.